CRY OF THE PANTHER

CRY OF THE PANTHER

ADAM ARMSTRONG

BANTAM PRESS

LONDON · NEW YORK · TORONTO · SYDNEY · AUCKLAND

TRANSWORLD PUBLISHERS
61–63 Uxbridge Road, London W5 5SA
a division of The Random House Group Ltd

RANDOM HOUSE AUSTRALIA PTY LTD
20 Alfred Street, Milsons Point, Sydney
New South Wales 2061, Australia

RANDOM HOUSE NEW ZEALAND
18 Poland Road, Glenfield, Auckland 10, New Zealand

RANDOM HOUSE SOUTH AFRICA (PTY) LTD
Endulini, 5a Jubilee Road, Parktown 2193, South Africa

Published 2000 by Bantam Press
a division of Transworld Publishers

Typeset in 11/13.5pt Times by
Phoenix Typesetting, Ilkley, West Yorkshire

Printed in Great Britain
by Clays Ltd, St Ives plc

1 3 5 7 9 10 8 6 4 2

For Margo Armstrong Fairbairn

The author would like to thank the Scottish Society for the Prevention of Cruelty to Animals and the Royal Society for the Protection of Birds.

PROLOGUE

Idaho, 1969

Ewan told Connla they couldn't take a girl with them.

Imogen had heard him say it last night when the two boys thought she was asleep. She had meant to be up in time to stop them going without her, but she woke to empty sleeping bags. Why didn't Connla wake her? He always stood up for her against her brother, so why not this time? She crawled out of the tent, the dew on the canvas flap damp against her skin, and stood barefoot in the wet grass. She strained to see if she could spot them, but the trees were dark and the trail empty, so she ducked back inside the tent and lay down again, aware of the silence and upset that they had left her behind.

She sucked at the corner of her blanky: eight years old and still sucking on a blanky. No-one at school knew about it. Even Ewan wouldn't tell anyone about that, and he told everyone anything that would embarrass his sister. She had given it up for almost a year, but her mom hadn't thrown it out and she had gone back to it for comfort when they told her they were moving back to Scotland. Today was the last day of the vacation before they went back to Jackson City. When they got there they would start packing. Her brother always bragged that he could remember Scotland, and that it was great and everything, but

1

she thought he was lying. If she had been only a year old when they'd come out here, he must've been four, so how could he remember?

She had really wanted to go with them this morning, as it was the last time they would ever be here together. The fishing was all done; they had caught a lot of steelhead and the boys were going after Indian stuff. Ewan said he reckoned there would be arrowheads; he thought that Indians had passed this way on hunting trips. Ewan loved arrowheads; he had a whole bunch of them back in his room, some older than others and some he had made himself. He told Connla there would definitely be arrowheads, but they might have to climb some, and they couldn't possibly take the Twaggle Tail. She had cringed at the nickname, hoping Connla would argue, but he didn't. He agreed: no place for the Twaggle Tail, not on a trip like that. So she had gone to sleep, determined to wake before dawn and tag along anyway. But now the sun was up and she had slept in and they were gone already.

The sleeping bag was warm but she could smell the chilled freshness of the morning. The corner of her blanky was soggy and she tossed it to one side and got up again. They had pitched their tents at a campsite deep in the trees. Scots pine; that's what her father called them. Tall and dark-leafed, with straight trunks that seemed to go up for ever before the branches sprang off them. She liked the trees; she could see movement in them, a quiet sort of unmoving motion, the way they must have moved as they grew. Crinkles of bark and the branches separating out from the trunk. She had looked closely and seen that two branches started as one, then split up and came back over themselves before reaching out in different directions. Movement. She could see it, though no-one else seemed able to.

It was chilly still, but she got her boots and put her coat on over her night-dress. She didn't know how long they had been gone and she sat down in Connla's sleeping bag and tried to tell herself it was still quite warm. Once in the night she had woken up and looked at him while he was sleeping. Her brother was on the far side and Connla lay in the middle, on his back with his

2

hands tucked out of sight and the sleeping bag up to his chin. His face as smooth as stone in the moonlight, hair a dark splash on the pillow. Looking at him made her feel sort of warm inside; she didn't really know why. He was just Connla McAdam, her brother's friend from across the street.

She buttoned up her coat and shook her hair. After three days at camp there was no way she could get a brush through the tangles. She dreaded going home later: the bathtub with shampoo and the comb. Her mother would spend hours trying to sort out the mess, only for her to sleep on it and have to start all over again in the morning. She laced her boots and looked for her hair band, but couldn't find it among the sleeping things. She looked at her blanky; thought for a moment, then left it.

A crow flew up from the trees, cawing loudly and startling her. She picked her way past her parents' tent; the door was zipped up and she could hear her father's muffled snores from inside. The remains of last night's dinner still clung to the skillets laid out by the blackened embers of the campfire. She could smell the steak-sauce marinade that Connla's mother had made. It was too strong for her, as was the elk meat. She didn't like the taste, or the thought of eating deer. How could anyone eat Bambi?

She made her way to the edge of the forest and stopped. The path, pale against the heavy green foliage, cut like a wide-bellied snake through the trees. They grew close together here, well back from the river and higher. The forest looked pretty dark and she hesitated. She had no way of knowing how long they had been gone or in which direction. Vaguely, in the distance, she could hear the rush and tumble of the Salmon River. Easter was only three weeks back and Connla's father, who fished for steelhead every year, said it was still pretty high with the snow melt. 'Gotta be careful on the Salmon,' he said. 'People got killed every year on the Salmon.' Ewan scoffed, rafters and canoeists maybe, not fishermen.

She paused at the tree line, looking into the darkness for a moment, then back at the tents. She heard someone stir, mutter, then snore again and she moved into the forest. The path was dusty, with silver-coloured stones pushing up through the dirt. Tree roots reached so far and no further. Her footsteps made no sound and she went deeper, glancing back every now and then to make sure the tents were still in sight. She would go as far as she could without completely losing sight of them, then, if she didn't see or hear the boys, she would come back. Trees grew up alongside her, close knit, the spaces dark between them. She paused and looked at the straightness of the trunks, how the wood discoloured here and there, how dark it was in some places and yet much lighter in others. The sun cut the odd shaft of light through the topmost branches to the forest floor, and she could see dust dancing. She couldn't *feel* the sun, though. No warmth; not enough space between the treetops for any heat to get through.

Something moved among the ferns to her right and Imogen saw a ground squirrel cracking nuts from pine cones. He watched her out of the corner of his eye, but didn't seem bothered. Imogen crouched on her haunches, one shoulder leaning against the comforting bark of a tree trunk. The squirrel went on cracking nuts, his little grey head darting up and down, snout twitching, whiskers like strands of a spider's web. Then something must have scared him, for he dumped the nuts and skittered up a tree with a tiny scraping of claws. Imogen stood up too quickly, and as she did her head swam, the world went dark and she saw Ewan up to his neck in water.

She stood very still and her head slowly cleared, but the image had been as vivid as if he were right there in front of her. It faded into nothing and she focused again on the trees. Only now it was darker, the sun was gone and she couldn't see the sky above her head. She looked back at the path, no tents in sight, and for a second she had to figure out which way the campsite was. Then she was walking quickly, back along the dirt trail, her heart rising in her chest. She walked and walked, further than she remembered, and for a moment she felt panic rising. Fear was taking hold when she rounded a bend in the trail and saw the canvas white of the tents.

*   *   *

She was sitting by the car when she heard a crash and clatter in the trees, then Connla's voice yelling for his father. The grown-ups were dressed now and drinking coffee. Her mother had given her a bowl of cereal, which she'd all but finished. She laid the bowl to one side and watched Connla come running down the trail, bursting from the tree line as if a cougar were after him. His father, seated by the fire he had nursed from last night's embers, got up, concern in his eyes. Connla ran into the clearing and dropped, breathless, into a heap.

His father crouched beside him. 'What is it, son? What's wrong?'

Connla was breathing hard, green eyes wide, chest rising and falling. He couldn't get any words out.

'Connla, what's wrong?' His father laid a large hand on his shoulder. Connla looked up now, the muscles of his face whitened against the tan of his skin.

'Ewan took off.'

Imogen sat where she was and watched. Her mother was beside them now. 'What d'you mean, took off?'

Connla dropped his shoulders. 'Just that, Mrs Munro. Took off and left me.'

'Back there?' His father jabbed a thumb towards the trail.

Connla nodded, not looking. His head came up, shaggy auburn hair across his face; he looked over the fire at Imogen. Their eyes met and locked, then he looked away. Her father was looking at the tree line, the wind was up and the points of the topmost branches drifted towards the south. Imogen looked at the pale blue of the sky, no sun now and broken up with cloud.

'You went off somewhere?' Her father was talking to Connla. 'You and Ewan, this morning?'

Connla looked at his father. 'Only as far as that clearing.'

'They went without me.' Imogen walked over, blanky in hand, trailing in the wet grass. 'I heard them talking last night.' She looked at Connla. 'You all figured I was sleeping, but I wasn't. I was right there listening.'

They all looked at her, then her father turned to Connla again. 'Where did you go exactly?'

'That way.' Connla pointed back down the trail.

'Where?'

'Just down the trail?'

'Towards the river?'

Connla, hesitating for a fraction, shook his head. 'Just that clearing, the one with all the rocks in it.'

'Arrowheads. They was looking for arrowheads.' Imogen sniffed the edge of her blanket. 'That's what Ewan said, anyways.'

'It's no big deal, Tom.' Connla's father was on his feet now. 'Ewan's just probably playing some kinda joke.'

Imogen's father nodded. 'Hey, Ewan.' He called into the trees. 'Come on out if you're in there. You succeeded in scaring your buddy.'

They all looked at the silent height of the trees. 'Ewan!' Imogen's mother this time. 'Come on out, Ewan.'

Nothing. Imogen looked at Connla. He stood with his head down, gazing at the red coals in the fire. She walked over to him and he glanced up, then he looked away, crouched down and hugged his arms round his knees.

'He's just kidding you around, Connla,' her father said.

'No, he ain't.' Connla's voice was no more than a whisper. 'I told you, he took off on me.'

Imogen's mother took her husband's arm. 'Tom, there's cougar in there, and black bear. Go and look for him, will you?'

He nodded and glanced at Connla's father, who reached for his coat. 'You wanna show us where he took off, Connla?'

Connla waved an arm. 'Just head down the trail. You'll come to the clearing where the big boulders broke off the mountain. That's the place.'

'You don't wanna come, huh?' His father cocked an eyebrow at him.

Connla shook his head. His mother splashed coffee into a cup and passed it to him.

'Come on, I'll get you some breakfast.'

Imogen sat in the entrance to their tent, watching him as he fiddled disinterestedly with his food. The two women sat on camp chairs, ate cinnamon rolls and drank coffee, talking in low voices. The forest was still, as though the birds had stopped singing, the animals stopped rustling in the undergrowth, even the snakes had stopped crawling.

The two men must have been gone an hour or so, and then she heard them, or at least one of them, coming back up the trail. It was Connla's father. His face was stiff and red at the cheek-bones, and in his hand he carried Ewan's baseball jacket. Imogen's mother got up slowly out of her chair. 'Tom's still looking,' Connla's father said. 'We found this on the trail.' He handed the jacket to Imogen's mother, then looked at his son.

'Connla, did he have his coat on when he took off?'

'Yessir.'

'You sure?'

'Yessir.'

'Look at me, boy.'

Connla met his eyes. 'Yessir, he did.'

His father pushed out his lips. 'I'm gonna take a drive up the highway, see if I can get a hold of the sheriff.'

The sheriff drove a white Chevrolet truck, with Custer County Sheriff written on the side. He leaned against the fender with his thumbs hooked in his belt. 'Where was he last seen?'

'A clearing, not far into the forest there.' Imogen's father had come back without any sign of Ewan. Her mother was pale, eyes ringed now, and she clasped a cup of coffee which she had long since finished drinking. They told the sheriff what Connla had told them. Imogen stared at him, his thick red-knuckled fingers with black hairs sprouting from the creases, nails chewed into ragged edges. Her mother had always told her never to bite her nails; bitten-down nails looked ugly. The sheriff was looking sideways at Connla, who squatted on a log by the fire. Imogen watched the sheriff, one boot resting on the fender, the other jammed in the mud by its slanted heel. She looked at the black gun that hung, weighted, on his right hip. His belly bulged at his shirt buttons and the skin of his neck was red above the collar.

7

She lost interest and walked over to Connla. He sat, knees drawn up, chin between them, scraping rough patterns in the dust with a stick. A turkey vulture squawked at the tree line, but he didn't lift his head. She looked at him intently, intently enough for him to look up, but he didn't. He just stared between his knees at the patterns he was making. His check shirt had a hole torn in the sleeve and Imogen could see a scuffed and bloodied scab on his elbow.

'Where's he at?'

He looked up sharply then. 'I don't know where he's at. If I knew where he was at I wouldn't be set here now, would I?'

She squatted on the log next to him. 'I guess not.'

The sheriff had the door of his truck open now. Imogen watched him lean his heavy frame against the jamb and unhook the radio transmitter. She could hear the crackle of static. 'This is Sheriff Truman. I'm down at the Grover campsite on the East Fork Road. We got an eleven-year-old boy possibly lost on the edge of the Sawtooth. I'm gonna need search and rescue.' He broke off, glanced to where Imogen and Connla were sitting, then spoke into the radio again. 'Can you notify the state police for me? See if they can send me a coupla troopers.'

Imogen looked sideways at Connla, who still hung his head between his knees, his shoulders shaking ever so slightly. 'You crying?'

He looked angrily at her again. 'No, I ain't crying. Quit talking to me.'

She got up and looked at him a moment longer.

'Quit bugging me, girl.'

Imogen shrugged, picked up the tail end of her blanky and walked over to her mother. She was sitting in the camp chair with the empty coffee cup still between her fingers. Imogen laid a small hand on her knee. She remembered what she had seen in the forest, the image of her brother up to his neck in water, and she must've blinked sharply because her mother squinted at her.

'What is it?'

Imogen shrugged. 'I don't know.'

'Imogen?'

'Nothing.' Imogen looked back at Connla. He was up off the log, arms tight across his chest, staring into the tree line. 'You think Ewan's all right, Momma?' Imogen chewed at her lip and looked, bug-eyed, at her mother. She could see the unease etched in her mother's features, the dark circles seeming to claw at her eyes. Her mother looked beyond her to the trees, where her husband and Connla's father had resumed their search a few minutes earlier.

''Course he's all right, honey.' She still had one hand on the empty cup; the other knotted into a small fist that rested between her thighs. Her legs were drawn up so she was balanced on the tips of her toes, as if she didn't want her weight on the ground. Imogen thought she looked fragile.

The team from Challis arrived in two red and white Search and Rescue trucks, six big men with short-cut hair and two women with them. They all wore baseball hats, thick jackets and heavily treaded boots. Their faces were serious, and when they spoke to the sheriff it was in low, all-but-inaudible voices. Connla was walking back and forward on the log now, arms out wide, balancing on the ball of one foot, then the other, like a tightrope walker. The sheriff had a large-scale map spread out on the hood of his truck; his hat was tipped back and beads of perspiration lifted on his forehead.

'He's in here someplace.' He tapped the map with a thick fore-finger. 'Connla!' he called over his shoulder then. 'Come over here a minute, will you, son?'

Connla stopped his balancing act and dropped off the log. His shoulders sat low and his chin seemed to rest near his chest. He stood a moment then shuffled over.

'You understand maps, son?' The sheriff made space along-side him. The other men moved back. Imogen was aware of the wheeze and hiss of somebody's breathing.

'Some.'

'We're here.' The sheriff jabbed at the map with his finger. 'You see? Grover campsite. The only one this far upriver.

Anything higher is frozen. See?' He pointed to the mountains in the distance, their summits hung with snow like slowly melting ice cream.

Connla nodded.

'This is the trail.' The sheriff spoke slowly, tracing the line on the map. 'In back of the trees here.' He tapped again. 'This is the clearing where your daddy found the jacket. This the same clearing he left you?'

Connla shrugged. 'I don't know. I'd have to see it.'

The sheriff looked across him at his mother. 'That OK with you, ma'am, if he comes along?'

She nodded.

'About a half-mile in, that about right, boy?' The sheriff spoke to Connla again.

'I guess.'

'Best put a jacket on. It'll be cold in there when you're outta the sun.'

Imogen sat on Connla's log and watched them head into the forest. Connla walked beside the sheriff, and a big man with a square back walked behind them. Connla looked small, disconsolate, lost. Imogen inched along the log until she sat in the exact spot where he had been sitting. Behind her one of the Search and Rescue women was talking to their mothers. Imogen wondered how it was that women always seemed to get left behind. Her mother lit a cigarette and the smoke drifted, smelling foul against the freshness of the air.

Imogen suddenly got up from Connla's log and followed the party into the forest. She didn't know how far ahead of her the men were, but she couldn't hear them. She could see the mess they had made of the path, a whole bunch of tracks in the dust, whereas this morning there had been nothing. She looked at the ground behind where she had walked and couldn't make out any of her own prints. It must be because the men were so big and heavy, she thought. They had the right boots on, too; she was only wearing tennis shoes.

She picked her way through the trees and listened to the sounds above her head. She could make out individual birdsong, though she couldn't put a name to the singers. At least they were singing again now, which did something for the blocked air that seemed to have lodged in her chest, taut, like a fur ball. She swallowed and swallowed, but just could not shift it.

She didn't know how far she walked, but the path climbed and the tree line fell back, giving more space and light between the trunks. The ground was covered with broken leaves, fern and bracken, and rock bulged grey against the sand-coloured dust of the trail. There were boulders, great hunks of broken rock in the trees, as if they had split from the mountains, rolled for fifty yards and then stopped. Imogen could see the sharp-sided cliff that climbed in a series of jagged ridges to the south. The boulders formed a clearing and Connla was sitting alone on a flat sheet of stone. He looked up as she came out of the trees. 'What the hell are *you* doing here?'

She shrugged. 'What're you doing?'

'You heard the sheriff. I came in with them.'

'Where they at now?'

He pointed towards where the cliff bucked at the sky, and Imogen frowned. 'How come you're set there then?'

'They didn't want me to go no further. Sheriff told me to go on back.'

'How come you didn't?'

'Didn't feel like it.' He scratched at the dirt with the toe of his boot.

'Is this where Ewan took off?'

He nodded.

Imogen looked beyond him to the circle of rock where dust-blown trails led off in a variety of directions. Far in the distance she heard the roar of Salmon River. She looked again at Connla.

'You sure?'

'What?'

'You sure?'

'About what?'

'That this is where he took off.'

He looked at her, his head slanted to one side. ''Course I'm sure. You figure I'd tell the sheriff if I weren't?'

Imogen shrugged. Something was wrong, but she didn't know what it was. She walked in a circle, trailing a flattened palm over the larger slabs of stone. She was aware of the texture against the sweat in her hand, and of the variety of different colours.

Connla sat where he was and watched her from hooded eyes; head down, trying to make it look as though he wasn't interested. Imogen stopped, palm flat against one particular rock, and cocked her head to one side. She frowned, then looked again at Connla.

'How come they went the wrong way?'

'What?'

'The sheriff and all those men. How come they went the wrong way?'

Connla stared at her. 'They didn't.'

'They sure did.' Imogen looked at the boulder, her hand still resting on it, and then across the clearing to a jagged slab that tilted awkwardly across the path. Anyone walking by would have to lean to avoid it. She stood very still, unsure of herself, then she crossed the clearing and paused at the leaning slab. It was very black, shiny almost, the surface looked damp but it wasn't. Connla sat where he was, watching her. Ewan had passed by this stone. Maybe he leaned a hand on it, she didn't know for sure, but she knew he had passed by.

'Ewan went this way.'

'He did not.'

She looked again at the stone, silent, smooth to the touch, cold; then, with a brief glance at Connla, she headed off down the trail. In her ears the sound of the river grew louder.

She walked slowly. The trees were thin again and the path climbed at a slight gradient, then split in two, one trail leading upward, running next to the cliffs, the other dipping in a wider curve which disappeared into the darkness of tree trunks. She slowed, hesitating, the trees seemed to gaze down on her, questioning. The wind moved in the lower branches. She stopped and, looking back, saw Connla twenty yards behind her.

'What you doing?' he called. 'Ewan never come this way.'

She ignored him now, knowing he was wrong, but not knowing how she knew.

'Come on back. You'll get yourself lost. Then what'll your momma say.'

Imogen gazed at him for a moment and he smiled. His whole face lit up when he smiled.

She shook her head. 'I won't get lost.'

His face fell; then he looked away, kicking at the dust with his toe. Imogen felt something, a sensation, a feeling, some kind of emotion she didn't understand. She stared at the stones on her left, then moved, as if drawn to them all at once. She stopped again, the fork in the path right at her feet now. She stared up and left, then down and right, bunching her small face and wrinkling her eyes at the corners.

'What you doing?'

She jumped. Connla stood at her shoulder. She hadn't heard him come up. He moved like a cat, silent, walking on the balls of his feet.

'What you doing?' he asked her again.

'Ssssh.' She was looking ahead.

'What you doing?'

'Listening.'

'For what?'

'I don't know. Something.'

He touched her lightly on the shoulder. 'Come on back. They'll be getting worried. You ain't but a kid. *I* shouldn't really be out here, never mind you.'

She didn't hear him. She was staring at the paths again. Which way? Right into the trees or left alongside the rock face, pitted and scarred with flinty indentations, copper coloured, and brown, blacker and darker as it rose and the sun reflected off it. She followed the left fork. Connla stared after her, then glanced over his shoulder. The search party was right across on the south side of the clearing. He looked ahead again and Imogen was already thirty yards up the trail.

Imogen walked more purposefully now. The river was getting louder; she could hear the familiar roar that had filled their ears

13

for the past three days while they dipped their poles for steelhead. High with the snow melt, the Salmon tore at its boundaries, cutting away clay and earth and little bits of stone from the banks. She could feel the breeze now. She was higher; the growing tightness in her calves told her she was much higher. Looking over her shoulder, suddenly needing comfort, she saw Connla following a short distance behind. Still the air stopped up in her throat, and the further she walked along the path the more the sensation grew. Trepidation, the beginnings of fear. It plucked at her body as something physical. Again she looked back. Connla seemed to be dragging, as if only following because he was worried about her. She could sense his reluctance, see it in the way he shuffled, the way he kept looking over his shoulder.

The stone on her left seemed to draw her. Her brother had passed this way; she knew it. She could sense him, in the air, the rock, the trail. She walked on, one hand on the wall to her left. The river grew louder. The path was narrow now, the trees falling away to her right. The sun dipped behind a cloud and the shadows faded into a thin grey light. She walked with stone walls to the left and right, as the path became a roofless tunnel where a section of mountain had broken away to form a slim, unnatural gully. She looked back again. Connla was still following her.

The rock climbed high above her head, blocking out the light, and the dust was damp underfoot. She could smell the river and almost feel the spray. Then the path widened and broke off to the right, cutting a new trail that wound back on itself, then dropped down the hill to the ragged edge of the trees. Imogen stopped again. Ahead of her was a clearing, perhaps a hundred feet long and fifty feet wide, ending in nothing – a bluff, a cliff edge, a ledge, she couldn't tell what. But she could see the expanse of the Sawtooth Wilderness stretching into the distance. The sky was carved into separate patches of blue by the height of the mountains. Now she had another choice: take the path down into the trees, or cross the clearing. She stood for what felt like a long time and then took a slow step forwards. Her heart was thumping, the river a tumult in her ears. She could see licks of spray leaping where the clearing ended. She didn't look back, but she knew Connla was behind her.

As she walked the fear grew and her legs felt heavier and heavier, as if they were gradually filling with lead. Her feet dragged in the dust and it was all she could do to place one in front of the other. The cliff climbed on one side of the clearing, and as the edge drew closer, pinion and juniper sprouted in scrubby, low-lying bushes. From somewhere inside her head she thought she heard voices shouting, but it might have been the river.

Ten feet from the edge she stopped. The fear gripped her like a cold fist. Breathing was hard and the tightness in her chest had become a physical pain. She wanted to turn her head, to look back and see if Connla was close. All at once she needed Connla to be close. But she couldn't look back; her eyes were fixed on the height of a fir tree climbing a mountain far in the distance. She was very close to the edge now. She had to get to that edge; she knew she did, but she couldn't take a step.

She sat down heavily. The ground was cold and damp, and she could sense the chill creeping through the meagre protection of her jeans. She couldn't get up, but she had to look over the edge. Rocking forward, she got to her knees, then leaned on her outstretched hands. Lying on her belly, she worked her way towards the edge like a snake, unable to get up, too afraid to try. Closer and closer, elbows in the dirt, hands curled into fists. Eight feet, five feet, four; she could almost see the far banks of the river. She stopped and sucked in a breath. She wanted to see, but her eyes seemed to close. She inched her way forward, eyes shut tight until she felt the rush of cold air on her face. She lay like that, prostrate, resting on her elbows with her fists against her cheeks and her forearms in the dirt. She didn't open her eyes, instead she imagined the river, tearing this way and that, white foam, huge waves, holes in the water where the currents clashed to drag you under. She felt somebody beside her and, opening her eyes, she saw Connla, his face white as stripped bone, his eyes like glass marbles in his head. He, too, was lying flat, but staring straight down. From somewhere behind them she heard voices shouting, real voices this time. She saw the sudden convulsion in Connla's throat, then looked down herself. She screamed.

Twenty feet below, her brother stared up at her. He was being thrashed about by the current, one of his legs trapped under a fallen tree branch which kept him from being swept downstream or dragged fully under. The leg was broken at the knee and it flapped back and forth like a hinge. His eyes were open, but his face was white and he stared without blinking.

Imogen sat hugging herself under the lee of the cliff while they fixed ropes. Connla sat a little away from her, his father by his side, talking quietly to him. Connla's face was ashen, but there were no tears. Imogen's father stood at the edge of the cliff like a broken puppet. He was buckled at the knee and his shoulders were hunched, hands in his trouser pockets. He watched as the rescue team went to recover his dead son. The sheriff was on the walkie-talkie back to the camp. Imogen's father looked round. 'Don't say anything to my wife,' he said quietly. 'I want to tell her myself.'

The sheriff nodded. Imogen's father bit his lip and his gaze met his daughter's. They looked at one another, and she thought he was going to come over to dry her tears and comfort her. But he didn't. He assumed the same ragged position and stared back over the cliff. Imogen looked at Connla, but couldn't catch his eye. He was far away, in some dim and distant place that only he knew about. The sun was out again, shining on his hair and casting his face in shadow so that he looked not of this world. Only his father looked real.

Imogen looked between her knees, suddenly sobbing again. Still her father did not come to her. She got up, wanting to go to him, to take one of the hands from his pockets and hold it, make him hold hers. She took a step towards him when something in a pinion bush caught her eye. She moved closer and squinted. At first glance it looked like a little wooden doll and carefully she picked it up. It was a doll, of sorts – an Indian, dancing with its arms above its head and a feather raised in one hand. It looked like there had been two, but one was broken off at the stem. Quickly she stuffed it inside her coat then, looking up again, she saw the stretcher holding Ewan being hoisted over the edge of the cliff and laid gently on the ground. Her father dropped to one knee, reached out with stiff fingers and touched the lifeless face of his son.

ONE

1998

IMOGEN WAS WOKEN AT FIVE O'CLOCK BY THE SOUND OF the cockerel crowing. That was when the sun, cresting the mountain, flooded the hen house. She had built it herself, and although it was serviceable and dry, it would hardly constitute a threat to either of the local carpenters. She yawned and stretched, then remembered what she'd planned to do later and a murmur of anticipation beckoned. She sat up, dragging crooked fingers through the tangles of her hair and stared at the shadows cast across the surface of the loch. There were two windows in the bedroom, one in either pitch of the roof, and neither of them had curtains. She hadn't bothered with them as one window faced the height of Sgurr an Airgid and the other Loch Gael, and anyway, her nearest neighbours lived fifty yards up the road.

She stood naked for a moment, considering the light. Her small easel was already erected just to the left of the window, which overlooked the loch. The window sill was wide and deep and cluttered with bits of crystal, dominated by two halves of Amethyst expertly sliced through the middle. The easel had been there a week now. Every morning the light was different, and she had to try to catch as much of it as she could before the sun got too high. She was working in oils and she squeezed fresh colour onto the palette. The sun was just high enough, casting the waters of the loch black in the foreground. This was what she needed, what she'd hoped for. Good old Charlie Abbott, waking her up like that. The hens had been a nightmare until she had driven over to Skye to buy him. They had nested just about where they pleased and she'd found eggs in the most unlikely of places. Now he shepherded and cajoled them around the yard and they laid their eggs in the nesting boxes.

She sat on the stool by the easel, still naked, the warmth of the sun from the south-facing window across her back. The light was perfect, and taking a number-twelve brush, she mixed colour and worked on the water in the foreground. Paint smeared the brush stem, blue and black on her fingers. She wiped them on her naked thighs. *Brush strokes are the voice of the painter.* Words from the past – her tutor at college, bending to study the composition she was attempting to breathe some life into. Edinburgh, when she was eighteen. She paused, mid-stroke. Nineteen years ago now, and it felt like only yesterday. Mr Montgomerie – an old man with bony, high-knuckled hands, resting against his thighs to steady himself. *Your style is your style, Imogen. Don't change it just because you change your subject matter. Your style says who you are.*

She sat back, resting a forearm across her raised leg. A boat moved on the mirror-like surface of Loch Gael, Morrisey crossing from one side to the other. He had a smallholding, rented from the estate, on the northern shore. He kept his tractor parked in a lean-to and rowed across the loch from his cottage every morning and every night. It saved him driving round the edge. She watched him pulling on the oars, no more than a speck in the prow. She didn't want him in the picture and, as she waited for him to pass, the light altered and she laid down her brush. She laughed and stood up again; this was going to be a long-term composition, no doubt about that.

She showered, brushed her hair into a single long plait and flicked it over her shoulder, still wet. If it dried that way then it was manageable for longer. Downstairs she put the kettle on, then stepped into the warmth of the morning and looked up at the sky. It was deep blue, like the sea is blue from an aircraft, with no cloud over the mountains. Shading her eyes she looked the length of the valley: nothing on the horizon to suggest anything other than a perfect day.

Charlie Abbott squawked as she unfastened the latch on the hen house. There were very few foxes round here, most of them had been shot or poisoned by the gamekeepers, but that meant that rabbits overran the place. The only thing that had troubled her chickens was the odd feral cat, and they were few and far between. Six hens and Charlie Abbott, she scattered corn and they squeezed out of the narrow doorway into the yard. It wasn't very big – not enough land on which to keep her horse – but it was big enough for the chickens to scrabble about in the dirt.

Back indoors, she ate breakfast and looked at the clock. Seven already. She had time to go up and check on her horse, but there was a lot of preparation to do at school this morning, especially if she wanted to get away sharp this afternoon. The horse would be all right: she had free access in and out of the stable at this time of year, so it wasn't as if Imogen needed to let her out. With half a slice of toast in her mouth and a cup of coffee balanced between her thighs, she drove up the bumpy road and round the south shore of the loch.

Loch Gael was shallow and flat, which was why the sunlight caused such a special effect early in the morning, and it was tiny compared to Duich or Alsh, which ultimately it ran into. Imogen had a seven-mile drive to the main road, single track, only laid with tarmac the previous year. That made a hell of a difference to how much coffee she spilled. The road wound past her neighbours' houses till she crossed the river for the first time; it was more of a tributary really, eventually linking Loch Gael to the sea between Skye, Scalpay and Raasay. She would probably have lived nearer the castle or school given the choice, but the house had been in Gaelloch. When her great aunt had finally passed away, with her parents content to remain in Edinburgh and Ewan long dead, it had come to her.

Ewan. She thought of him suddenly as she worked the heavy Land-Rover over the wooden bridge and across the cattle grid.

She hadn't thought of Ewan consciously in a long time. It was nearly thirty years since he'd died, yet the images of that day could be as vivid as if it were only yesterday. Sometimes his face would lift from where she housed it deep in the layers of memory. It was never as she remembered him alive, but always as in death, his skin white, eyes open and all of it underwater. She shivered and drove on, the Land-Rover bumpy and uncomfortable where a spring was sticking up through the vinyl seat. It was old and battered, but rarely let her down, and it pulled the horsebox over rough ground, which was absolutely vital.

Curving round Loch Long, she could see across Alsh to Glas Eilean, a flat, grassy island on the eastern side of the point. Skye almost linked with the mainland beyond it, where the narrow strait of Kyle Rhea took you out past the Sandaig Islands, southwest to Eigg and Rum. One time she had taken a boat to Rum to paint when the rutting season had begun. Apart from Redynvre, she had never seen red deer stags the like of which rutted on Rum. The school she taught at was in Balmacara, halfway to the Kyle of Lochalsh. Once upon a time there would have been a school in every village, but the Thatcher years put paid to all that. Now the buses ferried primary-school-aged children in from miles around.

Colin Patterson's green Volvo was parked in his usual spot as she pulled off the main road into the car park. He was always there first, partly because he was the head teacher and liked to show willing, but partly because Imogen generally arrived before the other two teachers. She sat for a moment with the engine off and drank the dregs of her coffee, aware of the traffic coming east from the Skye Bridge. At £4.60 a throw, it was no wonder half the islanders still didn't want to pay. She used to paint a lot on Skye, but it wasn't the same since the bridge had been built; at least with the ferry running they could limit the number of visitors.

She could see Patterson through the window of his classroom – tweed jacket, baggy at the pockets, with those leathery buttons and a strip of leather at the top of the breast pocket. He was from

21

Glasgow and had moved north with his family at around the same time as Imogen, half a dozen years ago. The word was that he had been deputy head at an inner-city primary school and hadn't quite been able to hack it. Still, that was nothing to scoff at, she had done much the same in Edinburgh, although perhaps she had left for very different reasons. Teaching, she would never have thought about teaching, not in the heady days of her late teens, when landscape and canvas were everything. Her art was why she hadn't gone to London with her fiancé after college. Well, that was what she'd told herself at least.

Patterson suddenly looked up, saw her sitting in the Land-Rover and waved to her, a broad smile on his face. Imogen glanced at her watch – still early; she was reluctant to go in on her own, but it would be a good twenty minutes before Jean Law arrived. She had her boys to see onto the bus and her husband's lunch to make. Why Malcolm couldn't butter his own sandwiches was beyond her. She sighed, stuffed the coffee mug under the windscreen and shoved open the Land-Rover door. It was stiff and creaked, and she daren't open the split window, even in summer, because she knew she'd never get it closed again. The door shut with an effort, and she noticed the rust chewing ever more urgently at the bottom of the panel. The Land-Rover was pre-suffix, so what could she expect. She had bought it from John MacGregor, the factor, when the Arabs bought out one of the McCrae estates. Mercifully, there were still some McCraes left and the castle hadn't been sold. MacGregor was another one to watch, but not in the same way she had to watch Patterson. MacGregor was far more obvious, and he had been kind enough to her, making sure the Land-Rover was serviced and road-worthy. He had also been instrumental in getting that hill land for Keira, her highland pony. He wasn't married, at least, but he was fifty years old.

Patterson came out of his classroom, all smiles as usual. 'Morning, Imogen.'

'Good morning.' She managed a smile.

'You're early.'

'Aye. There's stuff I need to get ready.'

He seemed to block her path, hovering before her like an expectant fly. Her classroom was adjacent to the one he had just come out of, and his position in the corridor stopped her getting to it without physically brushing against him. This was what made her hesitate, and what he wanted, notwithstanding the fact that his three young daughters attended the school and his wife ran the village post office.

'How are you?' He smiled again, showing all his teeth.

'I'm just fine. I'm very busy, though, Colin.' She moved to get past him.

'Anything I can help you with?'

'No. No.' She didn't look back, but stepped into the classroom and closed the door. It was obvious, closing the door like that with the day warm and everything, but what else could she do. He opened it. She knew he would. She hadn't even hung up her coat.

She looked round and he stood there, hand on the door knob, leaning in the space with one foot crossed over the other, baggy corduroy trousers over brown Oxford brogues.

'There's a staff meeting this afternoon, remember.'

'Yes, I hadn't forgotten.' She had forgotten, and it put paid to her plan to dash straight up the hill as soon as the bell rang. Her spirits fell. The ride to Tana Coire and back would have taken up most of the remaining daylight as it was. 'Have we much to discuss?'

Again he smiled. 'A few things, aye. End-of-term stuff, you know.'

She nodded, one hand fisted on her hip. 'Well, Colin. I'd best get on. No point in coming in early if I don't make the most of the time.'

'No.' He smiled. 'You should make the most of the time.'

He made her flesh creep with the obviousness of his arrogance. Some arrogance could be forgiven – when there was good reason for it, when the arrogant one had something genuine to be supercilious about. It was unnecessary but forgivable. Peter, her ex-fiancé, had had that kind of arrogance, a sort of smugness, based on his ability to make computers obey him absolutely, back when nobody else could. That was probably what finally broke them up, or maybe it was just another reason Imogen gave herself. That and London, of course. Peter had been English, studying at Edinburgh University. He played golf on Saturday mornings. Looking back, they had nothing in common.

Patterson left her alone then and she got on with preparing her day, aware that there were only two weeks left of the summer term and then each day would be hers until September. The mountains beckoned as always, but with the knowledge of what she thought she had discovered the pull was stronger than ever. Her parents would come up sometime in August for a week, as they liked to every year. They would let her be, however, having learned that particular art form years ago. She just had to work through these final couple of weeks and then the time would be hers.

The day dragged by and the children were particularly demanding. At lunch she had to watch them in the playground, along with Jean Law. Jean was west coast born and bred, older than Imogen at forty-five and heavy with red hair and freckles. Her eyes were pale blue and carried the expression of having seen a little too much of everything. They chatted about the up-coming vacation.

'I've got my kids at home, of course,' Jean said. 'Which'll put paid to any romantic notion of running off to the Riviera with some Italian lover.'

Imogen laughed. 'Is that what you'd do, Jeanie, if you had the chance?'

'Of course I would. Sun, sea, sangria. Lots of suntan lotion and some bronzed god to rub it on me.'

'You don't get sangria in Italy, Jean.'

'Chianti then. Darling, I'd settle for Lambrusco.' Jean watched the football some boys were kicking fly over the school gates and land in the soft grass by the loch. She nodded as the kicker looked her way imploringly then raced off after it. 'What will *you* do?' she asked.

Imogen thought about it and smiled. 'Oh, I'll take my horse and ride and paint and listen to the silence.'

'Solitude?' Jean squinted at her. 'I'm jealous of you, lassie. But I'm not sure it's all that good for you.'

'You think I spend too much time on my own?'

'I didn't say that.'

'What're my options, Jeanie? MacGregor, or an affair with Colin Patterson.' She shook her head. 'It might be just me, but I've not noticed the plethora of quality males in Galleoch.'

'There's always Andy McKewan.'

'Oh, yes, I forgot about Andy.' Imogen rolled her eyes to the ceiling. 'Now there's a man with conversation to enthral you.'

Imogen taught arithmetic in the afternoon, and then at a quarter to three she settled the children down for their story. Thirteen six-year-olds, all cross-legged on the cushions in the storytelling corner she had designed with some of her own paintings. She never used a book, but sat cross-legged herself and told them mythical tales of the Celts which she had picked up over the years. They loved the fact she didn't read them, but told them in the old way, from memory, with a conspiratorial edge to her voice. Jean asked her where she acquired the skill, and Imogen had to admit to too many nights in obscure highland pubs where the art of storytelling was still to be found.

'Miss Munro?' Connie McKercher, the daughter of a forester, put her hand up. 'Can we have the story of Olwen?'

'Not again, Connie. I only told you that on Monday.'

Colour brushed Connie's cheeks and she sat with her hands under her thighs and her head bowed for a moment. Imogen smiled at her. 'I'll tell you the story of Hudden and Dudden, two Irish scallywags, and the neighbour they tried to get rid of.' She glanced up and saw Patterson through the glass partition in the door. He smiled at her. She ignored him and looked into the children's expectant faces. Two of the boys were talking and, raising a finger to her lips, she silenced them.

'There once were two farmers called Hudden and Dudden,' she began. 'They had chickens in their yard, cattle in the meadows and dozens of sheep grazing on the hillside. In fact, they had everything a man could wish for, but still they were never happy. Now so it was that right in between them lived a very poor man indeed, so poor that he had but a hovel shack to live in, a tiny patch of grass and one bony old cow called Daisy. His name was Donald O'Neary.' The children listened, an innocence in their faces that delighted her. She told them how Hudden and Dudden plotted against Donald O'Neary and killed his only cow. But Donald was smarter than they were and took his quiet revenge by making them think his old tanned cow hides could produce gold coins by magic, knowing full well that they would steal the hides and make off. It all ended with their drowning in the Brown Lake. As she was finishing, Patterson opened the classroom door and listened. Imogen did her best to ignore him, but his shadow fell across the floor and she couldn't help but focus on it. She finished the story and looked up.

'I just wanted to tell you,' he said. 'The meeting'll be a wee while getting going. I've got a parent who wants to see me.'

Imogen's heart sank. That meant even longer before she could get away. She knew now that a trip to Tana Coire was all but out of the question.

She packed the children off with their parents, then wandered down to the staff room and found Jean making a pot of tea. 'You're a wonder, Jean Law. I could just murder a cup.' Imogen sat down in an easy chair. Tim Duerr was in the bursar's office next door and she could hear him on the telephone.

'Colin Patterson and his damn meetings.' She accepted a cup from Jean, who sat down opposite. She sipped her tea, watching Imogen over the rim.

'You're restless, today, lassie.'

'Am I?' Imogen made a face. 'To tell you the truth, Jean, I'd forgotten all about this meeting. I had plans for this afternoon.'

'What were you going to do?'

'Oh nothing much really,' Imogen lied with difficulty. 'I just wanted to ride Keira up the glen from the field. There's an outcrop of rock there I've always wanted to paint. I wanted to have a good look at it with the light as it is just now.' That wasn't what she was going to do at all, but the lie was a white one and told for good reason. If her initial instinct was right, she would be telling nobody what she had found.

'Light's important?'

'In painting? It is, yes, particularly if you're outdoors.'

Jean smiled. 'Why don't you try to paint for a living? Then you could take off whenever you wanted.'

Imogen thought about that. She could still hear Duerr on the phone next door. 'It's easier said than done, Jean. I sell enough bits through greetings cards. And besides, I'd only miss the children.'

Duerr put the phone down and came through. His face was the colour of rain clouds. 'Parents. Oh how simple life would be without the children's parents.'

Jean laughed at him. 'Then there'd be no children to teach, Tim. Have you thought about that?'

Duerr's face brightened considerably. 'Even better,' he said.

Patterson's staff meeting lasted an hour and a half, and it was almost six o'clock by the time Imogen turned off the main road, past the hotel and headed up the hill.

Eilean Donan jutted from its little island, grey and brown between the chilled waters of Loch Duich and Alsh, a perfect vantage point against any would-be invader. Imogen had always marvelled at the structure, originally a Pictish fort, which gradually evolved into the castle the McCrae's had rebuilt in the Twenties.

The Land-Rover climbed the hill in second gear, the engine whining a little. It had been smoking a bit lately and Imogen wondered if it needed oil. Long ago she had learned to decipher such requirements herself rather than constantly have to ask a man in the village. The road wound steadily higher, climbing the hillside, past the houses that belonged to Colin Patterson and his neighbours. She had often thought about their view of the loch, with the castle in the foreground and Skye across the water. Patterson had invited her round more than once, always when his wife was away in the city, and she had declined. It was getting worse of late, and more and more people were beginning to mutter about it.

Keira was at the top of the field, chewing at the longer grass as Imogen pulled off the road and parked outside the five-bar gate. One hinge was loose and the gate hung at an awkward angle, its bottom in the mud on the right-hand side. Imogen kept a battered horsebox parked in the field, and she had perfected the art of swinging wide on the narrow road and backing it in. It wasn't so much of a field as a hillside really, and a steep one at that. Land only fit for sheep and a solid highland pony. Keira was hardly a pony, standing well over fifteen hands and sturdy as a mountain goat. She looked up nonchalantly when she heard the rumble of the Land-Rover. Imogen whistled to her, and she tossed her head once before returning to eating the grass. The stable was a ruined stone cottage that, once upon a time, had belonged to an enthusiastic crofter. The roof was good and it had garage-style wooden doors. Inside it was dry, though there was one permanently open window, just a gap cut in the stone, which overlooked the loch.

Leaving the Land-Rover where it was, Imogen climbed the gate and strode up the muddy path. She kept one stable door open in summer, allowing the horse free access, and a wheelbarrow rested against the other one with a shovel standing next to it. Keira watched disinterestedly as she set about muck-clearing, before hauling fresh bedding in from the horsebox. Part of the stable formed a tack room, an open section which the horse had access to. She could have chewed the leather off her own saddle if she had a mind. Fortunately she didn't.

Imogen caught her and led her down the hill, where she stood patiently while she was saddled. Her ancestry reached back to the islands, but Imogen felt sure there must have been some mainland horse in her somewhere to account for her size. Like all highlands, though, she was short-headed and broad between the eyes. Grey in colour, her mane was black and flowing, and an eel stripe ran the length of her spine. The feathers on her legs were silver and ended in little tufts at her fetlocks. Imogen had had her since Keira was a baby and had given her the Gaelic name meaning, black haired one.

She brushed her now before she saddled up. There were still three hours till darkness fell, but that wouldn't be enough time to reach the coire and get back again. There was nothing she could do about it. It would have to wait till the weekend, or even till the beginning of the vacation. The yearning to find out was intense, but there was nothing to do but accept it. She just prayed to God that no-one else had seen them.

Keira needed exercising anyway, so Imogen took her down the hillside to the path that ran the length of Loch Duich. It was stony and a little steep in places, but Keira was more than sure-footed and Imogen had her trotting through the shallows all the way to the bridge. There she climbed to the main road, meaning to cross and follow the foothills of Sgurr an Airgid on the way back, but she met John MacGregor in his Land-Rover Discovery, coming from the Shiel Bridge. He waved to her, and she waited while he slowed, the chattering of the diesel subsiding to nothing. He rolled down the window and leaned his arm on the sill, his deerstalker hat perched a little too high on his head. He liked to wear a hat because it covered his missing hair. Imogen smiled at him. 'Good evening, John.'

'Hello, Imogen. Fine evening for a ride.'

'Yes, it's beautiful, isn't it.'

He nodded. 'On your way out or home?'

'A crossroads, I think you'd call it. I was about to turn back.'

He looked beyond her, his eyes a little awkward all at once. 'I've a wee bit of business at the McClachan hatchery, but if you fancy a drink later on . . .'

Imogen hesitated. In a way she felt sorry for him, but enough rumours abounded without adding to them unnecessarily. 'I'd love to, John. But I'm already running late. We'd a meeting after school today and I've done nothing but exercise Keira.'

He looked crestfallen, as if it had taken him all his courage to ask her. Guiding the horse forward, Imogen laid a gloved hand on his sleeve. 'Another time, John. Eh?'

He tried to smile. 'Aye. Another time.'

At home, she stood in the cool of the sitting room and took her book on birds of prey down from the shelf. Carefully, she flicked through it, tucking one loose strand of hair behind her ear, eyes thin in concentration. She ran her finger down the index, then flicked to the pertinent page and began to read. Only as far back as 1991 they had been listed as globally threatened, and they had been extinct in the UK since 1918. A reintroduction programme, with pairs selected from Norway, began on the Hebridean Island of Rum in 1975. She closed the book and smiled. She had painted stags on Rum. That's where she'd seen one before.

TWO

CONNLA WAS ON THE PHONE TO HIS EX-WIFE, SITTING IN his cabin in South Dakota. He had been writing notes for a lecture by the dull glow of an oil lamp when her call had broken his concentration. 'Have you decided when you're coming to Washington?' she asked him. He sat back and lifted the sole of one booted foot onto the roughly hewn edge of the desk.

'As soon as I've finished up here.'

'When's that gonna be?'

He sighed. 'A couple of days, I guess. Why?'

'I just want to make sure you get to that class, Connla. I know what you're like when you go native, and I don't bust my ass trying to get classes for you to teach just so I can look stupid when you don't show up.'

'When don't I show up?'

'When something more exciting happens. Like, you know, Siberia or the jungles of Africa.'

'Don't worry, Holly. I'll be there.'

She was quiet for a moment and Connla said, 'Was there something else?'

'Well, yes. There's a faculty dinner I have to go to and I don't have a partner.'

'What happened to Mario?'

'Mario's out of town. I think he's pissed at me for talking to *you* all the time.'

Connla laughed. 'Just tell him you feel sorry for me.'

'I do. Believe me.'

'But he still gets pissed, huh?'

'Male ego thing. It must be.' She was quiet for a moment. 'It's ridiculous that I can't find a partner, but everyone I know is busy.'

Connla frowned. 'Holly, you're not gonna . . .'

'I don't want to ask you, Connla. We see too much of each other as it is. But I really don't want to go on my own. I figured, what with you teaching here, that it wouldn't look so bad.'

'Aw, Holly. You gotta be joking. I hated faculty dinners when we were married.'

'Yes, Connla, I know. And I hated listening to lecture rehearsals on the consistency of mountain-lion shit, but I was the only one who'd do it. Am I right?' She paused for a moment. 'Anyway it's a fair trade: I get you work when you need it, now I need an escort for a dinner party. Believe me I don't want to show up with my ex-husband, but I don't have a lot of choice.'

Connla sighed. 'OK. OK. Seeing as you made the invitation so attractive, I'll come with you. But don't expect me to behave.'

'When did you ever behave?'

'I'm just saying so we know. When is it?'

'The evening of your lecture class, Connla, the day after tomorrow. The two things'll dovetail perfectly.'

'OK. I'll be there.' He smiled to himself. 'Can I stay at your apartment?'

'God, no. Surely you can afford a hotel. Get a Howard Johnson. They're not expensive.'

'Just kidding, Holly. But I'd like to see Mario's face.'

She snorted. 'Goodbye, Connla. Just make sure you're on time. OK?'

'OK. See you.' Connla hung up and shook his head. They had been divorced for two years now, but they still saw each other because of the work he did for George Washington University every now and then. Once or twice she had let him stay at their old apartment when money was really tight for him, but not since Mario had come on the scene.

Something scratched outside the back door, and he called into the shadows, 'Come on in, if you're going to.'

The door was pushed open and a large, feline head peered at him – black nostrils, whitened fur around the muzzle and dulled yellow eyes. Connla stared at the cougar and she flattened her ears and hissed at him.

'Oh, give me a break, Mellencamp. I've just had your mom on the phone. Come on. It's cold with that door open.' The cougar pricked her ears forward then slunk into the room, leaving the door ajar behind her.

'Your ex-mom's got a class for me to teach, so I'm outta here for a few days.' Connla squinted at the weight of her belly as he got up to close the door. 'She reminded me that she was the only one who'd listen to me talk about your scat. Funny what people remember about a marriage, isn't it.' He bent to his haunches and gently scratched her ears. Mellencamp rubbed herself against him like a domestic cat, then she stretched and sat down on the buffalo-skin rug in front of the fire. She remained there for a moment, blinking slowly at the flames, then looked over her shoulder at Connla. He studied her belly, where the fur gathered in whitened, almost woolly tufts.

'You just eaten, girl, or have you been fooling around?'

She lay flat on her side then, stretching out her paws, the claws suddenly extended, sharp enough to tear an elk's hide from its back. Connla watched her, head to one side. 'You gonna have babies, Mellencamp?' Again, she lifted her head, her tongue curling back over long, canine teeth. She half mewed at him. Connla stood up and, shaking his head, went to the refrigerator for a carton of milk.

The cabin was open plan on one level – bedroom, kitchen and living room all in one. He had tacked on a separate bath-room when he'd bought it ten years previously, but that was all he had done. Holly had always hated the place, and while they were married she'd only stayed when it was absolutely necessary. Connla poured a bowl of milk and laid it out for Mellencamp. She was already brushing against him, and she bent to drink, back sleek and straight, black-tipped tail flicking from side to side. Connla went back to his desk.

'Ought to be water for you, girl. Not good, all this domesticity.' He never forgot she was wild and she came and went pretty much as she pleased. The backyard was large, stretching up the hill and fenced all the way round. She could clear ten feet with no problem, however, and sometimes, when he woke up in the morning, he would find her sunning herself on the porch.

He had rescued her three years before, driving through the rain in his pickup truck one evening on the road out from Custer. It was March, the Easter tourists weren't yet flocking to Mount Rushmore and he had been enjoying the solitude. The rain was sheeting off the tarmac in a white spray, the wipers whipping back and forth across the dirty windscreen, obscuring the road ahead.

Connla was eagle-eyed, though, as observant as he had been as a child, and he spotted the yellow bundle lying by the side of the road. It was a female mountain lion, no more than a year old. He knew mountain lions better than just about anyone, having written a thesis on their habits for his Ph.D. at George Washington University. This one was unconscious but alive, having been hit by a truck. He scooped her up in his jacket and laid her as gently as he could on the bench seat of his Chevy. Back behind the wheel, he spun the truck round and raced all the way to Custer.

The vet took a long look at her and told Connla her ribs were broken, together with both her left legs. He checked for internal injuries, and the X-rays showed some intestinal damage, but nothing too serious. She had a large gash on her head, which would need stitching, as well as a hefty concussion. Eight weeks and a few hundred dollars later Connla took her home. Six weeks after that she got up from the bed he had made on the deck and hopped the fence. She had been coming back off and on ever since. He had been playing 'Jack and Diane' when he'd spotted her, so he called her Mellencamp after John Cougar.

Back at his desk he studied the bones of his lecture; it was only a week now before he had to deliver it. After that there was his English visit to look forward to. But he was still a long way from completing the lecture, and it needed to really hit the spot, because he was pitching for an environmental grant. Maybe Holly's dinner wouldn't be such a bad thing after all: he could pat the pockets of a few well-heeled faculty funders. But he hated Washington just about as much as she hated it here, and, like her, he knew they saw too much of one another. Divorced people with no kids didn't do that. Their trouble was that the whole thing had been completely amicable; no great rows or fights, no other people involved, just fundamental differences that wouldn't go away. Looking back, he wondered how they'd ever got married in the first place. Now they were divorced, the new lines drawn between them were far better defined than the old ones. Splitting their possessions hadn't been difficult. Holly kept the apartment close to the university at Foggy Bottom, and the Keystone shack had always been *his* home. Situated high in the Black Hills, *Paha Sapa*, the holy of holies to the Sioux. Red Cloud had fought tooth and nail to try and keep it after the whites discovered gold.

Mellencamp was watching him from the hearth rug. Connla picked up his notes, scratched the hairs on his forearm and smiled at her. 'Listen to this,' he said. 'Tell me what you think.'

Mellencamp yawned.

'Jeeze, I haven't even started yet.' Connla sat back and cleared his throat. '"Territoriality and the nomadic male". You don't like nomads, do you, girl? No, of course you don't. Go after your babies, don't they.' He looked back at his notes. '"A Lecture by Dr Connla McAdam".'

Mellencamp yawned again, got up and walked to the door. It was still open a fraction and, lifting a paw, she prised it the rest of the way, then disappeared into the night. Connla stared after her. 'That good, huh?'

He was woken by the telephone early the following morning and slapped the wooden nightstand until he located the receiver.

'Hello?' he said, sitting up.

'Dr McAdam?' A soft voice, Native American.

'You got him.'

'This is Joe Hollow Horn over at Manderson, Doc. I think I got a cougar problem.'

'You do?' Connla was fully awake now, pushing his hair back from his face. 'What kinda problem?'

'I got one taking my livestock.'

'Sheep?'

'Yeah.'

'You seen it?'

'I seen a shadow. I could've shot it, but I don't want to. Cougar's my animal totem, you understand?'

'Sure I do, Joe. You want me to come dart it for you?'

'Would you?'

''Course I would.' Connla swung his legs over the edge of the bed. 'I'll dart him and ship him some place else.'

'I'd be obliged, Dr McAdam.'

The drive to Pine Ridge took him via Rapid City. It didn't need to, but he was out of sedative for his dart gun. Stopping at the veterinary office downtown, he picked up a fresh supply and told the vet – who was sympathetic to his affection for cougars – about the call.

'Lucky he called you up, Connla,' the vet said. 'Most people would just shoot it.'

'No kidding. This guy's Oglala, though, and the cougar's his life sign. Kinda helps, you know.'

'Well, good luck, I hope you get him.'

'Yeah, so do I.'

He drove east out of town on Highway 44, through Caputa and the tiny, ridiculously named hamlet Scenic. Somebody must have liked a joke as it was half a dozen buildings falling to pieces on both sides of the street and tumbleweeds rolling across the road. From there it was a right turn off the highway and a two-lane through the Badlands – flat-topped bluffs, grassy on top and chalky white on the flanks. At Sheep Mountain he entered Pine Ridge Indian Reservation, home of the Oglala Lakota: the poorest place per capita in the United States.

Joe Hollow Horn ran a few head of sheep from a low-lying

cabin along the hill from the Manderson Cemetery, the Badlands side of St Agnes Church and Black Elk's old cabin. That was on private land now, but it was still just the same as when the old long-hair narrated his book to Neihardt in the Thirties. Connla parked the truck and a dog barked inside the house. The screen door swung open and a half-blood of about fifty came out wearing wranglers and a 'Junior Bonner' hat.

'Howdy. Thanks for coming out.'

Connla shook his hand. 'Glad you called me up.' He looked at the sky. Grey thunderheads were gathering and he could smell rain in the air. 'Fixing to let go,' he muttered. 'You wanna show me what happened?'

He followed Joe to the back of the house and a bundle of bloodied wool at the edge of the lowest sheep pen. Connla vaulted the fence and squatted next to the carcass.

'Didn't get it away, then?'

Joe shook his head. 'Me coming out musta scared him. I only saw the shadow, but I'm pretty sure it was cougar.'

Connla looked at the wound, the claw marks and the torn-open throat. 'Oh, it was a cougar all right; a big male by the look of it.' Standing up again, he straightened his hat and rubbed his neck where his hair hung below the collar. He gazed up the hill to the first line of trees, then turned to Joe once more. 'You mind leaving some sheep up that hill yonder, Joe?'

Joe squinted at the horizon. 'What you fixing to do?'

'I'm gonna hole up in that cottonwood right there.' Again Connla pointed. 'After what happened last night he'll be hungry and he knows there's food down here. He won't want to come too close to the house and I reckon I can get a dart in him up there.'

'It'll be dark.'

'It will, but I got a torch mount on my rifle.'

Connla straddled the boughs of the cottonwood tree, looking into the face of a horned owl who seemed just a little put out by the company. The darkness was all but complete, and the owl sat, wings tucked back, and looked at him with his head swivelled all the way round. 'Like sharing a tree with the exorcist,' Connla muttered.

It rained on him most of the night and he was glad of his weatherproof gear. It lived in his truck box, along with his dart rifle, which lay, assembled now, across his thighs. He could sit all night; he'd done it many times before, only this time it occurred to him that he was due to be on a plane to Washington in the morning. There was no way he would make it now. That first zoology class and Holly's party would have to go begging. Once darted, he still had to get the cougar loaded into the cage in his truck, then ship it back to Keystone. That was a two-hour drive at best. Then he had to find a suitable place to release the animal. Not easy. He was probably taking a dominant male from his home turf to new territory that would more than likely be occupied. There were very few free areas anywhere from the Black Hills to the Powder River Basin. Over the past two decades he had logged all the male and female turf and pretty much knew their boundaries. This guy would have to rove for a while. He might get his butt kicked a few times but, judging by the size of the claw marks he'd left in the sheep, he could handle it.

Just before dawn he felt the cougar's presence. They were the most elusive of creatures, most prevalent in Idaho, Colorado and California. In all, there were maybe twenty thousand of them scattered across the country, but very few hikers, hunters or would-be photographers ever caught a glimpse of one. Connla figured that after twenty years in the business he was as good a tracker as anyone, and he sensed the arrival of this old male long before he heard him.

The owl had left the tree, the rain had stopped and the wind was coming in from the north. Connla licked his finger and rechecked its direction, just to make sure his scent wouldn't be picked up by the cougar, then he eased himself back against the pale trunk of the cottonwood and readied his rifle. The cougar was still in cover, just at the tree line above him. Connla could hear him moving through the scrub and tangles of undergrowth

– slow, stealthy footpads, all but undetectable. Then he broke cover, keeping low to the ground.

A pale moon shortened the shadows and Connla's night sight was well attuned after the hours he had spent in the tree. The cougar was a dark shape against the thinly covered hillside. The sheep could smell him and they huddled together restlessly. There was no protection for them here; the lights of Joe Hollow Horn's house were a good 500 yards further down the valley. Connla lifted the dart gun, holding it lightly round the stock. The cougar had paused, one foot up like a pointer, his large flat head almost directly beneath Connla's position, ears back, flattened against his skull. He was big all right, tail whipping silently from side to side, shoulder muscles punching his hide as he moved forward again. There was no sound now, every movement was instinctive, as soft and silent as the night.

Connla settled the stock of the rifle into his shoulder and sighted it. He would need the torch mount, but only for a second. The cougar was beyond his tree now, perhaps thirty yards, and he wanted to hit him right behind the shoulder. He aimed, one eye closed, following the dark shape on the hillside. The sheep were bleating, shifting as one, packed against each other for comfort. Connla was aware of fresh lights in Joe's house, but he concentrated on the cougar, settling the gun and letting his breath ease out. Then he pressed the torch mount and squeezed the trigger gently. There was a dull thudding sound and the big male jerked up on his hind legs, rolled over and got up again. Connla kept the torch mount on him and saw the dart, still embedded despite the roll in the grass. The cougar snapped his head this way and that, then reached behind, trying to get at the pain in his shoulder.

The anaesthetic was strong and wouldn't take long to work, but Connla didn't want him loping off up the hill if he could help it. He seemed in two minds about what to do, slightly unsteady on his feet now, but still with the scent of prey thick in his nostrils. Connla sat where he was and watched him lurch a little, his great head swinging from side to side. Then he sat awkwardly on his hind legs and rolled over. Still Connla remained where he was, watching the cougar's side heaving up and down as his breathing slipped deeper into a rhythm. When he was satisfied, he slung the rifle over his shoulder and jumped down from the tree.

The cougar was long in the body and his tail more than doubled his size. A thick dark streak traced the length of his spine, and the very tip of his tail was frayed in black hairs. His mouth hung open, tongue over his teeth, and his eyes were half closed. Connla studied him for a moment. He would certainly need the Indian's help to haul him; he must weigh all of 200 pounds. Rifle over his shoulder, he set off down the hill.

Between them they manhandled the sleeping beast onto the sheet of tarpaulin that Connla fetched from his truck.

'Beauty, ain't he.' Joe nodded approvingly.

'He sure is. You ready?' Connla took the strain his side and they lifted him onto the tailboard of his pickup. The cage was ready and they guided the tarpaulin through the open door and laid it on the wooden base. Connla made sure the cougar was lying correctly and that his airway was free, then he snapped the fasteners on the door and stood back.

'You want some coffee?' Joe asked, tipping his hat back on his head.

Connla glanced at his watch. 'You got it to go?'

On the drive back to Keystone he mulled over the relocation problem. Like wolves, cougars could be released into new areas without any major detrimental effect. You could not do that with a bear. A bear had to know every inch of his territory from birth in order to scavenge enough food from it. A cougar, though, was a hunter, plain and simple; game and other cougars were the overriding factors.

He was trying to gauge it properly in his mind, thinking about the habitat and the other potential inhabitants. This guy was big and he would make good babies. There were lots of female territories up in the Black Hills, but no spare male ones that he knew of. He didn't want to let him loose close to the cabin because he would be a threat to Mellencamp's cubs when she had them. The resident male was getting old and would be no match for this fellow. The incomer would fight, win and then kill Mellencamp's cubs when they were born so that she would be ready to mate again quickly. Connla looked at his watch. He was never going to make it to Washington now. He'd had no sleep and he couldn't just drive anywhere and dump the cougar. He needed to go home, wash up and think about it properly. The cougar would be OK in the cage after he came round from the anaesthetic.

Back in his cabin he placed a pot of fresh coffee on the stove and studied the walls. More than half the available space was covered in large-scale maps of South Dakota, bits of Montana and Wyoming. The geographical area was vast, thousands of square miles. The rest of the space was decorated with photographs he had taken around the world. Shortly after gaining his Ph.D. he had realized that teaching wasn't really for him. He had loved photography since he was a child and the pictures of cougars, lions, tigers, leopards and some of the largest birds of prey were testament to his skill as a wildlife photographer. His most recently published photo, a Siberian tiger, was in the *BBC Wildlife Magazine*. He had taken it from up a tree while the tiger was climbing up to eat him. Looking at his watch, he wondered when he would have the courage to call Holly.

He yawned and sat back, resting one ankle over his knee, and looked carefully at the wall charts. He had to match the cougar in the truck with another male roughly his age and size, or find a vacant patch where the resident male had died or moved on. There were one or two possibilities, but all of them meant a few hours in the truck. His best options were in the Powder River Basin, but he didn't want to admit the drive was necessary. He closed his eyes, kneading the lids with stiff fingers, and yawned. Bed looked inviting; maybe he should sleep on it for a while.

He glanced at the wall again, his gaze just wandering now. Above the desk he had a collection of newspaper clippings from the United Kingdom, and he considered the face of a panther staring out of one of them. BLACK BEAST OF ELGIN was the headline. He had read it a thousand times, but still he reached for it and inspected the picture closely. With his UK visit coming up, his interest had redoubled. The panther in the picture had obviously been photographed at a zoo, but it was there to show the reader what the supposed Beast of Elgin looked like. Elgin was in north-east Scotland and at least four separate people claimed to have seen the cat. Their descriptions of size and colour told him that it was a panther, or, to term it correctly, a black leopard. Close up, you could see the rosettes against the black background. Leopards were smaller than cougars, weighed less and their hind legs were not enlarged. Their heads were a different shape and you could recognize individuals by the lines of small spots on their muzzle. He laid the piece down again and scratched the bristles crowding his jaw. Big cats running wild in the UK. The idea of it fired his imagination, because no-one was really sure they were there. It had never been proven beyond doubt. Were they real or only imaginary? Nobody had ever got the definitive picture on film, but there was plenty of evidence to suggest they were out there in the hills and forests of Britain.

Connla looked at his cameras, lying carefully in their cases beside his bed. If he could get a picture of a panther in the UK, he would really be on the wildlife-photography map. And the more that happened, the less he would need to teach in the class-room.

He was due in Britain in a few weeks' time. A zoo in the south of England was awaiting the arrival of two cougars, which were being shipped over from Banff in Canada. The owners had invited Connla to help get them settled in – something that happened from time to time since he was recognized as one of the leading authorities in the world. He stared again at the phone. What should he do: drive up to the Powder River Pass or wait a while and phone Holly? Picking up his hat, he headed out to his truck.

Once the cougar was safely released in Wyoming he had tele-phoned Washington. There was no answer at his ex-wife's apartment, so he'd left a message then tried the university, left another message on her voice mail and called her cell phone. There was no connection on that either, so finally he emailed her from his laptop and went to sleep. Rising early the following morning, he caught the first flight out of Rapid City. Holly hadn't called him back, which didn't bode well, and he assumed she was really pissed off about him missing the first zoology class. The trouble was, he thought as he hailed a cab in Washington, that what was important to her, or the university for that matter, was very different to what was important to him. They would never understand about the Indian and the cougar. Hundreds of cougars killed livestock, why didn't he just shoot it like everyone else.

The cab took him to the Holiday Inn close to the university medical centre and Foggy Bottom Metro Station. He wandered past their old apartment building and saw that Holly's car wasn't in the allotted space, so he assumed she was still at the university. In his hotel bedroom he tossed his bag onto the bed and twisted the top off a bottle of beer. The cab ride had been sticky, the traffic heavy and he wondered why he hadn't just taken the metro. The beer was cold and crisp in his throat, and he wiped his mouth with the back of his hand in satisfaction. Sitting down on the bed, he stared for a while at the telephone, then, picking up the receiver, he dialled her office at the university.

'Dr McAdam.'

He transferred his beer from one hand to the other. 'Hello, Dr McAdam. This is the other Dr McAdam, calling you up to apologize for putting the life of a cougar before a zoology class and a party.'

She didn't say anything for a second, then, 'Are you trying to be funny?'

'No, ma'am.'

'Don't give me the hicksville homeboy act, Connla. It doesn't wash any more.'

Connla smiled. 'Yes, ma'am.' He paused. No laughter. 'I thought that's what attracted you to me in the first place.'

'Attractions fade, or didn't you figure that out yet. Besides, I was very young then. I'm older and wiser now.'

She was softening; he could tell. 'You don't mean that. It was *always* the country-boy thing that got you.'

'I *do* mean that.'

'I am sorry, Holly. Really,' he said. 'But I'm here now and all set to teach up a storm to those students.'

'The faculty's pissed, Connla. They had to cancel the class.'

'I'll explain it to them, don't worry. Zoology in action; that's what I was doing. Hell, the students'll understand.'

'I hope so.'

'There you go.' He sucked on the beer. 'What time will you be done? I'm fixing to buy you dinner.'

'Late. I've got a meeting to go to.'

'Ah.' He smiled to himself. 'Payback time.'

'No. I've got a meeting, Connla. I'm a senior academic. D'you remember academe? We have meetings to attend.'

'Are you still mad at me?'

'Of course I am.'

'So you don't want me to buy you dinner then?'

'Connla, you go ahead and book an expensive restaurant. I just might not show up, is all.' She hung up without saying goodbye.

Connla grimaced at himself in the mirror. 'Yep,' he said. 'Payback time.'

THREE

I MOGEN ENDED THE LAST DAY OF TERM BY TELLING THE
children the tale of the sea maiden. She stood and chatted to
the parents at the school gate, but all the time she was itching to
get home and prepare for her upcoming trip. Events had
conspired against her over the last couple of weeks and she had
been unable to return to Tana Coire. Patterson was busy with a
parent and Imogen hoped to slip away quietly, but she could
tell by the way he kept looking over that he wanted to speak to
her. She never gave him the chance, however. School was
finished and the time was hers, and she climbed into the cab of
her Land-Rover.

Clouds were gathering west of the Skye Bridge, smoke
coloured and rolled like open-ended barrels. She drove back to
the turn for Gaelloch and saw Andy McKewan's Toyota truck
parked in front of the hotel – the fisherman from Kyle, another
one who wanted to get into her knickers. What was it about men
that they all seemed to seek women's company with some
ulterior motive? Feigning friendship only to try it on at the first
opportunity; so arrogant that they believed women would fall
for the little they were offered. An affair with Patterson, a date
with the ageing John MacGregor, or a quiet fumble with
McKewan. Was that merely cynicism or was it her experience?
She thought about it, mulling over her abortive relationships,

the half-hearted attempts since she broke up with her college fiancé. There wasn't much to analyse really, most of her encounters had been brief, to say the least. Was that a commitment problem on her part, or theirs? Or had they just been the wrong people. They say your past shapes who you are. She wondered if that had something to do with it.

Halfway along the seven-mile stretch to her house it began to rain, though the sun was still refracted in the waters of Loch Gael. It did that a lot here, mini rainstorms brushing in from the sea with the sun still strong in the east. The loch lay rumpled like black velvet, a perfect rainbow climbing above it. Imogen exhaled heavily and felt her soul freeing up at the sudden, silent beauty of the place. This is why she had spent every childhood holiday she could recall here. Her great aunt had seen what she saw and knew that she could see it, too. The first time Imogen remembered coming to visit her she had found some of her oil paintings in the attic. After that, when the old woman painted, Imogen sat and watched and learned. She had been more of a grandmother than a great aunt really; her mother's mother died long before Imogen was even thought of. They had had a special bond and Imogen remembered writing letters to her when she was a little girl in America.

Parking the Land-Rover, she gazed at the grey stone house and, for one fleeting moment, felt the old lady's presence. It happened now and again, and Imogen had always thought that she was somehow watching over her. She could picture her, sitting here in the garden with an easel and brushes, painting the loch from every angle in every kind of light or weather. Every summer Imogen would sit with her and watch. One gnarled, arthritic hand would grip a brush between the middle joint of her thumb and the flat of her forefinger; her fingers twisted with age, yet still able to respond to what her eyes beheld. She had never needed glasses. She'd never cut her hair and it had hung in silver lines to her waist. In her youth she had been beautiful. Charlie Abbott, ushering his hens across the grass, broke Imogen's thoughts. He looked up at her, head darting, chest out. He squawked at her.

'What's the matter with you?' she said. 'You're just like all the rest. How many women d'you need?'

He looked a little puzzled and Imogen went indoors.

The kitchen was spacious, warm in winter but cool in summer, and it opened on to a large, high-ceilinged lounge, with tall, thin windows facing south and north. Beyond it was the hall, with stairs climbing into the roof and the three large bedrooms. On the other side of the hall was her studio, stark and bare and very private. Her aunt had knocked down whatever crofter's cottage had been on the land originally and built this imposing house in the style of the eastern seaboard. Upstairs, the landing stretched, her bedroom at one end and the low-ceilinged bathroom at the other. Imogen filled it with plants and dried flowers. The bath stood on four lion's feet and was deep and enamelled, and you had to run the hot water first to avoid your bottom freezing in winter.

First thing in the morning she went up and saddled Keira. The sun was low still, but full and bright, and it reflected off the grey, flaglike stones of the cottage walls. The horse stood rattling the metal bit against her molars, saliva gathering in a yellowed froth at the sides of her mouth. Imogen flipped the girth strap over so it hung to the ground on one side, then bent under Keira's belly to reach it. Her mane hung unbrushed down one side of her face and she twisted her head back to nibble Imogen's thigh. Imogen wore jodhpurs and battered knee-length riding boots. She had saddlebags packed and ready, with her small easel folded into the rucksack set against the stable wall.

'Good morning.' The voice from behind made her jump. Keira shifted under her hand, half cocking one hind leg. Imogen looked round, shading her eyes, and her heart sank as she saw Patterson striding up the path from the gate. He must have seen her Land-Rover pass his house on the way up. 'Beautiful, isn't it,' he went on. 'Wonderful morning for a ride.'

Imogen still hadn't got the girth strap tight, but she wasn't going to bend for it now, with Patterson standing behind her. He smiled his Colin Patterson smile and his eyes were all over her. 'You look good.' He said. 'Jods. They look very good.'

Imogen dropped to her haunches, still half facing him, and tightened the girth strap. She waited for Keira to breathe, then pulled again and fastened it. She stood straight once more and lifted a stirrup, adjusting the strap behind it. She was suddenly aware of the smell of horse and leather and the fact that Patterson shouldn't be here, in her place, where the beauty was incredibly private.

'What can I do for you, Colin? I was just about to get going.'

'Where?' he said, leaning against the wall of the cottage. 'Where are you off to?'

'Just up the hill.' She did not point or gesture.

'For the day?'

'Probably.' Keep the conversation to the minimum, she told herself, and he might just go away. But he didn't. He stood there and chatted, listening to the sound of his own voice, oblivious to the atmosphere that must have been pretty apparent. All at once Imogen thought of her other would-be suitor, and wondered again at the quality of man who pursued her. What did they think they saw in her? Patterson married and MacGregor still living with his mother.

'I'd love to come with you one of these days,' Patterson was saying.

She fixed the other stirrup to the right length and reached for the saddlebags.

'Here, let me help you.' Patterson bent at the same time as she did and his fingers brushed the back of her hand. It was all she could do to stop herself from physically recoiling. She stood up quickly. He had the saddlebags, and for a brief moment they looked at one another. Patterson tried to smile, but Imogen's face was frozen. Suddenly self-conscious, he passed the bags to her. She fastened them quickly, then picked up her backpack and slung it over one shoulder. Patterson just stood there, looking from her to the view over the loch and back again. 'Such a pretty spot,' he said. 'Wonderful place to stable a horse.'

Imogen didn't reply. She guided the horse round the back of the cottage, past the old sheep pens to the path that led, at a calf-straining incline, between the cleft in two hills. Black-faced sheep cropped at the yellowing grass on either side of it.

'I have to be going, Colin.' Imogen turned without another word and began the stiff climb. She had to lead Keira the first bit, till she was out of sight at least. That would mean Patterson could stand there and watch the stiffening muscles in her limbs, the length of her legs under the boots, her hair flapping against her backside. She could feel his eyes on her every step of the way, determined, however, not to look back.

'You were lucky,' he called. And now she had to turn. He made an open-handed gesture at the field. 'With all this. Good old John MacGregor.' He looked very small and dark against the horizon, the expanse of Loch Duich and the foothills of Skye. That's how she would paint him – God forbid that she ever did – very small and dark. With a brief wave, he turned and trotted down the path like a puppy suddenly pleased with itself.

Imogen led Keira between the twin fingers and through the little gully with the sheep trails hewn out of its middle. She was glad of the rough path: the grass was greasy at this time of year, even when it was bone dry. It was long and tough, the stems sharp if you plucked them, and its length made it slippery. The heather didn't grow here. It started on the far side of the hills and climbed with the summer sun right into the mountains. She couldn't avoid thinking of Patterson and his parting shot about MacGregor. Patterson knew about MacGregor. Everyone knew about poor John; he made it so painfully obvious. Sometimes she would see him when he came out of the Kirk on a Sunday, black suit, black hat, like something from a bygone age. He always wore a hat, except when he was actually in church. On Sundays it was the antiquated homburg and the rest of the week the deerstalker. She wondered if he prayed to God to marry her.

She was angry with herself for allowing Patterson to interrupt her mood, the first opportunity she had had to get away since she had made the discovery on Tana Coire. She had meant to go long before now, but her mother had phoned from Edinburgh and then came up last weekend without her father, which was very strange. They had had one of their extremely rare semi-meaningful discussions, and her mother hinted that she feared Imogen's father was seeing someone else.

Imogen was shocked, watching her as she sat at the wide kitchen table, her hand fisted, the knuckles bumps of bone that reminded Imogen of her great aunt. Her eyes were tight, pocketed in wrinkles of flesh, her cheeks a powdered white, like parchment dusted with chalk. She hadn't seen her mother this close to tears since Ewan had died. Tears, indeed any form of emotion, were not something she showed very often.

'Why?' Imogen said. 'What makes you think that?'

'Oh, it's nothing really. I'm probably just being silly. It's just that I found a phone number on the bill which I didn't recognize, that's all.'

'So what?'

'I know, I know. But I always check the bill, and there's only so many numbers we call. You know how I am about keeping the costs down. I recognize numbers and I've never seen this one before.'

'Where was it, d'you know?'

'Edinburgh. Musselburgh, I think.'

'And you don't know who it is?'

Her mother looked up at her and shook her head.

'Have you phoned it? That'd be the best way to find out. I mean, it could be anyone: a plumber, a shop where he bought something. It could be just about anything.'

She shook her head. 'No. No, I couldn't do that. That'd be prying. Anyway, it's probably just nothing.'

'Why don't you ask Dad?'

Her mother got up then, still shaking her head. 'I'll make some tea, shall I.'

And that had been the end of it, the subject broached and dismissed again without anything really being discussed, just the surface scratched before emotion was dusted back under the carpet.

Imogen had wanted to ask what the number was, feeling positive her mother would have memorized it. Imogen had suspected the same thing for some time after finding an unknown Edinburgh phone number on her bill at the end of last summer. It had coincided with the time her parents had stayed, and when curiosity finally got the better of her she had phoned it herself. A woman answered and Imogen hung up.

She knew her mother would never phone it or ask her father outright. If it was another woman it would just be a fling. There was no danger that he would ever leave her, which is why she could brush it aside. Imogen's father blamed himself for Ewan's death, and to break up the family even more would compound that guilt beyond his ability to cope with it. Quite why he blamed himself, Imogen didn't know. How he could possibly begin to think that he was in some way responsible was beyond her. Maybe it was because, for a few years afterwards, her mother seemed to blame him, perhaps in the absence of anyone else.

Thoughts of the past clogged her mind on a beautiful summer's day when all she could hear were the burred voices of ewes calling to half-grown lambs, and the steady hoof beat of her pony. She paused at the height of the incline and looked back across the water. This was a spectacular view, the horizon bordered on either side by the greening walls of the twin-fingered hill. Dropping the reins, she stood for a long moment, gazing between Skye and the mainland at the grey-green channel of Kyle Rhea. The sun was high and the day shimmered in the still light of summer. From the copse of larch trees she heard wood pigeons calling. The horse carried on up the trail, pausing as she came out of the gully to crop the grass. Imogen remained a few moments longer, watching the colours change as the shadows shifted over the water.

Catching Keira, she mounted, leather creaking as she fitted her slightly built frame into the saddle. She kicked her feet into the stirrups and gathered in the reins, bringing the pony's head up without pulling harshly on the bit. She paused, looking between the mountains and choosing a path that would take her deep into the wilderness.

A couple of miles in she picked up Redynvre's tracks; he was ambling with a band of other stags, as always at this time of year. He liked to walk slightly apart, though, as if he knew he was bigger and stronger, as if he didn't want the fraternity to become too close in view of the rut to come later. His slot was easy to trace. Most of the red deer Imogen tracked had average-size hoof prints, Redynvre's were deeper and measured over ten centimetres from tip to base. He also had a chip on his right fore hoof which never seemed to grow out.

She caught up with the trail on the lower slopes of Corr Na Dearg, a 3,000-foot peak five miles north-east of the field. The heather clawed at the land here, climbing darkly from the lower slopes to the blue-grey granite bluffs. A small burn ran from the summit and the water was some of the freshest she had ever tasted; she could hear the rumble now in the stillness. No wind today, and the sun was working steadily higher. Redynvre had passed this way only a matter of hours before, and she knew she would find him maybe a mile or so further on, where the heather was thick on the upper slopes. He had paused to rub himself on the Seer Stone where the log bridge forded the River Leum. Imogen had no idea how she knew that; a thousand deer must have passed this way.

She found him where she thought she would, rounding a bend on the flattened track-strewn trail, muddied still in the middle by the last serious rainfall. The path opened into the sloping vale of Leum Moir, a vast mantle of ochre and green which crested in the savage, black tooth crags above Tana Coire. Maybe Redynvre saw her, maybe he scented or heard the approaching horse, but he lifted his great head, standing slightly apart from his peers, some younger some older than him, and bellowed across the land. Imogen stopped, the familiar thrill in her breast. She had trailed him for three years now and he seemed to know when she was coming. She had watched him cast his antlers in March and snort and dance away from his bachelor band as each autumn beckoned. She had watched him in the rut, when his great voice rang out so loud and long that he had up to twenty hinds in his harem. As far as she knew he had never been beaten in a fight, and he was in his prime at about eight or nine years old. Stags normally only roar during the October rut, but he always called when he saw her, as if he were practising, as if in some way he sensed her femininity. It was August now, and his antlers were still covered with velvet. They would start to fray in late September, and by early October they would be full grown, ten or twelve points, hard and sharp and strong.

Keira whinnied across the valley and the other stags, clipping at the heather, looked up. Redynvre stood chewing the cud, the wildness in his eyes, black nostrils flared. The horse and woman rode closer; the other, younger stags looked to Redynvre for the lead, but he didn't move away. Imogen slid from Keira's back and left her to browse the grass. For a moment she stood with the wind in her face, watching the deer, her pack still between her shoulders. Redynvre was on the downward slope facing her and beyond him lay the chilled waters of Loch Thuill, where the height of the sun reflected. Above him a clustered outcrop of granite sparkled with slivers of crystal. Imogen saw movement in the rocks above the coire and a pulse began at her temple. Sliding the pack from her back, she took out her binoculars and scanned the horizon. Then her breath stilled as she caught him in full flight, descending low over the loch. He was enormous, his body at least three feet long, wing span not less than nine from tip to tip. White fanned tail feathers, hooked yellow bill and yellow-skinned feet. His wings frayed into fingers against the pockets of wind. She knew he shouldn't be this far inland, but he was. *Iolaire suil na greine*. The eagle with the sunlit eye. He soared again, circled, and then, dropping like stone, he scoured the waters for fish.

FOUR

CONNLA SAT IN AN ARMCHAIR IN HOLLY'S OFFICE AT George Washington University, letter in one hand, TV remote control in the other. Holly was standing at her desk across the thick pile carpet, speaking on the telephone and watching him. From outside, in the corridor, Connla could hear the crash and clatter of students. He rewound the videotape, then ran it forward, stopped and froze the frame. Sitting straight now, sleeves pushed up, copper band exposed at his wrist, he squinted at the screen. For a moment the letter detailing his trip to the UK was forgotten as he studied the head of the leopard. Bigger than the female, and broader, he weighed half as much again. Right now he was squatting on a termite mound, surveying the sea of grass. His tail, longer than his body and white-tipped, curled behind him and pointed up at the sky. He was intent on a small group of impala, specifically two fawns. Game was good, but there were lion and hyena to contend with. A small impala could be hoisted out of harm's way up a tree.

'Connla, I wish you'd ask.' Holly had come in and found him in front of the TV screen. She was about to say something when the phone had rung. She stood behind her desk now, hand fisted on her hip, petite, with short dark hair, pale skin and high cheekbones.

Connla pressed the play button and spoke without looking round. 'I'm sorry, Holl; there was nowhere else to go.'

'That doesn't mean you can just waltz in here whenever you feel like it. I didn't even know you still had a key.'

Connla did look round now. 'You gave it me, remember?'

She pursed her lips at him. 'That was years ago.'

Connla lifted his shoulders. 'You never asked for it back.'

Holly blew out her cheeks. 'God, you're really amazing, you know that.' She looked at the TV screen. 'What are you watching anyway?'

'Steve Hutchings' film for *National Geographic*.'

'I suppose that's what you want to do?' She steepled her fingers, elbows on the desk before her. Connla looked at her. 'I'll always prefer stills,' he said. 'But six months in the Masai Mara with a film crew – yeah, I'd give it a shot.'

As Connla taught only infrequently, and wasn't an official part of any faculty, he used to share Holly's office when they were married. She had given him a key some two and a half years previously. 'Who was on the phone?' he asked.

'My father.' She had her fingers steepled to her chin, watching Connla, as if quietly deliberating. She swung herself lightly from side to side in the swivel chair.

Connla was looking at the leopard again. He was off the termite mound now and slinking through the swaying yellow grass, belly to the ground, shoulder muscles almost mechanical against his skin. 'God, would you look at him move.' Connla shook his head. 'They are so different to cougars, Holly. They move differently. A cougar's belly's lower at the front, or higher at the back, whichever way you look at it.'

Holly sighed then and shook her head. 'D'you have any idea how many times you've told me that?'

'Nope.'

'Well, a dollar a throw would be nice.' She stood up. 'Connla, you can't keep doing this: invading my life when it suits you, then clearing off when something better comes along.'

'That's not fair, Holl.'

'It's perfectly fair, believe me. Have you ever thought about getting an office of your own?'

Connla made a face. 'You mean getting the job that goes with

55

it? I couldn't do that, Holly. Besides, we create a lot of gossip round here. People wouldn't know what to talk about.'

'Not funny, Connla. It stopped being funny a long time ago.'

Connla flicked the television off and got up to pour some coffee. 'So how is your father, anyway? Does he still wanna be president?'

'My father's fine. He's another one who thinks I let you take advantage of me.'

'So what's new? He always thought that, even when we were married.'

'He's my dad, Connla. He looks out for me.'

'Yeah, right. Of course he does.'

'What's that supposed to mean?'

'It means he wants you to stay his little girl. You watch him, Holly. He'll do the same thing to Mario as he did to me.'

Holly laughed then. 'He gets on fine with Mario. I don't suppose it ever occurred to you that it might just be *you* he didn't get along with.'

Connla grinned. 'I guess he never did appreciate my charm, huh. My wit across the dinner table.'

'You mean your infantile sense of humour.'

'Infantile. Really! I thought you liked it.' He laid down the coffee cups and cracked a lopsided grin. He was tall, over six feet, with green eyes, like a cat. 'I thought that was why you married me.'

'Maybe,' she said, slowly. 'But I divorced you. Remember?'

He sat down again and picked up the letter.

'What've you got there?' she asked him.

'The invitation from England. You know those two Canadian cougars.'

She perched on the arm of his chair and Connla handed her the sheet of paper. It was from the Verwood Zoological Park in the New Forest.

'William the Conqueror planted that forest,' Holly informed him. 'It's a thousand years old.'

'Is that a fact?' Connla tried to remember his European history. 'Was he the guy that shot that other guy in the eye?'

Holly laughed. 'I don't think it was actually him, but you're close.'

Connla took the paper back. 'I'm really up for this, Holly. Should be a great trip.'

'Are you getting paid?'

'Something. Expenses, certainly.'

She looked at him from under her eyebrows. 'What about the summer school?'

'Who needs summer school? You've got me two semesters, starting September.'

'Yes, I did.' She let breath hiss between her teeth. 'Although, God knows why. But I tell you, I sure as hell expect you to be here for them.'

Connla flew into Heathrow airport in early August, the aircraft turning in a wide arc over London. He had been sitting next to a little old lady who told him she was from a place called Bagshot, and Connla had visions of some crusty English gent with a blunderbuss under his arm. London was multicoloured from the air: expanses of green dotted here and there, rugby posts, soccer nets and the odd tennis court amid the concrete. He recognized Hampton Court from old pictures he had seen in a magazine, and the woman seated next to him confirmed it. He had no idea where he was going once he hit the ground, but he had been wired his airfare and a rental car had been organized, so he guessed he would figure it out from there.

The airport was heaving. The plane landed at Terminal 3 and the crowds strained at the barrier as he came through, carrying his travel and camera bags. Nobody was meeting him and he wasn't due at the zoological park until the following morning, so he slowed things down, all at once weary from the journey. He bought himself a beer in the bar on the other side of the barrier, finding respite in the form of a metal-based stool. He sat and sipped at a Bud, his Pendleton hat, with its broad flat brim, upturned on the counter at his elbow. The bartender was polishing glasses and Connla caught his eye with a tip for the beer.

'How far is the New Forest from here, buddy?' he asked.

The young man, Asian with black eyes and black hair, scooped the coins into his waistcoat pocket. 'I don't know,' he said. 'About a hundred miles.'

'Is it easy to get to?'

'Are you driving?'

'I will be.'

'It's down the M3. Follow the signs west; it should be pretty straightforward.'

Connla thanked him, finished his beer and went in search of the rental company.

The zoo had organized a small car for him, and Connla studied the picture as the assistant did the paperwork.

'This isn't very big, right?'

The girl looked at the picture. 'It's an Astra. It's about average, I suppose.'

Connla smiled at her and leaned his elbows on the counter. 'What else you got?'

'The zoo only paid enough for this type of car, sir.'

'Yes, I know. But what else have you got?'

'A bigger car, you mean?'

'Car. Truck.' Connla was looking at the Land-Rover Discovery. 'I'm used to driving a truck. How much is this?'

'Quite a lot more, sir.'

He fished a Mastercard from his wallet and handed it to her. 'Upgrade it for me, will you?'

He negotiated the exit from the rental lot and followed signs for the M4. He couldn't decide which way to go, whether or not to try London itself or head south right away. In the end, he took the wrong turn at a roundabout and the decision was made for him as he found himself heading into central London. He got snarled up in the traffic and looked for an exit route. He came down a slip road, turned round and headed west again, out of the city. The map the rental company had given him told him to head for the M25, then the M3 towards Southampton. He drove more carefully now, wondering why London had beckoned at all, considering how much he despised big cities.

There was concrete everywhere. The M25 was thick with fumes, cars, coaches and eighteen-wheel trucks clogging the eight carriageways. The road looked as though they were trying to widen it further and he wondered if it would make any difference. People seemed pretty relaxed, however, considering all the congestion. There was nobody bruising anyone's bumper, not many horns blaring and no rifles hanging in the backs of any trucks. Some of the good old boys in Rapid City did that: hung a 30/30 in the rear window of their pickup. It sure put people off ramming your rear bumper. Connla had never bothered; the only rifle he owned was the kind that fired darts.

He found the M3 motorway only slightly less congested. London seemed to sprawl from its south-westerly limits all the way to the coast. He passed Basingstoke, witnessing a couple of twin grey towers on his right, and still the London overspill appeared to tail him. He missed Southampton and took the M27 west; then, at last, moorland rolled out on either side of him, and the forest that William the Conqueror had planted drifted against the horizon. It was late afternoon when he pulled off the road and into the car park of a pub that advertised accommodation.

The reception formed part of the bar, or rather the barman took the bookings, and charged him £25 for the room, which he worked out to be about $40, which wasn't too bad. The room had a shower and he stood under the hot water for a full half-hour. His hair was too long – Holly had been right about that at least – he needed to get it cut. When it was wet it stuck to the top of his shoulders and got cold really quickly. Towelling himself dry, he sat on the edge of the bed and spread before him the series of photographs the zoo had sent.

Two cougars: a big male and smaller, very pretty female. The pictures had been taken in Banff, where the two cats had been found as cubs when their mothers were killed – one in a rare fight with a grizzly and the other having been hit by a truck. Four cubs in all had been recovered from two different areas by park rangers. Two of them, a male and female from different families, had ended up in Banff. Connla knew them both well and had been asked to help out during their first weeks in Canada. The keepers over here shouldn't have too much trouble, so long as they treated them properly. He wondered how big their pens would be, and what kind of flight across the Atlantic they had had. He hated the thought of animals flying; it was just about the most unnatural thing in the world. Still, there were very few cougars in the UK, and the park had a good reputation. They were renowned for breeding Siberian tigers, which were all but extinct in the wild, now. The cougars ought to fit very well with their collection generally, and given a little luck they might begin to breed.

Downstairs, he laid his hat on the bar, and one of the locals made a crack about cowboys, which Connla took in good humour. He bought a pack of cigarettes, though he was trying to quit. A good-looking girl was serving and she seemed to take a special interest in him, much to the displeasure of a group of three workmen in their early twenties who came in at about nine o'clock. One of them commented on it and Connla told him it was only because he was American. 'Come on out to Rapid City,' he said. 'Same thing'll happen to you.'

It was enough to placate them. Connla was all but twice their age, and the last thing he needed was any aggravation on his first night in the UK. So he bought them a drink and they quietened down, and he ended up beating their butts in a pool game.

He got up at seven in the morning and drove straight over to the park. He could hear an African lion roaring as he parked the Land-Rover. The sun was up and he could feel the beginnings of the heat in the day. Already the thin cotton of his shirt was stuck to his back from the car seat. He took his cameras and made his way to the main gate. The park wasn't open to the public yet, and his was the only vehicle parked between the logs laid in the dirt. The lion was calling across the park as the early morning mist burned away, asserting his authority, or trying to. He would smell the antelope, zebra and giraffe, not to mention the other big cats. Connla slung his camera bag over his shoulder and stopped at the barred gate by the wood-cabin entrance.

A wall-mounted telephone faced him, and he picked up the receiver and listened: a buzz, a hum, then a female voice in his ear.

'Hello?'

'Hi there. Dr McAdam from the United States. I'm your mountain-lion man.'

FIVE

IMOGEN CAMPED ON THE BANKS OF LOCH THUILL, WITH THE coire – the ancient glacial flow – lifting to the uppermost crags. Keira was safely hobbled and grazed close by on the sweet, short grass of the mountain in high summer. The white-tailed eagle had been fishing for trout and, undisturbed by the presence of the woman or the horse, he soared and dived in turn at the loch. Imogen had had no idea there were trout here. For a long time she had sat and watched him, legs crossed, sketch-pad laid in the crook of her lap, marking the colours of bird, mountain and water. She'd had a real thrill when Redynvre, intrigued by her presence and perhaps the fact that she was all but ignoring him, had wandered to within ten feet of her. He had lifted his head, nostrils steaming as the afternoon temperature fell, and lowed at her like a cow straining to its calf.

Later in the afternoon the hunting eagle was joined by his mate, who was slightly smaller, her wing span less full, and they flew together, soaring on the up-draughts of the barely percep-tible breeze while Imogen watched them with one hand shading her eyes from the sun. They fished and fed until dusk, then lifted off from their perch on a withered tree to glide in one final loop over the loch before soaring to the massed height of the crags. Somewhere up there, she thought, they must be nesting.

Imogen looked at the sketch she had made, and the colours, which weren't yet filled in, were imprinted on her mind. When she got home she would paint the eagle in flight. She took her fishing rod from where it was stowed across the saddlebags, set it up and hooked some trout for her supper. It was too late to head home, and the sun was fading fast in the west when she cleaned and gutted two ten-inch rainbow trouts before setting the fillets on sticks to cook over the small fire she had kindled. She was deep in thought, at one with her solitude and the darkness, which quietly smudged the land. Redynvre and his cohorts were long gone, having roamed as far as the distant tail of the coire, no longer even dots against the ever-dimming horizon. The stars scratched like imperfect diamonds at the purpling haze of the sky, and Imogen sipped coffee, smoked a cigarette and considered. This was Atholl McKenzie's land, a tough, dour farmer who had bought about a thousand acres from the estate. It was virtually all sheep and she would bet her life on the fact that neither he nor any of his labourers knew that a pair of white-tailed sea eagles from Norway were nesting on Tana Coire.

She sat and stared at the sky, turning the fish now and then and sipping from her coffee cup. She wondered if she was the only person who knew about the eagles. She had seen nobody on her way there. She had watched closely and scrutinized the birds through her binoculars, and neither of them were ringed or wing-marked, as far as she could tell. She doubted, then, whether anyone else was aware of their presence, and she felt very privileged – the kind of emotion she experienced whenever she encountered Redynvre.

She debated what she should do. First, she ought to try to find out if they were actually nesting or just passing through, as was sometimes the case. Eighty-two of these birds had been reintroduced to Rum. Perhaps they had just been caught on a particularly strong westerly blown in from the Hebrides. On the other hand, they might be nesting here, though they were some miles from the sea. If they were, she ought to inform somebody – the Royal Society for the Protection of Birds or Scottish Natural Heritage, maybe. She determined that she would rise with the sun, ride Keira as far as she could up the coire, then leave her and climb in search of a possible site for an eyrie. The pair had been here for at least two weeks now, almost certainly because of the trout. Then it occurred to her that Atholl McKenzie had probably stocked Loch Thuill to supplement his meagre income from the sheep. She looked at the pair she was about to feast on and felt a little guilty. A sense of unease moved in the pit of her stomach. If McKenzie had stocked the loch, he wouldn't have done it to share the fish with eagles. But it was so remote up here. How often would he bring out parties of fishermen? She had no idea. Her emotions were probably doing all the talking; she was aware of that much at least. Happy, and yet disturbed, she unrolled her sleeping bag and slid it inside her bivvy bag, though judging by the sky it wasn't about to rain. She let the fire burn low and closed her eyes, listening to the gentle combination of water lapping on the bank and Keira cropping the grass.

In the morning she was up before dawn, heating coffee and eating a slice of malted bread from the small loaf she had brought with her. With Keira saddled and the gear stowed, she mounted and swung west up Tana Coire. An hour later, Keira was left hobbled to graze as far as she wanted to hop, and Imogen left her pack beside a stone, taking only a small bottle of water.

She climbed the rough path, and the sun rose to warm her limbs and set the sweat tingling against her skin. By mid morning she was as high as she could go and the western view took her all the way to the sea. She moved with great care, making as little sound as she could. The eyrie, if there was one, would not be as inaccessible as it would on a sea cliff and she didn't want to stumble on it inadvertently, especially if eggs had been laid. She had no idea how many eggs a white tail would lay – one probably, two at the very most. Every now and again she would pause and squat among the rocks to watch and wait and listen. But nothing stirred, nothing flew and no cry came to her. She used her binoculars to scan the sun-dusted stone for any sign of nest-making.

By midday she had found nothing, and was on the point of turning back, having decided that the pair were merely visitors from Rum, when she saw them. Side by side they sat, crown feathers ruffled in the wind, watching her every move from their vantage point 100 feet across diagonally from where she stood. Imogen didn't move. They would have seen her long ago, but clearly she had not intruded far enough for any overt display of unease. They were merely content to scrutinize her progress. The male was massive, and she took up her binoculars and studied his wings for letter markings. Nothing; this pair were not tagged. Quite what that meant definitively she didn't know, but they were here and, from what she could see in terms of twigs and twine and bits of bracken among the rocks, they were nesting. Instinctively she marked the spot in her mind – no need for a second glance – then moved slowly backwards until she was out of sight.

At home later Imogen sat on the floor of her studio, the soles of each foot pressed against one another, looking at the sketch she had set on the easel. She was at a loss to know what to do. She should tell someone, but the discovery was still fresh and private and full of silent emotion and she was loath to break the memory of the moment by sharing it with somebody else. Yet she feared for the location, knowing only too well the sort of battles that people had had with Atholl McKenzie in the past. Few farmers bought the land they leased and he must have fought tooth and nail to get his. He knew he had no right to stop people roaming across it, but he did have the right to protect his livestock and fish. Imogen was in two minds. If she told somebody she drew more attention to the situation, but if she didn't, the eagles would be offered no protection at all.

In the kitchen she made a cup of coffee and pondered her dilemma. Morrisey sculled Loch Gael in his red-hulled boat and Charlie Abbott led his hens around the yard, pecking at the corn seed she had laid for them earlier that morning. Imogen could see the male eagle in her head, the laconic ease with which he coasted above the chopped waters, casting his eye for fish. Maybe the eagles could be an attraction for McKenzie. Maybe he could not only offer sport fishing to his guests, but the chance to see a pair of eagles that had been extinct in the UK since the First World War. Imogen thought about that. Maybe she should just go and see him herself. It didn't take her long to decide against it, however. McKenzie was a miserable old man, not noted for his love of wildlife. He might listen to her, but she thought she ought to get some back-up first. Picking up the phone, she dialled the RSPB in Inverness.

The receptionist put her through to someone called Daniel Johnson, who told her he was the bird-of-prey expert for the region. Imogen hesitated for a fraction of a second, then said, 'I don't know if you're aware, but there's a pair of white-tailed eagles nesting in the crags above Tana Coire.' Silence. 'I know they were introduced on Rum,' she went on, 'but I wasn't aware they nested inland.'

Johnson remained quiet for a moment, then he said, 'No. Neither were we.'

He drove down from Inverness to see her that same day, arriving at two in the afternoon. Jean Law had come round for a cup of tea and a natter, and Imogen had to shoo her out the door before he got there. It was very important that nobody knew about the nest, not even Jean. Tongues had a terrible habit of wagging, and there were egg collectors everywhere. Johnson had warned her about not speaking to anyone, so they were clearly taking the find as seriously as she was.

He was in his early fifties, but fit-looking with a ruddy-brown quality to his skin, grizzled grey hair cut close to his skull and circular gold-rimmed glasses. Imogen made coffee and they sat at her kitchen table with her bird-of-prey book open at the pertinent page.

'And that's what you saw?' Johnson asked her.

She nodded.

'Did you photograph it?'

'No. I paint, I don't take pictures.'

He smiled. 'But you're sure?'

'Positive. I spent two days watching him and his mate. Why are they so far inland? I thought they were only found on Rum.'

Johnson sat back then, tapping at the table top with his fingernails. 'We introduced them to Rum first, but since then we've had some breeding pairs on the mainland. Not many, and only on the west coast. They nest in the sea cliffs.' He shook his head. 'We've never had them inland before. Their primary source of food is fish.'

'Atholl McKenzie's stocked Loch Thuill with trout,' Imogen said.

'Has he indeed?'

She nodded. 'He bought a thousand acres of hill land for sheep from the estate. I don't suppose he thinks he can make enough money from them alone. Fishing permits can bring in quite a bit of money, although you'd need a four-wheel drive to get to the loch.'

Johnson sat forward then. 'Imogen, this year's been the worst in the last five for illegal poisoning of raptors. So far we've had twenty-two buzzards, four red kites, two golden eagles, as well as peregrines and a hen harrier, killed. White-tailed eagles are on the world's near-threatened list. If these two are nesting close to a loch stocked with trout, they're going to be in danger.'

SIX

CONNLA CROUCHED ON HIS HAUNCHES AND WATCHED THE male cougar pacing back and forth behind the heavy wire mesh. Hat pushed back on his head, eyes skinned, he studied the gait, the movement of muscle, the way the tail flicked from side to side. The cougar watched him as he paced, head low, neck down, the muscles of his shoulders fluid against his skin. The female sat in a separate section of the enclosure, cleaning herself.

Jenny, the young keeper with whom he had been working all week, handed him a can of Coke and Connla smiled at her. The sun was high, the centrepiece of a perfectly blue, perfectly cloudless sky, and the sweat gathered in his hairline. Taking the rag from his back pocket he wiped the moisture away, then, snapping off the ring-pull, he downed a long draught of ice-cold Coke and wiped his mouth on the back of his hand.

'What do you think?' Jenny asked him.

Connla looked once more at the twin open-topped enclosures containing tree trunks, waterholes and plenty of shade. The male cougar had stopped pacing, and was now perched among the branches of the tree set right in the centre.

'We tried to model it on what they had in Canada,' Jenny went on.

'I think you've done a real good job.' Connla finished his drink, crushed the can and tossed it into the bin on the edge of

68

the footpath. 'A real good job. This guy's finding his feet already.'

The male was down from the tree again and moving around the enclosure, scraping and spraying his mark. 'You'll need to give them a few weeks to settle properly, but I don't foresee any problems.' He glanced at Jenny. 'You got a good vet?'

'We think so. Local chap. Certainly the best in the area. He spent a lot of time in Africa right after he finished his training.'

'Good. Has he seen them yet?'

'No. He's coming over this afternoon. You can meet him, if you want to.'

'That'd be good.' Connla looked at the sun. 'Let me buy you lunch,' he said.

They ate in the staff canteen, which was tacked on the other side of the kitchen to the main customer cafeteria. Jenny was twenty-two and had just graduated from university with a degree in zoology.

'What d'you want to do?' Connla asked her, spreading hard pats of butter onto a crusty roll.

'Work here while I do my Ph.D.'

He smiled. 'That sounds familiar. And after?'

'I don't know. I really don't want to teach, if I can possibly help it.'

'Sounds familiar, too.'

'I might try to get a research grant.'

'Are big cats your thing?'

She shook her head. 'No, I'm just working my way round the park. You know, doing a bit of everything. Rhinos are my thing, actually. Black Rhinos especially.'

'Interesting,' Connla said. 'I'm told they're as intelligent as elephants.'

Jenny smiled. 'That's right. You wouldn't think it by looking at them, would you? You know, they can hardly see at all, yet a male can gallop full tilt around his territory without banging into anything.'

'Sounds like you're up for it,' Connla said. 'I wish you lots of luck.'

She smiled at him then, her head tilted to one side. 'I think I've seen some of your pictures. Was it you who took the one in Siberia?'

He sat back. 'The tiger? Yeah, that was me.'

She looked wide-eyed at him. 'What did you use? A delay switch, remote control or something?'

Connla grinned across the table at her. She was referring to his recent trip for *BBC Wildlife*. He and two associates had spent six weeks in the tundra trying to photograph the Siberian tiger in its natural habitat. It hadn't been easy; they were incredibly few and far between, their numbers having dwindled even further than Connla was aware. The Chinese medicine market was seemingly the largest culprit. Jenny was talking about the picture of a massive male, taken from above. The tiger was climbing a tree, its ears back, teeth bared, eyes like burning coal in his head.

'Nope,' he said slowly. 'I was about one branch ahead of him. Lucky he weighed more than me or you wouldn't have seen the picture.'

She stared at him. 'What happened?'

'Oh, he climbed too high and too fast, the branch snapped and he took a tumble. Fortunately, he scared himself and took off.' He smiled. 'I, on the other hand, sat in that tree for a long time after.'

A television was on above the counter showing the lunchtime news and Connla heard something that made him look up. 'The creature apparently crossed the path of a young helper at the SSPCA rescue centre in Balerno,' a reporter was saying, 'at the northern end of the Pentland Hills.' Connla stared as shots of an animal-welfare centre filled the screen, then a young girl dressed in a blue short-sleeved shirt and slacks was interviewed. Connla got up from the table and asked the woman behind the counter to turn the volume up. He listened intently as the girl told how she had been on her way to work that morning at about 6 a.m. when a large black cat ran out in front of her car. She'd almost crashed into the banked side of the road.

'This wasn't a domestic cat?' the reporter asked her.

She shook her head. 'No way. It was much too big.'

'A wild cat then?'

'Och, no. A wild cat is tabby and not much bigger than your domestic one. No, this was big. I mean really big. And black.'

Connla felt the hairs lifting on the back of his neck. He watched till the reporter handed back to the studio, and then he sat down again, slowly. The woman behind the counter brought some coffee and he sipped at it thoughtfully.

'You interested in that stuff?' Jenny asked him. 'I suppose you're bound to be, doing what you do.'

Connla looked across the table at her. '*Are* there big cats running wild?'

'I think so. There's too many sightings for some of them not to be true.' She shifted her shoulders. 'Look at her, SSPCA. She's not going to make it up.'

'Where's Balerno?'

'Somewhere near Edinburgh, I think.'

He sipped at his coffee again. 'Nobody ever got a picture of one, did they?'

'Not that I know of. If they did it would be all over the TV, the papers, everywhere.'

'Yes,' he said, 'it would.'

'People used to keep them as pets, you see,' Jenny told him. 'Leopards, pumas, black leopards. The government passed the Dangerous Pets Act or something, and some of the owners just let them go. There's plenty of game for them up there – Roe Deer, Muntjak, Red, hundreds of thousands of hares and rabbits, and all the right kind of habitat.'

Connla set down his coffee cup and nodded. 'There are probably twenty thousand cougars in North America, Jenny,' he said. 'But you only get to see one if it decides to let you.'

He drove back to the small pub he was staying in. The vet had been out to have a look at the two new guests in the park and he and Connla had spoken at length. Connla advised him on a couple of things he might look out for and the vet had seemed capable enough. Connla had been in the UK for a week now, and had accomplished all he had set out to. He really ought to be heading for home, but as he pulled into the car park other things were on his mind. He sat in the bar and drank a pint of beer, watching the TV as the same report from earlier was reshown on the evening news. He ate dinner, then retired to his room with his camera bag and road map. Piece by piece, he laid out his equipment – his two favourite Canons, both equipped with standard 105-mm lenses but he also had a 180 mm, 300 and 400. Both the Canons were permanently camouflaged, with black electricians' tape covering all the shiny bits. It was amazing how far away an animal or bird could detect the sun on a shiny surface. He had a shoulder stock to help support the bigger lenses, as well as his infra-red remote release and tripod. He sorted it all and cleaned it, all the time considering the news report on the TV. Lighting a cigarette, he flicked through the road map the rental company had furnished him with. He found Edinburgh, and finally Balerno, just off the A70, on the north-western flank of the Pentlands. It took him all of five seconds to make up his mind.

He got lost on the M3 the following morning, missing the turning that would have taken him north to join the M40 for Birmingham and then up to Scotland that way. He ended up on the M25, with the M1 signposting the way north, but he checked the map and decided that the A1 would give him a more direct route. He drove slowly, biding his time until the congested traffic eased, then he slipped the Land-Rover into the outside lane.

He knew he shouldn't be doing this. He had stuff to do at the university in Washington. But the whole thing gripped him – the thought of finding wild animals in a place where they shouldn't be. Exploration; real-life discovery. It occurred to him that if the majority of big cats had been released as far back as the Seventies, then they could be breeding. He had no idea how many had been set free. Nobody did. His initial research back in the United States had been totally inconclusive. No-one in the UK knew how many people were keeping leopards or pumas as pets, and anyone releasing them illegally into the wild would never admit it.

He considered the information that Jenny had been able to furnish him with, which wasn't much. She told him that, officially, most zoological parks were sceptical about the idea, but she thought the evidence was pretty overwhelming. Sheep had been killed, their throats torn out in a manner that wasn't compatible with large dogs, the only other possible predator. There was also the way some animals had been eaten, their hides licked back with a very rough tongue. Dogs and wolves didn't do that; they plucked the hide with their short front teeth. She had told him there had been sightings all over the country: the Beast of Bodmin, the Elgin Beast, one in north London, another in Kent and Norfolk. Clearly, most of these would be hoaxes or people not knowing what they were looking at. She gave an example of a woman in the New Forest who'd dialled 999 claiming there was a leopard loose in her kitchen. Jenny and another keeper had rushed out to join the armed policemen racing to the scene, but when they got there they found a slightly confused weasel.

This new sighting yesterday, however, was different. The girl on the television was calm, collected and a helper in the animal-welfare centre; not the sort of person to be easily fazed. Her face was white when they spoke to her; she had clearly seen something. Connla considered it all as he drove. Most people in the UK had no experience of such animals, particularly in a wild environment; they wouldn't know what to look for if they tried to track them. Connla, on the other hand, had been doing it all his life; his only problem was that he didn't know the country.

He drove steadily north, passing signs for Sherwood Forest. Images of Robin Hood sprang to mind: Little John on the log, Kevin Costner and Errol Flynn, the Sheriff of Nottingham cancelling Christmas. He stopped for petrol outside Darlington and then left the A1 for the A68, his map indicating it as the more direct route, avoiding the large conurbation of Newcastle. The road was twisty, however, and one section seemed to be a succession of hump-backed hills that left his stomach in his mouth.

73

By the time he hit the Scottish border he was tired and it was getting late. There was a border overlook point beyond the massive hunk of stone that had 'Scotland' written on it, and he pulled off the road. Various cars and motorcycles were parked, with people enjoying the dubious delights of a roadside hamburger van. Connla put his hat on and stretched his legs, then strolled across the road to get some coffee. It was much fresher up here, the sky dotted with cloud and the sun less fierce. The breeze was sharp, and he rolled his shirtsleeves back down to the wrist.

Sipping a polystyrene cup of instant coffee, he stood with one foot on the stone wall and looked out across the valley. Barren but beautiful, the hills were undulating rather than high; smooth-topped and reaching as far as the eye could see. The colours were spectacular – green and grey, streaked here and there with russet as two hills converged, and shot through with purple where the sun dug out the valleys. The air was clean and clear and reminded him of the Black Hills, and there didn't seem to be anything like the same volume of traffic as in England. He remarked on it to the man serving in the burger van and was informed that the population of Scotland was only five million, compared to the fifty odd million down south. Refreshed, he drove on, but time was against him and he knew he wouldn't make Edinburgh before the welfare centre closed for the day. He followed the winding path of the River Tweed as it led him through the deep, tree-lined gorges to Jedburgh and its magnificently ruined abbey. Weary from the drive, he checked into the first hotel he came to.

SEVEN

IMOGEN WASHED HER HAIR OVER THE BATH, NAKED TO THE waist, her breasts chill against the enamel rim. It was a major undertaking as her hair was thick and wavy, to the point of natural curls, and it hung down below her waist. During term time she plaited it or tied it up, but when she wasn't working it hung free and messy and tangled. She wrung out the last of the shampoo suds and wrapped a towel round her head. The skin of her face felt like it was stretched across the bones, the aftermath of two days in the hills. She opened her eyes wide, blinking at her reflection in the mirror.

She stood there and massaged her scalp, working at the hair to get the bulk of the moisture out. She never coloured it, never put a dryer anywhere near it, letting it dry naturally in a warm room or outside in summer. She rubbed moisturizer into her cheeks, neck and around the collarbone. Her breasts were full and shapely still and the lines in her skin were minimal. Not at all bad for thirty seven years on the planet.

Yet to what avail? She shut herself away up here, from the world, from cities and people and men. Her main contact, apart from the visits to Edinburgh and her parents, was the greetings card publisher she painted for. Watercolour mostly, but they had made the odd print from oil and sometimes acrylic. They wanted Scottish landscape and she did not know anyone who had a feel for the land like her: even the oldest, most canny game-keeper. Oh, they might know it better, its trails, its natural landmarks, even its weather, but she doubted they were aware of its soul like she was. To her the land breathed, it was alive, vibrant and vital in a way not understood by many people. She always knew where Redynvre would be, and he somehow seemed to know she was coming: what a thrill the other day when he bellowed out his greeting. She felt at peace with the land, the mountains, lochs and wildlife. The majority of the time she was content with that, comfortable with her privacy and silence. But then there was the school and the village and the unwanted attention constantly heaped upon her. It was at those times she felt lonely. Never in the hills when she had Keira and landscape and canvas, but back in the company of people. It was there that some explanation for her life was demanded, not just by others but oftentimes by herself.

Downstairs, she boiled the kettle for tea and sat for a moment in her studio looking at the sketch she had done and thinking about the eagles. She had the hillside in her mind, the brutal weighted crags above which Redynvre had been grazing.

A vehicle on the track outside made her look up, and she smiled as Jean pulled up in her battered old Citroën. Imogen splashed tea into the earthenware pot and stepped out into the sunlight. Jean clucked her tongue at Charlie Abbott, who came strutting over the grass to challenge her. Imogen leaned in the doorway, arms folded, hair still loose and damp against the material of her T-shirt. Jean waved to her, shooed away the cockerel and came over.

'Your timing is wonderful, as always,' Imogen said. 'I've just made the tea.'

'Sixth sense. I can smell it a mile away.'

'Sit there.' Imogen gestured to one of the canvas-backed chairs she had set round the small garden table that had belonged to her aunt. 'I'll bring it out.'

She laid out mugs, milk and sugar and the two of them sat down in the sunshine.

'I just had to get away,' Jean told her. 'I hope you don't

mind. I know how much you value your privacy in the holidays.'

Imogen laid a hand on her freckled forearm. 'You're an exception,' she said. 'The only one, mind.' But her thoughts were elsewhere. Daniel Johnson, the man from the RSPB, had promised to phone her today with the upshot of yesterday's discussion. He was going to consider the situation with his colleagues and phone her as soon as they had reached a decision on what to do.

'Men,' Jean said, breaking in on her thoughts. 'I have to tell you, Imogen. It *has* to be evolution. Nobody could've created them. I mean, how could you think up a man? Or why even, for that matter?'

Imogen glanced at her. 'What? Oh, yes. How is Malcolm?'

'Och, I'm not talking about Malcolm. He doesn't qualify.'

'As a man?'

'As anything. Malcolm's Malcolm. He just is.' Jean sipped tea and gazed across the waters of Loch Gael, which was still today, with barely a ripple against the banks. 'I think I'll move out here and live with you. It'd be so much easier.'

Imogen sat forward, concentrating now. 'What's going on, Jean? What's happening?'

'Och, the usual.'

'Gossip?'

'Aye. I was in the post office just now and Mrs Patterson was very off with me. She asked me if I knew what her husband was doing in your horse's field the other morning.'

Imogen felt her mood sour. The sun still shone, but it seemed a little darker to her. She closed her eyes for a moment, her cup halfway to her lips.

'Take no notice,' Jean said. 'It's just villages for you.'

'But I get so sick of it.' Imogen stood up, flicked the rat-tails of her hair away from her back and looked across the loch. Morrisey was in his boat, crossing to his patch of vegetables. Colin Patterson and his leching. He made it so obvious, so ugly. How was it that some men could be like that? What was it about her that attracted them? Patterson was by no means the first. What did they see, these men? What vibes did she give off, and why? Imogen had no idea, but conversations like this were the bane of her life. There must be something deep-seated within her that attracted wasters like Patterson. 'I have absolutely nothing to do with him, Jean. His wife ought to know that.'

'I know, lass.'

'And it's not just him, is it. It's MacGregor, and that stupid lump of lard from Kyle.'

'McKewan?'

'Aye, him, with his cronies and their infantile giggling when-ever I go in a bar.' She let the air rush from her cheeks. 'You know, Jean, sometimes I think *I* should move, never mind you.'

Jean smiled at her. 'Don't do that, Imogen. I've got a better idea.'

'You have?'

'Oh, yes. Much better.'

'What?'

'A man.'

Imogen frowned. 'I thought we'd just agreed they're worth-less.'

'They are.' Jean leaned forward, elbows resting on the table top, the chickens scratching for crumbs at her feet. 'But I'm not talking about any old man, dearie. I'm talking about the best.' She tapped her skull with a fingernail. 'I think we should make one up.'

For a few moments Imogen just looked at her, not totally sure what she was talking about, and then a slow smile spread across her lips. 'Oh, I see; to stop the gossip, you mean. If you give me a boyfriend you take away the threat to the women.'

'And keep the lechers at bay.'

'So you mean, make one up.'

'Exactly. Make-believe; pretence. We'll give him a name, an identity and an occupation. We'll make him live in Edinburgh or Glasgow, and you can visit him for the weekend.' Jean laughed out loud, then. 'It'd be fun, Imogen, and a sure-fire

78

way to stop the gossip mongers in their tracks.'

Imogen wandered barefoot across the lawn, which ran in a gentle slope right to the shores of the loch. She stopped halfway and looked back. 'Jeanie, I think I've got better things to do. Who cares if they gossip? I'm used to it, had it all my life. I must give off some scent or hormone, or something that attracts it.'

'You're just different, Imogen. That's all. Look at you; you're beautiful.' Jean was out of her chair and had crossed the grass to join her. 'You don't conform. You go your own way. You take off for days at a time on your horse. It's them that has the problem, not you. They're jealous because you're absolutely nothing like them.'

'You think that's what it is?'

'Yes, I do.' Jean slipped an arm through hers and together they walked to the shore.

'They're small-minded folk from a small-minded place. Your only saving grace, as far as they're concerned, is that you are at least Scottish. God help you if you truly were an outsider. They want you in a box, Imogen. That's the nature of the kind of people they are. They have to label everything. Right now your label is single and alternative, and that's dangerous in a small town. So, let's change the label, give you a boyfriend and shut them all up. It'll be a laugh, if nothing else.'

'I don't know, Jean. Isn't it just coming down to their level?'

''Course not. Come on. We should think of a name first.'

'All right, what about James?' Imogen said, trying to enter into the spirit of it. 'I like James.'

'James is good. Nice and strong and Scots. Let's give him a really good job. I know, an advocate.'

'Or a doctor.'

Jean shook her head. 'Advocates earn more money.'

Imogen laughed then. 'Money's irrelevant, Jean. It's make-believe. No, I'd prefer a doctor. Bedside manner and all that.'

Morrisey was in the middle of the loch now and he lifted his hand to acknowledge them. 'Men like Morrisey are all right,' Imogen said, waving back briefly.

'Yes, because they just exist. They don't do anything; don't say anything.' Jean gazed across the lightly tufted waves, kicked up by a new breeze coming in from the west. 'They just are. They're easily manageable. Sometimes they even have their uses.'

They wandered back to the table and finished their tea, then whiled away an hour or so joking about the make-believe man. After Jean had gone, Imogen sat with her shoes off and her sketch pad on her knees, watching the colours change on the surface of the loch. Morrisey was still there, fishing this time. Imogen wondered about the daft conversation. Perhaps it wasn't actually so daft. Maybe the only way to stop the vicious, wagging tongues *was* to create a mythical man. The past clawed at her then – Peter and university, so long ago now and yet he had been her last serious boyfriend. More than a boyfriend; she had nearly married him.

It scared her to think of how much time had passed between then and now. Years ago, at university, when she did art and he did computing – back when computing was still in its relative infancy – he had pursued her, and she'd barely noticed him at first. That was nothing new, though; throughout her youth she had never noticed when somebody was interested in her. Invariably a man asking her for a date took her completely by surprise. It was as if she had no confidence in herself.

But she did have confidence in her work; in her ability with a paintbrush, clay or stone. Maybe it was because she was so engrossed in her work that Peter's approach came completely out of the blue. Later, after the two of them had got together, his friends told her he had done nothing but moon over her for weeks before he'd plucked up the courage to ask her out. Imogen had had no idea. She had known who he was, had seen him around the campus, in the refectory or, on occasions, the students' union bar. He had always said hello, and perhaps once had bought her a drink, but nothing more than that.

He made her laugh, and he wasn't unattractive, despite being fractionally shorter than her, but that only bothered her when they got more serious and marriage was mooted. Somehow she had always imagined her man being taller than her, protecting her in a way, perhaps. But in the early days, when they were both footloose students, ambitious in their own way, he had been fine. He'd wooed her, bought her flowers, taken her to dinner at a pizza bar in Edinburgh, which was all he could afford on the meagre student grant he received.

She liked his company; he was witty and intelligent and pleasant looking in a blond-haired, blue-eyed sort of way. Sex was awkward initially. Imogen had had a couple of interludes prior to meeting Peter, neither of which were serious and both of which she'd regretted later. How experienced he was, she couldn't really tell, but the first time was in his room and it was fumbled, buckles and belts, jeans round their ankles, not romantic at all. Maybe she never thought about it, maybe she did, but the romance, the real passion, if that's what she was looking for, never came.

Her parents met him and seemed to like him; he was a good sensible boy. But Imogen always felt that deep down they didn't really care one way or the other. There was a vacancy about their attitude, particularly her mother. Ever since Ewan had been killed she had felt that about her mother. As if the best part of her life had been taken away so what did the rest matter. It was the same when she'd told her the wedding was off. Notwithstanding the preparations and the money that had been spent already, her reaction wasn't much more than indifference; a sort of silent Whatever you think is best, dear.

Since Peter there had been the odd fling, little relationships here and there, but nothing that could even vaguely be described as serious. Down in the depths of her soul, though, for all her independence, Imogen missed it; she knew she did. It was the closeness more than anything. Not just being able to curl up in bed with someone; it was the deeper closeness, the knowledge that there was somebody out there for you, some-one who knew you and cared about you. She shook her head and laughed at herself. The kind of relationship she wanted didn't exist. Women themselves perhaps, in their bid for freedom, had changed all that. The rules were gone, not that they were ever efficient rules in the first place. But women had forged ahead and she got the impression that most men had no real idea of their role in life any more. So many of them just seemed to wander around lost, or had mid-life crises, like Patterson and MacGregor.

She didn't want a half-hearted relationship, one that most people considered normal. She wanted something more, something deeper, something that didn't get lost in the humdrum nature of daily existence. She wanted to be aware of someone else's soul, and for them to be aware of hers. She wanted to be moved, really moved; the way the land moved her, and the way Redynvre moved her. Whoever he was, he needed to feel as she did, to see things the way she saw them, to think deep in his soul as she did.

She closed her eyes and was back in the valley with the Seer Stone, bent and wizened like an old woman gazing into the future; the rattled passage of the Leum in her ears and Redynvre roaring across the hillside. She imagined him as September dwindled and the velvet spilled from his antlers, an adversary, suddenly, to those who ran with him most of the year. His harem, come October: fought for, defended and cared for. The way he would run alongside each hind and nuzzle her, always watchful for would-be suitors, sending them skuttling for cover with a savage dip of his head. He always kissed his women before he mated, gently, muzzle to muzzle, tongue against their faces. Imogen tipped back her head and laughed at herself. If that was the kind of man she wanted, no wonder she was alone.

Inside the house the phone was ringing. She jumped up and ran in to answer it.

'Hello?' she said.

'Imogen? This is Daniel Johnson from the RSPB.'

'Hello, Daniel. Have you come up with anything?'

'Yes, we have. We wondered if you'd like to keep an eye on the eagles' nest for us.'

'I'd love to. But what about Atholl McKenzie?'

Johnson was quiet for a moment. 'I want to visit the site with you, take in the lie of the land. I'll make a decision about him when I've had a chance to see it.'

EIGHT

CONNLA CROSSED THE SOUTHERN UPLANDS AND PASSED through Peebles. Beyond the town the road mimicked the path of the river at the bottom of the steep-sided gully, where the sun broke through the trees only occasionally. Then Neidpath Castle reared up on his left like some savage window on the past. He had to stop, could see nowhere obvious, so bumped the Land-Rover up against the barrier and walked back to a gap in the trees. For a long moment he just stood there, hands loose at his sides, the breeze that lifted from the white necks of water ruffling the weight of his hair. The castle seemed fixed in time, silent grey stones rising as part of the rock that secured them deep in the river bed. The stillness was awe-inspiring; no cars passing, no man-made sounds for a full five minutes. It was the kind of stillness he associated with the Powder River Pass back home; 9,000 feet above sea level and only the souls of dead Indians for company. The stillness was something that hooked into your being, and for a brief second in time Connla felt the history in the core of the land. Then a car rattled by, snapping him from his semi-trance, the reverie he had slipped into. His ancestry was Celtic, he was sure of that. Connla was very much a Gaelic name and he felt a oneness with this place. He had experienced it, subconsciously perhaps, the moment he'd crossed the border, like a gently soothing salve seeping into his soul.

He turned and walked back to the truck, glancing behind once more to see the castle gradually disappear, shrouded again by the trees. He sat for a few minutes behind the wheel and then turned the engine over. He drove slowly, taking in every curve in the road, every shaft of sunlight – God's sunlight coming through the trees, the kind of brilliance associated with the covers of religious books. At length, he came out of the narrow valley, and the low-lying Pentland Hills took shape on his right. Farmland gave way to moors, scattered here and there with deciduous forest, the perfect habitat for a panther.

Balerno was at the northernmost tip of the Pentlands, an affluent suburb of Edinburgh on the south side of the city by-pass. He came upon it suddenly at the bottom of a hill and swung right past the fire station and the school, following signs erected by the SSPCA. Jenny, at the Verwood Zoo, had told him that the SSPCA was the same as the RSPCA, only Scottish, which made sense given that they were in Scotland and were no doubt fiercely proud of their independence.

He left what appeared to be the main road behind as he passed the tiny town centre on his right. The tarmac narrowed ahead, then the central white lines disappeared, and for a moment he wondered if he might have missed a turn. But instinct kept him going and all at once the welfare centre appeared on his left, a series of stable-like buildings with the shop and offices set on the other side of a paved courtyard. Behind the shop a field stretched and a hundred dogs barked as one from the labyrinth of cages. He had to park the Land-Rover on the stretch of open ground close to the road and walk down to the shop. A concrete ramp lifted to the door, which was locked. For a moment Connla stood peering through the glass, then someone scraped their foot over stone behind him.

'Can I help you?'

He turned and looked into the face of Lydia Dodds, the helper he had seen the day before yesterday on television. He smiled broadly and pushed the hat back on his head.

'Yes, I think you can.' He jumped off the ramp and crossed the yard. A small horse moved behind Lydia and Connla smiled again. 'What's with him?' he asked, nodding to the pony which was secured by a rope rein and swayed from side to side like the ruined polar bear he had once seen in Auckland Zoo.

'He had a touch of colic. Nothing to worry about. He's OK. Just likes the attention.'

'Rescued?'

'Oh, aye.' She lifted her eyebrows. 'All the animals here have been rescued.'

Connla held out his right hand and she took it somewhat cautiously. 'My name's McAdam,' he said. 'Connla McAdam. I'm from the United States. I saw you on TV yesterday.'

She blushed. 'Oh, God. That interview. I looked just awful.'

'No, you didn't. You looked fine. Besides,' he said, 'you'd had a bit of a shock.' He broke off and looked back at the shop. 'Listen, I'd like to talk to you about yesterday. Is there somewhere I can buy you a coffee?'

They sat in the small staffroom behind the shop, Connla in a dusty armchair, ankle across his knee, watching her as she filled the kettle. 'It was just about a mile from here,' she said. 'I live in a wee cottage up on the hill. It was very early. Not long after dawn, in fact. I do the morning shift. I'm late today. You're lucky to have caught me.'

'What happened?'

She turned to face him then, leaning against the work surface, and hugged herself. 'It scared the living daylights out of me, I can tell you.'

'A big cat.' Connla cocked his head to one side.

She stared at him a little oddly for a moment, and then something like recognition spread across her face. 'I know *you*,' she said. 'You did that picture of the tiger; the one for the BBC.'

Connla grinned at her. 'Fame,' he said. 'I knew it'd get me in the end. You're the second person in as many days who's remembered that.'

'Anyone'd remember it,' she said, turning back to the boiling kettle. 'Anyone who had an interest in wildlife would, anyway.'

'You wanna tell that to the people back home? I could sure do with the publicity.'

She laughed then. 'Didn't it chase you up a tree?'

'Yes, ma'am. It most certainly did.'

Her eyes widened. 'A Siberian tiger.'

'Yep. I was on the ground to begin with. Till he charged me, that is. Then I climbed, thinking he wouldn't. Only he did, so I figured I might as well get the picture before he ate me.' He made a face. 'Then he fell out of the tree.'

'You were lucky.'

'No kidding.' Connla got up then and took the mug of coffee from her. 'Yesterday,' he said, 'what happened?'

She shrugged. 'Not a lot, really. Not when you compare it with your tiger.'

'Now wait just a minute.' Connla raised an index finger. 'There's a fundamental difference, Lydia. Number one, I got paid. Number two, I went there deliberately looking for tigers. You, on the other hand,' he sipped coffee, 'you just got the pants scared off you.'

She nodded, cupping her mug with both hands. 'You don't expect it, not in Scotland. It was a black panther, Dr McAdam. I know what they look like and it was definitely a panther.'

Connla stared at her for a long moment, feeling a little bubble of excitement in his chest. 'Lydia,' he said, 'you wanna show me where it happened?'

The road was a track, muddied and unmade, but the ground was pretty hard. He could see the tyre marks from her car, but nothing else. He bent to his haunches, looking carefully at the ground, and decided that she must have driven over any prints, if any were left in the first place.

'Right here?' He looked up at her, index finger pointed at the ground.

'Aye.' She was leaning out of the open doorwell of the Land-Rover, her eyes suddenly hunted. Connla stood up, knees creaking, and listened to the sound of the starlings in the trees. The track led from the paved road up the hill to three small cottages, one of which was Lydia's. Hedges grew on either side, not thickly set and with gaps here and there, plenty big enough for a leopard to get through. Again he glanced at her. 'Coming left to right across the road, yeah?'

She nodded.

Connla screwed up his face and climbed the far bank. Fields met his gaze, stretching to the slope of hills against the horizon. He thinned his eyes, the sun bright all at once and the wind nipping at his cheeks. He inspected the skinny, chipped twigs of the hedge with an expert eye, knowing exactly what he was looking for, some sign that an animal had passed this way. He glanced back at Lydia. 'Black leopard, you say?'

'Yes. They're the same, aren't they? A panther is just a black leopard.'

Connla nodded and looked back at the gaps in the hedge. There were various ones at various heights and he checked each possible way off the road. There were tiny hairs tacked to the edges of a few branches, some of them black, but he could tell at a glance that they weren't from a panther, a badger perhaps or some smaller animal. If the panther had passed this way there was no trace of it now. He felt a little downcast, foolish when one considered the possibilities. Panthers were as elusive as animals get; you saw them by chance or not at all. Lydia moved at his elbow.

'No sign then, eh?'

He shook his head. 'I didn't really expect there to be. Come on, I'll drive you back.'

He pulled back into the car park outside the welfare centre and left the diesel engine running. A four-hundred-mile drive on a whim. He had done it before; no doubt he would do it again. 'Who do I speak to?' he asked. 'In Scotland, who knows about big cats?'

Lydia looked puzzled. 'I don't know really. You'd best go on to Edinburgh and ask at our headquarters. It's on the left, opposite the Crammond Inn, on the road out to the Forth Bridge. Not the motorway, mind, the other way.'

Connla thanked her and reached across to open the passenger door. 'Don't worry about what happened to you,' he said. 'The chances of a panther wanting to eat you are very slim indeed.'

He glanced towards the hills. 'There's enough game up there to keep a forest full of them happy for ever.'

The drive to Edinburgh was straightforward and hardly any distance. He followed the route on the map, locating the series of roundabouts off the city bypass until he came to the road sign-posting the Forth Bridge. He almost missed the offices of the SSPCA, which were hidden behind a farm-type gate just off the main road. He swung the wheel hard left without indicating, and a frustrated motorist hooted his horn behind him. Connla smiled and waved politely at him, muttering under his breath, then parked the truck against the wall on the left. He stopped for a moment at the main doors and studied the statue of James V being attacked on his horse by brigands. The king's nose had rusted off.

The woman behind the reception desk was in her late forties, small boned, with dyed blond, almost yellow hair and perhaps a fraction too much make-up. She wore gold chains on her wrists and dangling from the loosening skin of her neck. She smiled at him.

'Good morning. Can I help you?'

Connla leaned his elbows on the counter. 'I hope so, ma'am. My name's McAdam.'

'You're American?' Her eyes lit up. 'I love America. New York, Los Angeles, New Orleans.'

'You like the cities, huh?'

'Och, yes. They're so vibrant, so full of life, so—'

'Dangerous?' he finished for her.

She laughed then. 'I suppose so. Me, I was brought up in the tenements o' Glasgow, so I'm used to all that.'

'There you go,' he said. 'Listen. This may sound stupid, but I want to talk to somebody about the big cats that people have reported running wild up here. You've got one over at Elgin.'

'We've had one in Balerno.' Her eyes were suddenly conspiratorial. 'One of our helpers spotted a black panther.'

Connla smiled. 'I know. I was just there. I saw Lydia on TV down in England. I drove up to speak to her.'

The woman looked impressed. 'You're that keen, then?'

'Oh, yeah. I'm sorry. I should've introduced myself.' Connla wiped a palm on the thigh of his jeans. 'Connla McAdam. I'm a zoologist cum wildlife photographer. Big cats – pumas specifically – are my specialty.'

'Just give me a moment, Mr McAdam. I'll get someone to talk to you.'

Connla sat and waited, flicking through the newsletters and magazines. The SSPCA had a link with the FBI on something called First Strike. Apparently there was a theory that people who were violent towards animals were potentially violent towards people. Soon a pleasant-looking woman in her early forties came down the corridor and introduced herself as Mary Warren, the press officer, and took him to an empty office.

'What can we do for you, Mr McAdam?' she asked when they were settled.

Connla explained the situation to her and she nodded and smiled, then clasped her hands on the desk in front of her. 'Well, actually there're a number of people you could talk to. There's John Williamson at the Royal Scottish Museum, or the people at the zoo. Then there's Glasgow Zoo.' She broke off for a moment and tapped her forefinger against the desktop. 'You know what, though, if it's the wild-cat sightings you're interested in, there's really only one man.'

Connla sat forward now. 'Who's that?'

Mary frowned, sucking her teeth. 'We have a man in Perthshire,' she said, 'who's logged every sighting there's ever been in Scotland. We don't use him officially, and he's got something of a reputation with the police, I believe.' She paused. 'I'm not sure what you'll think of him, but he would be the person to talk to. I think he lives somewhere near Dunkeld. His name is Harry "Bird Dog" Cullen.'

NINE

IMOGEN MET DANIEL JOHNSON ON THE FOOTHILLS OF CORR
Na Dearg, a good landmark which was easily recognizable
to hill walkers. That is what they were today: a couple of hill
walkers enjoying the splendour of the Western Highlands.
Imogen felt a little naked without her horse, and wasn't able to
recall the last time she had actually *walked* here. It was different,
however, and she thought she might do more of it, especially if
she ever had company. It occurred to her that she was always
alone in the mountains; the only people who had asked to come
with her she didn't want along.

She walked slightly ahead of Johnson, aware of every inch of
the ground, every landmark along the trail, leading the way
beyond the Seer Stone and the river to the Leum Moir. Here they
rested, on the edge of Atholl McKenzie's land, and Imogen
sipped from her water bottle. Johnson was twenty years her
senior, but he was fit, and he stood now and gazed up Tana
Coire through binoculars. 'There's people at Loch Thuill.'

Imogen jumped up and took her binoculars from her pack.
Johnson was right. She counted at least three dark shapes on the
edge of the loch. 'They don't look like they're fishing.'

Johnson lowered his glasses. 'Let's go and see, shall we.'

As they got closer, it was clear the men were not fishing. They
had a tractor and a small trailer and Imogen looked hard to see
if she recognized any of them. She didn't. 'They must be some

of Atholl McKenzie's labourers.' She muttered it more to herself than to Johnson. They walked round the loch, Imogen scanning the sky for telltale black dots against the clouds. She saw nothing, though. The wind cut and the day was grey, threatening rain. The three men were working, although Imogen couldn't tell what they were doing; they had some sort of fence posts and what looked like chicken wire in the trailer.

'Saplings.' Johnson nodded to the group of young trees on a flat patch of grassy land close to the loch. 'They're putting up wire to protect them.'

Imogen paused and looked again. 'They look like larch,' she said. 'Strange place to plant larch trees. What d'you think McKenzie is doing?'

Johnson made a face. 'I haven't any idea.'

They walked on barely twenty paces and Imogen almost stepped on a dead lamb which lay half hidden under a slab of loose rock. She stood a moment and stared. Johnson followed her gaze and neither of them said anything. One of the labourers' voices lifted from across the water as he shouted something to one of the others. Imogen stared at him, but he was bending down, tying a section of chicken wire around the trunk of a sapling.

Johnson was inspecting the lamb. 'This was very young,' he said.

'They lamb late this high.'

'I know.'

Imogen sighed then. 'D'you think it's been placed there deliberately?'

Johnson scratched his scalp. 'It's hard to tell.' He stood up. 'Let's see if there's any more.' The three men were watching them now from across the loch. 'Don't point,' Johnson went on. 'But whereabouts is the eyrie?'

Imogen looked up the coire, bunched her eyes and scanned the uppermost crags.

'There's a little promontory', she said, 'straight ahead of us, about fifty feet from the summit, where those three crags stick up like fingers.'

Johnson followed her gaze and nodded.

'The nest is between two small buttresses, well out of the wind.'

'You didn't see if there were any eggs, though?'

'I wasn't that close.'

He turned and looked beyond her to where the three men were still watching them. 'Let's walk round the loch,' he said. 'See if we come across any more dead lambs.'

They paced the circumference of the water but found no more carcasses. The labourers were bent to their work again, and Johnson glanced at Imogen. 'I'd like to try and get a look at the nest. Let's have a word with these lads, ask them if there's a path up the cliffs. That way we might get an idea if they know about the eagles.' They came full circle and approached the piece of ground where the men were busy with another section of chicken wire. A tall thin man in his forties seemed to be in charge; his limp black hair hung over his eyes and a cigarette was clamped in the corner of his mouth. He looked up as they approached.

'Afternoon,' Johnson said.

The man nodded and eyed Imogen, but didn't speak.

'I was wondering if you could help us,' Johnson went on.

'Oh, aye. Lost, are you?'

Imogen shook her head. 'No, nothing like that.' She smiled. 'We were wondering if there was any way up and over the cliff face there.'

The man looked beyond her, narrowed his eyes, and seemed to stare at the rock, hazed in silver now with sunlight breaking the clouds. He looked at their footwear – both of them wore walking boots – and he nodded, as if in affirmation to himself. 'There's no path,' he said, 'but it's not that steep.'

'What's on the other side?' Johnson asked.

'More of the same. Eventually the sea.'

'Have you climbed it?' Imogen took a small pace closer to him, and he looked at her again, then shook his head. He half-turned and spoke to one of his colleagues. 'Hey, Donald. You've climbed yon wall there, have you not?'

The one called Donald, younger and red faced, looked up. 'Aye. It's no' bad. Stick to the left-hand side as you look at it. It's all big jugs and gullies. You'll not have any bother.'

'Are there any deer up there?' Johnson asked.

The first man shook his head. 'The odd goat maybe. Sheep perhaps, but no deer that I know of.'

'Thank you.' Johnson smiled, half turned away and then looked back again. 'Tell me something else,' he said. 'Is there anywhere round here we can fish?'

The man laughed. 'Not without a permit.' He stuck his hands in his pockets and thrust his chin at the waves breaking the bank. 'You can fish right here if you get yourself a permit.'

'From Mr McKenzie?' Imogen asked.

'Aye.' He paused then. 'There's trout in the loch now. Most of the season's booked up already, though. You'll have to wait till next year.'

Johnson nodded, smiled and pointed to the trees. 'Is that larch you're planting?'

'Aye.' The man glanced behind him. 'We've a few to put in the ground. This'll be a bonny place for a picnic next summer. If you can afford the permit.'

They thanked him and turned again, walking back the way they had come, round the loch to the foot of the cliff. 'There is a path,' Imogen said. 'And it's a walk not a climb. That Donald doesn't know what he's on about.' She glanced sideways at him. 'Just go where I go.'

They made their way up, Imogen glancing back every now and again to check the activities at loch side. But the men were busy, their heads bent, working away at the wire. She paused halfway up to rest and indicated the promontory, temporarily hidden from view now. 'They don't know about the eagles,' she said. 'I reckon that lamb's just one missed by the foxes.'

Johnson looked at her. 'You think they'd have said something, then.'

'Don't you?'

He made a face. 'Farmers aren't going to broadcast it if they're killing birds of prey.' Imogen stared at the rock between

94

her feet. Her hopes had been high for a moment, but Johnson's caution checked them. 'Come on. I'll show you the nest,' she said.

They climbed on until they got to the point where she had spotted the eyrie. Looking diagonally up and right she caught a glimpse of brown feathers lightening the black of the rock. The sun had gone in again and the first spots of rain began to patter the stone around them. 'There,' she said quietly. Johnson followed her gaze and gave a low whistle. 'They're nesting all right,' he said. 'And that's a very large male.' He scratched his head, took a notebook from his pocket and jotted down a description of the location. He wriggled out of the straps of his backpack, set it on a ledge and then bent to retrieve his camera. Imogen scanned the valley below. She could see for miles, well beyond the three labourers who had loaded up their trailer and were heading down to the clutch of farm buildings that nestled in the cone-shaped valley in the distance. Behind her, Johnson was screwing in a zoom lens. He took half a roll of film of the birds, the nest and their immediate vicinity.

'What do you want to do about it?' Imogen asked him.

He sighed. 'Nothing. I think you're right, Imogen. I don't think the farmer knows. The nest looks freshly assembled. The pair are young; this is probably their first year together.' He glanced back down the mountain. The tractor was almost to the first stand of pine trees and in a moment or two it would be out of sight. 'How often can you come here?' he asked her.

'Within reason, as often as I want.'

'Would you be prepared to keep an eye on the nest, say, once a fortnight for a while?'

'Of course.'

He smiled. 'If anything changes we'll speak to McKenzie. But what he doesn't already know, I don't think we should tell him. At least not at the moment.'

Imogen sat in her lounge the following evening with a small fire burning in the grate. She didn't need the warmth particularly, although the wind that whipped across Loch Gael could be raw, even in summer. A cup of coffee steamed on the small round table beside her and outside the evening was waning. Light rain spattered the windows, creating tiny vertical rivers. The glass was always clean; she didn't consider herself particularly house proud but the windows were a priority. Without them there was no light and no view of the loch and, to her, light and views were everything.

Earlier in the day she had finished the painting of the eagle – very simple, in watercolour, a moment in time as it flew above the loch. She stared at it now, set on the chair opposite – the hooked yellow bill and the way his talons hung beneath him in the glide rather than up and back as he soared. She remembered the words of her tutor at college: 'Choose your brushes carefully. Use a palette knife, if you want to. Think. You don't paint a picture, you write it.' She knew exactly what he meant: to capture the life, the soul, the story that was in a painting. She always experienced a tingle of delight when a composition like this came together so quickly. But the delight was blighted. She knew Atholl McKenzie, and the powers of the RSPB or the police would be an irrelevance to him if he decided that raptors were harming his living. He wouldn't care if they were white-tailed sea eagles or sparrowhawks, he would get them off his land.

Her attention strayed to the TV. Another walker had gone missing in the Cairngorms and the mountain rescue teams had been out looking for him. He had left details of his Monroe trek in his car, so they *should* find him. She shivered then, remembering the lecturer from Stirling University who had been missing for four days. He, too, had left details of his route in his car, but then he had deviated from it. The mountains in Scotland were dangerous – far more dangerous than many people thought – and more walkers than actual climbers lost their lives because they didn't take enough care. It happened every year, winter and summer. The man from Stirling had fallen into a gully, and the search was within twenty minutes of being called off when he was spotted by the RAF helicopter as it made one final fly-by.

Imogen stared at the screen now, hoping they would find this man alive, and soon. She was aware of aged emotions and knew she really ought to avoid watching the news. Her gaze dulled and she no longer saw the screen. The newscaster's voice became a drone, and the drone a rumble in her ears, and the sound was the rushing, tumbling, terrifying Salmon River. And Ewan was missing. Her mother's fractured features, the pale fear in her eyes. Connla McAdam, sullen and silent on his log, and her father, crooked and stooped as he stared over the edge of the bluff.

Imogen stood up suddenly, hugging herself and pacing a moment before the fire. Her mother's emotions, and those of her father, had been separate from one another, separate from her own. There was no shared grief, no mutual comfort in their loss; each of them faced it alone. That was fine for them, independent of one another, if that was how they chose to deal with it. Father and mother feeling different things, experiencing differing moments of memory. But Imogen had been only eight and she, too, had had to face it alone. Her eyes were the first to see him, washed out, broken beyond repair, a husk of a person, lost to the Salmon River.

Neither of them hugged her, neither of them held her – not right then when it really mattered, the moment in time when her fear was at its height. Later, perhaps, when it didn't really matter, dreaming and waking in the night, the dark and the silence and night outside the window. She didn't need the comfort then. When she had needed it most, all the years of trust she had placed in her parents had proved to be false.

And it was always the same when someone was lost in the hills; she would sit there, watching and hoping that whoever it was would be found, because if they were not, then perhaps . . . She shook the thoughts away as the images from childhood began to swell again, pressing the fragile walls of her mind. She picked up the coffee cup, sipped from it and reached for the remote control. Silence descended immediately, save for the crackle of salty logs on the fire.

At eight thirty, she got in her Land-Rover and headed up to the field. Keira needed settling down and would be looking for

97

her hay net. Darkness was falling as she parked beside the broken gate. What was left of the sun dipped in the west beyond Skye. A distinctive engine note rumbling up the hill from the other direction told her it was MacGregor, and Imogen waved to him as she vaulted the gate. He slowed, but she was already halfway to the stable. He gunned the motor and drove on. Imogen fastened the hay net and stroked Keira's nose, delighting in the sudden breeze that broke through the empty window.

There was a movement at the door. Keira snorted and Imogen turned sharply. Patterson stood there, shoulders hunched into his neck, hands rooted in his pockets, his smile almost a leer. Imogen lifted a hand to her throat. 'Colin,' she said, 'you startled me.'

He looked at her, said nothing for a moment, then smiled again. 'I was just out for a wee walk. I saw your car, so I thought I'd say hello.'

'I'm just on my way home.'

He nodded. 'Was that John MacGregor I saw going down the hill?'

Imogen looked at him now, her head slightly slanted. Something in his eyes unnerved her. 'Aye, it could've been.'

'Did you see him then?'

'Not to speak to, no.' She adjusted the strings on the hay net.

'I thought he might've stopped.'

She turned again and he was staring, eyebrows stalked, eyes full and round.

'Why?'

'Oh, come on, Imogen. John's got a crush on you. Don't tell me you hadn't noticed.' Imogen was aware of the blood beginning to pulse at her temple. She stared coldly at him.

'I'm sorry.' Patterson held up his hand. 'But it's true, isn't it.'

Imogen stood with one hand on her hip now. 'Whether it's true or not, Colin, I'm not sure I understand why it's any business of yours.'

He stared at her then, colour burning his cheeks. 'No,' he said. 'No, of course. You're right. I'm sorry.'

She took a pace towards the door. He stepped in her way and took her by the upper arms. 'I am sorry,' he said. 'Really. That was rude of me.'

Imogen stood there, just a little uneasy now. Behind her, Keira sensed it and snorted, looking back at them with her eyes wide under the fall of her mane. Patterson still held Imogen by the arms. She shook his grip away. 'I've got to go, Colin. I've already had one indirect lecture about being alone here with you.'

He stared at her then, shock standing out in his eyes. 'I beg your pardon.'

'Jean Law.' She stepped past him, aware of the smell of sweat on his body, as if he had been running not walking. And then she knew. He had seen her car, then seen MacGregor's and ran all the way up here. No wonder he was sweating. She could see the redness about his eyes close up, hidden initially by the shadowed interior of the stable. 'Jean told me your wife had a few words with her in the post office.'

'My wife?' Patterson stared at her.

'Yes, Colin, your wife. The mother of your children.' She stopped. 'Where does she think you are now?'

All at once he was flustered. Her feelings for him shifted from general indifference to something more like disdain. He was a pitiful middle-aged man. MacGregor was a far better specimen in comparison.

'Do you know what, Colin,' she went on. 'I don't think you ought to come up here any more. I mean, people talk, don't they. You've got your children to think of, and I teach one of them.'

'Imogen, I—'

'I can do without the gossip and innuendo. I can do without your wife giving me the evil eye every time I go in the post office.'

'Imogen, I'm sorry. I had no—'

'I've got to go home now, Colin. I think you'd better go, too. Your wife will be wondering where you are, won't she.' She held the door open for him.

TEN

CONNLA BOUGHT A COKE AND A PACK OF CIGARETTES AT a service station just north of the Forth Bridge and climbed back into the truck. Unscrewing the top of the Coke bottle, he studied his road map. Dunkeld. Mary Warren had thought Cullen lived in or near Dunkeld. She had explained her slight hesitancy: Cullen was an ex-slaughterman and he was too comfortable around guns for her liking, but he was well known to the SSPCA because he turned up at virtually every big-cat sighting. Nothing slipped by his attention, and not only in Scotland; he had visited various other parts of the UK. He was a firm believer in the theory of multiple release after the laws changed in 1976. He also believed that, given the twenty-two years that had passed since, and the fact that the average life span of a leopard in captivity is twenty years, the cats had to be breeding.

Every time there was a sighting that warranted any kind of TV coverage Cullen was spoken to, although, for some reason the recent one at Balerno seemed to be the exception. All the time Mary had been speaking Connla could tell she didn't like him. He confronted her about it and she squirmed a little, as if she was hesitant to admit dislike for a person she was trying to introduce him to.

'No, I suppose I don't like him very much,' she had said. 'He's not really my kind of person. As I think I told you, he has a bit of a reputation and he's been interviewed by the police a few times – for poaching, I think, or suspected poaching anyway. I'm not sure if he still works as a slaughterman, but he used to come to sites where livestock had been killed, and quite often we had young inspectors there, some of them women. Don't get me wrong, Mr McAdam, our inspectors are all pretty tough. They have to climb, swim, dive and handle all manner of animals and people.' She had paused then. 'But Cullen had this way about him, as if he enjoyed upsetting women. You know, almost misogynistic. He loved to describe firing the bolt into a cow's head at the abattoir.'

Connla studied the map. Cullen didn't sound like his kind of person, either, but Mary had advised him there was nobody better qualified in the country when it came to big cats. Cullen had lived all over the place and knew the countryside better than most. Not content with kills and the locations of kills, he had tried to track the beasts, unsuccessfully so far, but he was something of a self-styled expert on their habits and behaviour. Connla thought of his own background and knew it would be an interesting meeting. He had asked her why Cullen was nicknamed 'Bird Dog' and she had told him he had a penchant for pitbulls and peregrines.

Connla drove north on the M90, avoided Perth, and took the A9, which was signposted to Inverness, some hundred or so miles further north. The afternoon was waning now and he hoped to find a hotel in Dunkeld for the night. He had discovered over the years that locating people in small towns wasn't really a problem: if Cullen did live in the area he would, no doubt, have a favoured drinking hole, either in Dunkeld itself or in nearby Birnam. Connla chewed over that name. *Though Birnam Wood be come to Dunsinane . . . and thou opposed being of no woman born . . .* or was it Birnan Wood? He never could remember his Shakespeare.

He entered the small town from the south, driving through Birnam before crossing the River Tay on an old humpback bridge. Twin towns, one all but running into the other; they were bunched against heavily forested hillside, with chunks of exposed rock rising above the houses. Dunkeld was more twee and affluent-looking than Birnam. Connla drove slowly across the bridge, pulled over on the main street and switched off the engine. It had begun to rain, the windscreen being slapped here and there by heavy, individual spots. He fetched his jacket from the back seat and got out. He could smell the river and bread baking somewhere, and he pulled a face at the weird combination. There were two hotels that he could see, both on Atholl Street, which ran north, away from the river. He strolled up Bridge Street, glancing left halfway along, where the high street ran to a square and then on to the roofless cathedral. He paused there, considering whether to get somewhere for the night first then look round, or vice versa. Deciding on the former, he walked the length of the high street; white buildings huddled together in an ever-widening line. The rain stopped, and within minutes a pleasant evening sun was reflected off the slate grey of the rooftops. He paused at the fountain, watching a French couple taking photographs, then looked around the ruins of the cathedral. There was a gentleness about the place, a slowness that appealed to him. A couple of people glanced curiously at him – his hat maybe; hats were not so common in the UK, he had discovered.

He checked into the Atholl Hotel for one night initially and asked the receptionist if she knew a man named Harry Cullen. She looked blankly at him and shook her head. 'I'm sorry,' she said, 'I don't.'

'No problem.' He smiled again. 'Where's the best place in town to get a drink?'

'The Taybank Hotel. Dougie Maclean's place.'

'Dougie Maclean?'

'Aye, the singer. It's down by the river there on the Meikleour road. Go down to the bridge and turn left. You'll not miss it.'

'Thanks. I'll give it a shot.'

The room was pleasant and not overdone, with a view to the woods that climbed steeply at the back of the building. Connla dumped his bag on the bed, took out a fresh shirt and a pair of underpants, then showered. With his hair still wet, he went to the dining room, ate a brief dinner, then headed for the Taybank Hotel. On a Tuesday night there weren't many people in the bar, but the few who were there looked quite an alternative bunch. One of them, a man in his fifties with white hair, a white beard and a large gold earring, tweaked on the strings of an acoustic guitar. Connla noticed a fiddle hanging on one wall and a strange, flat Irish drum, the name of which he could never remember but always felt that he should, hung on another. He bought a pint of Caffreys and sat at the bar. The girl who was serving was slim, young and very attractive, with blue eyes, angular features and a tumble of blond hair piled up on her head. Connla sipped his drink, lit a cigarette and smiled at her.

'Where're you from?' she asked him.

'The United States.'

'I know that, silly. I mean whereabouts?'

Connla laughed. 'South Dakota.'

'I've never been there.'

'Mount Rushmore. You know the presidents' heads?'

'Oh, aye.'

'Well, it's also got Crazy Horse Mountain, but most people don't know that.'

Her name was Isabel; she was from Dundee and was only working in the bar for the summer. She knew the owner from his music shop in the high street. Connla had to admit, once again, that he had never heard of him. He asked her about Harry Cullen. Again he got a blank look, which he'd half-expected. 'Jimmy might know.'

'Jimmy?'

'Aye, the manager. Hold on a sec' and I'll ask him.'

She disappeared out the back and then reappeared with a squat-looking, yellow-haired man with a deep suntan. He wore a silver stud in his ear and his muscles pressed against his shirt at the bicep. 'You want "Bird Dog"?' he asked.

Connla nodded. 'I'd like to talk to him, yes.'

The man looked at him, head slightly to one side. 'What d'you want to talk to him about?'

Connla looked back at him evenly, thinking that he ought to

103

tell him it was actually none of his business, but knowing that would get him precisely nowhere, and as he had nothing to hide it would achieve equally as little. 'Panthers,' he said.

The man grinned. 'You're American.'

'There you go.' Connla offered his hand. 'McAdam. Connla. I'm a zoologist and photographer. The SSPCA told me Harry Cullen was the main man in these parts as far as big cats are concerned.'

The manager laughed then. 'Oh, Harry's the main man, all right. At least *he* thinks he is.'

'D'you know where I can find him?'

'He comes in sometimes. The weekend mostly. He lives over in Meikleour. Got himself a cottage on the estate.'

'Meikleour?' Connla frowned.

The manager pointed to the door. 'Take a left and keep going. It's about fifteen miles. Spittalfield and then Meikleour. You canny miss it.'

Connla thanked him and ordered another beer.

The following morning he took the Meikleour road, which bordered the Tay for a few miles before lifting through open farmlands with Caputh Castle to the south. Connla liked the Tay, wide and deep and gentle in a way he could never associate with any of the rivers back home. The Salmon came to mind, fast and fierce, and he shook away the sudden shadows the memory brought with it. Spittalfield was a minute, blink-and-miss-it sort of place, and Meikleour seemed to be no more than a post office and a bus stop for schoolchildren. He checked the directions the manager from the Taybank had given him and made a left turn opposite the post office.

The road narrowed into a single unmade track, with potholes everywhere still filled with last night's rain. Farmland opened out on either side, and he saw Friesian cattle and black-faced Scottish sheep separated by lines of electric fencing. A cattle grid rattled under the wheels of the Land-Rover, and to his right was a sprawling brownstone building, broken only by an arch. This must be the converted stable block the manager had mentioned. Cullen's cottage lipped the river itself at the far end of the track.

Halfway down, Connla's truck was greeted first by barking, then a pitbull, or something that looked extremely like it, running full tilt towards him. He thought pitbulls were illegal in Britain. Maybe he was mistaken. Slowing the car, he looked down at the leaping dog, which had spittle flying from its frayed black lips and a meanness in its eyes that he usually associated with people.

Up ahead, the narrow track arced between the trees and opened into a clearing with a small stone house at the far end. Connla could see the way the land dropped to the river beyond it. A battered Volkswagen pickup truck with a steel-coloured camper top on the back was parked askew in front of the house with what looked like years of dried mud climbing above the wheels. A man appeared in the darkness of the doorway wearing jeans, work boots and a thin cotton parka of military green. He was balding; his black hair was wispy at the sides, lifting above his ears to border the crown, and he had a moustache covering his upper lip. He nipped the end of the hand-rolled cigarette he was holding between forefinger and thumb and stepped out into the sunshine. With one hand in his coat pocket, he regarded the brand-new Land-Rover with suspicion. Connla switched off the engine and the man called the dog to heel. It stopped barking immediately and trotted behind his legs, where it stood with its chin resting on one exposed boot top. Connla opened the cab door and got down.

'Good morning,' he said. 'How you doing today?'

Cullen, if it was Cullen, just looked at him. 'Not bad,' he muttered, his voice deep and gravelly, without much trace of an accent. 'What can I do for you?'

With a glance at the dog, Connla stepped closer. 'I'm looking for Harry Cullen.'

'Oh, aye.' The man put a fresh match to the stub of his cigarette. Connla noticed that his fingernails were long and yellowed, like animal claws. He could smell something resinous from inside the door to the cottage, but couldn't say what it was.

'Are you Cullen?' he asked.

'Depends.'

'On who I am? Connla McAdam. Zoologist. The SSPCA told me you were the man to speak to about big-cat sightings.'

Something sparked in Cullen's eyes and he dipped his hand back in his jeans' pocket.

'And you want to know about them.'

'Panther, lynx, puma. Whatever it is that's out there.'

Cullen smiled then; he had long teeth, but only across the front. Connla could see by the shadows that all his molars were missing. 'Oh, there's everything out there,' he said.

Connla followed him into the darkness of the main sitting room, which was furnished crudely with a battered leather sofa with half a rug thrown over it before the empty fireplace. In the shadows just to the right of the front door, a Harris Hawk perched on a stand tearing at the flesh of a large brown rat. It was that which Connla could smell from outside. He glanced at Cullen. 'Bird Dog,' he said and grinned.

The little room at the back was a shrine, a testament to years of study. There was no wallpaper, and no need of it as every spare inch was covered, pasted, with newsprint. It was in chronological order, as if he had begun at the doorjamb with 1987 and continued right round the room, going from top to bottom until he got to the final sighting at Pentland. News stories from hundreds of different sources, with pencil marks on them and circles here and there round specific words. Below the window Cullen had a free-standing bookshelf stuffed with books and magazines. Connla could see that the newsprint continued behind it. The small desk had a map of the UK pasted on top, with a multitude of different-coloured pins stuck into it at various locations.

'My own system,' Cullen explained. 'Black's for panther.' He pointed. 'Red is for spotted leopard or jaguar. Nobody can tell the difference, so I put them all down as leopard. I put lynx in with leopard, too, because everyone thinks they've seen a leopard, and as far as my research goes it was mostly spotted and black leopard that got released back in the Seventies. Yellow is for puma. You know the difference?'

106

Connla half smiled. 'I wrote the thesis for my doctorate on the North American mountain lion.'

Cullen looked unimpressed. 'Green is for lion,' he went on. 'That's African lion.'

'Two?' Connla stared at the map.

'One really.' Cullen tapped London with a long fingernail. 'There've been two sightings in Barnet, north London. But I reckon it can't be a lion, or even a lioness. A lion's a big animal, you know. If there was one roaming around London, I think the police would know.'

Connla glanced at the other green pin in the south-west of the country. 'And there?'

'That's Dartmoor.' Cullen showed his teeth again, scraping a blackened palm over the stubble that clung to his sagging jaw. 'It's possible. We had two sightings in May. Two different people both described what I'd call a young male lion.'

Connla leaned his knuckles on the desk and looked sideways at him. 'Paw prints?'

'They took a plaster cast. Some fella at a zoo down there confirmed the prints were big enough. No claw marks, you know the sort of thing.'

'And the rest?'

'Fawn coloured, beginnings of a mane. Young male lion.'

'Running wild on Dartmoor?' Connla raised his eyebrows.

Again he looked at the clippings of virtually every sighting for over ten years. He glanced at the big-cat books on the shelf – tiger, lion, leopard – then back at the map once more. 'How many of these have you checked out?'

Cullen popped the air from his cheeks. 'About seventy-five per cent, I'd say.'

'All over the country?'

'As much as I can. I've been doing only Scotland for the last three years.'

Connla looked through the open door to where the brown-feathered hawk was swallowing the last of the rat. 'Does she catch her own food?'

'Of course she does. She's not a pet, Mr McAdam.' Cullen

squatted at the desk, brushed the toe of his boot along the pitbull's flank and rolled some fresh tobacco. 'Now, what is it I can do for you?'

Connla moved back into the sitting room, finding the confines of the study suddenly very stuffy. Cullen followed him and made his way to the tiny kitchen area beyond the stairs, which climbed to the open mezzanine above. Metal rattled as he poured tap water into a kettle.

'I'm an expert on pumas,' Connla told him. 'I'm also a photographer. Big cats mostly, but I do other stuff. Sharks, salt-water crocs, alligators, the odd snake here and there.'

Cullen laughed, a guttural sound in his throat. 'Anything that's dangerous, huh?'

'I guess.' Connla flapped an arm at his side. 'Never really thought about it that way, but, yeah, I guess you're right.'

'You want to get a picture of a panther in Great Britain.' Cullen stepped out of the shadows, a greyness in his face which Connla hadn't noticed before.

'Yes.' Connla folded his arms and looked across the short distance between them. He felt strangely uncomfortable in this man's presence. It was an alien sensation. He always got on with everybody, and he had been in some rough places with some very rough people. 'I can track better than anyone I know,' he said.

'But you don't know the country.'

For a long moment Connla stared at him. 'No,' he said, 'I don't.'

ELEVEN

IMOGEN HUNG THE PAINTING OF THE WHITE-TAILED SEA
eagle on the wall at the bottom of the stairs, adjusted it,
stepped back and took a good long look. The eagle stared back
at her, his eye catching the sun over the loch. She folded her
arms, cocked her head to one side and knew this was one of the
best watercolours she had ever painted. Normally the really
good ones went to Glasgow for prints and then reduction for
greetings cards, which brought in enough money to buy winter
feed and shoes for her horse. But this one would remain here.
Eventually, perhaps, she would allow them to print from it, but
she wanted to do nothing that would draw attention to the presence of white tails on Tana Coire.

As soon as she had let the hens out and spread enough corn
to keep them going for a day or two, she loaded her gear into the
Land-Rover and drove up to the field. Keira, perhaps sensing
the urgency of their mountain rides now, trotted down from the
top of the hill and stood waiting to be saddled. Imogen ran her
hands over her head and kissed her where a lock of her mane
hung between her eyes. Fifteen minutes later they were through
the gap in the fence at the top of the field and riding north for the
coire.

On the far side of the log bridge that spanned the River Leum
she met William Morris the gamekeeper. He was a short, chubby
man with red and roughened cheeks – skin persistently gnawed

by Scottish weather. He was on his own, wearing a tweed jacket and tie, as was expected by the new Arabian laird. Morris spotted her as she approached the bridge through the pass, standing as he was on a hilltop, shotgun broken and crooked under his arm. He wore stiff-soled boots and gaiters and a flat cap pulled low to his eyebrows which sprouted stray hairs at various angles.

'Ms Munro.' He touched his cap with an index finger. Imogen felt clammy fingers of sweat at the nape of her neck.

'Hello, Mr Morris.' She eased Keira to a standstill and looked down at him. Keira champed on her bit, rattled the metal against her teeth and tossed her head.

'You still like to ride, I see.'

'Aye, I still like to ride.' Imogen had never liked Morris. He was a grandfather three times over yet leched after just about any woman with a pulse. He shifted the gun from one arm to the other and rubbed his jaw with thick dirt-grained fingers.

'What brings you this way?'

'Nothing in particular.' Imogen walked the horse around him. 'I'll see you, Mr Morris.'

'Not if I see you first.' He cackled at his joke and watched her till she rounded the bend in the trail.

One hundred yards south of the loch, Keira almost stepped on a peregrine falcon. She shied suddenly, nearly unseating Imogen, who gripped with her legs and steadied the horse beneath her. Keira regained her footing, shook her head and whinnied a lament that echoed across the valley. Imogen slipped out of the saddle and walked back to the bird. It was dead. She touched it with gloved fingers; it was stiff and cold. Carefully, she prised apart the feathers. There was no sign of any wound, no birdshot or animal marks, and anything hunting would have eaten it long before now. The area around where it lay seemed to reek of death; her imagination was fired by the fear Imogen suddenly felt. She looked back down the trail. Morris, although gamekeeper to the estate, was a long-time friend of Atholl McKenzie and kept vermin under control for him as a favour. It was no skin off Morris's nose, as he had looked after this area when it was still part of the estate.

Quickly now, scouring the landscape for movement, Imogen stripped the saddle bags from Keira's back and rummaged for the hessian bag she used to stow the horse's carrots in. It was empty and just about big enough to house the dead peregrine; Imogen wrapped the bird carefully, then transferred everything else from the bag to the other one before refastening the straps. She stood and caught Keira's reins, and the horse wheeled in a circle as she mounted, hopping for a moment on one foot. She hoisted herself up and, as she did so, she caught sight of Morris striding back along the trail. He was 100 yards behind her and had rounded the curve of the hill. When he saw her he stopped. Imogen, her heart beating fast, ignored him, and with a squeeze of her legs, eased Keira into a trot.

She knew now she would have to be careful not to arouse suspicion. Morris was heading back this way, albeit some distance behind her. She wanted to get to the coire as quickly as possible to check on the eagles. But at the same time, she didn't want to be spotted doing so by him. It was a dilemma, and one that made her angry. She would bet her life that the bird in the saddlebag had been poisoned. As soon as she got home she would contact Daniel Johnson and get the society's lab to check the carcass. It was illegal to poison falcons, especially peregrines, which were still few and far between. If McKenzie was killing peregrines he wouldn't hesitate to poison eagles.

She rode on to Tana Coire, determining that if Morris or McKenzie or any of his men showed up, she would openly challenge them about the eagles. But nobody did, and she let Keira graze the banks of the loch while she sat in the afternoon sun, which bled weakly over the land, and watched the sky for movement. She sat for three hours and saw nothing, and was contemplating climbing the crags to check the nest itself when all at once a patch of darkness gained definition against the height of the mountain. Closer and closer it came, and the shape became a bird, and the bird an eagle; Imogen sat transfixed as it dived for trout. She was thrilled and terrified at the same time. All it needed now was for Morris to show up. But he didn't. The

111

white tail fished in peace and then soared, taking the final catch, impaled on its talons, back to the relative safety of its eyrie.

As soon as Imogen got home she dialled Johnson's number. They agreed to meet halfway between Gaelloch and Inverness for Imogen to hand over the peregrine's carcass. They met at a pub, had a brief drink together, then Imogen gave him the dead bird. Johnson took the hessian bag gingerly. 'How close to the loch was it?' he asked her.

'About half a mile.'

He nodded and grimaced. 'If this is poison, we'll go and see Atholl McKenzie.'

TWELVE

CONNLA CALLED HIS EX-WIFE FROM THE PAYPHONE IN THE hotel lobby. Before he had left Washington the biology faculty had been on to him about teaching summer school again. He had considered it, needing the money badly, but there was no way now he would be back in time.

'I just thought I'd let you know there's no way I'm gonna be able to do it. Can you tell them for me? This is a great opportunity, Holly. I've got a chance of getting one of these cats on film.'

'How much of a chance?'

'Well, I'm not sure yet. But there was a sighting only the day before yesterday, and I ran into a fella I figure can help me out. It's a chance I gotta take. Nobody's ever got a definitive photograph before. The interest here is huge. I mean national-TV huge. If I can be the man with the camera, it'll put me on the map.'

There was a short silence and then she said, 'Why are you telling me, Connla? Why don't you call the faculty direct.' She paused then. 'This isn't your way of warning me you might not be back for the first semester, is it? It damn well better not be. I've put my neck on the block for you here.'

'No, it's not that, Holl. I just wanted to keep you informed.'

'Why exactly?'

He had no answer for her. All at once he wondered at himself.

Was this to do with the teaching, or just keeping a link with the past. 'Are you telling me we talk too much?'

'Yes. Don't you think so?'

'I don't know. I guess. Yeah, if you wanna look at it like that.'

'Look, I'm busy, Connla. I don't mean to rush you off, but I've got meetings.'

'OK. I'm sorry.'

'Just don't let me down. OK?'

'OK. Bye.' He hung up, pushed back his hat and scratched at the sweat in his hairline.

He took a walk into town, his thoughts shifting restlessly about in his head. Why *did* he call her so much? What was it about him and the past that he never quite wanted to let things go? It had never occurred to him until right at that moment, but that was how it was: a fear of letting things go. He recalled how gutted he had been when Holly had told him their lives were too separate to stay married any longer. He knew she was right, but that didn't stop the sudden emptiness inside him. Maybe he ought to talk to somebody about it, because no doubt it had something to do with his parents and Ewan Munro's death. But that would mean heavy discussion, and he couldn't bear the thought of raking old coals. He shook his sudden depression away, walked up the high street and stopped at a little craft shop.

The trouble with Holly was that all the time they were married she had never got away from the idea of him making chair of the faculty in some Ivy League university. Yet it had been his very wildness of spirit, his dishevelled restlessness, that had attracted her in the first place. She had told him as much after they'd got together, while he was finishing his doctorate. Ironic, then, that she had spent the entire duration of their married life trying to ease the wilderness out of him.

He browsed among the knick-knacks, the little bits of Scotland for sale. Nothing appealed to him, it was either too twee or too crass, then he noticed a spiral display of greetings cards with various highland scenes depicted on them. One in particular caught his eye: a painting of a red deer stag, his head high, the last of the velvet fraying from his antlers. He glanced at some of the others; they looked like the same artist had painted them, though none of them were signed. A mountain scene where the rock was black and grey with a great fissure running through it. Hillsides, lochs – all beautifully painted.

He was about to pick up the one of the stag when he stopped. His mouth went dry and a shiver prickled his hair. Another card – a loch, with the surface ruffled into white horses and the hills rising beyond it. It was viewed through a four-paned window, and it was the window that caught his attention. There on the sill, half hidden by a yellow-and-blue curtain, was a little wooden figure. Connla stared at it and felt sweat break out on his palms. A native American Indian, arms to the heavens, head thrown back, an eagle feather and the broken stem of another clutched in his right hand.

He walked outside, the atmosphere in the shop suddenly stifling; it stopped up his throat like an infection. For a long moment he stood on the pavement, looking through the faces of the meandering tourists. The world pressed in on him, darkness at the edge of his mind, a darkness he hadn't experienced in years. He could feel how quickly his heart was beating, and the confines of the small town seemed to press him against the earth. He started to walk, avoiding the pavements, moving up the road towards the bridge on the outside of the parked cars. He walked quickly. The sun seemed to have gone, yet he could see it still high in the sky.

A wind ruffled the waters of the River Tay, high with the spring rainfall, soaking the long grass at the edge of the banks. Connla picked his way down, moving past the children's playground, where mothers pushed their infants on swings and watched nervously as the younger ones climbed the steps of the slide. He heard their laughter, and yet he did not hear them, only the stillness in his head and the loose slap of water. Crouching to his haunches, he sucked in breath and looked to the far bank. A fisherman drifted under the bridge in a boat, trolling for rainbow trout. The river seemed to roar and yet the sound was not from there; it was wedged deep in the past and Connla knew it.

Surrounded by Douglas Fir trees, their height accentuated by the tenderness of his years and the knowledge he suddenly carried. Knowledge that nobody else knew and, no matter how much he wanted them to, nobody could ever share. Running through the trees with the branches picking at him like the fingers of witches from story books. The path twisted this way and that; boulders, great hunks of rock, faces etched in the stone, watching him as he fled, accusing him with their silence. He paused and panted, and for one moment thought it couldn't be, but then the stitch in his side, his parched and swollen tongue, the reddened sand that clung to the soles of his shoes. They would never believe what he told them. He knew they would never believe him. At that moment, barely ten years old, he knew he was blighted for ever. He had slowed to a walk, knowing that running was useless now, yet run he must, sweat he had to. He lingered for a moment to catch his breath and the face of the sun seemed to be missing from the sky; the trunks of the great trees crowded the path and forced it, dwindling into darkness.

He stood again, watching the current pluck at reeds beneath the surface of the Tay. Someone had walked on his grave. That's what it felt like. Memory flooded back as if his finger had been snatched from the dyke and the whole thing had collapsed in seconds. He saw the face of his father soused with whisky, the broken veins in his cheeks red, blue and black in some places. The bulbous swelling of his nose and the watered yellow eyes that belonged to a man twice his age. He saw his mother, sitting nervously in the chair she always sat in, clicking her teeth and rubbing one hand over the other in a state of perpetual agitation. He saw the sheriff's face, cropped hair, dark patches of sweat under his arms, thick red-knuckled fingers and white straw hat. He heard again the questions, hours and hours of questions, and smelled the stain of chewing tobacco on his breath. He saw his mother's frightened red eyes from the other side of the table. He saw Ewan Munro's face and felt again the terrible silence at school.

That first day back in Wyoming, before the funeral or the memorial or anything, when he had walked into school on his own and every eye had turned his way, as if they could see right through him. There was suspicion in his own mother's eyes, she who had brought him into the world, so why not in those of his peers. Ewan had been his best friend, and when you were Ewan Munro's friend there was something selfish about it. So Connla had walked into school that first morning on his own, and he would remain on his own for as long as he stayed there. Nobody spoke to him, nobody said a word, not pupil or teacher. They just looked on in that peculiar silent way, unease etched in their faces.

He leaned against the side of the bridge for a moment, listening to the excited shriek of the children playing behind him. He fumbled in his pocket for the pack of cigarettes he had bought but hardly smoked. He had to steady his hand as he lit one. He eased the smoke into his lungs, held it and exhaled, then felt giddy and a little sick in the same moment. He almost tossed the burning cigarette into the river, but he sucked again and the nicotine seemed to calm him. He took two more powerful drags and then flipped it away, exhaled through his nose and stuffed his hands into his pockets.

He saw Imogen's face, as clear as if she still stood before him with that yellow blanket dragging over her shoulder. Her eyes were clear and cool and they looked into his soul in a way that no-one had ever done before. She looked at him while he sat on the log; she looked at him in the Sheriff's office and every day at school. The other kids looked with suspicion and unease, but Imogen, Imogen looked with certainty.

And now this, like the hand of God all at once on his shoulder, stopping him in his tracks and wheeling him round to face a past he had denied. Slowly he walked back to the shop, and the assistant smiled at him from behind the counter. Connla did not smile. He stopped at the card display and looked again at the scene. Breath caught in his throat, and he hesitated a moment before picking up the card and laying it on the counter. 'Would you know who painted this?' he asked, suddenly unsure of his voice. The woman picked it up and inspected it for the signature he already knew was missing. 'I really couldn't tell you.'

Connla nodded. 'You figure there's any way of finding out?' He gestured to the others. 'I think the same artist painted them all. They must be reductions of larger paintings. This stag was done in oil, for sure.' He paused to show her. 'I'm only here for a while and I'd like to maybe buy a painting to take back to the States.'

The woman frowned for a second and shook her head. 'I really don't know,' she said. 'I suppose I could ask the whole-saler, get them to ask the card publisher maybe.'

'Could you do that for me? I'm going to be away for a few days, but I can pop in when I get back.'

'Fine,' she said. 'I'll see what I can do.'

Connla thanked her, paid for the card and went back to the hotel.

Harry Cullen was waiting for him, sitting in the open doorwell of his battered VW truck. The pitbull poked its head out from under the camper top, saliva dripping in big gobs from its jaws. Cullen flipped away the butt of his cigarette and leered. It must have been intended as a smile but definitely came out as a leer, and Connla began to wonder at his choice of travelling companion. Cullen hefted a bag from the passenger seat and made his way round to the back.

'We'll take your wagon,' he said. 'I'll have to drive if we go off road.'

Connla glanced at the battered VW. 'No problem,' he said. 'Guess you're bringing the dog, huh?'

'Of course. I don't go anywhere without him. He's a good tracker, Mr McAdam. They use them to hunt wild boar in New Zealand.' Cullen showed his grey-and-yellow teeth again and called to the dog. It jumped from the tailgate and sat down at his feet.

'He certainly does as he's told,' Connla said.

Cullen smiled again. 'He does what *I* tell him, right enough.'

Connla felt the shiver down his spine. 'Right enough,' he mimicked under his breath, and opened the back door of the Land-Rover. 'Dump your stuff in here.' He already had his overnight bag and camera equipment set out in the back. Cullen laid his travel bag next to it, then hefted a much longer rifle bag alongside. Connla stared at it, hands on his hips. 'What've you got there?'

'Magnum.'

'A sniper's rifle?'

'Hunting rifle, Mr McAdam. We're going after leopard, remember.'

Connla looked at him squarely then. 'We're not going to shoot one, though.'

Cullen turned back to him, a sour expression on his face. 'Are you telling me you don't take a gun along when you track your mountain lions?'

Connla thought about it then. It was true, he borrowed an old 30/30, just in case of trouble. If a mountain lion wanted to eat you, he could. But he looked again at the long leather rifle case and two things struck him: first it was incongruous; he didn't associate guns with the UK, even if they were trying to track down a leopard. Second, his old 30/30 was a short-range self-defence weapon; the gun that Cullen had brought was the kind an FBI sniper might use.

Cullen rolled another cigarette and cupped his hands round the match. 'Are we going then, or what?'

They drove east on the Blairgowrie road. Connla was paying Cullen. Not a great deal, but he was paying him. Cullen was going to take him to the most recent sites. 'Elgin,' he mused, smoking as they drove; his window down just a fraction. Connla glanced at where the pitbull sat, with its backside on the rear seat and its legs on the floor, head jutting between them. Those incredibly powerful jaws gaping open, white teeth hung with saliva that bubbled against leathery black lips. Every now and again the dog would glance up at him, and Connla noticed again that meanness in its eyes. 'Aye, we'll head up that way,' Cullen went on. 'Go over the Lecht and through Glen Rinnes Pass. There's a farmer near Dufftown who phoned me two nights ago. Had a sheep killed up there; he's still got the carcass.'

Connla glanced sideways at him. 'How was it killed?'

'Spinal cord snapped. Bite to the back of the neck.'

'Was it eaten?'

'No.'

Connla cocked an eyebrow. 'Sounds like a dog to me.'

'You mean the bite, or the fact it was left?'

'Either. Both.'

'Tigers kill with a single bite to the back of the neck.'

Connla nodded. 'I know they do. The tiger's the cleanest killer of all the big cats. If you're gonna get killed by one, make sure it's a tiger.' He squinted sideways at him.

'Are you telling me we've got a tiger loose in Scotland?'

'No.' Cullen pressed the stub of his cigarette through the gap in the window and wound it up again. He folded his arms across his chest. 'Leopards have been known to kill that way. You ought to know that.'

'But the carcass was just left, you said. Sounds more like a dog to me.'

'That's a point, right enough.' Cullen shifted himself in the seat. 'But there were bite marks round the snout, Mr McAdam. How many dogs do you know that try to suffocate their prey?'

They drove north out of Blairgowrie, on a steep winding road through the Bridge of Cally and up the Spittal of Glenshee. The heavily wooded land gave way to spartan hillside and the southerly fringe of the Grampian Mountains. Connla saw ski lifts and a lodge as they passed.

'It snows up here in the winter, Mr McAdam,' Cullen told him. 'Do you ski, yourself?'

Connla smiled. 'Badly. I prefer climbing.'

Cullen looked impressed for the first time. 'Climbing, eh. Rock or snow and ice?'

'A little of both.' Connla eased the truck into a lower gear as the road got steeper. 'I do a lot of rock work in the summer. Plenty of mountains in North America, Bird Dog. Sometimes you gotta climb if you want to take good pictures.'

'Got your boots with you, have you?'

'Never go anywhere without them: boots, harness and

cameras. Always two, always loaded. That way I'm ready.'

Cullen laughed a harsh burble in the back of his throat. 'Sounds like me and my guns.'

They drove on, up through Braemar, with the Grampians shouldering them to the north-west. Scottish towns were grey, Connla decided, the architecture not quite matching up to the splendour of the natural surroundings. Dour was a word he would have used, even with the sun bouncing off their white-washed walls. From Braemar they carried on up the A93 as far as Crathie. Connla frowned and looked at Cullen.

'Isn't there something I should know about Crathie?' he said.

Cullen curled his lip. 'The Queen, God bless her. She visits the church, aye. Balmoral's just up the road.'

At Crathie they turned north into the hills. 'We're going over the Lecht,' Cullen told him, 'really wild and windswept. Not a place to be driving in winter. It's the first major road to get closed when the snow comes. That and yon one to Grantown from Tomintoul. We'll stop in Tomintoul.'

Gradually they got higher, the hills were smoother, brown and green with just a handful of shallow crags, and mottled here and there with man-made forests of pine. Cullen explained that 90 per cent of the old Caledonian forest had been ripped out during the Industrial Revolution.

'Is that when they forced out all the Highlanders?'

Cullen shook his head. 'No, much later. *You're* talking about the clearances.' He rolled another cigarette. 'That all happened after Culloden in 1746, when Bonnie Prince Charlie fled to Skye with the Duke of Cumberland at his heels. The Highland clans were broken up by the English and shifted down to the lowlands. Gaels, man. Scottish Celts. Gone. No language, no tartan, no nothing.'

'Flora McDonald?'

Cullen laughed drily. 'Aye, he certainly dumped her, so he did. Not quite as romantic as the story is told, Mr McAdam.'

They drove through a second ski area and crested the Lecht Road, then wound down a low hill where Connla saw a pair of red deer stags, their antlers coated in velvet, a short distance from the roadside. 'Beautiful,' he muttered.

'Aye. They make good eating, too.'

'You hunt them?'

Cullen nodded. 'In the season I do. Got a permit from two or three estates. We've got about a hundred thousand too many up here, Mr McAdam. The land canny sustain them. No natural predators, you see.' He glanced back at the stags. 'Even so, it's not often you see them at this time of day.'

'Dawn or dusk,' Connla said quietly.

'Aye. Dawn or dusk.'

They drove on and Corgarff Castle seemed to spring from the hillside below them, a square stone fort with a pitched-slate roof.

'Garrison for the soldiers,' Cullen explained. 'English soldiers. The Duke of Cumberland built this road after Culloden.'

'They kept coming up here, the English, didn't they,' Connla said.

'Aye. And have you noticed how they're still at it?'

Cullen told him that Corgarff was an eerie place at night, especially when lit up in the winter. Snow on the hills, the land wild, empty and barren, and this ancient fort rising from nothing like a lone candle to pierce the darkness. 'The Wolf of Badenoch used to raid up and down this pass,' Cullen told him. 'Clansman from Speyside. Nasty piece of work, so he was.'

'I heard a rumour that they were considering reintroducing *real* wolves in Scotland,' Connla said. 'To take care of the deer.'

'That's a rumour, aye. But the farmers are all against it. Think about it, Mr McAdam. If you're a hungry wolf, what're you going to go after, a light-footed deer or a sheep?' They left the Lecht Road and drove into Tomintoul. 'Highest village in the highlands,' Cullen said. 'I've got a lot of friends here. If we get a sniff of anything we can stay in the hotel.'

The town was small and grey, with single-storey houses bordering the sides of the road that led down to a small square with three pubs or hotels and a tourist-information shop. Cullen indicated the hotel on the far side of the square which had an upmarket-looking coffee shop directly across from it. A small patch of green was decorated with park benches, and by the time they got there the rain was falling as fine drizzle. Cullen directed Connla to stop and they went into the hotel for something to eat.

The bar was spacious and decked out in quality wood panelling. A pair of ancient skis hung on one wall, along with carefully selected pictures depicting Highland scenes. A sign hung above the optics: 'Vagabond Bar'. This'll do, Connla thought. A handful of men were seated on wooden-backed stools, one of them in the boots and gaiters of a gamekeeper. Connla noticed a powerful torch poking out of the canvas bag at his feet. Cullen knew them all; they shook hands with him and he nodded to the torch.

'Been lamping?'

'Aye, last night.'

Cullen turned to Connla. 'Lamping,' he said. 'For foxes.'

Connla nodded. 'Shine the light to dazzle them, then shoot them like sitting ducks.' He glanced at the three men. 'You get a lot of trouble with foxes?'

'The estate owners don't like them.'

Again Connla nodded. 'You got a lot of rabbits?'

'Millions of the bloody things.'

Connla nodded to himself this time, sat on a stool and ordered coffee. Cullen introduced him to the men and told them what they were doing. The gamekeeper lit a cigarette and regarded him thoughtfully. He had cropped sand-coloured hair, blue eyes and the permanent facial tan of a man who spends his life out of doors. 'Black Panthers, eh?' He made a face. 'Yon beast of Elgin. Bird Dog's certainly your man for that.'

'You ever see it?' Connla asked him.

He shook his head. 'No. I've seen the odd wild cat and plenty of ferals in my time. Nothing bigger, mind.'

'I've seen traces.' One of the younger men, with a parka and mop of tousled black hair spoke up. He sipped from his thin beer and rattled the glass against the bar. 'Tracks and that, ken. Big toes. No claw marks.' He sat back. 'That's all I've seen, mind, and I beat for grouse every year.'

123

'But they are out there,' Connla said.

'So everyone tells us.'

Cullen looked wistfully through the window. 'Och, they're out there all right,' he said.

The farmer showed them the sheep's carcass. 'Lucky you came just now,' he said. 'I was about to burn this before it stank the whole place out.' He had it laid under a sheet of tarpaulin behind an old machinery shed in his concreted yard. Two collies gambolled at their heels. The pitbull remained in the Land-Rover. Connla lifted the neckerchief he wore to cover his nose as he pulled back the tarpaulin and inspected the foul-smelling carcass. The spinal cord had been severed with what looked like a single bite, but the teeth marks were inconclusive and could have been made by a dog. Rolling the carcass over, he looked at the indentations around the muzzle – burned-looking holes amid the short black fur of its face, where pinpricks of blood had congealed. He worked out the pattern, then rocked back on his haunches and rested his forearm across his thigh. 'Something certainly tried to suffocate it,' he said.

Cullen squatted then and began to probe the tightly woven wool with his fingers. Connla worked at the other side. 'Here,' he said. 'And here.' He counted four tears in the skin which had initially been hidden by the wool. He looked at the spacing carefully, having witnessed similar scenes a hundred times before. 'Leopard,' he said and stood up.

The rain had stopped but the wind was stronger, and it dragged the weight of the clouds across the hilltops, smothering their upper flanks in smoke. It was mid-August, but all at once Connla was cold. He looked out across the fields of grazing sheep to the foothills and ridges of Glen Rinnes Pass – wooden stretches, rocky outcrops, and thick, deep bracken; a million and one places for an animal as silent and stealthy as a leopard to be hiding.

'Have you ever seen anything?' he asked the farmer.

The man nodded. 'Once,' he said. 'Aye, just the once. A long way off.' He pointed due west to the first line of wooded hills.

'Yon tree, standing slightly apart from the rest. Like a black shadow, it was. I only saw it for a moment.'

Cullen rested his back against the door of the Land-Rover, rolled a cigarette and then licked the gummed edge of the paper. 'This is the area where there's been the most sightings,' he told Connla. 'From here to the Lecht Road.' Connla had the map laid out on the bonnet. Cullen spoke without looking at it. 'Due south you've got a passage of land through the hills. Highest peak's about twenty-five hundred feet. South of the Glenfiddich Lodge there's the Blackwater Forest; plenty of cover there. Then there's the Ladder Hills, with woodland both east and west.' He lit the cigarette, letting thick smoke drift from his nostrils. 'We've had more sheep taken from more farms in this one area than all the rest put together.'

'More than one cat,' Connla stated.

'Maybe a whole family.'

'Panthers are solitary, Bird Dog. Young stay with the mother for just over a year, then move on.'

'You know what I mean. There's loads of territory space.'

Connla folded his arms and rested the heel of one field boot against the toe of the other. 'You think they're breeding then?'

Cullen made a face. 'Nobody else does, but ninety per cent of them were released twenty-two years ago. How long do leopards live?'

'In the wild? Normally, twelve to fourteen years.' Connla twisted his lip. 'But then you gotta take account of natural predators in that equation. Cougars live twenty years; that's because nothing really hunts them. A panther living up here would have no natural predators. There's no record of anybody shooting one, so you can't even count man. Not only that, there's good habitat, excellent water and a multitude of game. I figure a leopard could live twenty years and change.'

'That doesn't explain it, Mr McAdam. It would mean all of them were about to pop their clogs.' Cullen shook his head. 'No,' he said, 'they've got to be breeding.'

THIRTEEN

IMOGEN KNEW WHAT DANIEL JOHNSON WAS GOING TO TELL her long before the telephone call came through. She was in the kitchen, resting her backside against the dresser, holding the receiver with her free hand clutched in her armpit. 'It was poisoned, wasn't it,' she said.

On the other end of the phone he sighed. 'Strychnine.'

'I knew it would be.'

'I'm going to telephone Atholl McKenzie.'

'Why don't we just go up there? It might be his own land, but McKenzie's pretty much a full-time shepherd. He'll be nowhere near a phone.'

Johnson seemed to ponder for a moment. 'OK. Let's meet up on the coast road and go in one car.'

Imogen had the shorter drive to Attadale, where the unmade road wound five miles due east to McKenzie's isolated sheep farm. She had never been onto his land this way before and she waited for half an hour in a lay-by before Daniel Johnson's Royal Society Land-Rover rounded the bend and passed beneath the slabs of broken granite that crowded the road. Imogen slipped out of her truck, pushed the door to with a creak and heaved it again to shut it completely. Johnson watched her with a smile.

'The old ones were always the best,' he said as she climbed into the passenger seat.

'Tell me that in January when there's a foot of snow on the ground.'

He laughed, engaged first gear and pulled back onto the road. One hundred twisted yards further was the turning for Atholl McKenzie's farm.

'Have you met him before?' Imogen asked as they bumped their way along the rutted track, furrow deep with rainwater in places. Johnson shook his head. 'I know of him, though.'

'Then you'll have heard what a cantankerous old goat he is. I've come across him once or twice. When he first bought out the farm he tried to stop me riding on his land. He claimed my horse tore up the ground too much.'

Johnson looked sideways at her. 'What did you do?'

'Nothing. I still ride on his land, but I keep to the deer trails wherever I can. McKenzie drives around on a quad, Daniel, and there's no way anyone can tell me a horse's hooves do more damage than tyre tracks.' She lifted her eyebrows then and grimaced. 'I think the last time he saw me he called me the horsey hippy bitch.'

McKenzie wasn't home. The farmyard was deserted. It was a cluster of grey stone buildings with corrugated rust-coloured roofs; all except the house, which had been fitted with new slate. No smoke curled from the chimney and nobody came to the door.

'Has he not got a wife?' Johnson asked her.

Imogen shook her head. 'Not that I know of.'

Johnson looked around the yard. 'A thousand acres, you say. He could be anywhere.' Imogen peered through a greasy window into the kitchen. Pots and pans littered the sink and draining board and more were stacked on the table. She turned to Johnson again. 'Let's drive up to the loch. Check the area for lambs' carcasses. Those men might be working again.'

They lurched their way up the track that pitted the hillside, roughly worn by a parade of different vehicles. Johnson had the Land-Rover in four-wheel drive and they bumped and bounced their way up and down a succession of low hills until they came to a pine forest. The track led them right through the middle of it. On the far side was a clearing, then more thinly spaced trees, and beyond it the coire and flat waters of Loch Thuill. They saw a tractor and quad bike parked by the loch side, but there was no sign of any humanity. Imogen sat forward, gripping the rail on the dashboard, thinking that they were already too late and imagining the eagle and his mate lying prostrate on a boulder somewhere, shot or poisoned or worse.

Johnson pulled up next to the quad and switched off the engine. Imogen sat still for a moment and the two of them peered across the expanse of the loch to the foothills, the edge of the coire and the buttresses rising above it. No movement, not much wind, all was still, and when they got out of the cab the silence seemed to settle against them like something chill yet living. Again Imogen was visited by the sensation that something was wrong. She looked sideways at Johnson and then took her binoculars from the cab and scoured the crags at the point where she knew the eyrie to be. She could see nothing and almost panicked, but then told herself that she wouldn't be able to see it from that angle anyway. Lowering the glasses, she stood in silence for a moment, then heard voices among the trees.

She turned as four men walked out of the wood carrying two logged tree trunks between them. Imogen recognized William Morris the gamekeeper and two of the labourers from the other day. The fourth man was Atholl McKenzie. He squinted at their Land-Rover, and then his eye caught hers and he leaned to one side and spat.

Johnson stood and watched them, arms folded as they skirted the edge of the loch fifty feet away. They carried the logs to what would become the picnic area and stopped. McKenzie dropped his end and shifted his shoulders before turning to face them. Imogen and Johnson walked over. Nobody said anything, but McKenzie, a big powerful man in his fifties, looked them up and down with the faintest curl of his lip.

'Mr McKenzie?' Johnson looked into his wide, flat features. He was heavily bearded, red with grey flecks. His hair was red under his wool cap and red where it curled like fur on the exposed muscles of his forearms.

'Aye. What d'you want?'

Johnson carried a small leather satchel and, opening it, he took out a report with a photograph of the dead peregrine pinned to it. 'I'm from the RSPB,' he said. 'And this is Imogen Munro.'

'I can see that.' McKenzie scowled at the white Land-Rover. 'And I ken who the lassie is.' He looked her up and down. 'The weird one with the horse.'

Imogen shook her head sadly. 'Now I know what happens when cousins marry,' she muttered.

'What was that?'

'Nothing, Atholl. I didn't say a thing.'

Johnson showed the paper to McKenzie. 'This is a peregrine falcon, Mr McKenzie. Ms Munro found it on your land the day before yesterday. She brought it to us and we tested the carcass. Our veterinary pathologist found traces of strychnine. The bird had been poisoned.'

McKenzie ignored the proffered sheet of paper and looked Johnson right in the eye. His gaze was stiff and glassy and, from a man of his build, unnerving. 'And?'

'It's illegal to poison birds of prey, Mr McKenzie.'

McKenzie took half a pace forward. 'Are you suggesting it was me?' He poked his own chest with a fat thumb, looking from Johnson to Imogen and back again. He took the paper then and shook it out, inspecting the report before slapping it back into Johnson's hand. 'That bird could have come from anywhere. It could've flown onto my land.'

'Yes, you're right. It could.' Johnson folded the report away. 'Nobody's accusing you of anything, Mr McKenzie. The bird was on your land, and I'm just informing you that we know about it, that's all.'

McKenzie was ignoring him again and looking at Imogen. 'This is your doing, isn't it. Interfering wee—'

'Mr McKenzie.' Johnson plucked his attention back again. 'The other reason I'm informing you is that it's come to our attention that you have a pair of very rare eagles nesting here.'

Now McKenzie thinned his eyes. 'Eagles?'

'White-tailed sea eagles.' Imogen spoke now. 'They've built an eyrie above the coire.'

McKenzie looked sourly at her for a moment and then frowned. 'Sea eagles. What're they doing this far inland?' Then the light of comprehension dawned in his eyes and he looked sideways at the loch. 'Oh,' he said, 'I see.'

'You stocked the loch,' Johnson said.

'Aye. Rainbow trout.' McKenzie flapped one gnarled hand at the hillside. 'You think a man can scrape a living out of just the sheep?' He snorted. 'Not a cat in hell's chance.' He glanced at his men. 'Did any of you know about this?' They shook their heads collectively and McKenzie looked back at Johnson. 'Are you telling me you expect me to share my fish with eagles?'

'They don't eat much, Mr McKenzie. There are only two of them.'

'Sea eagles maybe. But they're not all, are they? D'you have any idea how many lambs I lose to kites and hawks and golden eagles over a year?'

'They're all protected species, Atholl.' Imogen stepped in front of him. 'They've a right to be here.'

'Pay rent, do they? Pay land taxes?'

'Oh, for goodness' sake. Listen to yourself. Why don't you think of it differently? You're the only farm in the highlands with a pair of white-tailed eagles from Norway nesting by your loch. It's an added attraction for your fishermen.'

'She's right,' Johnson said.

McKenzie just snorted. 'Fishermen like to fish,' he said. 'They're not interested in looking at birds, especially ones that scare the fish.'

They drove back to the main road, both of them quiet and thoughtful. 'What d'you think?' Imogen asked him when he dropped her back at her Land-Rover.

'I don't know. McKenzie knows *we* know, which is important. Not only that, but he doesn't know the exact location of the eyrie. He'll think twice, Imogen. Apart from mounting an armed guard that's all we can hope for. He knows that if he does try to poison them, we'll prosecute him.'

Imogen stared through the windscreen at the silent black crags. 'They'll still be dead,' she said.

She tried not to think about the eagles, working in her studio on the large oil of Redynvre under the crag. He truly was a magnificent beast, alone on the hillside, the heather and shadows of the short cliff above him. The phone ringing in the lounge distracted her. She ignored it, but she had no answerphone, and whenever she let it ring off she regretted it. In the end she went through and picked it up.

'Hello?'

'Imogen, this is Morag Ross from Dickinsons.'

'Hi, Morag. How are you?' Morag was her greetings-card publisher: they knew each other from art-school days in Edinburgh.

'I'm fine. Listen. We've had a call from a shop in Dunkeld. Apparently some American has been asking about your cards. The shop thinks he might want to buy an original painting. Can we tell him who you are?'

Imogen thought for a moment. 'I don't sell my originals, Morag. You know that.'

'I know. I just thought I'd ask.'

'Did he give his name?'

'I don't think so. No.'

Again Imogen thought about it. 'No,' she said. 'Thanks anyway, Morag. But I don't want to sell any paintings.' She hung up, reminding herself that the point of not signing her work in the first place was to maintain the privacy she had cultivated so carefully.

Late that afternoon Jean Law phoned her. Her husband had taken the two boys on an all-night fishing trip and she was at a loose end – sudden freedom wasn't something she experienced very often. She suggested a drink at McLaran's bar in the village, where they had an Irish folk band playing. Imogen agreed, albeit reluctantly. It wasn't often that Jean got a night off.

They met there and Imogen was first to arrive, which irritated her. She hated going into pubs on her own, especially the local ones, but she was damned if she was going to sit in the car park and wait. It was already crowded, with fishermen, hatchery men and foresters thronging the place. Patterson was there with Tim Duerr from school, obviously both having a night off from their wives. Imogen wondered if Patterson had thought she might be there and arranged it specifically. He spotted her immediately, as if he had been watching the door, like a cat sitting at a mouse-hole. After the other night she wanted to avoid him, but Tim was with him, so she couldn't really do so without it being obvious. Andy McKewan, the fisherman from Kyle, was standing at the bar with his crew. He saw her, grinned like a wolf and asked to buy her a drink.

'No, thank you,' she said. 'I'm waiting for a friend.'

'So? does that mean I canny buy you a drink?' McKewan was big and bearded, his hair permanently greased with fish oil and his teeth inky black at the edges. Imogen stood back from his breath. 'No, but thanks all the same, I'll buy my own drink.'

Mercifully, Jean walked in and Imogen grabbed her. 'Can we go somewhere else?'

'Why? this is where the band's playing.'

'I know, but the atmosphere stinks.'

'Why?'

Imogen jerked her head towards McKewan.

'Och, just ignore the big jerk. Don't let him spoil the evening.'

Imogen took a cigarette from her handbag and fumbled for a lighter. There was the flash of a zippo and the smell of petrol under her nose as McKewan offered the flame to her. She had no choice but to accept and she blew a steady stream of smoke at the ceiling.

'Can I get you a drink?' McKewan asked, suddenly smiling at Jean.

'Thanks very much. Gin and tonic, please, Andy.'

'Imogen?' The smile said it all, lips lifted over blackened teeth, showing the red of his gums.

'Go on then. I'll have a Glenlivet. Double. No ice.'

They found a table to themselves, the way to Patterson's mercifully barred by groups of people standing. In the far corner the three-piece fiddle band was preparing to play. Imogen sank gratefully into the seat with her back to the rest of the bar. Jean sat opposite her and smiled over her shoulder at Andy McKewan. 'You know, he's not bad for a fisherman.'

'Good God, Jean. Have you been married that long?' Imogen stared at her. 'His hair looks like it's washed in a fryer and his teeth could be piano keys.'

'Aye, but he's dead rugged with it. He's big, too. I like big men.'

'Then why did you marry Malcolm?'

Jean laughed then. 'I'm just teasing, lassie. Trying to lighten you up. I wouldn't touch him with a bargepole.' She sipped her drink. 'It's just good to be out without Malcolm or the kids. I feel young again, Imogen. You've never been married. You wouldn't know what I mean.'

Imogen sipped her whisky and thought about that. Never married, no children, barren. What chance was there of children when she was single, and what chance of the right man coming along in a situation like hers. Maybe that was how she wanted it. Why she had *really* settled out here in the middle of nowhere. Maybe it was nothing to do with painting and the land and wildlife; maybe that was just an excuse for the inadequacies of her emotions.

'Did you ever want children?' Jean asked, as if guessing her thoughts. Imogen stared at her. 'What d'you mean, *did*? I still could. I'm only thirty-seven, Jean. Women have kids well into their forties these days.'

'Yes, but not their first one.' Jean looked awkward all at once, as if she had struck a nerve and regretted it.

Imogen sat back. She did want children. She just hadn't met the man she wanted to have them with yet. She had always told herself that, when she did, she would know. She knew it hadn't been Peter, which was another reason to call off the ill-fated wedding plans. And she knew it hadn't been any of her infrequent lovers since. 'I need the right man. I don't want just anybody,' she said aloud.

'Och, everyone says that.' Jean swallowed gin and swirled the ice in her glass. 'We settle for what we can get in the end.' She looked beyond Imogen then and half smiled. 'I'm sorry. I didn't mean to sound sharp just now.'

Imogen shook her head and laughed then. 'Don't worry, it's not a major issue. If I really wanted children, I daresay I'd have *settled* for someone by now.'

In the morning she was wakened by the sound of Charlie Abbott crowing from the henhouse. It was five o'clock and the sun was already up. She slipped out of bed and crossed to the open window, where she bent to look at the loch. The light was perfect and she settled on the stool and picked up a size seven brush. Holding it at the very end of the shaft, she began to work on the patterns the sun spread on the surface of the loch. She worked till seven, lost completely in what she was doing; melding landscape with water and sunlight and the shadows cast as it shifted. Meticulously, she painted exactly what she saw, everything coming together with an ease she recalled from her student days. She had lost none of it: the passion, the desire, the way an image gripped her and held her attention, while allowing her mind to roam and wander across the landscape, drawing in emotions that other people didn't seem able to sense. Depth. She had been told many times that she brought out the depth in the land. Not just the physical depth; somehow she got to grips with the soul of things, the essence of the lives that had mingled with it: animals, plants, people. She captured the history in a piece of stone, a mountain, a loch.

She laid down the brush at seven thirty and wandered downstairs. Making coffee, she stood in the open doorway and sipped it. Still naked, she crossed the yard, delighting in the freshness of the morning against her skin. She picked her way between the chicken droppings and opened the latch on the henhouse. Morrisey was on the water in his red-hulled boat, but he was too far away to see her as anything but a blob. Back indoors she ate a bowl of muesli and thought about the previous evening – how she was viewed and lusted after by a bunch of men who knew nothing about her. Then, all at once she was reminded of the phone call from Morag and the interest of the American. Was he, she wondered, just one of those Americans who wanted to take bits of Scotland home with them? Or did he, perhaps, see in her work what she might have seen when first she sat down to paint? At nine fifteen, she did not know why, but she picked up the phone to her publishers. 'Morag,' she said when she got through, 'that shop in Dunkeld. If the American comes back they can tell him who I am.'

FOURTEEN

CONNLA SPENT THREE DAYS IN THE COMPANY OF HARRY Bird Dog Cullen, and together they visited a further four farms within a radius of 100 square miles. They talked to various farmers, shepherds and gamekeepers, who claimed to have seen tracks or patches of hair or the animal itself. They always gave the same description: four to five feet long, with a tail the same length again, always from a good distance and always the same colour. Bagheera the black panther. Connla figured it would be the same one, given the size of the territory. They spent the nights in the hotel in Tomintoul, and a local skiing and climbing guide told them he had come across what he thought were a big cat's paw prints not far from the Shelter Stone in a boulder valley a few miles to the south-east.

Connla figured that three days was enough of Cullen and his slavering dog, which only seemed to not attack him because Cullen didn't actually order it to. They returned to Perthshire and he paid for the three days and dropped him back at Cullen's truck.

'Are you leaving now?' Cullen asked as he hefted his rifle case from the Land-Rover. Connla shook his head. 'No. I want to stick around for a bit longer, see if we hear of anything. Maybe we'll luck out and get a lead on a spoor.'

'We'll be lucky up there at this time of year.'

'I know.' Connla laid a hand on his shoulder. 'But I've tracked cougar in the Arizona desert, Bird Dog. I know you think I'm just some dumb-assed yank, but I know my stuff. Believe me.'

Cullen regarded him dispassionately. 'We'll see, eh.'

Connla left him then and went back to the hotel. There was one message for him on email when he checked his laptop: Holly, with a reminder of the semester start dates and a list of meetings he needed to attend first at GWU. Connla shook his head with a smile; his phone call must have really unnerved her.

With hot water falling on his head and hair plastered against his neck and shoulders, he thought about Holly and, even now, the crazy aspirations she seemed to have for him. Their relationship had been a contradiction, and it was still that way. None of it made much sense. He was thirty-nine years old and she figured it was time he thought about growing up. But what was growing up when you felt seventeen inside. He was lean and fit; no gym necessary when you spend half your life hiking through the Rocky Mountains. Growing up made him think about his parents, long gone now, but their faces still clear in his mind. He had no need of photographs.

His mind wandered to the greetings card he had bought and, switching off the shower, he wrapped a towel round his waist and took the card from the cabinet by the bed. The windows were open, late afternoon sunshine pouring in, and he rested his elbows on the sill and studied the picture again. A Scottish window scene, and yet with a beautifully carved figure of a ghost dancer set upright on the sill. Shoshone; he was pretty certain it was Shoshone. They were from the basin area and probably moved as far north as the east fork of the Salmon in the summer. It was either that or Nez Perce; possibly Bannock, but he doubted it. The Shoshone had sent warriors to Walker Lake and had been part of the ghost dance phenomenon: the last great insurrection against the incursion of the white man at the end of the last century. So many warriors from so many tribes, whole nations coming together in one united cause. He stared at the right hand held aloft, one eagle feather where once there had been two.

Holly and her sanitized life had known nothing of this,

nothing of his folks or what had happened to them. She knew nothing of the Boys' Club in Rapid City, where night after night he had lain in fear of crawling fingers, a spider's walk between his thighs. Dark memories, all of them. He stepped away from the window and placed the card back in the cabinet. Fetching a fresh shirt from the closet, he pulled on his jeans and field boots and went down to reception.

The same thin-faced girl with auburn hair was behind the desk. 'Excuse me, Dr McAdam,' she said. 'You have another message.'

'I do?'

'Yes. Well, I think it's for you anyway.' She fumbled amongst the paperwork in front of her. 'The craft shop. McCleod's in Dunkeld. They called and asked if we had an American staying here. The description sounded like you.'

Connla leaned on the desk. 'It is me. I never left them my name.' He smiled. 'What did they want?'

'They asked if you could pop in when you get back.'

'That was kind of them.' Connla glanced above her head to the clock on the wall.

'What time do they close?'

'I don't know. About five thirty, I'd imagine.'

He thanked her and stepped outside. It was five fifteen already. A brisk walk and he was outside the little shop, and then he went in, the bell tinkling above the door as he opened and closed it. The same elderly woman was sitting behind the counter, knitting what looked like a child's sweater. Connla smiled at her and recognition fired in her eyes.

'Ah,' she said, laying down the knitting, 'you got the message then. I wasn't sure. You didn't leave me your name.'

'No, or where I was staying.' He laughed. 'Great piece of detective work on your part.'

'I got on to the publishers myself in the end and they contacted the artist.'

'Did they give you his name?'

'Aye, they did. They phoned me back with it.' She smiled. '*He* is a *she*, actually, and she lives in a village called Gaelloch up by the Kyle of Lochalsh.'

Connla felt gooseflesh on his cheeks. 'What's her name?' he said.

'Imogen Munro.'

He checked out of the hotel the following morning, taking his luggage with him. He phoned Cullen and told him he was heading west and would contact him in a few days, then he took the Land-Rover and drove up the A9. He did not drive quickly; after nearly thirty years he wasn't in any hurry. His mind wandered off by itself, sometimes quiet, sometimes dragging him into myriad thoughts and emotions. Memories, things he had left hidden and wanted to remain that way. On the passenger seat next to him was the greetings card. He knew whose window it was now, only he remembered her as a little girl from Jackson City, Wyoming who had a crush on him.

He took the A9 beyond Pitlochry and up through Glen Garry; the countryside rolling out on either side till he came to Dalwhinnie. Here he turned off, skirting the northern lip of Loch Ericht, where the road narrowed considerably, climbing past farms before plateauing for a few miles. It was empty, with no other cars to disturb him. The sky seemed low here and the sunshine was only just beginning to work on the early morning mist. At the fork in the road, with Laggan signposted to his right, he turned west for Spean Bridge. It was a two-lane road and it weaved in gentle and not-so-gentle curves, passing through various tiny hamlets, and then the expanse of Loch Laggan opened out on his left.

The beauty of the place was incredible. The western United States had some of the most spectacular scenery on the planet as far as he was concerned, but each section went on for an eternity. Mountain after mountain, valley after valley, forests drifting like a sea of green waves to edge the very horizon. Here the scenery was tranquil then suddenly savage within the space of just a few miles. The hills rose steeply above Loch Laggan, and halfway along its northern flank he made out the spires of an isolated church jutting between the trees across dark and choppy water. He could feel the history, sense the souls of generations that had shaped the land, fought for it, shed blood and died for it. He could almost hear the clash of steel, the shouts of Celtic voices, the old Gaelic of the Highlands. He paused briefly at Moy Lodge to look at the water pressing against the dam, then drove on with other thoughts in his head.

Custer County, Idaho, 1969, the sheriff's office in Challis, a small town with one main street of old West buildings, rising into the foothills north of the Sawtooth. Two deputies with blue shirts, blue pants and massive pistols hanging from gunbelts which made them look like something out of a John Wayne movie. Silence, save for the clicking keys of a typewriter and the gloop and bubble of the water-cooler that stood next to a token rubber plant. His dad sitting opposite him on a grey plastic seat, with his arms folded across his chest and his features matching the colour of the chair. His mother standing, unable to sit, moving back and forth, pacing, feet tapping like a nervous dancer on the chipped linoleum floor. The sobs rising from Mrs Munro's throat. The haggard exhausted look on her husband's face. And Imogen, Twaggle Tail, with the dark piercing eyes that stared at him as she sucked the corner of her blanket.

He pulled off the road where the hills rose grizzled and craggy from the banks of Loch Lochy. He needed to breathe. The sun was high, the mountain air clean and fresh and he needed to clear his head. He stood for a long moment, looking over the water at the black-faced sheep chewing the stepped hillside.

The sheriff had sat him down, a great pad of foolscap paper on the otherwise empty table. 'Now, son. You wanna go back to the beginning here and tell me exactly what happened.'

Connla's lowered eyes. Even now he could see them, and feel again the weight in his chest, as if somebody very strong were squeezing the breath out of him.

'We got up and went into them woods. Ewan dumped his jacket to go climbing, then he took off, is all. That's why I come running back.'

140

'You sure that's it?' The sheriff, with his head cocked to one side, stared into his eyes.

Connla lifted his shoulders. 'That's it, sir. I swear there ain't no more.'

The sheriff sighed and eased his bulk back in the chair so Connla was aware of the sound of it straining. He shifted his plug of chewing tobacco to the other side of his mouth and looked at Connla out of half-closed eyes. 'You know, son,' he said, 'when I was a little bitty kid there were things I got up to that I wouldn't tell my folks no how.'

Connla watched him, holding his gaze with his own bunched eyes.

'You understand what I mean?'

'I think so.'

'Some things are just secret, aren't they.'

'Yessir. I guess.'

The sheriff leaned his elbows on the counter and rubbed his hands together. 'Trouble is, though, son, sometimes what feels like a good secret to a child isn't that way to the child's mom or dad. You follow me?'

Connla shrugged his shoulders.

'There's certain stuff that moms and dads need to know which we kids just don't wanna tell them. But you know what, sometimes it's best if we do.'

'Yessir. I know, sir.'

The sheriff nodded and smiled. 'So, Connla. You wanna tell me any more about what you and Ewan got up to?'

Connla bit his lip, looking at the floor, his palms sweating where they dangled in his lap.

'Son?'

Connla shook his head. 'I told you everything there is, sir. There ain't no more to tell.'

He got back in the Land-Rover: shadows had fallen across the sun now and he could see storm clouds gathering like residue from explosions. He drove on through the pass, with Loch Lochy on his left, then climbed again, the road thin and twisting, with few cars, even in high summer. There was the odd coach ahead of him, but otherwise the land was still and empty. Then the mountains seemed to lean back and grow smoother. Another loch bending at right angles to the west, smooth-skinned hills rising to a good height, but gentle, with no buttresses of rock to scar their flanks. The banks of the loch were shallow . . . and then Connla was back home in Jackson City, with the death of Ewan Munro the word on everyone's lips.

Smalltown USA, wagging tongues and a memorial service at school, where student after student offered a eulogy to him. The number-one man was dead, and there were weird circumstances: a drowning in Idaho at the weekend. His parents were flying him home to Scotland, where he would be buried among his ancestors. It was as if some great chieftain had gone and a void was left in his place. Connla stood in it alone, flanked on either side by his parents, but as alone as anyone could ever be. Ewan had been the apple of the whole community's eye, one of those kids that couldn't put a foot wrong, even though he might be a selfish, spiteful sonofabitch. Best in class, best on the sports field – the Munro family had a million and one reasons to be proud of him. Connla McAdam was just darned lucky that a fellow like Ewan singled him out for a buddy.

He stood by the car once more, smoking a cigarette; eyes closed, he saw again that white face, drained of life and yet staring up in accusation. He and Imogen, laid flat out on their bellies for fear of toppling over the cliff. One of Ewan's legs caught in the rotten cottonwood bough, broken at the knee and being thrashed back and forth by the current. The roaring, shrieking, rock-pounding Salmon River, which claimed ten lives at least a year. He glanced once more at the passenger seat and the greetings card with the picture on the front that sparked a thousand memories.

*   *   *

Jackson City after the Munros had gone: the silence of a small town, the stilted nature of school life, the suspicion, overt in some eyes, less obvious in others. The way his father slipped deeper into the Jim Beam bottle and his mother's nerves grew more and more brittle, till they cracked and finally snapped, and she muttered and stuttered her way into a sanatorium. And coming home from high school one afternoon, aged fourteen years, three months and sixteen days, to find two welfare officers waiting for him.

'Your daddy's in the hospital, son. And your mom's not coming home. We're here to take you to South Dakota.'

He had physically trembled. He was young still, but the deterioration of his parents had warned him of something like this. And yet the warning was not enough. Here were two people he had never seen before, dressed in their neat, official clothes, a man and a smiling woman telling him they were taking him away. And he knew that when he got in that car with them that would be it, his life in Wyoming was over, everything about childhood would be gone. Nothing to hold on to, no-one to comfort him. He would be alone in the world, the aloneness he had first experienced when he arrived back at school from Idaho.

Connla let go a stiff breath, standing on the hillside with the twisted road behind him and the might of the Western Highlands before him. Words from the past that still rang like a death knell in his head, words that he could have foretold the day Ewan Munro died. And then everything being rushed and having to pack and being strapped in an unfamiliar Buick that smelled of the freshener dangling from the mirror on the windscreen. The drive through Wyoming to Rapid City and his new home at the Boys' Club, with the woman talking in soothing tones to him about what he might expect and the special new school the government had organized for him. His mouth was so dry he couldn't reply.

The new home was a dormitory full of other kids, some tough, some not so tough, everybody looking for a new place in the world. Nobody with anything or anyone to fall back on, so you fell back on yourself, and sometimes you had to fight to do it. He recalled thinking, as he dusted himself down from a fist fight and washed the blood from his lip, that he had two distinct choices: he either got busy and tough with himself or he would slip into the gutter and stay there for the rest of his life. He dabbed at his bloodied features and looked in his eyes as they stared back from the mirror. People sank or swam in here. There had been Boys' Club people in Jackson City; they were always the best fighters, and always the first people the cops called on when there was trouble in town.

Boxing. A lot of the boys went boxing, but Connla had no time for that. He was left to his own devices, put in a new high school where every parented kid looked at him like he had some kind of disease. But he had been bright, much brighter than either his parents or his school tutors had given him credit for, back in the days when he had stood in Ewan Munro's shadow. He remembered it as clearly as the loch he stared at now. Fifteen years old, nine months into his time at the Boys' Club, his birthday gone by with no present or card, just two distinct choices. Some of the kids were already into petty street crime and he was being dragged along with them. But he was bright and he knew it. Sink or swim, buddy, he told himself. Get on or get out. That's all there is to it.

He put himself out on a limb, buried his head in his books and graduated with honours from high school. Then it was college and a part-time job in a photographer's studio, where he fell in love with the camera. Every weekend he would ride his bicycle into the Black Hills, where Sioux warriors sought *Hanblecheyapi*, the vision quest for their people. His first pictures were of a mountain lion crouched on a rock in the forest, watching white-tailed deer through the tree trunks.

He gained a degree in zoology, then a Ph.D., and won his first photographic assignments. Gradually he established a slightly off-beat reputation, with his Gaelic name and Celtic eyes and the wilderness etched in his soul. That was when he had met Holly the senator's daughter, and he'd craved her social acceptability as much as she'd craved his restlessness of spirit. Their paths had converged like twin branches of an oak tree, only to pull away from each other as the years took their toll.

FIFTEEN

IMOGEN RODE KEIRA BACK TO ATHOLL MCKENZIE'S LAND.
There were other things she had planned for these summer
weeks, other trips, landscapes she had wanted to paint, but the
discovery of the pair of white tails had changed all that. There
was a purpose in Keira's stride, trotting along the deer trails,
cantering once they got beyond the Seer Stone and the Leum,
and Tana Coire dominated the horizon. Imogen had a tent with
her and plenty of food. She didn't know how long she would stay
out here, but she was prepared as best she could be. She trusted
McKenzie about as far as she could throw him. The poison for
the peregrine would have been laid by him or one of his men, or
possibly by William Morris the gamekeeper. The bird hadn't
been poisoned elsewhere and just flown on to McKenzie's land
to die. McKenzie was a hard old hill farmer. He was trying to
make a thousand poor-quality acres pay, and the price of lamb
was rock bottom. No wonder he'd thought of stocking the loch.
But there were only two eagles, and the reason they'd become
extinct in Britain in the first place was because men like
McKenzie poisoned them.

There was no sign of any work being done as Imogen
approached the water, easing Keira from a canter to a trot and
finally a walk. The area set aside for picnicking was deserted.
The logs from yesterday had been added to; a further four lay
crosswise on the original two. But apart from that there was no

sign that anyone had been there. Imogen reined Keira in and sat for a long time, holding her head on a tight rein and scanning every inch of the loch side for movement. She saw nothing and climbed down from the saddle.

The wind was fierce this high, tearing at her clothing and whistling through the trees on her right. She studied the edge of the pinewood, where McKenzie and his men had been working yesterday. Perhaps they were in there hauling more logs. There was no sound, though, and no movement. Keira was cropping the long grass at the loch side, browsing among the stones for the juicier patches. Imogen wandered to the water's edge and surveyed the coire and the crags through binoculars. She sectioned the area, beginning at the bottom of the cliffs and gradually working her way higher, breaking up the rock piece by piece. She saw nothing and, clicking her tongue at the horse, she started round the loch. Keira followed, walking a few yards behind her, pausing to nose at the grass now and again. Imogen got as far as the edge of the coire and stopped. Once more she studied the land, the way the hills broke gently around the water, then reared suddenly in the savage outcrops above the coire itself. The waters were roughened flakes of flint, sliced into breakers by wind that blew from the north.

Again she was visited by the strange sensation she had experienced yesterday, as if something was wrong. The land felt barren and empty. That was ridiculous. The land *was* barren and empty. But she knew it was more than that. Somebody else might rationalize it as emotions running high in view of the precariousness of the recent discovery, but Imogen knew herself better than that. She gazed up at the rocks and searched with the naked eye. Nothing. She scanned the loch and the hills to the east and south. She shaded one hand over her eyes and looked the length and breadth of the chilled and whitened sky. She saw nothing. Looking down again, she saw Keira watching her. 'What do you think?' Imogen asked her. Keira tossed her head and snorted.

Imogen squatted in the shelter of two boulders and thought for a moment. The wind had risen yet further and the whistle had become a howl. It dragged over her shoulders, clawing at strands of her hair, which was tied back from her head and tucked inside the collar of her jacket. She thought she saw movement, thought she heard a cry, and stood up sharply. It was nothing; some trick of her imagination. Shaking her head at herself, she started to climb the narrow path. Halfway up she again thought she heard a cry, but once more she was mistaken. Her heart bumped against her ribs and she knew then that something was wrong. The rock seemed to be alive, and she walked with one palm pressed against it until she got to the point where, diagonally, she should see the eyrie. She stood and stared, the saliva drying in her mouth.

Nothing. No movement, no sign of dark-brown feathers cresting into the wind, no hint of yellow, not even the mass of mossed twigs that made up the eyrie. She moved much more quickly now, picking her way across the buttresses in a traverse. She got closer and closer and, as she did so, she found bits of stick and leaves and then more twigs and sections of packed moss, and she felt the cry welling up in her throat. The eyrie was completely destroyed. She stood right over it now and she could sense the coldness, the silence that was all that remained. Looking back down the mountain she could pick out more bits and pieces, flotsam and jetsam that had been part of the nest. And then she saw something else, flat and speckled like a piece of broken china. She moved down to it carefully; the going was very steep here. And as she got closer, she supported herself with one hand and her fingers closed over a coarse brown feather. Imogen stopped, aware of her own breathing. She lifted the feather, brought it close to her face and smelled it – a resinous oily odour. She looked again at the little piece of china, and all at once she knew what it was.

Atholl McKenzie's quad was parked outside his house when Imogen rode into the yard, Keira's hooves announcing her arrival with a clatter of iron shoes. Dogs barked and over by the barn two collies strained at the lengths of rope that held them. Imogen pulled Keira up sharply and she snorted and stamped her feet, sweat foaming her flanks from the gallop down the hillside. The farmhouse door was thrown open and McKenzie stepped outside, face red, sleeves pushed up, vein pulsing like cord at his neck.

'What the hell have you done?' Imogen shouted at him from where she sat on the horse. He squinted slightly, then cocked his head to one side. She opened her closed fist and showed him the piece of broken shell clutched in her palm. 'What have you done to them, Atholl?'

McKenzie folded his arms and leaned in the doorway. He was chewing, jaws working against each other like a cow at the cud. He watched her, saying nothing, eyes tight and pig-like in the pockets of flesh that held them. Imogen looked into his face. 'You knew about them all the time,' she said, 'didn't you. Yesterday. You already knew. You'd been up there and smashed their nest already. Where are they, Atholl? What did you do with the bodies?'

McKenzie shook his head at her. 'You know, if I had a tape recorder I'd be suing you for this,' he said. 'You ought to learn to keep a civil tongue in your head. You can't go around accusing people of things, lassie. It's against the law.' He shifted his position, spat between his feet and leered at her. 'Now, get out of my farmyard before I fetch a shotgun.' He banged the door after him and Imogen was left alone, impotent, the horse shifting beneath her.

She wrote a long letter to her mother; she wasn't quite sure why, but all at once she needed to. They spoke on the telephone quite often, but every once in a while she felt the need to sit by the still-ness of the loch and write. Taking paper and envelopes from the bureau she had kept when her aunt died, she wandered down to the shingled beach. Mid-morning, the sun stretching, no breeze at all coming in from the sea. She sat on a large flat stone, black-ened at the edges by a skirt of water reed and jutting strategically from the shingle. She rested the pad of paper on her knee, bare-foot, the stones not bothering her, and gazed across Loch Gael to the grey green of the hills. No movement, no sign of life, just the handful of houses and the water. Sometimes canoeists would venture this far on the twin rivers; not today, though; today there was a perfect sense of peace. And yet she felt no peace. Her peace had been invaded; the peace in her soul, which she only achieved during the solitude of her summer sojourns, had been interrupted. Yesterday – the terrible discovery on Tana Coire, Atholl McKenzie's wanton act of destruction. She had informed Daniel Johnson as soon as she'd got home, but he told her there was little they could do about it. He would speak to the police, but without any evidence he doubted they would act. Their relationship with farmers was fractured at the best of times. They wouldn't want to exacerbate things without concrete evidence. So the eagles were gone, and with them Imogen's peace.

She would try to indicate her feelings to her mother in an implicit way, hoping that she might sense her disquiet from the general tone of the letter. Her aunt would have sensed it; not a word would need to be spoken. She paused, pen poised, looking at the whiteness of the page, and wondered how she could convey the sense of emptiness she felt this morning. Her mother was not the least bit intuitive, unlike her aunt, who many people believed had the second sight of the Celts. Imogen remembered how they had returned from seven years in the United States with her brother travelling in a coffin. Her mother, of course, had been on the telephone and told everyone what had happened, and that they were flying Ewan's body back to be buried in Edinburgh. Her aunt had come down to the funeral and, arriving at the church in Corstorphine, she had taken Imogen's hand and held it for the entire service. When Imogen looked up at her there was a light of recognition in her eyes, as if she understood things that only Imogen knew.

She laid the page aside and watched a cormorant dive into the loch. He had flown in from the sea in search of salmon. He wouldn't find any in Loch Gael, of that she was certain. The sun warmed her face and she crossed her legs and leaned back, hands buried deep in the cooling shingle. Closing her eyes, she lifted her face to the sun and allowed it to seep into her skin. What could she tell her mother? She felt a terrible sense of loss, as if something precious had been stolen from her. But maybe that was not all; maybe it was an accentuation of a deeper, old loss, a long-term loss. Perhaps she was reminded of the something that had gone out of her when her brother had died. She didn't know exactly *what* it was, but she needed to share it with somebody. The more she looked at the letter, however, the less she thought that somebody was her mother.

She finished it, though, not very hopeful that any of the vibes she wanted to impart would find their mark. She considered trying to explain her feelings in an explicit way, but ever since Ewan had died her mother had found explicit emotion of any kind too hard to handle. She had spent the rest of her emotional life skirting round difficult situations. If she felt she had happened upon something, discovered it for herself, she would dig away like a terrier at a burrow. If, on the other hand, something was laid bare before her, she shrank back from the confrontation.

Imogen addressed the envelope and drove down to the post office. Colin Patterson's wife was serving. It was Thursday and there was a small queue for pensions; Imogen had to wait her turn. Morrisey was there, paying his electricity bill, and a couple of lads from the McClachlan Hatchery were also hanging around. They nodded to her and she nodded back, then she stood in the queue, aware of their roving eyes on her hair, her back and her legs beneath the cotton dress. Her turn came to be served and Mrs Patterson looked up, smiled, then saw who it was and glowered. Imogen flinched, recovered and considered telling her exactly what she thought of her and her husband's pitiful, unwanted attentions. But she decided against it. Open confrontation with a middle-aged frump in a post office was not her idea of a good time. Instead, they regarded each other as if they were both experiencing the same bad taste in the mouth. Imogen smarted at the idea that this woman could conceive of her being attracted to a man like her husband, and by the time she stepped outside again the colour had risen like thunder in her face. She walked straight into Jean Law.

'Imogen.' Jean looked at her, head tilted to one side. 'Do I detect a frown?'

Imogen took her by the arm and led her away from the post office. 'Yes, Jean, you do. Let's go and get some coffee.'

They drove to Kyle and sat in a hotel where nobody knew them, and there all of Imogen's frustrations boiled over. 'What is it, Jean? What's it all about?' She shook her head. 'I couldn't care less about Colin Patterson. She ought to know that. Why is it that a single woman in a small town is the butt of everyone's imagination? What do they think I get up to, for God's sake?'

Jean laid a hand on her arm. 'Don't let it bug you so much. You're letting them win.' Imogen exhaled harshly through her teeth. 'They're not winning, Jean. But I am losing.' She sat back. This was much more than Patterson's wife. This was the hopeless letter to a mother who could never be there for her; a mother who only had room for the son who'd died thirty years previously. This was everything she had gone through from that day to this, every tiny emotion, every failed liaison. Dealing with males like Patterson and the pathetic John MacGregor, boors like McKewan and downright bastards like Atholl McKenzie.

Losing, that was exactly how it felt, quietly, gradually losing, slipping away into some dark corner where she could sit and hug herself. She looked out of the window and Skye rose in sharp grey contours, the water choppy and broken before it. Sea and land and sky, and yet she felt as penned in as she had ever been. Jean was watching her over the rim of her cup. 'There's much more to this than just Patterson's wife, lassie. What on earth is going on?'

Imogen looked at her then, and all at once she felt weary. 'Oh, Jeanie,' she said, 'I wouldn't know where to begin.'

Connla drove round the bend in the road and Eilean Donan Castle dominated the point. Built on a green isle flat against the surface of the loch, a great expanse of water before and beyond it. A single-track bridge – three arches fixed it to a point on the mainland – gave it access and a vantage point like no other. He slowed the truck and pulled into the car park, recognizing the scene from somewhere, but not remembering where. People were buying tickets for a tour, but he had never been one for tours so he just walked to the edge of the loch. Seaweed choked the shallows beyond the boulder-strewn banks and Connla stared at the castle walls reflected in the stillness. The weed gave way to more rock, and then darkness as the bank dropped away sharply. He looked at the fortress once more – grey stone bleached almost white in the sunlight.

Gaelloch, according to this map, was a little further on towards the Kyle of Lochalsh and the Skye Bridge. A right turn, then a few miles back into the hills beyond Loch Long to the smaller Loch Gael. He had no address other than the village, but it didn't look very big on the map. It occurred to him that he had no idea who Imogen was now, or what kind of person she had become. Was she married? How many children did she have? She might not even remember him, and then all at once he wasn't sure he wanted her to.

He spotted a white-faciaed hotel in the village, just along from a bar called McLaran's. A young red-haired Irishman called Billy in a pale green shirt and darker green tie served him. 'What name would it be, sir? And is it just the one night?'

'I'm not sure about the one night,' Connla said slowly. 'I guess I can stay longer if I want?'

'Sir, you can stay as long as you like. But we are expecting a party up at the weekend.'

'I'll know by the weekend,' Connla said. 'My name's Brady. John Brady.' He paid for the room in cash.

Upstairs he could see the loch and, if he craned his neck, a tiny bit of the castle. He sat on the narrow single bed, gazed towards Skye and wondered at himself. Where had John Brady come from? He didn't know anyone called Brady. Perhaps it was his own Irishness, or the evident Irishness of his host, but the name just popped into his head. All of a sudden he didn't want to be Connla McAdam here, not yet anyway. He wasn't sure why, and the thought of lying had no appeal, save some misguided sense of safety. Imogen Munro – after thirty long years. What could he possibly say to her?

For a long time he sat there, wondering quite why he had come. All thoughts of photography and panthers were gone. All he could see was the past and her face as an eight-year-old, with her jet-black hair and that old yellow blanket curled around her fist. It was an unnerving image. It had been then, and it was now, and yet that card in Dunkeld: it triggered other memories, not just of how things had been that day by the Salmon River, but before that, little Imogen the Twaggle Tail, who trailed after her brother and had a crush on Connla. There were two years between them, and he had felt protective over her, especially when Ewan was being his most spiteful self. She had been so bright and clear-eyed, and everyone loved her for her tumbledown hair and trailing yellow blanket. He wasn't the slightest bit surprised that she could paint so beautifully; the Indian figure was exactly as he remembered it. The shock still set his skin tingling as he thought about it. Imogen had always had an eye for detail. He remembered the way she talked about the trees in the forest during the days before Ewan got killed. She saw things in their shapes that he had never heard anyone else talk about. There was an affinity there, the kind of affinity he imagined she had with this beautifully savage place. He longed to see her, and yet in the same breath he was full of trepidation.

He went back downstairs and ordered some lunch in the bar. A couple of locals came in for a pint. They were noisy, laughing and joking among themselves. One of them, a tall, bearded man with oily hair and bad teeth, nodded to him.

'How you doing?' Connla said.

The man squinted. 'American?'

'South Dakota.'

'Oh aye. Over here on holiday, are you?'

Connla swallowed beer. 'Yeah, I guess you could call it that. But I'm looking for somebody actually. An artist. Her name's Imogen Munro.'

The man stared at him for a long moment, and there was silence from his companions. Connla got the distinct impression he had said the wrong thing. The man continued to stare and he rested one elbow on the bar. 'You know her?'

Connla shook his head. 'No. I saw her greetings cards in a store in Dunkeld. I thought I might buy a painting from her.'

'So you're not a friend then.'

Connla could see the stickiness of the ground. 'Never met her.'

The man seemed to brighten. 'She lives in Gaelloch.'

'Aye, teaches school at Balmacara,' one of the others put in. The big man stilled him with a glare and looked back at Connla. They were about the same height, but the Scot was broader, thicker set, heavier. 'So you're not a friend then,' he repeated.

Connla made an open-handed gesture. 'Like I told you just now, I never met the lady. I'm just your average Yank tourist looking to take a piece of Scotland home with me.'

They laughed then and the big man bought Connla a drink. 'Andy McKewan,' he said. 'I keep a fishing boat at Kyle.'

Connla shook hands with him. 'John Brady. I take pictures of wildlife.'

'Well there's plenty o' that round here. Red deer, roe, fox, otter, badger, eagles, not to mention the ospreys.'

'How're the ospreys doing now? I heard they were well guarded.'

'Och, they're breeding fine just now.'

Connla's food came and he moved to a table by the window to eat it. Clouds swept in from the sea and rain rattled the glass, yet he could see the sun was still shining over part of Skye. When he was finished, he ventured another question of McKewan.

'You got any idea where I can find Mrs Munro?'

'Miss, you mean. Well, *Ms*, I suppose it would be. She's not exactly a stripling any more.' McKewan cracked another grin. 'She lives by Loch Gael. Cross the bridge there and take the first right, all the way back to the hills. Carry on till the road ends and you'll not miss it. There's only the one way in and out.'

Connla took the truck and headed towards the bridge that split the three lochs, Duich behind with the castle at the juncture with Alsh; and Loch Long, much smaller and narrower, off to the right. He could see the road snaking a path round the lip and he assumed that Gael must be further inland. He trundled across the bridge with the windscreen wipers flicking back and forth as the rain hove in from the sea. He could see the concrete arc of the Skye Bridge and made a mental note to cross to the island before he left, if only to see where Bonnie Prince Charlie had landed. It was weird, he knew the old story about the Stuart Prince and Flora McDonald, but you got the impression that the sea crossing was a hell of a voyage. Not if he went from here, it wasn't; you could all but spit and hit Skye.

He took the road, as directed by the fisherman, and gently skirted Loch Long. It was single track with passing places, but he had to pull in only once. After seven or eight miles the mountains closed around him, then he crossed two bridges over the river. The first one was wooden, and for a moment he wondered how stable it would be. Beyond the second bridge cattle roamed loose, the black and white Friesian, not the shaggy red-haired long horns he had seen on the way up here.

Loch Gael was small even compared to Loch Long. It was wider though, and more rounded, with smoother shingle-strewn banks and flat, clear water. Gaelloch was no more than a clutch of houses, mostly white and single storey, without so much as a shop. The last house, though, whose front yard ran down to the beach was the grey-brown stone of the larger dwellings he had seen. It looked like it was a single storey, but the pitch of the roof was steep and he could see that it had been converted. Dormer-style windows faced both north and south. He pulled up, got out of the Land-Rover, scratched his head and looked for someone to ask. Then he saw a metal mailbox nailed crudely to the gatepost. Munro, it read, and he knew that he had found her.

There was no vehicle in the drive, just hens wandering loose and a big old rooster with a scarlet crown who stalked up to him; chest puffed up in challenge.

'Hey, buddy,' Connla cooed at him. 'Take it easy. I just want to know if your momma's home.' He looked at the backyard, lawned, although pretty much unmown, with the odd shrub here and there. Wild rather than well kept. A wooden chicken coop was perched on stilts behind the house, and the drive beyond the initial gravel was hard-baked dirt, rutted here and there and runnelled by rivulets of rainwater. He rapped on the side door and waited. Nothing. He knocked again. Still nothing. She wasn't there. Connla studied the front aspect where the loch stretched to the mountains which rose purple and blue in the gradually lowering cloud. He got the distinct impression that a storm was blowing in.

SIXTEEN

CONNLA DRANK IN THE PUB THAT NIGHT AND MADE CONversation with the locals. He found out that the estate was owned by Arabs and the salmon hatcheries weren't doing so well. There seemed to be little work, save forestry or taking to the sea, as with Andy McKewan. He and his crew were out in force again, and Connla got the impression that he was something of the big man in the community. He listened to their tales of fishing off the Rockall in weather that sent lesser mortals scurrying for the shelter of Hebridean harbours. In the morning he paid his £4.60 and crossed the bridge to Skye.

Imogen rode home in the lee of the Kintail Sisters, following the River Shiel with the main road on her left. A full day out, trying to shake off the depression generated by the plight of the eagles and yesterday's events. Jean had listened while she rambled on about her life, probably making no sense as she left so much out. There were things in her past that had remained secret and would do so still. But it had been good to talk nonetheless, particularly given the impotency of her letter to her mother.

August was beginning to wane and thoughts of the September term loomed like little spectres in her mind. She had left at dawn this morning and ridden beyond the Five Sisters through the Kintail Forest. It had rained more than she would have liked, but that didn't overly bother her, although the thought of a long hot soak in the bath had a certain appeal. She rode at a trot, Keira sensing how close her stable and a hot mash supper were. They skirted the southern edge of Loch Duich and took the Keppoch Road. At the field Keira whinnied at the black-faced sheep which had invaded her pasture yet again. The Land-Rover was backed up on the hill, so if there was a problem with the starter motor Imogen could trundle down and bump start it. The nearest house to ask for help was Patterson's, so she made sure she never left herself with a potential problem.

She led Keira to the old stone cottage, unsaddled her and broke away caked mud from her legs with the grooming brush. Keira loved every moment and her left hind leg quivered at the steady caress of the bristles. Loosed once more she made her way up to shoo off the sheep, while Imogen drew water from the hand pump and heated it on the stove she kept in her Land-Rover.

Connla had learned, by way of gossip more than anything else, that Imogen kept a horse on the hill road overlooking Loch Duich and that right now she was away in the mountains. He didn't ask many questions, just listened to the bar-room banter and discovered that they all thought her a bit weird, taking off as she did whenever the opportunity presented itself. She was unmarried, no children and he got the impression that every man in the bar would like to get in her knickers. On his return from Skye he had driven up the hill road until he came across a battered Land-Rover and a horsebox in an empty field with a stone cottage standing. He parked his truck and sat for a long time, glimpsing part of her life and thinking back over thirty long years. A hundred different memories crawled from the fissures of his mind.

Now he sat in his room, watching the road as a new storm blew in from the loch, kicking the smoothness of the surface into a mass of bone-coloured breakers which battered the stanchions under the bridge. He saw the short-wheelbase Land-Rover drive by and his heart stirred in his chest. He watched it cross the bridge, buffeted by the sudden strength of the wind, then disappear round the corner. He lay back on the bed for a few minutes, his arms stretched above his head, then sat up sharply, shook away the past and went out into the storm. The rain was almost horizontal, flashing across the tarmac in great breaths of spray, soaking him in seconds. He jumped behind the wheel of his rented truck and swung out onto the road. He hesitated, then turned left instead of right. Imogen had only just driven by and he would let her get settled at home before he ventured out to Gaelloch.

But he was restless and the tiny hotel bedroom was cramped, squeezing him between its walls like a cougar in too small a cage. He drove down to the castle, now closed and spectacularly sombre against the storm that raided its seaward walls. Connla drummed his fingers on the steering wheel, then turned back on himself and climbed the hill road for the second time that day. He pulled over in front of the field and switched off the engine, then, taking his coat from the back seat, he got out and vaulted the gate.

The horse was nowhere to be seen and he guessed it must be sheltering in the stable. It was a ruin of a cottage; he wondered who had lived there and for how long. How many generations of Western Highlanders, islanders, perhaps, who had shifted across the inlet to the mainland? One room, it would have been; grey stone, like the dry-stone walls that encircled the farms he had seen in the north. He paced up the path, aware of the smell of mud churned by the rain, and paused to look back at the loch. As he did so, he saw the headlamps of a car coming up from the gloom of the village.

The horse was in the stable, tugging at the hay in her net. She looked back as Connla moved in the window space, snorted, then settled back to her dinner. Connla spoke softly to her, as he had spoken to Mellencamp when he'd scraped her battered body off the Keystone Road. The horse blew through her nostrils and lightly stamped her foot, as if to tell him his muttering was just fine but not to come too close. Behind him the car slowed and Connla melted into the shadows, not wishing to have to explain his presence in someone else's field. The car was a station wagon; it slowed to a crawl, then stopped, engine idling, and the driver's door was opened. He saw the shaggy head of a man inspect his truck over the roof, then glance towards the stable before dropping back behind the wheel. Connla was in the lee of the half-open door and couldn't be seen from the road.

When the car was gone he went into the stable and looked at the racks of tack hanging from pegs on the wall. There was an Australian stockman's saddle; it had been a long time since he had seen one of those. He looked more closely at it and saw the Queenstown stamp, not Australia, New Zealand. Imogen had got about. He stroked the horse's long dark mane and eased his fingers along the length of her flanks. The skin felt a tiny bit pinched where the cinches had been. 'Bet you're glad that saddle's off, huh?' Connla flattened her ears and then left her.

He was climbing back into his truck when the same car pulled up. The driver's window was rolled down and Connla looked into the face of the shaggy-headed middle-aged man whose jowls were just beginning to sag from his jawbone.

'Can I help you?'

'Excuse me?' Connla was half in, half out of the seat.

'Ah, you're the American I've been hearing about.' The man switched off his engine. Connla lifted one eyebrow. 'Word sure gets around.'

The man stepped out onto the road, looked at him closely and then glanced at the field. 'Have you been out walking?'

Connla pointed across to the scrubby gorse on the loch side of the road. 'Down there. I wanted to sit a while and watch the storm.' The rain rattled off the shoulders of his coat. The man lifted his eyebrows. 'I suppose it can be spectacular,' he said. 'You're the chap who's been asking about Imogen.'

'The lady who paints, yeah.'

'She doesn't sell her pictures. Well, not her originals anyway. You're wasting your time.'

Connla stared at him for a moment. Was this another guy warning him off?

'I figured as much,' he said. 'You can always hope, though,

161

so I guess I'll talk to her anyway.' He paused. 'I'm told she's away. You have any idea when she'll be back?' The man squinted at him for a moment. 'She is back,' he said. 'She was only gone for the day. This is her field. You came by this afternoon, I believe. Her Land-Rover was parked here.'

'Really? Well, there you go. I just wanted to see where the road led. Spent most of the day on Skye.'

The man nodded, then opened his car door. 'She won't sell you a painting,' he said. 'Believe me, you're wasting your time.'

Connla drove out to Gaelloch, wondering just how many men in this tiny place had staked their claim on Imogen. Then he wondered if she would recognize him. It had been thirty years. As far as he was concerned he didn't look anything like he had done as a child, not even around the eyes, which they say don't alter much. He doubted he would recognize her. As he drew closer his heart began to race and he slowed his speed almost to walking pace. What would he say to her? He had told everyone he was John Brady and he still hadn't figured out exactly what had made him lie. But then he remembered Imogen's eyes from way back when and he knew; even at the age of only eight her eyes were like twin dark drill bores.

Imogen lay back in the bath surrounded by lighted candles, her head in the water and her hair spreading like the snakes of Medusa. The water was hot and shot through with Radox to ease the quiet cold from her muscles. It had been a good day, yet she couldn't shake off the image of Atholl McKenzie's brutal face and the knowledge of what he had done. A diesel engine sounded on the gravelled section of road between her house and the Morriseys and she sat up in the water. The bathroom window faced north over the loch, and her aunt had deliberately set it low in the wall with the glass unfrosted in order to maximize the views. Leaning on the chilled enamel and straining her neck, she could see twin headlights through the gloom of the storm. It was a Land-Rover, she could tell by the engine note. John MacGregor? He was the only person she knew with a Land-Rover. What the hell did he want? But then MacGregor never came out without phoning her first.

162

She didn't want to see him and resolved to lie in the bath and ignore any persistent knocking. The Land-Rover seemed to pause, though, as if the driver was hesitating at the gate, then slowly it crawled up the drive. She looked more carefully now, and watched as the door opened and a man stepped out. Tall and lean, he flipped the door closed behind him. It wasn't John MacGregor; she would know his uninspiring bulk anywhere. Who then? And then it occurred to her: the American.

She jumped out of the water, wrapping her head in a towel as the first knock sounded downstairs. She reached for a second towel, then decided that she couldn't answer the door to a perfect stranger like this. He knocked again, and she opened the window and called out through the rain: 'Just give me a minute.'

His face was caught in the porch light, longish hair, falling in shadow. She saw him smile. 'Hey, you're in the tub,' he said. 'Look, I can come back.'

'No.' She flapped a hand at him. 'Just give me a sec' and I'll be down.'

Connla stared up at the partially lighted window, seeing her head swathed in a towel, but unable to make out her features. She had a softly undulating accent, cultured and gentle, not guttural like some of the Scots women he had heard. The last time he had heard that voice the accent was more small-town hick than his own and the owner was eight years old. So many memories; he had a knot now in his gut like a heavy immovable stone. Why had he come here after all these years? And with a lie on his lips already. He wanted a cigarette, but didn't wish to light one now that he was here and had disturbed her, and any moment now she would be down. So he waited in the gradually easing rain, watching droplets of water glinting like crystal as they fell through the arc of light round the porch. The upstairs window was closed and he stood with his hands in his pockets, shifting his weight, almost subconsciously, from one foot to the other. The waters of the loch were tossed by the wind behind him and he could hear the waves chewing at shingle.

Inside, Imogen rubbed at her hair with a towel, then shook it out and slipped on a bathrobe. It reached to just below her knees and she made sure there were no gaps at the front, then she went downstairs. She really ought to get dressed to receive a guest, but if he came unannounced like this then he would have to take her as he found her. He was wasting his time anyway: there was no way on God's earth she would sell an original painting. Everything she had ever done was either hanging on her walls or stored in the loft with the work left by her aunt.

Connla waited on the step, butterflies fluttering in his stomach, as the light grew through the glass rhombus at eye level. He heard the pad of bare feet, then locks were turned, the door swung open and he looked down at the smooth, even features of Imogen Munro. Her skin shone with the heat of the bath water and her eyes were large and dark and oval.

There was character and depth in her face rather than obvious beauty. Her hair, though, was jet black and hung long and wet to her waist, where already it gathered in ringlets.

'Come in,' she said. 'I've sort of been expecting you.'

She could smell the rain on him, mixed with the scent of his hair and skin; it nibbled at her senses. He was tall, with angular features and stubble on his chin. She put him at about forty, maybe slightly less, it was hard to tell.

'Come through.' She nodded to the kitchen and Connla moved past her.

The house exuded a warmth that was nothing to do with heating or insulation; there was a peacefulness about it. Strangely now he was inside he felt fractionally easier. She need never know who he was; he could just be there, see her. Perhaps he might lay a few ghosts to rest. He paused in the kitchen, not sure if she meant him to go on to the lounge, and rested his palm on the back of a pine chair. The room was large, lived in and dominated by a huge table in the middle of the floor with six chairs round it. There was an old gas range against the wall and wooden units and draining board. Connla's eyes, though, were drawn to the walls where her original paintings were hanging. He recognized the same hand immediately, not just from the subject matter, which was far more varied than what he had seen in Dunkeld, but from the tone of each composition.

He stepped closer, staring at one picture then the next. Imogen watched him, the way he moved, the way his gaze roamed the walls as if she wasn't there. His eyes bunched slightly, wrinkling the skin at the edges as he studied her work without speaking. He moved easily, long limbed and graceful, almost like a cat. His hair was thick and dark auburn in colour, accentuating the green of his eyes. He had a straight, almost aquiline nose and skin tanned to a light fawn colour. He looked round at her suddenly and she felt colour burning her cheeks.

'I'm sorry,' he said. 'I guess that was kinda rude. Walk right into your house and gawp at your pictures without so much as introducing myself.'

She smiled. 'No, it's all right. I was flattered.'

'They're very good.' He looked again at the stag. 'You paint a lot of pictures with red deer in them, don't you.' He cocked his head to one side. 'Is it the same stag?'

She smiled again and lifted the kettle from the ring on the stove. 'Would you like some coffee?'

'I'd love some.' He shook his shoulders. 'Get this rain outta my bones.'

'Here.' Imogen held out a hand for his coat. He slipped it off and passed it to her, then watched as she reached up, stretching one foot to her toes, and hung it on the back of the door. The robe lifted slightly against the smooth skin of her calf. She turned and he smiled at her, then extended his hand.

'John Brady,' he said. 'I'm the guy the store called you about.'

'I thought you must be.' She laughed then. 'They said you were American.'

'Did they?' Connla smiled, nodding a little knowingly. 'You figured some Yankee tourist looking for Braveheart, huh?'

'No, no. I don't know what I thought. But everyone likes to take memories of a place away with them, don't they.'

He nodded his head slowly. They shared memories of a place, although they were different, at least in perception. Right now she had no idea, and that fact ought to give him confidence, but it didn't. 'I guess they do, at that,' he said quietly.

She gestured to the chairs round the table. 'Take a seat.'

'Thank you.' Connla sat down, one leg stretched out in front of him. He wore Levi's, Timberland boots and a denim shirt. He pushed the hair away from where it fell across his eyes. Imogen leaned against the Welsh dresser and folded her arms. The sleeves of her robe were dragged up, and Connla couldn't help but notice the rich smoothness of her skin, tanned quite dark with just a dusting of fine hairs.

'Where are you from?' Imogen asked him.

'South Dakota. The Black Hills. A place called Keystone. I've got a one-room shack up there.'

'Really?'

'Well, I guess you could call it a cabin. And the room *is* pretty big. I could've divided it up a bit, but I've never gotten round to it.'

'What do you do there?'

'There particularly, or just any place?'

She smiled. 'What do you do for work, I mean?'

Connla pulled a face. 'Well, I guess you could call me something of a hybrid. A cross between a lecturer in zoology and a photographer.' Again he looked at the picture of the stag on the wall. 'Is that the same guy?'

Imogen sat down opposite him. 'Redynvre. Yes.'

'Redynvre?' He smiled. 'D'you always name your subjects?'

'I did him. After the Stag of Redynvre in the story of the Wooing of Olwen.'

'Celtic mythology, isn't it? King Arthur or something.'

Her eyebrows shot up. 'You know it?'

'A little.' He tugged at his hair. 'Got some Irish in me. I think we're pretty much the same stock, aren't we. Scots and Irish.'

The kettle boiled and Imogen got up and poured water into the cafetière. Connla watched her as she placed two earthenware mugs on the table and bent to get milk from the fridge: Imogen Munro after almost thirty years. His head was choked with memories, images from the past, some of them disturbing, and yet the longer he sat there the less disturbed he felt. In a weird way it began to feel strangely comforting, almost like some kind of affirmation. Part of him wanted to tell her who he was

166

right then, but it was simpler this way: just to see her, say hello and then leave. She would not sell a painting and he didn't really want to buy one anyway; it was just a ruse to see her after the shock he had received in Dunkeld.

'What brings you to Scotland, Mr Brady?' she asked him as she sat down again. Connla looked at the plunger on the glass cafetière, watching as the particles percolated beneath it. 'I was visiting an animal park in England.' He sat forward. 'I specialize in big cats; pumas in particular.'

'Is that what you do in South Dakota?'

He nodded. 'I've tagged most of the population of the Black Hills and Powder River Basin and got their territories mapped. Habitat, game availability, that kind of thing.'

Imogen looked at his long slim fingers, which were spread before him on the table, empty of jewellery; no tell-tale band of white on the third finger of his left hand. She was amazed at herself; her eyes had strayed almost instinctively. Who was he? Was he married? These were the first questions to pop into her head. Perhaps it was the circumstances of the past couple of days? Perhaps it was the innate sense of aloneness she felt as the summer grew longer? She didn't know, but all at once it seemed strangely important.

'How long have you lived in South Dakota?' she asked him.

'Off and on for twenty years, I guess.'

'In a one-roomed cabin?'

'Yep.'

She smiled. 'I don't suppose you're married then.'

Connla laughed. 'You got that right.'

Imogen flushed, shaking her head. 'Excuse me,' she said. 'I have no idea why I said that.'

'That's OK. There was somebody once, but you're right, she didn't like the cabin. Having said that, I didn't like the apartment, either.' He indicated the plunger on the cafetière. 'Do you mind?'

'Be my guest.'

He poured coffee for them both, then added milk and sugar to his own. 'Are you married?' he asked her.

'No.' Imogen sipped coffee, self-conscious all at once. She had taken the conversation too far much too quickly. 'I thought all you American men drank your coffee black and sugarless,' she said, trying to change the subject.

'I like to break with tradition.' He sipped and smiled, then looked beyond her once more to the paintings. 'You're very good, you know.'

She twisted her mouth down at the corners. 'I'm OK. But it's nice of you to say so. Do you know much about painting?'

'I know about pictures. I know how to make a good photograph. The principles aren't dissimilar.'

'Light, character, feature.'

He nodded and scraped back his chair. One picture, hanging by the open doorway to the lounge, intrigued him. It was a mountain scene, with a single shaggy-coated goat high up on a precipice. He moved closer to it and stared for a long time. The rock was black and grey and purple in places, with cracks running through it, shadows where the sun fell across it, the detail immaculate. He wanted to reach out and touch the texture. He didn't. He turned, looked her in the eye and said, 'What's the main subject here, the goat or just the rocks?'

Imogen stared at him, aware of her heartbeat all at once. There was something about him, familiar maybe, but she didn't know what it was. She got up and stood next to him. She was much shorter, her head reaching no higher than his shoulder. She gazed at the picture and knew when she had painted it, knew exactly where it was.

'Devil's Rigg,' she murmured.

'Pardon me?'

She looked into his face. 'That's Devil's Rigg. South of here; very steep, very rugged.'

'I can see.' Connla was aware of how close she stood; he could smell the drying of her hair, the faint hint of shampoo, the heat in her skin. He looked back at the picture. 'You paint rocks real well, you know that.' And then he stopped and stared. He was standing all but against the door jamb of the lounge and he could see a window and curtains and he knew the loch and the hillside were beyond it, even though now they were obscured. The Indian carved in wood rested on the window sill, upright against the inner wall, just as it did in the picture, half hidden in the fold of the curtain.

Connla felt his palms begin to tingle. His mouth was dry, despite the coffee, and he stood rooted for a moment.

Next to him, Imogen was still; she was aware of his breathing, the proximity of his maleness. Glancing up at his face in profile, she could see he was no longer looking at the picture. 'What is it?' she asked.

Connla twisted his head round, memories suddenly broken. 'Nothing. Pretty room, that's all. You've got good taste.'

Imogen looked where he was looking and frowned. The twin couches before the open fireplace had been bought from charity shops and were covered with a couple of old throws. The floor was the exposed wooden boards her aunt had insisted on, and her only consideration to comfort was the Persian rug she had bought at a car-boot sale in Inverness. More of her pictures hung on the walls and Connla stepped into the lounge.

'Do you mind?' he said.

'Not at all.' Imogen followed him, watching as he moved; his close-fitting jeans were frayed where they dragged at the heels of his boots. He was well shaped, without being overtly muscular, and all at once she imagined wrapping her arms about his waist from behind and holding his warmth against her. Again she felt colour rush to her cheeks and again she had to look at the floor. She was barefoot and naked beneath the towelling robe and he was a stranger in her house.

Connla moved to the window, his gaze shifting restlessly from picture to picture. He stood side on to the glass, where the rain streamed against it. Before him, on the wall, was another picture of the stag. 'Redynvre,' he said. 'This is the one they made reductions from, isn't it?'

Imogen moved alongside him again. 'Yes. That's on a peak north of here. Ciste Dhubh.'

Connla looked sideways at her. 'You paint when you're out there?'

She nodded. 'I take fairly lengthy trips in the summertime. I have a horse, a highland pony. I keep her up on the hill overlooking the loch.'

'In that stone cottage?' Connla said. 'I thought it looked like a stable.'

Imogen stared at him; again there was a hint of something about him. She half screwed up her eyes. 'Have you been up there?'

'I took a drive. I went there while you were still away. That road looked interesting. I figured the views would be good.'

'And were they?'

'Yes. They were spectacular. I never knew the Isle of Skye was so close to the mainland.'

'A lot of people say that. I suppose when you had to take the boat across it seemed like more of a distance.'

Connla was looking at the Indian figure, his thumbs hooked in his pockets, sweat in his palm, heart high in his chest, though his face betrayed no emotion. Imogen was silent beside him, still looking at Redynvre. Carefully, Connla picked up the figure, and his mind raced back, tumbling over itself. He could smell pine trees and Douglas fir and the cottonwoods close to the river; he could see the trail and hear Ewan Munro yelling. He felt Imogen's gaze. 'This isn't Scottish,' he said quietly.

She looked at the carving against the palm of his hand. Her mind stilled and she took it from him and replaced it on the window sill. 'No, it's just something I picked up.'

'Do you know what it is?'

She had turned away from him, hugging herself, and moved to the fire that wasn't there. It was chilly tonight and she wished she had built one earlier. 'I don't know what you mean.'

Connla picked it up a second time, and she turned and wanted to take it from him, but didn't. He seemed to weigh it in his hand. 'It's Native American,' he said, 'but then I guess you figured that already. Possibly Sioux or Shoshone. Cheyenne, maybe. I've seen something similar once before.' He pointed to the broken feather. 'I think there were two of these originally; they're eagle feathers. The Thunderbird – Wakinyan Tanka –

170

the embodiment of the great spirit himself. This guy is a ghost dancer. Somebody carved it in memory, I'd say; in memory of what might have been.'

Imogen looked from his eyes to his hand and back again. 'What d'you mean, in memory?'

'After the event. Looking back with too much hurt, maybe, to reflect on.' He paused and pushed out his lips. 'In the late 1880s, at Walker Lake, Nevada, a Paiute Indian called Wovoka had a vision of the messiah. The vision was of a reunion with the dead, where all was as it had been. With the first new grass of spring the dead would rise up and the white oppressor would fall away, the buffalo would return and the sacred way of living would be restored to the red man. Warriors came from all over the west; literally thousands of them, from all the different tribes, converged on Walker Lake. They wanted to hear the message from the Wanekia – that means 'one who makes live'. They met with Wovoka and he instructed them in the steps of the ghost dance, which he had learned in his vision. The dance would issue in the new beginning. It was passive insurrection. No more farming, no more labouring, just dancing day and night till the hoop of the nation was whole once again. In the dance, they would meet with dead relatives and cement the return to the old ways. Wovoka gave each leader two eagle feathers and some sacred red paint for their faces. Later, Black Elk of the Sioux made ghost shirts at Pine Ridge, close to where I live.' He stopped talking and set the little figure down again. 'It all ended in tragedy.'

'What tragedy?'

He looked round and could see the disturbance in her eyes. His tongue was suddenly tied; there were things he wanted to say but could not. He looked away. 'In 1890 the Sioux had been dancing under Black Elk's direction and the authorities were getting nervous. The Indians would not work. Sitting Bull was arrested and then killed, and still the people danced. None of the whites could understand it and their ignorance bred fear. In the end, the remnants of Custer's Seventh Cavalry massacred three hundred and forty women and children at a place called

Wounded Knee. The dance went on at other reservations but, symbolically, that's when it ended.'

Imogen watched him, and all at once she felt her space had been invaded; there was a stranger in her house. That hadn't happened in a long time.

'I'm sorry. I'm taking up your time,' Connla said.

Imogen half smiled. 'I have to dry my hair.'

'Look, I'll go. I should never have come out so late anyhow. Insensitive of me.'

'It's OK.' But she was weary all at once. 'They should have told you, I don't sell my originals.'

Connla picked up his coat from the back of the kitchen door, working the collar between his fingers. 'Listen, thank you very much,' he said and turned. 'Oh, by the way, they did tell me. About the pictures, I mean.' He smiled then and stepped out into the night.

He sat in the truck for a few moments, trying to gather his emotions. Everything seemed messy. He hated to lie. But right now lies were his only protection. Imogen Munro after thirty years. The little girl from Wyoming, whose brother had drowned in the east fork of the Salmon. The thoughts dribbled away, but Imogen's face filled his mind: the sheen of her hair, the clarity of her skin and the sharpness in her eyes. Her nose was fine and straight, her lips full and red. He could smell the bath on her even now and imagined her naked, as he was certain she must have been, under that robe. He widened his eyes at himself in the rear-view mirror and started up the diesel.

Imogen leaned with her back against the door and heard the engine turn over. There was quite a pause before it did, as if he was sitting there with the rain pressing him into his seat and nowhere for his thoughts to flee. She sensed the thought in him, the great depth of it. She didn't know why. She had never met him before, and she had sensed nothing vaguely like it in any of the men up here. So why now? And what was it exactly that she thought or felt or sensed? Green eyes and that fire in his hair; it was all she could see as she stared blankly in front of her. She thought about the contours of his movement: the slight swing of his arms as he walked, the way his jaw worked when he spoke, the way he had bunched his eyes while gazing at Redynvre. She shook herself physically and told herself not to be so stupid. Then she went back through to the lounge, paused a moment and stared at the broken feathers held by the Indian on the window sill. So now she knew what it was, after all these years. She stood by the sill and remembered, and the rain beat against the window.

Connla drove slowly back to the hotel, a cigarette burning between his fingers. So many thoughts, so many emotions, old and new and clashing like waves under the bridge. Rain still pounded the windscreen and the wipers worked furiously. He parked the truck outside the hotel and sat for a long time just thinking about what had happened. It was hard to take in after thirty long years – Imogen Munro grown into a beautiful woman and that little ghost dancer on her window sill. Outside, the wind howled and the rain rattled the bodywork of the truck. Connla shivered where he sat and stared into the blanket of night. Was that it? he wondered. Come up here, see her and go? Was that enough after all these years? He had no answer and the chill seeped into his bones. He climbed out of the truck and ducked into the bar.

McKewan the fisherman was there, seemingly a permanent fixture, and also the man with the shaggy hair whom he had seen up at Imogen's field. Connla nodded to both of them and felt the cold stare of a third older man, with a Sherlock Holmes hat on his head. He slid onto a vacant stool and ordered a pint of Guinness.

'Wild night, so it is,' the barman said.

'You're not kidding.' Connla watched as he poured the dark beer into a straight glass.

'Did you find her, then?' Andy McKewan's bulk was all at once at his shoulder. Connla glanced at him and caught both the man from the hillside and the older man watching him. He frowned to himself. It was like being in the Slaughtered Lamb.

All he needed now was a pentangle on the wall. 'Yes, thanks,' he said.

'Any good?'

Connla squinted, his mind wandering elsewhere. 'Sorry?'

'The pictures. Were there any good ones?'

'Lots. I don't think she's going to sell any, though.'

'I told you she wouldn't.' The man with the shaggy hair spoke from further down the bar. McKewan, leaning on his forearms, swivelled to stare at him. 'And what would you know about it, Mr Patterson?'

Patterson seemed taken aback, either by his own interjection or the sharp retort from McKewan. Connla sipped his Guinness and watched.

'I work with Imogen, Andy. I know all about her painting.'

McKewan laughed then, loud and raucous, and glanced at his crew for favour. 'No,' he said, 'but you'd like to.' He cackled again. Patterson reddened and Connla caught the older man's eye across the bar. Something vaguely resembling a smile itched away at his lips.

It was only then that Connla noticed there were no women in the place. He took another cigarette from his pack. He must be flustered, nerves frayed out; he only smoked like this when his nerves were shot to pieces. McKewan snapped a zippo under his nose and Connla cupped his hand to the flame.

'So what're you going to do now, Mr Brady?' McKewan asked. 'Now that wee Imogen won't sell you a picture. Are you going on back to America?'

Connla hunched back on the stool, his hands resting in his lap. 'I guess.'

'Straightaway?' Patterson was too eager again.

Connla glanced at him. 'No, I've got some stuff to do over here first.'

'So you'll be around then?' The older man spoke for the first time from across the bar, where he nursed a tumbler of pale whisky.

'For a coupla days maybe. Figured I'd go over to Skye.'

'I thought you said you'd been.' Patterson again.

Connla was beginning to enjoy this. They were like a band of nomadic lions stalking the only female in season. 'I might go again,' he said.

McKewan rubbed his meaty palms together. 'We could take you fishing, show you some real Scottish weather.'

'You know what?' Connla said, nodding to the rain that spread like a sheet on the window. 'I think I've seen it already.'

McKewan laughed and clapped him on the back, nearly knocking him off the stool.

'Get this man a dram,' he said. 'Make it a good one, Billy.'

The barman took a tumbler and spun it in his palm before lifting it to the optics.

Connla watched as he poured a measure of malt whisky, then McKewan tapped the bar with a blackened fingernail. 'On ye go,' he said, and the barman shot in another.

'Ice? Water?' McKewan said to Connla.

'Straight.'

'Good man.' Again McKewan clapped him on the back. Connla took the glass, toasted them and knocked it back in one. The others gawped at him. 'Mr Brady,' McKewan said, 'we sip our whisky in Scotland.'

'Mr McKewan,' Connla rested an elbow on his shoulder, 'we slam it in South Dakota.'

SEVENTEEN

IMOGEN WOKE LATE, SOMETHING SHE NEVER DID IN THE summer vacation: there was always too much she wanted to do. But this morning she slept in, and when she woke up she wasn't refreshed but weary, as if weights were attached to her limbs. The rain was gone and sunshine stretched across the loch, and she lay there in the silence listening to fragments of birdsong which carried from the trees on the hillside. Last night she had dreamed of her brother up to his neck in water. She could see him now: head jerking this way and that, as if unseen limbs were frantically trying to keep him afloat. Imogen could feel the tightness of her skin about the eyes and she knew she had been crying in the dream. Slowly, lethargically, she eased herself out of bed. She got as far as the edge and stopped, a great cloud of depression moving in on her. She had a sudden desire to speak to her mother and contemplated telephoning her. But then her phone started ringing and, grabbing a robe, she went down to the kitchen to answer it.

'Hello?'

'Hello, Imogen. It's me.'

Imogen sat down on a stool, pushing a hand through her hair. 'Oh, hi, Jean.'

'Are you only just up?'

Imogen yawned, weariness in her face. 'Yes. What time is it?'

'After ten.'

'Och, I must've been tired.'

'Well?' Jean said in her ear. 'Did he come?'

'Who? Oh, the American. Yes, he came.' The previous night flooded back to her: his face, his voice, the way he looked at her pictures. 'Jean, I can't talk on the phone this morning. My head's not in gear.'

'Make some tea. I'll come round.'

Imogen was not at all sure she wanted company, but she put the phone down and the kettle on to boil, then she went to let the chickens out. Jean had wasted no time and was pulling up in her car as she got back to the kitchen. The kettle was singing and the room gradually filled with steam. Absently, she dropped a couple of teabags into cups and carried the whole lot over to the table. Jean let herself in without knocking, her face red, eyes bright and inquisitive. Imogen felt anything but enthusiastic, Ewan's face haunting her every move.

Jean saw the state she was in and clicked her tongue. 'Sit yourself down, lass. Let me do this.' She poured tea, then made some toast, buttered it and set a plate in front of her. 'You're not all there today, are you.'

Imogen took her hand and squeezed it; tears broke against her eyes and she blinked them back. Jean looked suddenly shocked. She sat down next to her and took her in her arms like the big sister Imogen had never had.

'Hey,' she said, gently. 'What's the matter? He couldn't have been that bad.'

Imogen wiped away the few tears that had dribbled onto her cheeks, sat up straighter and exhaled harshly. Jean stirred her tea and passed it to her. She gripped the cup in both hands, the warmth of the enamel feeding into her skin.

'I'm sorry,' she said. 'It must be my hormones. I don't know what's the matter with me this morning.'

Jean laughed. 'That's OK. We don't have to talk.'

And then Imogen smiled. 'All you want to do is talk,' she said. 'You want to find out what happened. Me with a man in my house.' She could feel the clouds lifting. Laughter: the best ante-dote for anything. That was something her aunt had always taught her.

'Oh, go on then,' Jean said with a coy smile. 'What was he like? Big and fat with a wallet to match?'

'No, actually.' Imogen stared out of the window. 'He was tall and slim and good-looking in a characterful sort of way.'

'Characterful?'

'Yes. You know, strong features – nose, chin, hair. Not a pretty boy, deeper than that.'

'What colour eyes has he got?'

'Green.'

'Hair?'

'Auburn, I guess. Very dark. It looked like it was burned.'

Jean made a face. 'Are we talking James Lawton?'

'No. God!' Imogen said. 'He was a customer, Jean.'

'No he wasn't, dearie. You never sell your pictures. You knew that before he came.'

Imogen got up then and wandered to the window, resting both palms flat on the sill. Jean followed and slipped an arm about her shoulders. 'You're really missing a few brain cells today, aren't you.'

Imogen leaned against her. She wanted to tell her about the dream, about her brother, about the way she had telegraphed his death to herself. Her aunt had had the gift of second sight, but it had not happened to Imogen before that day in Idaho, and never again since. She had looked it up because she had heard people talking about her aunt in almost witch-like terms after she died. She found a book on Celtic mythology and discovered the dubious gift of second sight. A vision of somebody up to their neck in water meant they were going to drown. They weren't dead when you saw it, but they would be soon after-wards. She remembered sitting in the library in Edinburgh with a shiver running up and down her spine like a startled spider. It had depressed her for weeks, the strange knowledge that when she had seen her vision in the forest on the edge of the Sawtooth, her brother was still alive. She wrapped her arms round Jean's waist then and held onto her. She desperately wanted to talk to her mother, but her mother wouldn't understand, or if she did, she wouldn't allow herself to share again the moment of tragedy with her daughter.

Connla woke with a thick head from drinking too much whisky. Normally he drank very little, so when situations like last night arose he didn't handle them well the following morning. A pulse thudded at his temple. He felt sick and had to roll over and lie on his back. The blankets seemed to press him deeper into the bed, adding to the swimming sensation in his skull, and he kicked them off and lay there, naked, looking up at the ceiling. Imogen's face filled his mind, that look of old in her eyes, as if she could see right inside someone.

He sat up and his head reeled, but he forced himself to the bathroom and doused his face in cold water. He gravitated to the shower, where he stood, limbs loose and weighted head to his chest, while the water drummed the ache from his brain. Dressed, and with a cup of coffee inside him, he felt much better, but every sensation, every thought was directed towards Imogen. Yesterday's storm had gone, and he stepped outside to a warm breeze coming in from Lochalsh. He wandered aimlessly towards the castle, pausing to watch the sunlight reflecting off the water. Skye looked inviting today and very green. He sat on the rocks and watched the boats trawl up and down to the salmon hatchery.

Jean had gone and Imogen had got herself together. She needed to muck out her horse, so she pulled on an old pair of dungarees and a T-shirt and got the Land-Rover started. She drove round Loch Gael with her head clearing, pulled out onto the main road and crossed the bridge towards the village. The traffic was quite busy and she had to slow right down before turning off to climb the Keppoch hill. She saw the American sitting on the beach with his back to her, looking out to sea. He wore a short field jacket and the wind caught his hair, blowing it about his shoulders. Imogen pulled off the main road and stopped, engine idling. She sat there for a moment just watching him. Somebody hooted a horn loudly at her and she started. MacGregor came trundling down the hill in his Discovery. When Imogen looked back at the beach, the American was watching her.

She sat there, hand on the gear stick, foot depressing the clutch. He climbed over the rocks and stood on the far side of the main road, waiting for a gap in the traffic. Then he crossed purposefully towards her. She was going to wave and just drive up the hill, but she didn't, she sat there, aware of a weakness in her stomach. She could sense him, feel the probe of his eyes through space and glass and metal. He came alongside and she leaned over and opened the passenger door.

'Morning,' he said.

'Hello.'

'Beautiful, isn't it. After yesterday.'

'Yes.' A short pause; awkward little silence. He smiled at her, she back at him, eyes on each other for a second, then on anywhere but each other.

'Well, anyway,' he said, looking across the bonnet. 'It was nice to meet you.'

'You, too.'

He stuck out his hand. She looked at it, did not respond, then her tongue snaked over her lips and she stared at the castle through the windscreen. 'I'm going up to sort out my horse. If you're not doing anything . . .'

'No.' He said it hurriedly; too hurriedly, but he didn't care. 'I'm doing nothing at all.'

'Jump in then.' She scraped Coke cans, papers and empty cigarette packets onto the floor from the passenger seat. 'It's a bit messy, I'm afraid.'

'Hey, no problem.' He slammed the door, and rested against the vinyl seat. She gunned the motor and they drove up the hill to the field. On the way, they passed a green Volvo estate car and Connla recognized the shaggy-haired man from yesterday. Imogen saw Patterson, their eyes met and she smiled at him and waved. Patterson looked suddenly startled.

At the field, Connla walked beside her up the soft muddied

path to the stable. The horse was at the top of the field, chasing sheep. Imogen nickered to her and she looked round, then trotted down to greet them.

'She's a Highland,' Imogen said, noting his silent interest. 'Bred for the mountains and as sure-footed as any goat you could mention.'

'She's pretty. What's her name?'

'Keira. It's Gaelic. It means "dark-haired one".'

'It's a beautiful name.'

They stood looking at one another for a moment, neither of them moving, then Keira pushed between them and nuzzled against her mistress. Imogen rubbed her neck, tracing stiff fingers through her mane and whispering softly to her. Connla moved along her flanks, stroking her with a flat palm. Imogen watched him and smiled.

'Have you spent much time around horses?'

'Some. I guess I can ride a bit.' He looked up at her once more. 'How far do you ride?'

'Oh, as far as I can. The longest I've been in the hills is a week. I don't know why really, it's just worked out that way.'

Connla stroked the horse's mane. She was sniffing at Imogen's pockets.

'Carrots,' Imogen explained. 'I didn't have my head on right this morning. Normally I bring some for her; it's the only reason she's pleased to see me.'

Connla helped her shovel the muck out of the stable, then he took the wheelbarrow round the field, which was very steep in places, almost a climb, and scraped the rest of it up from the grass. He dumped it all in the pile beside the horsebox at the gate. Imogen watched him working, suddenly delighting in the company. When he was done he wiped his hands on the wet grass. 'All set?' he asked.

She nodded. 'Job done for the day.'

'What're you going to do now?'

'Well, I was going to go home and paint.'

'D'you paint every day?'

'I try to. But I'm not working to anyone's timetable.'

'You just do it for yourself.'

'Yes,' she said. 'I think that's the only way.'

For a few moments they stood in silence, then Connla smiled. 'Can I get a ride back?'

'Of course.'

She dropped him outside the hotel. 'Thank you,' he said. 'That was nice.'

'Yes.' She sat there, with him half in half out of the truck. She could smell him: his hair, the sweat on his skin from the exertion. She flared her nostrils slightly.

'Right,' he said.

'OK.'

Suddenly he smiled. 'Would you have dinner with me tonight?'

Imogen looked at him. 'Yes,' she said. 'I'd love to.'

His face lit up. 'What time shall I come for you?'

'It seems a long way to come out given that we'll only be coming back again.'

'That's true,' he said slowly. 'But, you know, I'd like to come and get you.'

She smiled. 'Well, that'll be fine then. Make it seven thirty.'

He closed the door and waved as she drove away, then he walked back into the hotel.

Upstairs, in his room, he sat for a long moment, looking at the waters of Lochalsh through the window. Again his lies haunted him and he wondered what he was doing. She stirred something in him, and while he had clogged it up with a lie, he didn't really know what it was. Angry with himself, he got up, took another shower, then paced the room with a towel wrapped round him. She had no idea who he was and all the time that was the case he was playing with her emotions. She felt something; he could sense that much. *He* felt something. When she was a kid she had had a crush on him, and perhaps he, too, in his own way, had had one on her. But that was years ago and things changed radically when Ewan was killed. To come here now, like this, and tell her lies about himself was unfair and told neither of them anything. So why was he doing it? Fear?

Cowardice, perhaps? Wanting to face the truth at last and not being quite up to it.

He sat on the bed with a sigh and switched on the lunchtime news. He saw a bloodied sheep lying at a farmer's feet. He turned the volume up loud and listened to the man being interviewed. 'Aye, I saw it. This time I did. No question. There's bloody great beasts out there and it's time someone did something about it.'

Connla spotted the blue SSPCA vans, and then the camera panned to the uniformed inspector checking over the carcass. He felt his pulse begin to race.

Downstairs he phoned Harry Cullen, who seemed to be expecting him in his own particularly superior way. 'You saw the TV then?'

'Yes. Just now. Where was that?'

'Corgarff. Not far from the castle. I'm on my way up there now, see if I can pick up any tracks. The kill's awful fresh, so my lad might get a sniff.'

Connla thought about Imogen. 'I'm in the Kyle of Lochalsh,' he said.

'That's nice.'

'I've got to stay here tonight.'

'Oh, aye.'

The innuendo irritated Connla. 'Look, the earliest I can get over there is tomorrow.'

'No bother. It's your party, Mr McAdam. But if we find something, I assume it'll be the same terms as before?'

Connla let go an inaudible breath and considered his ailing bank balance. 'Yes,' he said. 'I guess so.'

'Excellent. See you tomorrow then.'

'Wait, wait,' Connla stopped him. 'Where are we gonna meet up?'

'Best place would be the hotel in Tomintoul. We'll probably need to spend a couple of nights there anyway.'

More money, Connla thought. Thank God Holly had got him those semesters.

*   *   *

Imogen painted, but her thoughts were elsewhere – something else that never happened to her. She stuck at it for an hour or two, then she wandered down to the loch and sat on a blanket, soaking up the sunshine, and realized that she was whiling away the hours until it was time to get ready to go out. She had phoned Jean and told her about the date. No, she didn't know where they were going, but she imagined it would be somewhere local. In fact, she wanted it to be somewhere local.

'We talked it up,' Jean told her.

'How d'you mean?'

'All that guff about James Lawton, the make-believe doctor from Edinburgh. We talked it up and then in walks Mr good-looking America.'

'I don't know that he's that good-looking.'

'Well there must be *something* about him. And by the way, now you've told me, don't be surprised if I pop out for a drink tonight.'

'Jean!'

'No, no. All's fair in love and war. It wouldn't be right if he left without me ever having clapped eyes on him. Besides, evidently like you, I want to see the local reaction. This is an event that could be talked about for decades.'

Imogen didn't mind. She didn't mind at all. Jean had been a good friend. Then she wondered if she was doing this just to spite the locals. She didn't think so, but it was possible. Everything had been so muddled today that it was very hard to tell. She was looking forward to him coming, though, and the fact that he was driving the seven or so miles just to pick her up delighted her. That hadn't happened in years.

EIGHTEEN

CONNLA DROVE OUT FIFTEEN MINUTES BEFORE EIGHT,
dressed pretty much as he always was, although he had put
on a fresh shirt and brushed the dirt from his boots. He was
showered, shampooed and had that knot of butterflies in his gut
that he last remembered experiencing in high school.

Imogen was ready at seven fifteen, smoking a cigarette
nervously in her kitchen, wearing a simple cotton dress with only
knickers underneath. She wore shoes with a slight heel, accentuating the shape of her calves, and her hair was brushed and
tied over one shoulder. She waited, had a cup of coffee, stubbed
out the cigarette and lit another one. Then she heard the rumble
of diesel and the clank of wheels on the second bridge and imagined him picking his way through the loose sheep and cattle. The
sun was fading in the west, but the evening was still bright and
warm. She didn't wait for him to get out of the truck, but slipped
a bag over her shoulder and stepped into the yard.

Connla watched her through the windscreen, the dress
hugging her breasts and falling just above the knee. She wore
black leather shoes and her hair was tied in a single Native
American-style plait. He switched the engine off and jumped
down, meeting her as she walked across the yard. They were two
feet from one another – no touch, just a smile and a look, and
he opened the door for her and watched the way she brushed her
skirt under her thighs as she sat down. The material rode higher

now and Connla was aware of a little tightness at the back of his throat. Climbing behind the wheel again, he turned the truck round and headed back to the main road.

'Where would you like to eat?' he said. 'It's gotta be your call, I'm afraid. I'm pretty new round here.'

'Do you know what,' she said. 'I'd be quite happy eating in the hotel.'

'Fine with me. Bar or dining room?'

'The bar will be just fine. The dining room's too stuffy.'

'Whatever you say. You're the lady.'

Nobody was in the bar yet, which displeased Imogen. Don't say this would be the one night when no-one would show up. It was early still, mind, and all she needed was one local, man or woman, and the word would spread like a forest fire. They sat at one of the window tables and Connla got her a drink. Imogen waited, watching him at the bar, one eye on the door. Jean would definitely be in. She was honest enough not to deny her nosy-parker tendencies.

He sat down opposite and she noticed the copper band on his right wrist. 'Do you always wear that?'

Connla squinted at it. 'I guess. Don't need to, but I'm out in all weather and I probably worry about the rain getting into my bones. Call me superstitious, I don't know.'

She smiled, sipped gin and felt in her purse for a cigarette. 'I don't normally smoke like this,' she apologized. 'But today . . .'

Connla took a pack of Marlboro from his shirt pocket. 'Today, I guess you're nervous, just like me.' He lit her cigarette for her and sat back. 'How long have you lived up here?'

'Oh, about seven years, I suppose.'

'And before that?'

'Edinburgh.'

'I've only ever been as far as the city limits,' he said. 'Driving up the other day.'

'It's lovely. You should visit before you go back to the States.' She paused then. 'When are you going back, by the way?'

Connla grimaced. 'I'm not sure yet.'

186

'But soon?'

'Sooner rather than later, I guess. Come September there's two semesters of teaching heading my way, but I've got no inclination to acknowledge them.'

'You sound like me.' She traced a finger round the rim of her glass. 'I live for the summer holidays.'

Connla leaned his elbows on the table. 'You, your horse and your paint tin, huh?'

She smiled. 'Something like that.' And then the memory of this morning's dream was there again, like a raw nerve at the back of her mind. She bunched her eyes.

He noticed. 'You OK?'

'I'm fine. I just had a bad dream last night. It keeps coming back to me, that's all. They do that sometimes, don't they.'

Connla nodded. 'Yes,' he said, 'they do.'

Imogen finished her drink and Connla got up to fetch another round. When he sat down again she told him she used to live in the United States.

He sat back, thinking about how much of a coward he was for carrying on this pretence. Bad dreams, old wounds reopened. He had lingered too long at her window sill. He should tell her; he needed to tell her. He should do it now, but his own wounds had been scratched and he knew, for the moment at least, that he had no choice but to carry on with the lie. He eased his tongue over suddenly dry lips.

'Whereabouts did you live in the States?' he asked her.

'Jackson City, Wyoming.'

'I know it.'

'Do you?' Her eyes widened and he saw himself reflected in them for moment, as if he were inside her looking out.

'Of it anyway. It's the northern side of the state, isn't it?'

'That's right. Across the line from Idaho.' She looked at the tabletop then, remembering. He could see it in her eyes. She was picturing the little town, junior high, her old house on River Street, a block down from his. 'We moved there when I was one.'

'How come?' He hated himself for asking.

'My dad was a contractor on the dam they built.'

He looked blank.

'His firm was working on the construction. Anyway, we lived there for seven years and then the contract ended and we had to come back to Scotland.'

'So you were still pretty young when you left,' he said.

'Yes. America was my home. I knew nothing about Scotland, and when I got here I had an accent worse than yours.'

He laughed out loud then. 'You got it. I know just how those Wyoming hicks talk.'

The food came and then Jean walked into the bar and, right behind her, McKewan. Imogen felt a little thrill in her breast. She was going to enjoy this. She introduced Jean to John Brady, and she sat for a moment with them before going back to the bar and her drink. Connla spotted his erstwhile bar-room buddy and nodded to him. McKewan responded with barely an incline of his head. Imogen thought this was wonderful. All she needed now was Patterson to come in. But he didn't, and neither did MacGregor, and she forgot about them. Jean only stayed for the one drink and then left. McKewan and his cronies propped up the bar for a while before moving on to McLaran's.

The two of them sat across the table from one another and Imogen found herself telling him pretty much everything about her life. When she'd returned to Scotland as a child it had been very hard at first. Her parents had found things awkward as well, difficult to make the adjustment back after living a different way of life for so long. She'd found the school system very different and her accent didn't help, singling her out for ridicule with the kind of cruelty that only children can muster. After that it was secondary school, then her highers, where she excelled in art. She lost herself in it. Her tutors saw her talent and encouraged her, gently advising without stifling her creativity. At college she had been told she was good enough to go all the way, wherever 'all the way' was.

'To be professional? Paint for a living?' Connla said.

'I suppose.' She finished her drink. 'I suppose I could've gone-further, but I loved landscape and wildlife and didn't really want to experiment in the way I would've been forced to. Artists are expected to be outrageous these days.'

He laughed then. 'And you didn't want to be outrageous?'

'Not for the sake of it, no. Anyway, somehow I got into teaching, then my aunt died and left me the house in Gaelloch. I gave up my post in Edinburgh and applied for the school at Balmacara.'

'And do you like it?'

'Oh, yes. I love the children. I only teach the young ones, mind; the ones who haven't begun to be conditioned yet. And I love the country. The west coast is everything: white beaches, the Atlantic and the mountains, of course.'

'Not to mention the deer.'

'Yes,' she said, smiling. 'You know, you're very perceptive.'

'Am I?' Connla rested his chin on his palm. 'You think so?'

'You seem to be. You seem to have an eye for what I'm about when I'm painting.' She hesitated because she knew it would sound silly, then she said, 'It's weird, but I feel as if there's something familiar about you.'

Connla sat back. 'Maybe I've got a double somewhere. Maybe you saw me in a former life.'

'Maybe.' She arched her eyebrows. 'Do you believe in former lives?'

'I don't know. Perhaps. Nobody knows what's out there, do they. We've only ever got what other people have told us; society, religion, other people's experiences and opinions.' He rested his arm on the back of the chair, not wanting the evening to end, but guilt ridden again and all at once feeling fraudulent.

'You're leaving tomorrow, aren't you,' she said.

He nodded.

'For good?'

Connla looked at her for a long moment. 'I don't know. There's some work I have to finish.'

'And then?'

He sighed. 'I guess it's back to the States. I've got those semesters to think about.' She glanced at the clock. The barman had called last orders. 'I'd better get back,' she said.

'Right.'

They drove in silence, skirting the loch to the twin bridges and finally the gravelled road, bereft now of wandering livestock. Connla pulled into the drive and stopped, leaving the engine running. Again they sat in silence, neither of them looking at the other. Connla was about to switch off the engine, but he didn't know what his motives were. He desperately wanted to tell her who he was, but somehow he just couldn't.

'Thank you for a lovely evening,' he said quietly.

'No.' She rested a hand on his forearm. 'Thank you. I really enjoyed talking to you.' Connla was aware of the warmth of her hand on his flesh. He looked into her eyes.

'I'm glad. I really enjoyed talking to you, too.'

She nodded and smiled, then gazed through the windscreen to the quiet waters of the loch. She opened the door. 'It's a beautiful night. D'you fancy a walk?'

'Why not.' Connla switched off the engine and they walked side by side, close but not touching, across the lawn and down to the shore. There was no cloud tonight; the stars were led by a brilliant Venus and the moon was a pale shadow caressing the surface of the water. Connla pointed at the sky. 'Look,' he said, 'Venus is lying directly under the moon.' He looked sideways at her. 'That'll bring you luck.'

Imogen smiled at him. 'Just me?'

'Well, me too maybe. But you for sure. This is your home.' Connla looked into her face then. He wanted to kiss her, but she bent for a pebble and skimmed it across the water. She turned to face him again and the faintest breath of wind lifted the weight of her hair. He stepped closer, then gently laid a hand on her shoulder and kissed her. Arm in arm, they walked back to his truck. 'Guess I'd better be going,' he said.

'Have you a long drive tomorrow?'

'The other side of Grantown-on-Spey.'

'Far enough.'

They stood again by the truck and Connla held her just above the hips, her flesh warm under the cotton of her dress.

'Goodnight then, John,' she said.

'Goodnight, Imogen.'

They looked at one another, neither of them knowing quite what to say or do next.

'Anyway,' she said, 'if this is goodbye, it was great to meet you.'

He smiled and kissed her lightly. 'It isn't goodbye. And it was great to meet you, too.' Then he pointed again at the sky. 'There was an old Cherokee medicine man called Rolling Thunder. He said, if you want to have good dreams, pray to the grandmother moon.'

NINETEEN

CONNLA DROVE EAST, WATCHING THE DAWN BREAK WITH one hand on the wheel, slumped half sideways in the seat with the window rolled down. The crispness of the air caught the breath in his chest and he stared at the mountains which bordered the road on either side. It might be hot today; it was so hard to tell up here, one moment the sun was shining and the next storm clouds rolled off the sea. He felt a strange numbness inside, as if part of his emotions had been awakened and part of them anaesthetized. Imogen's face had dominated his dreams for the past two nights now, as clear as day – every line, every contour and the great depth in her eyes. He still couldn't tell himself exactly why he had lied to her. He could see the snippets of recognition in her face, although he knew she had no idea what they meant. Sometimes you got those feelings about another person; the affinity with them could be so strong, so familiar, that you felt you knew them already. She would put it down to that. He drove on, slightly numbed now and very unsure of his motives. Perhaps this was all some kind of macabre voyeurism on his part? Perhaps it was a pathetic attempt to exorcize the past. Whatever it was, none of it was fair on Imogen. She had probably forgotten all about the past and busily built a life for herself, and here he was quietly ruining it for her.

*　　*　　*

Cullen was waiting for him at the hotel in Tomintoul. Connla had turned north on the A9 once he hit Dalwhinnie and had driven beyond Aviemore, then east through Grantown-on-Spey. He pulled up behind the battered VW and saw the pitbull slobbering at him from the tailgate. He climbed out, stretched his limbs and went into the hotel. Cullen looked up from his perch on a bar stool, a cloud of grey cigarette smoke like mist around his head. He had a tall glass of beer in front of him.

'Ah, you made it then.' He glanced at his watch. 'The spoor'll be cold by now.'

Connla was irritated, other thoughts clouding his brain this morning. 'No it won't.' He sat down on a stool and ordered a cup of coffee. Cullen cackled suddenly and squinted at him. 'Frosty this morning, eh. Whose bed did you get out the wrong side of?'

Connla ignored him and stirred two packets of sugar into his coffee. He looked sideways at Cullen, who was unshaven and toothless. He could smell gun oil and grime on his parka, and one trouser leg was stuck in his workboot, as usual. 'So what did you find out?' Connla asked him.

Cullen's face was suddenly serious. 'We've definitely got tracks.'

'You mean a paw print?'

'No, I mean tracks. If you want to finish your coffee I'll show you.'

They took the Land-Rover as before, only this time Cullen insisted on driving. Connla didn't mind; he was weary after his restless night and the four-hour drive he'd already done. He sat in the passenger seat while Cullen took the wheel, the dog a semi-silent barrier between them.

'Where we headed?' Connla asked.

'A farm out by the castle.'

'The one on the TV?'

'Aye, John McIntyre's place. He's a pal of mine.'

Connla shook his head and smiled. 'Who isn't a pal of yours?'

Cullen grinned wickedly, showing the gaps in his teeth. 'Oh, not many people, Mr McAdam.' He looked forward again. 'I make a bad enemy.'

Connla sat up straighter then, glanced at the dog and hunched himself into the door.

'Have you got a sleeping bag with you?' Cullen asked him. 'If we pick up the trail we might need to stay out.'

'I always carry a sleeping bag.'

'Boy Scout were you?'

'Something like that.'

They took the road south-east, following the line of the Conglass Water till they came to the northern end of the Lecht. Connla stared left and right out of the window; hills greened to brown on both sides of the road, and ridges of new heather and bracken stretched in waterless ponds of black. The farm was north of Corgarff Castle, along a pitted dirt track at Cock Bridge. The track ran for perhaps half a mile before the straggle of grey stone buildings settled between two gentle summits came into view. Cullen had an unlit roll-up between his lips, which flapped up and down as he spoke.

'McIntyre's had trouble before,' he said.

As they entered the farmyard the pitbull pricked up its ears and spittle drooled from the side of its mouth. Connla watched it splash against the vinyl panel between them.

'Stay here,' Cullen growled. The dog whimpered, glanced at its master, then cowered against the back seat. Connla opened his door. The afternoon had clouded over considerably, and at this height the wind was brisk and teased out the gaps in their clothing. Connla zipped up his field jacket and looked round at Cullen. 'Did he keep the carcass?'

'Aye. He was going to burn it till I persuaded him that you should look at it first.'

'Thanks.' Connla looked around for the farmer.

'He's a busy man, Mr McAdam. Not much money in farming these days. He's away in the hills with the sheep.' He led the way into the barn.

Connla could smell the flesh beginning to rot as soon as they entered. The barn was dark inside and hung with cobwebs as thick as cord. Bits of broken machinery cluttered the concrete floor, and the hayloft above his head was loose and full of holes. Cullen bent by a sheet of tarpaulin, which lay across a bale of straw. 'I told him we'd burn it for him after.'

The ewe had a long tear in its throat, edged by a stiffened flap of skin, and bloody, blackened tissue hung from the folds of discoloured wool. There were no other obvious wounds, but Connla eased the wool aside and looked at the deep scoring he knew he would find on the flank. He gauged the depth and position of the claws in his mind. 'I'd say this was a female leopard. She attacked, but the sheep got free and ran some before it died.' He pointed to the dried blood on the ewe's legs and the spatter marks on the underside of the belly. Then he indicated the scoring of the claws. 'See the depth, the spread? That indicates a female to me.'

Cullen looked sceptical. 'You can tell the sex of a cat by its claw marks?'

'I reckon I can, if it's a mountain lion. A leopard's pretty similar, Bird Dog. I'd say this baby weighed about a hundred pounds.'

'The ewe had two lambs,' Cullen told him. 'You think maybe she tried for her, got it wrong and took the lambs?'

'I don't know. Are the lambs missing?'

Cullen nodded.

'Then maybe that's what happened.'

'Well,' Cullen got up with a cracking sound from his knees. 'We'll find out if we catch her.'

Connla looked up at him. 'You told me there were tracks.'

Cullen crooked his index finger.

Outside, they crossed the yard as the first spots of rain began to slap the concrete. Connla turned his collar up and tugged at the brim of his hat. He followed Cullen past the elbow of the buildings and over a five-bar gate. The field had been used by sheep, although it was empty now, and their droppings littered the shortened grass by the fence.

'The ewe was attacked here,' Cullen said. 'McIntyre had brought the flock down so he could check their feet and dip them.'

'This was dawn yesterday morning?'

'Aye. He was just on his way out when he saw the panther run off up the hill.' Cullen pointed into the distance. 'That's where the tracks are.'

'Have you followed them?'

'Only as far as the tree line.' Again he pointed, this time to where a grove of larch trees straddled the hillside, white trunked and heavy with foliage.

They climbed the hill and the grass grew thinner, mud taking over where the ground had been churned by a hundred cloven hoofs. The mud was smoother, however, the closer they got to the trees; and about fifty yards out Cullen stopped and pointed at the ground. Connla recognized it immediately; it wasn't deep, but there was no sign of any claws – the print of a big cat. He felt a surge of excitement and dropped to one knee. This was the best he had come across yet, not just one track, but a well-spaced group of them, and he imagined the panther, black against the hillside, loping into the trees. He stood up and looked at Cullen. 'You want to wait here?' he said. 'I've got stuff to make a plaster cast in my truck.'

'Go ahead.' Cullen rolled a cigarette. 'The trail'll be cold by now, but we might as well follow it anyway.'

'Can you track through woods?'

'If there's something to track.'

They looked at one another for a moment, silent competition between them. 'I'll get the gear then,' Connla said.

He laid his camera equipment, collapsible tripod, shoulder stock and remote exposure gear on the hillside while he made a plaster cast of the first paw print. Silently, he congratulated himself on his expertise; twenty years of studying cougars had not left him without knowledge. This was a female leopard all right; melanistic, if that's what the farmer had seen – black fur with the spots, or rather rosettes, still visible. It wasn't uncommon for a spotted mother to give birth to one black and one spotted cub, or even two black ones.

He checked the consistency of the ground, which was quite hard, the mud having formed from just a light rainfall. He considered the depth of the print and decided one hundred pounds would be about right. When he was finished he stood up, took off his hat to wipe the sweat from the leather band and waited for the cast to dry. He marked the exact spot where they'd found it on his map, then slipped the cast into a clear polythene bag and labelled it. Cullen stood watching him, his back to a larch tree, the butt of his hunting rifle on the ground between his legs.

'You got a gun in that pack?' he asked.

Connla shook his head. 'We won't need a gun, Bird Dog. If we find the leopard, which I very much doubt, we certainly won't need a gun.'

Cullen smiled then, showing his receding gums. 'Better to be safe than sorry, though. Eh, Mr McAdam.'

Connla shouldered his pack and looked again at the prints. They led directly into the thinly spaced trees. Cullen had his dog sniffing around already. Connla doubted it would be much use as a tracker, though he did think, if they were lucky enough to find it, the dog might just tree the leopard long enough for him to photograph it. But he would rely on his own instincts and abilities to track it. He had tagged a whole heap of cougars in South Dakota and he had never used a dog for tracking.

He followed the line of prints into the trees, then stopped. The farmer had startled the leopard and it was probably carrying a lamb in its mouth. Lambs were born in the spring, so this one would be plump and fat by now. No problem; a leopard could haul three times its own body weight up a tree if it had to. The trees thickened further into the copse. Connla studied the undergrowth and figured out which was the most instinctive path to follow, the one with the least resistance, yet cover. The prints were smaller spaced as they trailed through the trees: the leopard had obviously slowed to a walk. Connla followed them as best he could, though the ground was much drier here. He paused at the far side, with Cullen alongside him, where the hillside rolled into a valley; there was no cover other than bracken. He turned to Cullen, whose dog seemed to be getting nowhere. 'Goes on like this, huh, the territory?'

Cullen half smiled and waved his arm in a circle. 'Aye, it does. Exactly what you see, Mr McAdam. Mountain and valley, the odd wee loch, a burn here and there. Yon heights are the Grampians. Keep going west and you're in the Cairngorms.' He looked back at the tracks himself now and pushed out his lips. 'If I was yon beastie, I'd make for the higher ground.'

They both looked west then, where the hillside climbed steeply to a ridge of exposed rock. Connla nodded and they struck out for it. Halfway across the valley he paused and dropped to his haunches, the grass was weak and bent back and scarred with a brown stain.

'Sheep's blood.' He glanced up at Cullen, again the excitement building. Cullen shifted the rifle from one shoulder to the other and pressed his dog's snout to the spot. This time it ran off a little way, heading for the line of rocks, where it paused and came back again.

'Could do with a bloodhound,' Cullen muttered. But then the dog lifted its head, looked at both of them for a moment and scampered over the ridge. The two men exchanged a glance and followed.

The ridge continued along the length of the hilltop with an ever-steepening drop on either side. The dog had definitely seized on something and led them between the rocks to where the slope began to dip. Here Connla paused, something darker than the grey of the stone catching his eye. He bent and scraped at a rock, then showed his fingers to Cullen. It was a tiny patch of loose black hair, no more than a few strands. He tested the coarseness against his skin. 'I need a microscope,' he said, 'but I'd bet a hundred bucks it's her.'

Now he stood and looked out across the valley, brown and grey against the weighted clouds above them. He half closed his eyes, scanning every nook, every dark patch on the land. From his field pack he took another polythene envelope and slipped the strands of hair inside. He checked exactly where they were on the map and logged the co-ordinates.

'You're really up for this, aren't you?' Cullen said.

'Bird Dog.' Connla had a new-found enthusiasm for the man

and laid a hand on his shoulder. 'If I can find a leopard out here, then maybe, just maybe, I won't have to go back to teaching.'

They went on, climbing ever higher, moving up through gorse and bracken and heather. When they had gained a couple of thousand feet they stopped and Cullen produced a small petrol stove. They rested and made some coffee. Connla always carried dried rations so they would not be stuck for food that night. Cullen told him to forget dried rations, he'd shoot a rabbit or two.

The dog appeared to have lost the scent, but Connla was not unhappy with their progress. The land was stunningly beautiful, even in the drab weather. It would more than likely rain again tonight and he wondered what sharing a tent with Cullen would be like. A mile further on, they stopped as Connla came across some more tracks. They were much smaller, though, and ran in single file. He stared at them and scratched his head. Cullen chuckled to himself. 'Fox, Mr McAdam.' He bent down and pointed. 'A fox places his hind feet into the prints of his front ones and draws them into a line under his body. Looks like he's hopping, doesn't it.'

'I'm more used to coyotes than foxes,' Connla said. 'I'll bow to local knowledge, Bird Dog. Always a good policy.'

Cullen motioned with the barrel of his rifle. 'He was hunting rabbit. Look.'

Connla saw the rabbit tracks then – twin sets of tiny fore prints – and the longer, flatter hind feet.

'It's a mountain hare, in fact,' Cullen corrected himself.

'Sure scared him off, too.' Connla nodded to where the prints suddenly changed, the little indentations of the fore feet appearing behind the larger ones, where the hare bounded away. He looked at the sky, which was blacker now than ever. 'What time does it get dark up here?'

'Oh, not for ages yet.' Cullen rubbed a calloused palm over his jawline. 'Crack on, shall we?'

They climbed higher still, the dog no use to them now, Connla using his instincts and Cullen's knowledge of the country. He was working on gut feeling and applying his intimate knowledge of cougar habits to leopards. He doubted whether they would see anything, for all he knew they might have walked right by her on a dozen occasions already. If she was downwind the dog would be none the wiser.

They camped out, Connla erecting the lightweight hoop tent just as the rain began. Cullen was as good as his word and shot and skinned a brace of rabbits, fed the offal and intestines to the dog, then roasted the carcasses on a small fire.

'Your field craft's good, Bird Dog,' Connla admitted as he chewed on a skinny hindleg.

'Bloody well ought to be. I've spent half my life out here.' Cullen produced a silver-topped hip flask and took a heavy swig. He offered it to Connla, who sipped somewhat more gingerly.

'Take a dram, man. On you go.' Cullen flapped a yellow-nailed hand at him, then set about taking his gun to pieces. Connla swallowed more of the burning whisky and rescrewed on the lid. He watched Cullen with his weapon and could see the love the man had for it. He had watched similar men in similar circumstances all over the world; their most prized possession their rifle. Once upon a time he, too, had been a hunter, but he had swapped his rifle for a camera on the day he'd turned twenty. He hadn't shot anything since, except of course with a dart gun.

Cullen's face, darkened by the firelight, intrigued him. Its swelling bald dome, shiny now, with shadows lying under quick, dark eyes, and the habitual roll-up cigarette clamped between his teeth. Connla rested on his elbows and gazed through the firelight to the lighter mass of the sky, scratched by the crests of mountains; they weren't very high but there were a hell of a lot of them. This area was prime cougar country, although a cougar could survive in just about any terrain, so long as there was enough for him to eat. Once upon a time they had been scattered throughout the whole of the American continent, but now they were confined pretty much to the western states. They could survive anywhere from the forty below of the northern Rockies to the deserts of Arizona and New Mexico. They had adapted to new habitats, evolving to cope with change. They ranged in size according to their living conditions and could be anything from tan to blue-grey in colour, with all manner of red and brown in between. Unlike leopards, their hindlegs were considerably longer than their forelegs, which was ideal for mountain terrain. Like leopards, they lazed between hunts, cleaning and licking their fur, giving the dual benefit of hygiene and the extra vitamin D absorbed from the sun by their coats.

The rain was easing against the nylon tent and Connla took a cigarette from his pack. Cullen looked on longingly and Connla tossed one to him. His thoughts wandered away from his companion and his preoccupation with his rifle, and away from the pitbull lying just inside the flysheet. They drifted to Keystone and his cabin in the hills, then Washington and the upcoming semester. Finally they settled on the Kyle of Lochalsh, the tiny hamlet of Gaelloch and Imogen Munro's face. Throughout the day he had been elsewhere, concentrating on his craft, endeavouring to track the untrackable and only too aware of the little bursts of excitement the various finds had given him. Yet for a moment it seemed less important, other than, perhaps, keeping him in Scotland. And remaining in Scotland was now important less because it kept him away from the university than for other reasons.

He shook his head to clear it, but Imogen's face remained – the gentle darkness in her eyes, the Celtic sheen of her skin and that improbable tumbling hair, like a massed black waterfall.

'I'll give you a penny for them, Mr McAdam.'

Connla glanced across the flames. Cullen had finished reassembling his rifle and it lay across his knees; his gaze centred on Connla.

'Oh, I was just thinking.' Connla lit his cigarette and breathed smoke at the dying fire. He motioned to the rifle. 'You look like some Highland gunman with that thing across your lap. Something from the old days?'

Cullen squinted. 'In the old days it was cap and ball, Mr McAdam, and not enough of that. This whole place was cleared after Culloden. I told you about the clearances. Bastard English again. Did you see that film *Braveheart*, with the lairds and prima nocta?'

'The women on their wedding days, you mean?'

'Aye. They used to do stuff like that. It's all true, you know.'

'It sounds pretty familiar, apart from the first-night stuff, maybe.' Connla sat up a little straighter. 'We did it with the Native Americans; cleared them out and moved them on some-where else. Took their language, their traditions, their whole way of life.'

'Yon Indians. Aye.'

Connla made a face. 'I live pretty close to Pine Ridge, Bird Dog. That's the Oglala Sioux Reservation. Right now it's the poorest place in the United States, and only a hundred and fifty years ago the seven tribes of the Teton were the proudest, most prevalent race in the west.'

'Life, Mr McAdam. Life, politics and religion.'

'You're not kidding.' Connla stopped talking, all at once watching the dog. It was sitting up now with its ears pricked forward.

'Sometimes I think—' Cullen started, but Connla lifted a finger to his lips and silenced him. The air was still, the rain gone and the wind less than a murmur. Connla thought he heard a sound he had only heard once before, on the edge of the Kalahari. He strained hard to listen, convinced that his ears deceived him. But then he heard it again, and as he did a shiver puckered his cheeks.

Cullen stared at him. 'What is it?'

'Ssshh.' Again Connla strained his ears. The wind picked up then dropped to nothing. Still the pitbull sat where it was. It had heard the sound, too, but couldn't smell anything. Silence again and Connla half stood, thinking he had been mistaken. But then he heard it a third time and he knew it wasn't his imagination. It was a coughing sound, almost a grunt, like a pig snuffling away at the trough.

'You were right, Bird Dog,' he whispered.

'Right about what?'

'About them breeding in the wild.' Connla stared at him. 'Hear that grunt? That's a leopardess calling her cubs.'

TWENTY

CONNLA WOKE BEFORE CULLEN, THE VOICE OF THE leopardess still in his head. In his dreams she had come and looked down at him where he lay. She wasn't black, but spotted, and he recognized her like an old friend, counting the marks on her face. She called to him as if she were calling her cubs, but when he tried to scramble up the hillside his feet kept slipping. For a long time she watched him, shoulders hunched, the white tip of her tail flicking from side to side, then a dog barked and she rose and backed away, her ears suddenly flat. Connla lifted himself on one elbow and stared at the pitbull terrier.

Wriggling free of the sleeping bag, he crawled outside; the grass was springy and soaked with dew. He set up the stove, then walked the short distance down the slope to the burn. Yellow water spilling over lichen-rich stones, and pebbles of orange and brown had been thrown up by the peaty earth. Connla bent to fill the water bottle, delighting in the sudden warmth of the rising sun on his scalp. Then he stopped and stared.

On the far side of the stream, no more than five feet away, he saw fresh prints in the mud bank. He squatted there for a long moment in silence, letting the implications sink in. He recognized the print of the leopardess, but along with hers he made out what looked like two sets of smaller ones. They were definitely breeding. Last night he had heard the proof and now he was looking at it. He got up slowly, realizing then that there was not only a female here, but somewhere also a male. Female and male territories overlapped, and out here, with the numbers so few, they would be vast. The largest cougar patch he had logged was over 150 square miles in the Powder River Country of Wyoming. That had been a male, and he had heard of even larger territories in Idaho. This one, sprayed and scraped, could easily be as large.

Cullen was awake and rubbing his eyes when Connla got back to the tent. He set the water on the stove and lit it. 'Make the coffee, will you, Bird Dog? I've got some prints I wanna cast.'

He crossed the stream carefully on stepping stones, making sure he was a good way down from the print markings so as not to disturb them if he stumbled. Setting up his gear, he mixed fresh plaster and set the casts. Cullen wandered down the hill, crossed the stream and handed him a tin mug of coffee. 'It's hot,' he said. 'Don't burn your lips.'

Connla set the mug down and worked again at the plaster. 'They're definitely breeding,' he said. 'We've got cub prints right here.'

Cullen looked out of half-closed eyes and sipped noisily at the coffee. 'Could be just wildcats.'

'You mean the ones with the round-tipped tails?'

'Aye. The real wild ones, not feral.'

Connla shook his head. 'No chance of that.'

'How come?'

Connla smiled and pointed to the large print, right at the water's edge. 'Here's where momma was standing.'

Cullen watched as he labelled and bagged the casts, then worked away with his tripod and camera, making sure he took pictures from every angle. He marked the area on his map, and took shots of what he considered pertinent landmarks. When he was finished he folded the tripod away.

'If they're breeding there has to be a male,' Cullen said slowly.

'Yep.'

'Any sign of him?'

Connla shook his head. 'There won't be. His turf could be

huge. He'll only come across the female when it's time to make babies.'

'How big?'

Connla looked up at him. 'Daddy? A lot bigger than this girl, for sure. I don't know, maybe a hundred and fifty pounds, maybe more. There's plenty of food up here.'

'How big is the biggest?'

'Leopard? I guess around one ninety. They're smaller than cougars. I've seen male cougars in the Yukon at up to two fifty.' He picked up his coffee. 'These cubs are pretty young still. Look at the size of their prints.'

'So?'

'So somewhere there's gotta be a lair.' Connla smiled then. 'Tell me something, Bird Dog. If you were momma leopard, where would you hide your babies?'

Imogen painted the oil of Redynvre and was reminded again of the sea eagles. She was in the studio with the massive Velux window open above her head. There was as much light as possible in the room, with windows facing both south to the hills and north across the loch. It had rained the day before she had made the sketch, but the rain had stopped that morning. When she had come upon the grazing stags the afternoon had been still. She had commented on the weather conditions in her sketch notes, which were laid out on the table next to her.

She always stood when she painted in the studio, especially with a big canvas such as this one. She had wanted to begin with the sky – powder blue with a hint of grey in it, grainy almost. The clouds were slow moving but ragged, the edges diffused in the foreground and flatter and thinner in the distance. But she had painted the mass of rocks first, making harsh, thick lines with her palette knife, starting with black paint and then adding touches of greyed white as they took on more definition. She surprised herself. This was not how she painted. She always started with big blocks of colour, forgetting anything vaguely resembling line or character or definition. That would all come later. Half the pleasure was starting with a mass of colour, yet knowing that from the initial colour all that was in your head would finally break free.

But today it wasn't like that. She had painted the rock in detail, and, at the base, as if it were part of the stone itself, she had fashioned the figure of somebody standing. She stared at it now, aware of the strangest feeling: that it was somebody else's hand, not hers, that held the brush, as if she were standing back and being shown how it looked through someone else's eyes. She was aware of a sudden clamminess on her skin. Sunlight flooded the room, yet she was strangely cold. For some reason she thought of Hugues de Montalembert, the French painter who lost his sight in 1982. Two muggers broke into his New York apartment and threw paint stripper in his eyes. A few weeks before he had painted a self-portrait with a horse in the background: neither he nor the horse had eyes.

She had to leave the studio and go outside. She wandered to the shores of the loch, vaguely aware of gulls crying in the distance. She stood with her arms folded behind her, the wind pressing the cotton of her dress against her legs, framing material against muscle. Why think of that now? Why paint something like that just now? For a long time she remained there, alone with the water, the mountains and the handful of silent houses. The wind got up and clouds rolled intermittently across the sun to darken and lighten the day. Imogen stared blankly into the distance and thought about the past few days and the memories awakened by a man she had never seen before.

John Brady's face filled her mind. She could see his eyes, the arch of his brows, the hair that looked as though the sun had set in it. She could feel him, sense him, smell his skin, right there on the loch side, as if he were standing next to her.

Back in the house she pottered, straightened the throws on the settees, considered dusting and went to the cupboard under the sink in the kitchen. She worked away at the surfaces and the mantelpiece, and at the lounge window she paused. She picked up the little carved figure. Ghost dancer. That's what the inside of her head felt like today: a mass of confused emotion and memory, like a macabre dance of the ghosts. Shoshone, he'd said, or Sioux. It couldn't be Sioux, not on the east fork of the Salmon. She thought it might have been Nez Perce, Chief Joseph's tribe, who had almost made it to Canada before they were finally beaten back. She traced her finger over the single remaining eagle feather and images of the white tails flashed through her mind – the male, wings back, talons out, reflected in the water. Carefully, she set the figure back in its place.

In the studio again, she selected a brush and had to look hard to identify the image she had set in the rock: a splodge of black paint. She was about to smear and start again, but something stayed her hand and she laid the brush down.

Connla and Cullen hiked north-west towards the Ridge of Caiplich. They forded the River Avon, amid 2,500-foot peaks which were still mottled with snow in the shadows. Cullen was leading, with Connla falling in behind him, his pack heavy all at once between his shoulders. Cullen marched purposefully, the dog trotting at his ankles, panting in the sudden heat of the sun. The route took them along ridges, through tree-lined gullies and back again to the barren height of the hills. Cullen walked with no map and no compass, using only the sun and his innate knowledge of the land to guide him. They crested another hill, using the well-worn deer trail as their path, and he stopped. Connla had been deep in thought and almost bumped into him.

Cullen was gazing down on a valley strewn with boulders, some of which must have been thirty feet high. It stretched for mile after mile, a great cleft in the land, littered with broken rock, as if a pair of giants had been having a stone-throwing fight. One particularly large slab was pressed against the base of the far hill. Cullen pointed towards it. 'The Shelter Stone,' he said. 'It forms a natural hawf.'

'What's a hawf?'

'House. Home. Shelter. There's a space under the rock, a cave. A door was fitted years ago. There's always firewood and candles. I've stayed there many a wild night.' He rolled himself a cigarette and sat down on a flat sliver of rock. Connla remained standing, shading his eyes from the sun.

'There're more holes and caves down there than you could shake a stick at,' Cullen told him. 'If I was a panther wi' bairns, I'd hole up in one of those.'

Connla sat down next to him and pursed his lips. The valley was not only littered with boulders, there were clumps of trees, deep bracken and undergrowth. They were six or seven miles north-west of last night's camping spot. The leopard could easily range that far, even burdened with cubs. They would still be young enough for an eagle to snatch, but no doubt she was mindful of that and would move them at dawn and dusk, when deer and other game were feeding. Right now they would be laid up in a tree or deep in the bracken, soaking the sun into their skin.

Cullen had the stove out and was brewing tea. He seemed to stop every other hour to do this, like some kind of unspoken ritual. Connla didn't mind. They had come across no other signs of spoor that morning and he wanted time to think. He had successfully tracked cougars in mountain country without any significant trail to follow, not just in South Dakota, but in Arizona, Canada and the redwood forests on the California/ Oregon line. The cougar and the leopard were relatives. The cougar was bigger, having evolved to suit the needs of the Western Hemisphere, whereas leopards suited the East. The same cat was found anywhere from Africa to the jungles of South-East Asia. It had learned to adapt to very different climates and habitats, from jungle to open grassland. The ones on the loose in the UK were originally from captivity and they would have adapted in different ways again. Up here they ought to be more spottable, as they had no predators once they got beyond kindergarten age and there was plenty of game.

Movement on the far side of the boulder valley caught his eye and he picked out a group of roe deer leading their young through the rockier patches. He looked at the size of the fawns, getting bigger all the time, but still no problem to the leopardess. She could bring down a stag if she had to. He had seen Mellencamp take out a 600-pound bull elk up by Sylvan Lake last winter, right alongside the Sunday gulch trail. It would have frightened the life out of any overzealous hiker who happened to be testing the ice that day.

Cullen clipped the end of his cigarette, his rifle across his lap, his legs drawn up, and his face carved as if from stone. Connla could all but see the wheels of his brain working. 'Deer, rabbit, stoat, weasel, pine marten.' Cullen twisted his lip. 'What's with the lambs then, Mr McAdam?'

Connla made a face. 'She's just walking the territory. She'll do that. Keep the marks fresh by scraping up new dirt and leaves to scent. The cubs'll know the boundaries well enough to be pushed over them when they're older. Maybe McIntyre's farm's a marker, Bird Dog, and she figured on an easy meal while they were there.'

'How old would the cubs be?'

'Two or three months, I guess.'

'Could *they* have killed the lambs? Sort of a learning curve.'

'It's possible, but I doubt it.' Connla looked out once more across the valley.

'Momma maybe took the lambs for them to practise on, but she'd have killed them first.' He finished the last of his tea. 'They do that from time to time when they're all but done weaning. She'll show the youngsters how to open up the carcass and get at the meat.'

They continued round the steep inclining hillside, following the course the deer had taken, contours of dirt creating thin footpaths like tiny snow block trails. They got lower and the rocks got larger, and then, purely by chance, Connla found a fresh set of prints in the lee of a boulder. It was a plateau of rough, flat ground, with a muddy drinking hole seeping from under the stone. The sun could not get in and the grass had only grown so far. There was a patch of grey water with soft squashy banks to it, and in them were the imprints of two fore feet where the mother had bent to drink. Connla felt the hairs stand up on the back of his neck. 'These are very fresh,' he said.

Cullen had his dog's snout to them. 'Go on, boy. Get her scent.'

'Bird Dog, I think you ought to keep him close,' Connla told him. 'He's big enough to kill the cubs if we run across them.'

Cullen looked sourly at him. 'D'you want to find them or not?'

'Sure I do. But I don't want to find them dead.'

They looked at one another for a long moment and Cullen leaned on his rifle. 'Why don't you leave my dog to me, Mr McAdam.'

'I will. I'm just saying, what d'you think he'll do if he finds them?'

'He'll do exactly what I tell him, like he always does.' As Cullen was speaking the dog suddenly yelped and took off. Connla stared after him, then into Cullen's eyes. Cullen hefted his rifle in his left hand and they took off in pursuit. The deer trail climbed the hillside now, curving away from the valley. The pitbull galloped along it, vanishing just as the two men turned the corner. Connla ran in a half-crouch, the weight of his pack bearing him down. Cullen was not so encumbered, and for a man of his age he could move very quickly. Connla found himself being left behind. The hill curved and dipped sharply, becoming almost sheer at the edge of the path, and he had to slow even more, pressing one hand into the hillside to steady himself. He heard sudden barking up ahead and bent his legs and ran faster.

The path opened again, with shale to his left and the hill climbing starkly to his right. He ducked past a great slab of stone and saw Cullen standing square in the path, staring down the hill. Connla followed his gaze and spotted the hindquarters of the dog pressing between two rocks close to the valley floor. Then he saw a sudden flash of yellow and heard a guttural squawling, like two alley cats in a fight. There was no wind and the valley created a natural echo chamber. He grabbed his binoculars and swung them in an arc. A flash of something and he looked back again. His gaze settled on a spotted leopard cub, backed up against a rock with the pitbull bearing down on it. He looked sideways. 'Cullen, call the dog off. Call him off now.'

Cullen suddenly grinned. 'He's too far away, Mr McAdam.'

For a moment Connla was frozen, all thoughts of his camera

and pictures forgotten. The dog would rip the young leopard to pieces.

And then, with a flash of black and a half shriek, the pitbull was reeling, toppling head over heels. It happened in a second; a blur of flying paws and the dog was yelping and screaming, up on its haunches, bred to fight but with no chance against this. The panther slapped it hard, paw flattened, claws extended, tearing a hole in its side. Seconds later the dog was hanging from its jaws by the throat, its body limp and flapping about like a doll.

'Bastard!' Cullen stared down the hill. The panther had the dog pinned now and in its death throes. Cullen had his rifle hunched into his shoulder, eye to the sight, finger already squeezing the trigger.

'No!' Connla lunged and jerked the barrel up with his forearm. The shot cracked away, echoing off the rocks. Below them, the panther dropped the dog and shooed its young into hiding.

The bolt action on the gun had smacked Cullen's nose, and his fingers came away bloody when he touched it. For a long moment he stared at Connla. 'You're going to regret that,' he said.

'For Christ's sake, man. What were you thinking of?'

Cullen dabbed at his nose with the heel of his thumb.

'I told you to keep the damn thing on a leash. The mother was protecting her young, Bird Dog. What did you expect?'

Cullen dabbed again at his nose and spat a gob of blood from his mouth. 'I expect to be able to look out for my own dog,' he said quietly. 'I don't expect some Yankee tree hugger to interfere.' He worked a fresh round hard into the breech, and Connla stared at the gun.

'What? You're gonna shoot me now, right?' He turned away, shaking his head. 'Give me a break, Cullen. And while you're at it, get a life.'

TWENTY-ONE

T HEY HIKED BACK TO THE FARM AT CORGARFF, CULLEN carrying the shattered body of the pitbull in his arms. He walked ahead, back straight, not speaking. Connla had inspected the area thoroughly, but there was no sign of the panther or her cubs, only the torn-up grass soaked red. The attack had been ruthless – a mother protecting her young. She had ripped away the pitbull's jugular vein, sending ropes of blood spraying into the air like geysers. Some of the rocks looked as though they had been vandalized with paint. Cullen had taken a spare army shirt from his pack and wrapped the dog's body in it. Connla had suggested they bury the dog there and then, but Cullen told him to mind his own business. So now they marched in silence, walking by the light of the head torch that Cullen took from his pack.

Back at the farm, Cullen insisted on loading the dog into the Land-Rover and they drove to the village of Tomintoul in silence. Connla, exhausted from the day's exertions, booked into a room, took a shower and went to sleep. Cullen stowed the body of his dog in the back of his truck, then sat at the bar with the landlord, drinking into the small hours of the morning. Finally, the landlord yawned for the umpteenth time.

'Harry,' he said. 'I'm away to my bed. Lock the door before you go.'

Cullen shoved his glass across the bar for one last shot of whisky.

When the landlord was gone, he sat and smoked and brooded. For eleven years he had been monitoring these sightings; eleven years trying to find a big cat and be the man who caught or shot it, to prove beyond all doubt they were out there. He had imagined the newspaper stories, the book about his life, the rounds of chat shows – TV and radio alike. Years of careful, painstaking work – finding the locations and checking prints and carcasses at kill sites. Then this American waltzes in with his big ideas and his bloody great cameras and his twenty years of tracking pumas. Now his dog was dead and the best chance he was ever likely to have of shooting one of the panthers was gone. He thought of the paltry hundred pounds McAdam had paid him. He had lost a thousand pounds' worth of dog and, with the current government legislation, he wasn't likely ever to replace it.

He finished his whisky, then climbed over the bar and lifted the glass to the optic. A double. He sipped at it and topped it up again while the beginnings of an idea slowly took shape in his head. Leaving the glass on the bar he went outside, being careful not to let the front door close on him. He staggered slightly as he scrabbled in his pocket for his car keys and then he unlocked the door of his VW. His canvas pack lay on the front seat where he had chucked it on transferring the dog from McAdam's Land-Rover. He blinked in the moonlight as he tugged at the straps and eased open the drawstring. He delved now, one hand feeling amongst the clothes, the cold tank of his petrol stove and the soft piece of oilcloth. He smiled and lifted it clear. He closed the car door and held the cloth in both hands before peeling it back like the skin of a banana. Cold steel glinted blue in the fall of the streetlight. He thought he heard a noise and started: the village copper lived just across the square.

He stood for a moment and listened, but he was alone; he ran a practised, if inebriated, eye over the pistol. It was a throwback to his days in the slaughterhouses – sometimes the bolt gun was no good and he would revert to this. He had filed off the serial number long ago, back when all handguns had to be given in because the government overreacted after the shootings in Dunblane. A 357 Magnum revolver that no-one knew he had – short-barrelled; the sort of weapon you see in American films. He weighed it in the palm of his hand and considered his options.

Connla slept fitfully. In his dreams Imogen stared at him with her dark eyes, questioning the lines in his face. Then she faded and the leopardess sat over him again, but this time she was black and there were no cubs with her. He could feel the heat of her breath and hear the squawling deep in her throat. Her lips were drawn back, whiskers down, her face wrinkled like a male scenting flehmen. And something else was there, some darkness moving at the edge of the dream, the shape of a man. It faded and only the leopardess remained, and then her face became Mellencamp's, staring at him in the way she did when entering the house unannounced at dawn. Gradually she faded, but he could smell her scent where she had dragged dried leaves into a scrape, then spray-marked it as part of her territory. A nomadic male would kill her cubs. She hadn't got any cubs. Yet she had, they were tawny and spotted, with black streaks on their backs like lion cubs in Africa. The nomad would kill them to make her ready to mate again. There was nowhere she could hide them. The nomad stood on two legs and his mouth was the barrel of a gun.

Connla woke sweating before the dawn, and he had one thought in his mind: to get in his truck and drive to the Kyle of Lochalsh.

He didn't hesitate, pulling on his jeans, shaking his arms into the sleeves of his shirt and lacing up his boots. He had paid for the room last night, so he didn't have to worry about waking the landlord, and he stepped outside and closed the door quietly. It was just beginning to think about getting light, fingers of grey scratching away in the east. He saw Cullen's truck and then Cullen himself, snoring, face pressed up against the window, slumped behind the wheel in the driver's seat. His pack lay open next to him, the rifle, encased again now, across his knees.

Connla studied his aged seamy features; there was grime above his eyes and stubble bruising his chin. He really didn't like this man; and it was a feeling he had had from the start.

He started the noisy diesel-engined Land-Rover and drove slowly round the square, then headed west down the road to Grantown. From there it was south and west, and then Gaelloch, and when he got there he didn't know what he was going to do. There was something there, he told himself, something there from the past. Words to say, perhaps, maybe things to sort out. Yet he had put that chance even further away when he'd told her his name was Brady. So why was he going back? He could see her face; every tiny line, every shaped contour memorized from across the table in the hotel bar. He compared it with the little girl from Wyoming who had had a crush on him and recognized only the eyes. They had grown bigger and perhaps a little darker, but their shape was as he remembered. He could see her and smell her, that heated quality in her skin. It felt as though she had invaded his soul and so held part of him that he needed to get back. He had no idea what he was going to say to her, only that he had to see her again.

Imogen walked her horse along the edge of Tana Coire. She could see Atholl McKenzie and his labourers bent double as they shaped the pine logs into the base of a table. She could imagine the fishermen next year – waders and umbrellas and tackle boxes and strings of nets and barbecues, with drinks laid on by McKenzie. She closed her eyes, the wind nipping at the corners, forcing them to run with uncried tears. She imagined the eagle inches above the loch, feet thrust before him, talons reflected in the black of the water, wings back to steady him, the tips spread into six magnificent fingers filtering out the wind.

Looking up, she saw that McKenzie had spotted her. Both he and his men were watching and Imogen could only gaze beyond them at the crag in helplessness. They had beaten her and they knew it; beaten her before she even knew of the competition. Those eagles had been killed or scared off, their nest destroyed, before she and Johnson ever got to McKenzie's farm. She knew

215

it and they knew she knew it, but there was nothing she could do about it now. One of the men suddenly waved, then a wolf whistle pierced the silence and Keira half reared and whinnied. Imogen wheeled her around and galloped down the valley.

She rode back through the Vale of Leum Moir. It had been raining all morning and it was raining now, the sweet summer rain that makes the grass lush and rich so the stags can gorge themselves before the exhaustion of the rut. The big bucks would be high now, right up where the summits scraped the clouds and the heather was moist and thick and new. Imogen guided the horse one-handed, the other hanging at her side like a cowboy, the flat-fronted pommel of the stockman's saddle gentle against her pelvis. It was more padded, more compact and more shaped to her body than the standard English one. She rode often and over long distances, so she'd invested in something designed for the sheepherders of Australia and New Zealand. This one had been ordered from a shop on the banks of Lake Wakatipu and sent back twice before it fitted Keira's back properly.

She climbed now, Keira's forelegs sinking less deeply into the grass as the valley gave way to hillside, which grew sparser with each upward stride. The path wove a pattern through the brown scrub of the bracken, sand-coloured and snake-like, lipping the hillside in ever-tightening bands. Imogen moved out from the shelter of a stand of trees and the wind hit her full on, the rain gaining in strength. She wore a wide-brimmed waterproof hat which she pulled closer to her nose. The wind was chilly, but she was warm enough. Her long waxed coat kept her dry and Keira's flanks sweated against the inside of her legs. She headed south, crossing the River Leum and cutting between the mountains. The going was less steep and much easier on Keira, not that she minded; she fairly relished being saddled up, and horses like her had been used to haul wood and peat and all manner of things over far rougher ground than this.

An eagle called above her and Imogen looked up, the brim of the hat shading her eyes from the sudden white of the sky. Cloud blown, grey and cream, she scanned the horizon for the bird, then spied it soaring far to the north. She watched as a second, slightly smaller one, joined the first, and taking her binoculars from the saddlebags she scanned the pair for markings. Her heart began to drum in her chest. Their bodies were sleek and brown, not the tawny russet of golden eagles but a muddier, darker brown. They soared together like lovers, the updraughts catching in the sharpened hollows of their wings. She picked out the white in their tail feathers and felt the adrenalin rush.

They drifted gradually closer, circling lower and lower, as if they'd spotted her and in so doing a kindred spirit. They were so close now that she could make out the paler patches on their breasts. She sat in the stillness and watched as they climbed one last time, before turning into the wind and heading out to sea in the west. And she thought of Gwrhyr and Eidoel seeking Mabon son of Modron in the tale of the wooing of Olwen:

So they came to the place where the Owl of Cwm Cawlwyd made his home, and enquired of him after Mabon.

'If I knew I would tell thee,' spoke the Owl. 'When first I came upon this place, this great valley you see before you now was a wooded glen. But the race of men came and tore it up by the root, and there grew a second wood and then a third. All this time passed and I remained here, and yet I know not of this Mabon you speak.' He ruffled his wings and said, 'Nevertheless, I will guide thee, emissaries of Arthur, to the place where dwellest the oldest creature of this world. Where he has not travelled there is no such place. I'll take you to the Eagle of Gwern Abwy.'

As she rode home the rain had been replaced by clear skies and a sun that picked out the flattened pieces of exposed rock and heated them. Warmth spread through her veins and she knew the image of the breeding pair would remain imprinted on her mind for ever. She rode back to the field and unsaddled the horse, then shovelled the muck from the stable. Keira stood while she groomed her, Imogen taking the brush to her mane and tail as well as her flanks. Then she loosed her and sat for a while with the sun on her face, looking across Loch Duich to Skye. When she finally got home she found the American parked in her drive.

Connla had been there for an hour already. He had driven straight to her house, not thinking about food or where he would stay for the night. He knew she wasn't home as soon as he saw the Land-Rover was missing, so he'd turned the truck around and headed up to the horse's field. She wasn't there, either, and he had hesitated for a long moment, sitting by the five-bar gate with the engine idling. The man with the shaggy hair had gone by in his green Volvo and given Connla the eye, so he'd decided to drive back to her house and wait.

He didn't know why he had come other than on that morning's impulse; he had followed such urges all his life and had never really regretted it. But as he sat there and the time dragged by he wondered if he might regret it now. It was two in the afternoon and he lit a cigarette, something he never did unless his head was up his ass. He was staring at the loch when he heard the rumble of her old oil-burning truck. He saw her cross the second bridge and then disappear into the trees before coming round the headland, past the last of the whitewashed houses. He waited, aware of the tension in his gut. He really had no idea why he had come here and less still of what he was going to say to her. But her truck pulled up and there she was in her heavy work boots, grubby dungarees, and yet with a femininity about her that took his breath away. He opened his door and slid to the ground. She looked into his face and smiled.

'Hello,' she said.

'Hello.'

She hauled her pack from the back of the truck and led the way to the house. For a second Connla paused, waiting to be asked in, but she just looked over her shoulder and smiled once more. He followed her into the kitchen, where she laid down her pack and went straight to the kettle.

'Would you like a cup of tea or a beer?' she asked.

'Tea would be great, thanks.'

'Sit down.' She gestured to the pine chairs at the table and Connla eased one back. He slipped his field jacket from his shoulders and set it behind him. The kitchen was warm, with the sun streaming through the window, setting the particles of dust dancing.

He watched her at the sink, sleeves pushed up, revealing the smooth skin of her forearms, the hair over her face hanging in a braided curtain of black. She washed her hands, shook them out, then turned to face him, flicking her hair over one shoulder as she dried her hands on a towel. She watched him watching her and she could feel a hint of butterflies in her stomach; not fear, not apprehension, just that strange nervous fluttering when someone you like has their attention fixed totally on you. Neither of them spoke. She finished drying her hands, then turned from him again, aware of his gaze even more intensely as she reached for mugs from the dresser. She placed tea bags in the mugs, then poured on the boiling water, fetched milk and sugar and set everything out on the table.

Connla was aware of the tightness in his throat as he watched her, the little smile edging her lips into creases. She held up the milk bottle and he nodded.

'And sugar?'

Again he nodded, studying her face, little crow's-feet just beginning to show at the corners of her eyes and laughter lines by her mouth. She glanced at him, her hair falling over her face. She hooked it behind her ear.

'What brought you back?'

'You did.'

She paused, the mug in her hand half extended towards him. Then, avoiding his eye, she set it down before him.

'Why?'

'I don't know. I woke up before dawn this morning and decided to come and see you.' He could see the movement in her throat as she swallowed a mouthful of tea, eyes still anywhere but on his. 'Where were you this morning?'

'Tomintoul.'

'Was your trip successful?'

'Yes and no.'

Now she did look at him and her gaze was clear and even. She considered his face: the lines in his forehead and around his

219

eyes from years of squinting in sunlight; hair hanging to his shoulders; eyes like slices of green crystal. She looked at his hands as they encased the mug, veins blue and prominent against the skin, a broken nail on the index finger of the right one. She could see the hairs on his forearm poking out from the sleeve of his shirt.

'I was tracking a panther that killed a sheep at Cock Bridge.'

She stared at him now, eyes suddenly wide. 'Really?'

He nodded.

'Did you find it?'

'Yes.'

'You're joking.'

He shook his head. 'A black leopard with cubs.'

'You're serious, aren't you.'

'Very.' He leaned forward. 'I wanted to get a photograph. To prove that big cats are running wild in the UK.'

'And did you?'

Connla shook his head.

He told her about the SSPCA and meeting Cullen, and the trips they had made together. Imogen was leaning forward now, the ends of her hair trailing on the tabletop. Connla had to fight the urge to lean over and caress that hair, run his fingers through that hair, drag that hair to his face and smell the warmth in it.

'What happened?' she asked him.

'We found the panther, or rather Cullen's pitbull did.' He told her what had happened.

'There's a male out there somewhere, and she's mated with him, which proves the numbers must be reasonably significant. The cub was pure leopard. I didn't get a chance to see the other one, but I think there were two. Leopards usually have two cubs at a time and there's nothing to kill them out here. I didn't get any pictures because, like I said, Cullen's dog went for one of the cubs. The mother killed the dog and Cullen tried to shoot the mother.'

Imogen stared at him then, her hand trembling slightly where she rested her wrist against the edge of the table. Her own recent experiences echoed in her head. Connla suddenly sat back and ran both hands through his hair. 'I'm sorry,' he said. 'I don't know why I'm telling you all this.'

'It's OK.' She smiled, and her smile was reassuring, urging him to go on.

'Anyway, I was too busy trying to stop Cullen shooting her to get any pictures.' He sighed, then thought for a moment. 'I've got some plaster casts of the paw prints in my truck, though. Would you like to see them?'

'I'd love to.'

She watched him cross the yard, long-legged, loose-limbed, hair picked up by the breeze. His shoulders were lean and sinewy, and not too wide. She watched him every step of the way; watched his back and the way his shirt bagged just above his bottom. She watched him open the boot of his truck, reach in and come out with his pack. She leaned in the doorway, arms folded, one dungaree strap hanging loose at her waist. Connla turned and caught a glimpse of her before she straightened up and lifted the strap over her shoulder. He had felt her eyes on him as he'd crossed the yard and he delighted in the intensity of the gaze. He felt warm and wanted and, above all, understood, as if something deep inside her knew who he really was, though the realization had yet to break her consciousness.

She made more tea and watched while he undid the draw-string on the old canvas bag. But his face froze as he reached inside, and then he closed his eyes, biting down on his lip.

'What is it?' Suddenly her hand was on his arm.

He lifted out the polythene bags. Imogen stared at them, filled with crumbling bits of plaster. Connla sat down heavily. All the casts were broken, shattered beyond recognition.

'Was it the journey?' she asked him.

He shook his head and lifted the pack to the light. Both of them could see it clearly, the dirty outline of a boot mark on the material. 'Cullen did this.' Connla frowned deeply. 'But how? I had them in my room with me all night.'

'Where were you staying?'

'Just a small hotel.' He forced the air from his cheeks with a hiss. 'I didn't lock my door. I never thought to. Thank God my cameras weren't in there.' He kept those separately in twin aluminium cases. Then another thought struck him. He still had the undeveloped film he had taken of the paw prints. He looked at his watch, nearly four o'clock. 'Imogen,' he said. 'D'you know where I can get film developed quickly?'

'There's a place in Kyle.' She smiled again, softness in her eyes. 'I'll show you, if you like.'

They took his Land-Rover and drove to the Kyle of Lochalsh. 'Could you track the leopard again?' she asked him.

He shrugged. 'It's possible, I suppose. But they're awful hard to find. This one's gonna be even more careful after what happened with the dog.' He sighed. 'I guess if I holed up in the Shelter Stone for a week or two I might catch a glimpse. The trouble is, I don't have a week or two.'

Imogen could feel her heart sinking. 'You have to go home?'

He glanced sideways at her. 'Yeah, I guess I do.'

He drove with his left hand resting on the gear stick. Imogen looked at it for a moment, then, almost unconsciously, she reached over and let her hand settle on his. Connla felt the breath catch in his throat.

'Stopping the cub being killed was far more important than getting a picture,' she said. 'You know they're out there now. You've seen them with your own eyes. Something tells me you're the kind of man to find a way round the problem of locating them again.'

'I hope so.' He furrowed his brow. 'But right now those two semesters I told you about are beckoning.'

Imogen stared out of the window at the loch, aware of a sudden inexplicable sense of loss. 'Do you have to go back?'

He entwined his fingers in hers. 'I wish I didn't. More than anything I wish that I didn't.'

They took the pictures into the photo shop and then went to a small cafeteria overlooking the loch which was full of coach-party tourists from Bournemouth. They sat opposite one another and drank thin but frothy coffee. It started to drizzle, then rain harder and harder until the loch and the sea and the

Isle of Skye were completely obscured from view. Connla longed to tell her the truth, aware that with every minute that passed it was becoming harder and harder to do so. Imogen told him about the eagles and how she had first discovered them and what had happened subsequently.

'I thought they were dead,' she said, 'poisoned like the peregrine. But they weren't.' She half smiled. 'This'll sound really stupid, but this morning, when I saw them again, I couldn't help thinking they were looking for me.'

Connla gazed across the table at the softness in her eyes. 'It doesn't sound stupid. They were a long way from the sea.'

She laughed then. 'Coincidence.'

'Why?' he said. 'The other night you told me Redynvre always seems to know when you're coming.'

Imogen shrugged and sipped coffee. 'Anyway,' she said, 'I know McKenzie didn't kill them; that's the main thing. Maybe they'll build another eyrie on the sea cliffs. He can't get at them there.'

They talked about Scotland and she told him then how sick she got of village gossip, how debilitating it could be and how she constantly had to fight off the attentions of men like McKewan and Patterson.

'I noticed they'd staked a claim,' Connla said. 'How come you never got married?'

She shook her head. 'I nearly did. To a boy I met at university. It would've been a mistake.'

'What was he like?'

She made a face. 'I don't know. He was quite good-looking, I suppose. Very studious, very aware of himself, ambitious. He was heavily into computers, which was much less common back then. No doubt he's made a whole pile of money since, married someone in London, had two point two children. You know the kind of thing.'

Connla sighed heavily. 'Tell me about it – regular everyday life. The kinda thing I never did very well.'

Imogen laughed. 'You and me both. Peter was nice enough, I suppose. But he was wrong for me. You know, you think you'll find your soulmate so easily when you're young, but it never works out like that. I'm just grateful I realized in time.'

'And what made you realize?'

She wrinkled her nose. 'I don't really know. Maybe it was the Saturday morning golf, or the endless evenings he spent in front of his computer, or the banking systems he prattled on about.'

'And you were busy painting?'

'Painting, sculpting, creating. Oh, don't get me wrong, I'm not decrying what he did. It was just so different. I don't know, there just didn't seem to be much soul in it.'

Connla rested his elbows on the table. 'I know what you're saying. When most of my contemporaries were thinking about corporate law or Wall Street or whatever, I was up to my knees in mountain-lion shit.'

'And how did you get into that? Metaphorically, I mean.'

Connla laughed. 'I don't know. I guess I found them fascinating. They go their own way, Imogen. They're solitary and they've withstood the advances of the American dream, unlike most anything else. I found one busted up on the highway one time and I managed to get her fixed up. She's called Mellencamp. Here.' He fished in his wallet and brought out a picture of the cougar. Imogen looked at it. It was just of the head: yellow eyes, white mouth and high black-tipped ears.

'She's beautiful.'

'Something, isn't she. Thinks she's queen of the hill.'

'And she's a pet?' Imogen looked up at him.

'Oh, no.' Connla shook his head. 'She's wild, all right. She just comes to visit me once in a while. I don't lock my doors in Keystone and I've woken up to a rough tongue on my face on more than one occasion. She deems to grace me with her presence now and again, but she could just as easily kill me if she had a mind.'

Imogen laughed then. 'You know what, most people carry a picture of their wife or girlfriend or children in their wallet. You're the first man I've met who carries one of a mountain lion.'

Connla squinted at her. 'You think I ought to see someone about it?'

They laughed again and looked at one another across the table, then Connla asked her how old she had been when she'd broken off her engagement.

'Twenty-three.'

'You know, you talked about finding a soulmate just now. I don't think many people of twenty-three have even begun to consider that. They might get married, be planning kids even, but a soulmate isn't what's on their minds when they set out. I think you come round to that way of thinking later on in life.'

'What, when you've had a lifetime of *soul*-searching, you mean?'

He smiled. 'I guess. Hey, what do I know? I'm the guy with the picture of a cougar in my pocket book.'

Quietness then: no words, just the hubbub of conversation from the elderly people around them and the rattle of rain on the glass. Connla glanced at his watch.

'Guess those pictures will be ready pretty soon, huh.' He looked into her eyes and saw his face reflected in them for the second time in his life, and for one tiny moment he was back in Idaho, sitting on a log with his head between his knees, staring at red ants crawling in sand at his feet. She was next to him, the little girl with brown skin and black tangly hair, that dirty yellow blanket hanging over her shoulder.

'Are you booked into the hotel?'

He looked up. 'Not yet.' Silence again, awkward this time. 'I'll get it organized on the way back.'

They collected the pictures and they were good, but Connla knew that Cullen wouldn't verify the geographical locations, and although he had taken landscape shots they could still be anywhere. Not only that, but pictures of paw prints had been doctored many times before and people had every right to shout 'hoax'. Damn the man to hell for smashing up the casts. Imogen seemed to sense his unspoken frustration.

'There's nothing you can do?' she said.

Connla lifted his shoulders wearily. 'I don't suppose there's a law against breaking plaster in this country.'

They drove back in silence and he felt the defeat begin to

225

weigh on him. His mission in coming here was a failure now and he had complicated his entire life with this new situation. He almost regretted walking into that store in Dunkeld. But when he sensed her next to him, when he glanced sideways and caught a glimpse of her face in profile, when he took in the easy manner with which she held herself, he didn't regret it. He gazed out of the window as they came back towards the castle – at the peppermint black of the loch, the way Skye lifted in a rumble of slow hills and the snaking canyon of water that separated it from the mainland.

'Where are you?' she asked him gently. Connla smiled and looked out of the corner of his eye at her. 'Oh, I don't know. Right here, I guess.'

He slowed up as the hotel came into view across the curving line of the bridge.

'Shall I drop you off or check into the hotel first?'

'I don't mind.' She thought for a moment, then asked, 'How long till you have to go home?'

'A few days, I guess.'

The turning for Gaelloch was approaching. Imogen hesitated, then said, 'I was going to take another trip into the hills with Keira. Would you like to come with me?'

Connla looked sideways at her. 'I'd love to.'

She cooked dinner and opened a bottle of red wine. Connla stood, leaning against the sink and watched her. She had tied her hair back now – one long plait wound snake-like on top of her head. He had no idea what she was preparing. He didn't ask, was merely content to watch the way she moved about the kitchen. She wasn't in the least bit self-conscious under his gaze. She moved easily, almost gracefully, as if she was very much at peace with her body.

'What're you painting right now?'

She looked sharply at him then and he thought he had said the wrong thing.

'Redynvre.' She hesitated and tugged her lip with her teeth. 'At least I think that's what it is.'

'Sounds interesting. Can I see?'

She looked at him again, panic in her eyes for a moment. He lifted a hand, palm upwards. 'Hey, it's OK. Forget it. I understand: artists and work in progress. It's the same for me, only I use rolls of film.'

She had never let anyone see her work in progress before, and her studio was the only room in the house she locked when people were staying.

'Honest. It's OK.' Connla got up and smiled reassuringly.

'No,' she said. 'I don't mind. You can see it, if you want to.'

She led the way down the hall, not knowing why, but aware that it was all right to show him, this American she hardly knew, though the picture disturbed her more than any she had ever painted. The studio was still lit by the setting sun and she didn't switch on any artificial light. The canvas was where she had left it, resting on her largest easel with a piece of muslin cloth draped over it. Her palette, uncleaned, lay alongside, with her brushes standing in a pot of turpentine that she should have emptied ages ago.

For a moment they both stood there and Connla took in the starkness of the room – such a contrast to the rest of the house. There was nothing on the walls, just white board painted white again, no drapes, a large Velux window in the roof and two in either wall. No pictures, no furniture, not even a chair; the only concession to comfort was a portable CD player with twin speakers attached by straggling wires. A pile of CDs lay on the floor beside it. He could see Otis Redding and Van Morrison, Mozart and Puccini's *Madame Butterfly*.

Imogen stood at the easel, suddenly unsure of herself. Was this all right after all? No-one but no-one was allowed in here. Her aunt had built this studio and nobody had been allowed in then, save her as a little girl. Connla looked at her, the way she picked at her lips with her teeth, her eyes avoiding his, slanted towards the ground.

'You don't have to show me, you know. I really do understand.'

'No. I want to.' She did. What disturbed her was not the

actual showing of the unfinished work so much as the why. Carefully, she folded back the muslin cloth, and Connla saw the outline of a mountain, the beginnings of the sky and a mass of black and grey rock. Imogen watched his face. He looked even-eyed, arms folded across his chest like an Indian.

He scrutinized the picture. This was important to her and he didn't know why. Clearly this room was private, so why had he been allowed in? And then he saw the image of a child in the rock. A shiver shook his flesh and he wasn't sure why. For a moment he wondered if this was just some charade, that somehow she knew everything and had tricked him in here to expose him for the liar he was.

He did not let it show on his face, but Imogen knew he had picked up the outline in the rock. He couldn't possibly know the significance, but she wanted to make sure she wasn't imagining it herself. 'It's nowhere near finished,' she said carefully. 'The stag will be in the foreground.'

Connla glanced at the sketchbook lying open on the floor: the outline of the deer, the mountain, sky, and then the colours and tones listed. Notes to herself, things that only she would understand. He looked again at the painting, the mass of black rock and the image of the boy within it. 'Thank you for showing me,' he said quietly.

Later, after dinner, they sat in the lounge on the twin couches before the unlit fire. The sun had gone and the wine had gone and Connla looked at his watch. 'What time d'you want to leave in the morning?'

'Early. I have to load Keira into the horsebox, and it's a good hour's drive to Loch Loynes.'

'D'you mind if we take two cars? I may have to go straight to London afterwards.' She looked beyond him into the darkness of the uncurtained window. 'Two cars is fine,' she said.

Connla shifted to the edge of his seat. 'I guess I'd better get moving then.'

'Why don't you stay here?'

He stared at her.

'I mean there's no point in going to the hotel now. They probably won't take your booking anyway; it's almost eleven o'clock.'

'Right.' Connla looked at her for a moment, then prodded the sofa with his knuckles.

'I've got a sleeping bag in the truck.'

'OK.'

'Right.' He stood up, stretched, and yawned. 'I'm beat.'

'Today was a long day for you.'

'I guess.'

She stood up. 'I'm really sorry about the plaster casts.'

'Ah, don't worry about it. I still saw what I saw. You got big cats in this country and they're breeding. If that keeps happening your government will have to change its whole attitude to the environment. Gotta be a good thing in my book.' He smiled at her. 'I'll just get my gear. Thank you for a great evening, Imogen.'

'Thank you for coming back.'

He wanted to kiss her again, but he didn't. He stepped past her and went out to his truck. When he came back she was still standing where he had left her, but the moment had passed.

'Would you like a bath or anything?' she asked. 'I'm afraid I don't have a shower.'

'In the morning, if that's OK. I'm beat right now.'

'OK. I'll have one then, too.' She smiled and glanced at the sofa. 'Will you be comfortable enough?'

'Oh, yeah. I've slept on all sorts of couches, believe me. And you oughta see my shack in Keystone. My bed makes this look like a four-poster.'

She smiled. 'I'd like to – see your shack, I mean.'

'Well,' Connla reached out and hooked a strand of loose hair behind her ear, 'maybe one day you will.'

She felt the fleeting warmth of his hand and she wanted to close her eyes and lay her cheek against it. But the touch was brief and then gone. She lifted a fist to her mouth in a yawn. 'Now you've started me off.'

'One question?' he said. 'You've only got the one horse.'

She nodded. 'I thought we'd walk and pack the gear on Keira.'

'Sounds good to me.'

She moved to the door; he wanted her to stay and to kiss her again, but the space between them was awkward all at once. She paused, looking back, and smiled.

'Sleep well.'

'Yeah. You, too.'

She closed the door and he sat down on the sofa.

He lit a cigarette in the darkness, the only light now that the candle had withered into wax on the hearthstone. He listened to her moving about upstairs; in the bathroom briefly and then her bedroom, which he hadn't seen but could sort of visualize from the footfalls above his head. He imagined her shimmying out of her dungarees, exposing brown legs and panties, sitting to take off her socks and shifting the shirt over her head.

Imogen sat naked in front of the mirror and took the brush to her hair, which was tangled now with sweat. She tugged at the roots, pulling her head to one side, twisting her neck muscles so they stood out like rope against the skin. All the time she watched herself and her nipples puckered under her gaze as she imagined him downstairs. She hadn't heard a sound since she'd come up, but she knew he wasn't asleep; he was probably still sitting where she had left him. Why had she shown him the painting? She had no answer. He had seen the image of the boy in the rock, like some faded cave painting from an age long past, when men were but a memory of what they would become. He had seen it and had said nothing. Maybe he'd just hated the painting. Maybe he couldn't see anything. Maybe he didn't wish to ask because he already knew it was only a work in progress and no doubt he thought all would become clear in the end. Not that he would be around to see it. A few days, he had said, a few days and he would return to America, and something told her she would not see him again.

She laid the brush down and rested both hands flat on her dressing table, staring at the dark almost brooding eyes that stared back at her from the mirror. So why was she up here with him downstairs? Why did she not just ask him to come up? Why not go down now and see him? Her breath grew short and a little pain began at one temple. She wanted to go down. At that moment she wanted to more than anything in the world. But it was as if she didn't know how. She sat there with no clothes on, looking at her face in the glass, and then she got up and stood before the full-length mirror, half in shadow, the room lit only by the lamp on the other side of the bed. She stood side on, her hair obscuring one breast, smudged darkness at the top of her thighs. She knew she was imagining other eyes on her: his eyes, green eyes, the eyes of the cats he loved so much. Again she felt the urge to slip on a gown, step downstairs and see him. A few days and then everything would be back to normal. School would be starting and Patterson's attentions, unfettered by the distance of summer, would be fixed on her once again. Life would go on and she would go on, alone as before. She stood up, reached for her gown and then she heard the sofa creak downstairs. Her hand fisted in mid-air and she climbed into bed.

Connla lay on the sofa in his underpants, the sleeping bag unravelled but unused on the floor. He heard the creaking of floorboards above his head and thought, just for a second, that a door would open and he would hear footfalls on the stairs, the squeak of the bannister as her hand traced the length of it. But the sounds did not come and he rolled onto his side. And then he thought of the level of his deceit and guilt stuck like a hunk of unchewed bread in his throat.

TWENTY-TWO

THE POLICE CAR PULLED INTO THE SQUARE IN TOMINTOUL and parked behind an old VW pick-up truck. 'Harry Cullen,' Soames said, indicating the truck. 'What's he doing here?'

Gray was driving; he was younger than his partner, with hair clipped to nothing above his ears.

'Who's Harry Cullen?'

'He's a poacher, amongst other things. Most people call him Bird Dog because he's always had a pitbull and a falcon of some kind.' Soames opened his door. 'He's crossed my path once or twice.'

They walked into the bar and found Cullen seated, grey-faced, on a stool. Soames shook his head. 'Well, well, Bird Dog. Fancy meeting you here.'

Cullen squinted at him. 'Fancy.'

'Is the landlord about?'

'I don't know.' Cullen jabbed a thumb over his shoulder. 'Try the kitchen.'

Soames made a face at his partner. 'Malt-based hangovers are always the worst,' he said, and pushed open the kitchen door.

He came back a moment later with the landlord. 'We haven't got any male cleaners, Mr Soames.' The landlord wiped his hands on a cloth.

Cullen rested his chin on his fist and studied their conversation in the mirror behind the bar. Soames scratched his head. 'Well somebody phoned us.'

'What did he say exactly?'

'He said he had just cleaned a guest room and found a pistol under the bed.'

'A pistol?' The landlord stared at him, eyes wide all at once.

Gray nodded. 'Aye, a pistol. We have to take it seriously, Mr Buchanan. There's no such thing as a legally owned pistol any more. Possession can get you ten years.' Buchanan rubbed a hand across his reddened features. He still wore the striped butcher's apron he used when he was cooking the guests' breakfasts.

'Which room did he say?'

'Number three.'

Buchanan muttered something, then wandered behind the bar and picked up the register. He had only nine rooms, but still couldn't remember who was in which. People came and went on a daily basis in the season. 'It's empty,' he said. 'There was somebody there last night, but he left first thing this morning.'

Soames sniffed the aroma of frying bacon that had followed them from the kitchen.

'What, no breakfast? I thought your fry-ups were folklore in these parts.'

'Folklore they may be,' Buchanan said, 'but he was American. I don't suppose he'd heard.'

'We'd like to take a look at the room anyway, please.' Gray held out his hand for a key.

Cullen waited while they went upstairs. He could hear booted feet on the boards and strands of conversation. Room three was right over the bar. There were more booted feet, a muffled exclamation and then a smile stretched his sallow features. All at once his hangover receded.

The three of them came down again, with Soames carrying a revolver by a ballpoint pen stuck up the barrel. Cullen knew it was loaded with six hollow point shells.

'This is very serious,' Soames was saying. 'Do you have any idea where we can find him?'

The landlord shook his head. 'He never left an address.'

'Not even one in America?'

'No. I should've taken it, I know. But he paid me in cash and he was with Bird Dog, here.'

'Bird Dog?' Soames gazed across the bar. 'Wherever there's trouble there's Bird Dog. Why *is* that, Harry, eh?'

Cullen shifted on the stool and squinted at him. 'Mr Soames. Does your wife know what you're on about? Because I never do.'

Soames stepped closer to him. 'What were *you* doing with an American?'

'If you must know, hunting leopards.'

'What?'

'Yon big cats. A sheep was killed over at Corgarff the other day. Even you must've seen the news. A leopard did it. A black one.'

'You mean the beast of Elgin?' Gray said.

Cullen gave him a withering look. 'No, I mean the beast of wherever else. Elgin's a bus ride away.'

'There's no beast of anywhere,' Soames said. 'They're just stories put about for the tourists.'

'Are they indeed. Well, tell that to John McIntyre out at Cock Bridge. Tell it to me, Mr Soames. I saw this one with my own eyes. If you take a look in the back of my truck you'll find my dog with his throat ripped open.'

The policemen fell silent then, exchanging a brief glance. Cullen fished the keys from his pocket and tossed them to Soames. 'It was a panther. That's a black leopard to the un-educated. I saw it kill my dog. Go on, take a look.' He scowled at them. 'The American was a zoologist. His name's McAdam. If you want to know, the SSPCA put him on to me.'

'He was looking for these beasts then?'

'Aye. He needed a guide; someone who knew the country.'

'Was he armed?'

Cullen sucked breath. 'I don't know. But I certainly was.'

'With this?' Soames held up the pistol.

'With my rifle. I've got a licence, Mr Soames. You should know, you've asked to see it often enough.'

'I thought you were living down in Perthshire.'

'What's that got to do with anything?'

'Paid you, did he, this American?'

'Aye.'

'How much?'

'None of your business.'

Soames held up the pistol. 'After Dunblane, everything's our business, Bird Dog. Did the American have this with him?'

'How should I know?'

'Did you see it on him?'

'He didn't wear a holster, if that's what you mean.'

'Don't be funny, Bird Dog. You know exactly what I mean.'

Cullen shifted his shoulders. 'I told you. I never saw a gun. But he's a Yank and we were hunting leopard. Put it this way, I wouldn't go without my rifle.' Again he shrugged his shoulders and turned to face the optics. Soames inspected the gun once more. 'The serial number's been filed off.'

'Well, of course it has. Pistols are illegal. You just said so yourself.'

Soames sat on the stool next to Cullen while Gray called the find in on the radio.

'What's his first name?'

Cullen shrugged. 'I don't know. Connor, Conroy or something.'

'Connla,' the landlord put in a little sheepishly. 'There. I remember that much at least.'

'Have you any idea where we can find him?' Soames looked back at Cullen.

'Nope.'

'OK. But don't disappear. We might need to talk to you again.'

'Now where have I heard that before?' Cullen watched them go and let them get to the door before he called out, 'When he came up here just now he'd been staying at the Kyle of Lochalsh.' He touched his index finger to his forehead and looked back at the bar.

*   *   *

Connla helped Imogen catch the horse and he slipped the rope bridle over her head while Imogen collected the pack frame from the stable. He rubbed an easy palm up and down the horse's neck to quieten her, then led her to the horsebox and coaxed her inside with a carrot. Between them they hoisted the tow bar onto the ball joint on the Land-Rover and made sure the lights were working, then Imogen jumped behind the wheel and eased the rig away from the field. Connla closed and locked the gate, climbed into his own truck and followed her east along the Keppoch Road. He wished they were riding together, wished he was driving and she was sitting next to him with her hand on his thigh in that easy manner of lovers.

He had to content himself with following her, though. He had used the bathroom after her this morning and had smelled her scented soaps as he lay back against the cold enamel, watching shafts of sunlight bouncing off Loch Gael. He loved bathrooms, at least those ones touched by feminine hands. Hers was spacious, with three massive rubber plants crowding it. Against one wall a rack full of ironed clothes and warm towels lay over the radiator. There were more plants on the window ledges, and some of her pictures – small ones – adorned the walls.

Connla followed her to the valley floor and they drove south-east along Loch Duich, wide and flat with the hills rising steeply on the far side. He glanced up as they passed under the shadow of the Sisters of Kintail, which dominated the southern fringe, and then through the steep-sided Glen Shiel towards Cluanie. He remembered Loch Loyne as the flat elbow-shaped expanse of water he had passed when he'd first driven up here. An hour later Imogen pulled off the road and they parked their vehicles in the shelter of the foothills with the water lapping to the north. There was little wind today and a clear sky that boasted the warmth of the sun. Connla jumped down and helped her with the tailgate of the horsebox. Working close beside her he could feel the rustle of her clothing, her blouse billowing at the neck, and could just see the top of her breasts. Her hair hung loose, half covering her face as she bent to settle the tailgate. Connla went inside and untied the rope rein from the loop that held it. He backed Keira out carefully and she snorted, tossing her mane, then whinnied at the loch, as if she saw the ghosts of dead ancestors trapped beneath the surface. Imogen quietened her and then she fastened the pack frame on her back. Keira watched with interest, unused to this change in weight and feel.

Between them they loaded the tent and sleeping bags and Connla's climbing gear onto the frame. Imogen motioned to the great loop of rope he had with him.

'Are you planning on going climbing?'

'You never know,' he said. 'I do a bit back in the States, mostly when I'm chasing cougars.'

'Do cougars go that high?'

'Sure they do. They're a lot better climbers than we are.'

Ready now, they left the vehicles and moved off, Connla noting that he would need to put some air into a tyre on his truck when they got back. Imogen walked free of any pack. He carried only his cameras, taped and fitted with a 300 and 180 mm lens respectively. He wore his Pendleton hat and she told him he looked like Indiana Jones, which he didn't mind at all. 'Harrison Ford's good-looking, right?' he said.

'Well, I suppose some people would say so.'

The horse followed them, her lead rein fastened to the pack frame. If she paused to crop grass Imogen would just nicker at her and she'd come trotting on. Connla walked with the sun climbing higher up his back, his face to the west, freshened by a breeze that breached mountain passes from the sea. There was no path to speak of; Imogen picked her own way through the gullies and clefts in the land, threading a path away from the loch, where the ground lifted and the colours changed every few hundred feet. Connla smelled the sweet scent of new heather, and ahead he could see a line of stags high on the ridge. 'I never knew there were so many deer in Scotland.'

'There are too many. The environment can't sustain them. They should let the wolves come back.'

'You think that'll happen?'

'With the prejudice of the farmers? Hell's got more chance of freezing over.'

'I know a gal that runs a sanctuary in Minnesota,' Connla said. 'She told me the people here aren't against it.'

'I didn't say the people. I said farmers.'

'You might be surprised. The same thing happened in Montana, but the ranchers finally bought into the idea.'

'I won't hold my breath.' She looked a little scornfully at him. 'If you can prove there really are big cats, d'you think they'd let the wolf come back?'

'You got a point there.' Connla paused and looked again at the ridge. 'Where does the stag you paint live?'

Imogen made a face. 'Oh, everywhere. North of here mostly.'

'Redynvre. The stag of Redynvre.'

She nodded.

'D'you know much Celtic mythology?'

She walked on, a stem of grass between her teeth. 'Some. Enough to tell stories to the children.'

'At school? Is that what you do?'

'Every afternoon.' She smiled, hunching her shoulders into her neck. 'In the last lesson, just before they go home. They love it.'

'I bet they do. Makes a change from Nickelodeon.' They walked on for a while and then Connla said, 'Do *you* want to have children?'

She looked sideways at him, shading her eyes from the sun. 'Perhaps. I've considered it now and then. But I ought to get them a father first.'

Connla laughed out loud.

'Seriously, I have thought about children,' she told him as they rested briefly below a craggy outcrop of rock. 'But I suppose being an infant-school teacher fulfils a lot of my natural urges.'

'And you can give them back.'

'There is that, of course.' She gazed back the way they had come, between the rising hills which stretched as far as they could see now. They had climbed maybe a thousand feet and the wind had risen a little.

'Remote up here,' Connla said. 'A man could get lost if he didn't know what he was doing.'

Imogen glanced at him. 'They do, frequently. We lose people every year, winter and summer. The mountains are far more dangerous than they look. More often than not it's walkers rather than climbers. They don't take the care that they should.'

'You've got search-and-rescue teams, though, huh?'

'Of course. Volunteers mostly, but backed up by the RAF with a helicopter.'

Connla looked from south to east to north, sweeping the rugged, broken landscape with an eye that had grown up in the lee of the Rockies. 'Bet this is bleak in winter.'

She smiled, appearing to guess his thoughts. 'It's not Rocky Mountain bleak, but it's bleak.'

'You know the Rockies, Imogen?'

'A little. I know I was young but I did live in Wyoming, remember.'

Connla stared into the distance. 'Of course. Can you remember much about it?'

'Bits and pieces.' Her face was shadowed all at once, the sun dipping behind a cloud. 'My brother got killed there.'

Connla felt as though somebody had jabbed a stick at his chest. His lungs tightened and he had to open his mouth to release the trapped air. She wasn't looking at him; her gaze had shallowed to where the ground fell away in slate and shale at their feet. The horse snorted and Connla glanced round and saw a brown-coated mountain hare squatting on its hind legs, cleaning its whiskers. Imogen followed his gaze. 'Their coats turn white in the winter. I'd get one on canvas if only they stayed still long enough.'

'How did your brother die?' he said it softly, hating himself, but knowing the question had to be asked.

Imogen didn't answer right away; she moved off the square of polished rock and stood looking at the trail between her feet. 'He drowned in the Salmon River.' She looked up suddenly, almost sharply. 'D'you know it?'

Connla nodded. 'I've fished there.'

'We used to fish there, too, with some friends of my parents. Steelhead trout.'

Connla watched the hare bound away. 'On the east fork. Some of the best fishing in the country. I know people who fly in from St Louis just for the steelhead.' They were quiet for a long time; Imogen was staring across the mountainside. Then she moved off again, nickering softly like a horse. Keira lifted her head and followed her.

They climbed and the sun climbed with them. Connla watched the horse, which was more surefooted than they were even hefting all the gear. He took some photos of her and some of Imogen, too, walking with her head down, that great mass of hair flying in all directions.

Halfway up the hill she stopped and, taking an elastic tie from her pocket, she dragged the hair back from her face. Connla watched her, then, almost unconsciously, he cupped the smoothness of her cheek with a palm. Imogen closed her eyes at his touch; she turned her face to him and he kissed her. She didn't move, both hands still holding her hair. Then she let it go and he drew her to him, the softness of her breasts against his chest. She held him, one hand sliding down his back to rest at the top of his jeans. They kissed and broke apart, and she looked into his eyes; neither of them said anything, but around them the mountains sang with a silence broken only by the horse cropping at grass.

Hand in hand now they pressed on; no words, just the dirt and stone and deer tracks under their feet, the horse trailing them and the sky clear again above them. That night they camped by a burn, which bubbled between flattened patches of dark heather before spreading into a pool about the size of a large garden pond. Imogen touched Connla's arm and lifted her finger to her lips; he followed her gaze and saw a pair of otters poke their snouts from a burrow. They sniffed cautiously at the air before slipping silently beneath the surface of the water.

Moving their campsite further upstream, Connla sought fallen wood until he had enough for a fire. He lit it while she watched him, feeding just the right amount of kindling to keep it small but bright with very little smoke. They had brought food and some wine and Connla cooked a kind of stew while he watched Imogen standing a little way off, sketch pad resting against her hip and working with a stick of charcoal as the sun sank beyond the mountains.

She came and sat down, laying aside her pad, and fed a little more wood onto the fire. 'What's that hill there?' he asked, pointing to a craggy buttress that jutted between the uppermost flanks of two hills several miles to the north.

'That's Devil's Rigg,' she told him. 'We lose lots of walkers up there. It's far more treacherous than it looks, full of crevices and ravines, some of which you can only see from the air.'

'Why do I recognize it?'

'There's a painting of it hanging in my kitchen.'

'With the goat on the bluff.' He nodded. 'I knew I'd seen it somewhere.' He laughed then. 'You know, you must be very good if I recognize it from your painting.'

He poured some wine; she tasted his stew and blinked several times, but ate it anyway. Connla laughed, nibbled at his and gave the rest to the otters. Then he lay on his back and looked at the darkening sky.

'It'll only get grey.' Imogen moved next to him, kneeling, one arm across his chest and looking where he looked. Her hair fell onto his face and he could smell it; he closed his eyes just to breathe her in. He felt the lightness of her lips against his and then she pressed harder and he tasted her tongue, her teeth, the wine-sweetened scent of her breath.

She stood up as the moon rose and the wind died to a whisper, then she peeled off her top as if it were a second skin. Connla lay where he was, one arm behind his head, looking up at her until she was naked and blurred at the edges, her back to the moon like a silhouetted sepia image. Her hair hung over her breasts so he could only see their outline; the ends frayed against her thighs and the shadows of her lap until she knelt once more and he felt her softness against him.

They lay for a long time, naked on the sleeping bags in the heather, Imogen's head against his chest, tracing patterns on his skin with her fingertips, saying nothing and thinking everything. Connla felt both elated and depressed in the same moment. He felt wrong. He was a liar, yet he knew he loved this woman. The panther and his pictures, his life and career were forgotten. There was just this place and the stars and the warmth of her body on his.

'Look.' Her voice was a whisper. Connla looked where she pointed and saw the northern lights, whiskers of faintly illuminated cloud tracing patterns at the edge of the world.

Imogen rested against him, warm, fulfilled, a woman, listening to the night sounds she knew so well, watching the firmament, aware of the shape of each breath that rose from his chest beneath her. She could hear the steady beat of the life inside him and she wanted to look into the well of his eyes and see herself there and hope that she always would. She knew this man, knew all about him. She didn't know how, but she could sense that she did. Maybe it was in a former life. Who knows what mysteries surround the moment of death? She could die here; she could die like this, tonight. She could happily go to sleep lying against the warmth of this man and never ever wake up. She had thought that such emotions were beyond her, that she delved too deeply, looked too hard into whatever it was that confronted her. She had looked at her husband to be and seen what she did not wish to see, and ever since then she had been walking backwards, facing things but backing away from them.

They woke at dawn and Imogen got up, walked naked to the stream and bathed while Connla watched her. She stood with the sun behind her and he could see the tiniest blond hairs lifting against her skin where they were caught between light and water. Later that morning they walked on and camped again in the afternoon. It was a perfect summer's day, where the sweat dried on their bodies after they made love, and Imogen rode Keira naked, hair to her thighs, and Connla photographed her like Lady Godiva. In the twilight she made him sit on a rock, one leg extended, arms across his chest with the wind in his hair, and then she painted him, naked – something she hadn't done in years.

Again they slept under the stars and talked long into the night. Imogen asked questions and Connla lied, hating himself more and more and more.

In the morning they lay together for a long time, and then Imogen said she really ought to get back, as there were things she had to do. Connla agreed and said he would return to the village with her to spend at least one more night before driving down to London. His ticket was open and he could postpone the flight just a little longer. They packed up the tent and cooking gear and he decided he would tell her everything that evening. He'd sit her down and explain, tell her the truth and why he had lied in the first place. He felt a little better after that, and he was determined that this thing budding between them would somehow not be spoiled.

They had just loaded everything onto the horse when two dark specks against the sky caught Connla's eye. He tugged the brim of his hat lower and Imogen followed his gaze. 'They're golden eagles, not white tails,' she said. 'A breeding pair. They've nested in this area for years.' Connla watched as the two birds drifted on the breeze, then swung towards the height of Devil's Rigg, disappearing into the folds of black rock. He looked round at Imogen. 'I've got to get some pictures.'

'I know.' She smiled, touched his face and handed him his pack with his boots and climbing gear. 'Be careful,' she said. 'I'll see you at home tonight.'

They had walked in a rough semi-circle and were only a couple of hours from the trucks. Connla stood watching as she headed back towards the loch, Keira trailing behind her. *Home*, she had said. I'll see you at *home* tonight.

TWENTY-THREE

IMOGEN LED KEIRA BACK TO THE VEHICLES AND SETTLED her in the horsebox. She secured the tailgate, then looked westward again, wondering where he was, if he was climbing, if he had got his pictures. Slow warmth eased through her knotted muscles as she got behind the wheel and felt in her pocket for the keys. The engine started first time and she smiled and wondered how she could make him stay. She could not. He had to return to America; she knew that. Take it for what it is, she told herself: a glorious interlude, one of those precious interruptions in your life that should be treasured not mourned when they're over.

The road alongside Loch Duich was busy, crowded almost with coaches; the world and his wife seemed determined to cross the bridge to Skye this summer. Imogen was glad her aunt had built her house on Loch Gael and not Duich or Alsh. She trundled up the Keppoch Road and let Keira loose in the field, then she backed up the horsebox and hung the tack in the stable. She was anxious to get home, anxious to get inside and close the door, open her book of watercolours and look at what she had painted. He would be a good few hours yet, and she wanted that picture on the easel in her studio so she could work on it some more. It would be nice to be able to show him what he looked like as an artist's model when he got home. *Home*. She must stop using that word; home for him was a cabin in the hills of Dakota.

She closed the five-bar gate and drove back past Patterson's house without so much as a sideways glance. She saw a police car parked outside McLaran's bar, but ignored it, crossed the bridge and took the turn for Gaelloch. Morrisey was out in his boat as he always was; he seemed to spend his entire life crossing and recrossing the loch. Perhaps it was just his method of keeping away from his wife. Imogen crossed the second bridge and took care with the cattle and sheep that always seemed to block the road, though she had never quite figured out where they came from. Then she saw the police car parked in her driveway.

Two policemen got out as she pulled up and one chilling thought struck her: they always send two policemen when somebody has been killed. The older of the two men came up to her, cap set high on his scalp, face seamed and tanned like leather. He cleared his throat very matter of factly.

'Imogen Munro?'

'Yes.'

'We'd like to speak to you, please.' He indicated the keys in her hand. 'Can we come inside?'

'Is it my father?'

He frowned and glanced at his colleague. 'Inside would be better.'

Her father then. Numbed, she fitted the key in the lock and let them into the kitchen.

'Tell me what happened,' she said.

The policeman took his cap off; he was bald underneath except for one wispy length of hair flattened against his scalp. 'It's not your father, Miss Munro, or your mother. So don't worry.' He squinted at her then. 'D'you know an American named John Brady?'

Imogen frowned. 'Yes.'

'D'you know where he is?'

'Yes. I left him this morning. He's in the hills west of Loch Loyne. Why?'

The policeman indicated one of the high-backed chairs at the table and she nodded. He sat down and took a magazine from his pocket. *BBC Wildlife*. 'We don't think his name *is* John

Brady,' he said slowly, 'although that's who checked into the hotel by the castle.'

Imogen could hardly take this in – fear and relief in as many moments. Here were two policemen sitting in her kitchen, telling her the man she knew she loved was not who he said he was. It was so unreal she almost looked around for the hidden camera. The policeman flattened the magazine on the table, then turned to a page with the corner bent over. It was a picture of a tiger, and next to it was a smaller one of the American.

'It's the only picture we could get. The SSPCA told us about it.'

Imogen wasn't listening to him. She was staring at the name beside the photograph: Dr Connla McAdam.

'Is that him?'

Imogen did not reply.

'Miss Munro.'

She looked up, eyes dull all at once. 'What?'

'I asked you if that was him.'

Again she looked at the picture. 'Yes,' she said softly, 'that's him.'

The policeman cleared his throat again and glanced at his colleague. 'As you can see, his name is *not* Brady. Quite why he told you it was we don't know. Have you ever seen him before?'

'Before when?' She was numb now, all her senses closing down.

'Before he came here to buy a painting.'

Connla McAdam. No wonder she felt she knew him. Connla McAdam from Jackson City, Wyoming. 'No,' she said, not knowing why she lied.

'Can you tell us exactly where he is?'

'No, not exactly. What do you want him for?' She fought to stop her voice from cracking.

The policeman sat back. 'Well, we're interested to know why he suddenly decided to change his name, for one thing. He seems to have been in Scotland for a while and he's not done so elsewhere. We've checked with two other hotels, one in Tomintoul and one in Dunkeld.'

Imogen could feel the colour in her cheeks. Her chest was tight all at once. Connla McAdam. Connla McAdam in Scotland. She sat very still, her hands trembling in her lap. She stared beyond them both till they blurred into hazy blue images. She focused on the window pane, the smear on the glass and the pink cherry blossom beyond it. She bit her lip.

'I'm sorry.' The policeman's voice came as if from faraway. 'This is obviously a bit of a shock.' Imogen bit her lip harder, blinked, then focused on their faces again.

'What d'you want with him? Changing your name's not illegal.'

'We found a pistol in his hotel room in Tomintoul. We'd like to know if it's his.'

'A pistol?'

The policeman nodded. 'It's serious, you see. You know they're illegal.'

'Of course. After Dunblane.'

He looked at her then, gently, like a father would his naive daughter. 'Clearly he seems to have lied to you.'

'Clearly.' She stood up suddenly. 'Is there anything else I can help you with?'

He seemed to consider that for a moment, then he got up. 'Well, no, I suppose not. Not at the moment anyway. We'll go and take a look where you said. West of Loyne, was it?'

'Yes.' She broke off again and sucked breath. 'When you catch up with him, tell him not to come back here.'

He glanced down at her then, a kindly expression on his face. 'I'm really sorry.'

She held up a palm, eyes shut tight.

'We'll let ourselves out, eh.'

They left her and she sat on a chair, listening to the ticking of the clock on the wall. Connla McAdam, the boy from Jackson City, Wyoming. The boy who'd sat on the log, staring at sand when the sheriff came looking for her brother. The phone rang. She stared across the room for a few moments then picked it up.

'Yes?'

'Imogen.' Patterson's voice.

'Yes, Colin.'

'I was so worried about you. The police have been in the village. That man you're seeing; he's not who he says he is.'

'I know. Thank you, Colin.'

'Are you all right?'

'Yes. Thank you.' She put the phone down and rested her weight on it, pressing until her wrist turned white with the effort.

She moved into the lounge, hugging herself, an emptiness in her gut, as if somebody were scraping at her with a palette knife. Her gaze settled on the window sill and the little Indian figure. Then all the lies hit her: everything he had told her, each little yarn he had spun. *If you want good dreams, pray to the grandmother moon*. She trembled physically, thinking what a fool she had been. Then another thought struck her and she climbed the stairs and the small ladder to the loft. It was dry and warm, with a single lightbulb, and most of the floor space, as well as the shelves, were solid with canvas or glass-framed watercolours. Imogen had no index system, but she knew which were her paintings and which were her aunt's, and she went straight to the one she wanted. A watercolour painted two years previously, the loch and the hillside from the window of her lounge, and there on the sill was the ghost dancer. She knew what had happened in Dunkeld now; he had seen the greetings card they had made of this picture and he must have recognized the figure. He had seen it before, which told her everything she needed to know. She remembered it as if it were yesterday, lying there among the thickened branches of the pinion bush as her brother's body was lifted out of the river.

Custer County, and the sheriff bustling through the doors to his office in the Challis. No sun now. The two-street town windswept and barren, a gale coming in off the mountains. One hand on Connla's shoulder, eyes stony, a nod to his deputy to lift the flap in the counter. Ewan's body already on its way to the hospital in Salmon for an autopsy. Her mother crying. Her father silent, scuffing the toe of his boot against the linoleum. The sheriff talking in hushed tones to Connla, who sat, elbows on the table, fists into his jowls, not looking at anyone. Then he slid over to his mother with unfallen tears in his eyes and she seemed unable to hold him.

And the sheriff looking puzzled, one eyebrow raised, a pad of paper and a pen before him, looking from left to right and then, after a glance at her parents, crooking his index finger at her.

She had climbed onto the seat opposite him, smelling his sweat, aware of the damp patches under the arms of his shirt and the way the shadow on his chin had darkened throughout the day. He looked tired, with little red lines in the whites of his eyes and hair flattened on his scalp from his hat.

'How'd you find him, honey? How'd you know where to look?'

Pushing out her bottom lip and thinking hard and being very frightened, she had no answer to give him.

And she had no answer now. Downstairs again, she went to the window and picked up the little figure, the heat of tears in her eyes. What kind of cruel game was this? She held it, cold against her skin. No wonder she felt she knew him. No wonder he seemed to know her. Lies; all of it nothing more than lies. And the time they had just spent together, that special closeness only ever experienced as a teenager with the freshening of first love. He had robbed her of the feelings, cheated her, taken them at a cost. Tears flowed now; silent, angry tears. She thought of the watercolour she had painted and felt prostituted, as if she had given up the only bit of self she had. Eagles. She shook her head bitterly. That was just his way of saying goodbye without saying goodbye. He'd be halfway to London by now.

She wandered the house – her studio, the garden, down to the loch – and the peace and solitude and privacy she had cultivated over so many years was shattered. Never had she felt so cheated. And the sheriff's face again in her mind and then tension in her throat and memory. Ewan up to his neck in water.

How'd you find him, honey? Tell me how you found him? Did you know where he was all along?

No, she didn't. But she couldn't tell him how she had found

him because she didn't know herself. The way he looked at her, the way the deputies looked at her – there were no women in those days. Hicksville USA, nothing like welfare workers or woman cops or anything. She had no answer for him and he didn't believe her, just like he didn't believe Connla. And in their way her parents didn't believe her, either, had never believed her. And here she was facing it all over again.

In the studio the large canvas haunted the easel. The black of the rock, no deer, no mountain or sky, just the stone and the image of her brother etched into it. Like he had been before she'd found him – his essence, his passing, his spoor or scent or whatever. It was that which drew her along the trail to the cliff, where she was so scared the only way she could look down was to lie flat on her belly. And the worst of it was to come later: the knowledge that when she had seen him up to his neck in water, Ewan was still alive.

Connla dipped his feet into rock boots and worked them over his ankles, wincing in pain. They were too small for him; his toes were mashed up against the edges, giving him maximum pressure points on the rock. His sit-harness and gear loops were laid to one side; dulled metal hardware in the sun. He stood at the base of Devil's Rigg and looked above his head. He figured the eyrie would be close to the top, maybe this side, maybe round the first of the heavy grey buttresses. Granite. He pressed one hand against it; it ought to be solid enough. Granite wasn't crumbly or liable to break off like some limestone. The rock was cold and polished under his fingers, but the first hundred feet of slabs looked easy, no more than a steep walk using your hands for holds only in the odd place here and there.

After that it looked more difficult, but even so it was nothing he couldn't handle. There were sheer patches and the odd overhang, but he figured he could avoid the worst of it if he was careful. He was basing all this on where he had seen the eagles appear to settle. It was hard to tell, russet and brown against black and grey, high up, the birds were soon lost amid the cliff face. Still, he had no pictures of panthers and he had spent a small fortune, all of which he'd have to earn back somehow. If he could get a couple of Scottish eagles on film he could think of at least one US publication that might buy them. It was only a pity they weren't the white tails that Imogen had seen.

He thought of her now, Imogen, whom he knew he loved with a vengeance. The little girl from Wyoming who'd had a crush on him as a kid, the girl he had protected from the jibes of her brother. Why did he love her? How could he love her? Thirty years, and only a few days together, days marred by the labyrinth of lies he had woven. Yet he did love her. He was certain of that. He wanted to remain here in Scotland, to be close to her, hold her, have her hold him; the only link with a childhood lost the day her brother died.

There was movement above him and the male eagle suddenly took to the air with a slow beat of his wings. Larger than the female, and darker in colour, with three wing beats he was riding the airwaves like a gentle surfer easing away from the wall. Pushing all thoughts of the past and future out of his head, Connla fixed the camera round his neck and started up the mountain.

After a hundred feet the going got much tougher. He decided he would traverse the first bulbous pillar to the next gully, where, from the ground, the climbing looked easier. He fixed a piece of protection into a crack and hung there for a moment, dipping his hands in the chalk bag which hung from his belt. He looked down; it still wasn't sheer, but if he took a tumble it would last a hundred feet, and the mountainside was littered with boulders. He made the traverse with no problem, however, congratulated himself and rested for a moment. The male eagle was long gone, not even a speck against the horizon, but his mate was still up there somewhere.

Connla climbed higher, watching the rock wall as it splintered into sections, grassy tufts like oddments of hair on a peeling scalp. As he ascended, he realized the shape of the rock formation was like a sleigh or a wheel-less wagon of some sort. Devil's Rigg. He climbed on, and then he saw new movement high to his right, 200 feet away, a ledge with the cliff falling sheer beneath it. It was the female eagle, the wind ruffling her feathers; he could see her clearly now through the lens of his camera. Her eye was bright and fierce, watching for pine marten and wall rats. She shifted her weight from one razored foot to the other; hooked beak ready to tear anything that threatened her baby to pieces. Connla looked at his position and hers, considering his best option. He could snap away from here, but the angles weren't as good as he would have liked – there would be too much wall in the background – and he knew that with stealth he could sneak a lot closer. Heck, he had done it with a Siberian tiger.

The wind had risen, though, and it was cold against the back of his neck. His pants felt all at once too thin, and his knees scraped the rock as he manoeuvred himself round. He decided his best bet was to climb a lot higher, maybe make the summit of this face, then shift along and sling an abseil rope, approaching her from the left and above. The mountain was sectioned. From the ground he had seen the way the rock pushed out and then dropped back to form grassy gullies and recesses of varying sizes. Imogen's words suddenly stuck in his head: *Lots of ravines and crevices.*

He climbed the next section, feeling the adrenalin surge in his veins. This pitch would be more difficult than the last, and he had no back-up from any belay, just the friction boots, the chalk and the strength in his own fingers. He bit the bullet and climbed, swinging over the outcrops and working his way round an overhang with a three-fingered mantelshelf to contend with. He was sweating and his muscles ached, but he was getting higher and higher. And then he was in the next, more gentle section, a grass-topped sloping plateau, and he breathed more easily. The eagles were still above him and a good distance to the right. The slope he was on wasn't steep, but it stretched for perhaps a thousand metres. It was littered with boulders and rocky outcrops bulging up from the grass. He could see crevices and thin, steep gullies, some small, some not so small. Devil's Rigg.

Again he checked his position and knew he would have the best vantage point if he got above the eagles and traversed. He could come down the largest, most imposing buttress and shoot his pictures with mostly sky as the background. With this in mind, he started up the grassy slope, ruing his friction boots all at once on the damp dew-laden grass. This plateau was north-facing, and most of it would perpetually be in shadow. He half walked half climbed, gear clanking at his waist. He should have left it below and just brought the odd rock or friend or peg to use for the belay. But he felt better with it and he needed the abseil rope. The next section was climbing again and the rock face was very smooth and polished. He would be exposed up there and he began to wonder whether it had been such a good idea after all. He paused to think for a moment, considering other options. There was clearly another way up somewhere because he could see goats grazing in the distance. He pondered briefly, then moved up towards the face. Suddenly the ground fell away in front of him in a very deep ravine, broken by clumps of grass and trees and large patches of exposed rock. There was no way across, so he had to go round, which was long and laborious when all he wanted to do was scale that final wall and traverse to where he thought the eyrie was.

He skirted the ravine and finally made it to where the grassy area rose steeply to the sheer wall of stone. Dipping his hands in his chalk bag he rubbed his palms together, took a breath and climbed. He had got maybe ten feet when the friction point on his right foot gave way and he stumbled, lost his grip and dropped to the grass. He landed and slithered, tried to grip and then started rolling. Sudden panic in his throat: he had no axe to break his fall. And the ravine. Within seconds he was in space, falling head over heels with the cry caught in his throat.

Imogen was woken by the sound of knocking. It was late evening sometime; she must have dosed off. Her neck ached where it was cricked in an awkward position, pushed against the armrest on the settee. Her first thoughts were of Connla, and they were warm and gentle, then she remembered he was a liar and that she had been cheated and that hollow feeling engulfed her again. She sat where she was, very close to tears. Get a grip, she told herself. Thirty-seven years on your own, you can do thirty-seven more. Could she? She doubted it. Bleary-eyed, she answered the door.

It was the two policemen again. She let them in and sat down at the kitchen table. The older one did the talking. 'We found the Land-Rover Discovery rented to McAdam, where you said at Loch Loyne. One of the tyres was flat and there was no sign of him.'

That was odd. If he had been planning to take off he would have done so in the car, surely. He could change a wheel. Imogen looked at the clock on the wall, ten already and dark outside.

'We've left a man out there in case he comes back,' the policeman went on. 'When did you say you left him?'

'Early this morning.'

The younger policeman sighed. 'Well, maybe he got out some other way.'

'What, and left a Land-Rover for you to find? That's likely.' Imogen got up, took an already opened bottle of wine from the fridge and poured herself a glass. She rummaged in the dresser for the packet of cigarettes she had broken open earlier. Behind her the policemen were leaving. 'We'll keep you posted,' they said. She spoke without looking round. 'Don't bother. He's nothing to do with me.'

When they had gone she sat and drank the wine, poured a second glass and lit a cigarette. The phone rang again. She looked at it, sighed and shook her head. It rang and it rang, and in the end she had to answer it. Mercifully it was Jean.

'How are you? Have the police been round?'

'Yes. Twice.'

'His name's Connla McAdam, not John Brady at all.'

'I know.'

'I'm sorry, Imogen.'

'Not as sorry as I am. Jean, I feel such a fool.'

'I know. I know. Don't, though. You weren't to know he was telling lies.'

Imogen sighed. 'How come the police knew about me?'

'I don't know for sure. Apparently somebody from the newspapers had been on to the hotel. I think it was Andy McKewan told the police, mind.'

'Good old Andy.' Imogen felt tears threatening again. 'You know what, Jean. I think I'm going to move.'

'Och, don't.' Jean tried to laugh. 'Who would I have to talk to? You're bound to think like that right now, but you'll get over it.'

Imogen debated whether to tell Jean that she'd known Connla as a child in America. Not now, not on the phone. Another time, perhaps, she might tell her the whole story. She said, 'The police found his car by Loch Loyne.'

'Is that where the two of you went?'

'Yes.'

Jean paused. 'Did you . . . you know?'

'Yes, Jean. We did.'

'Och, Imogen. I really am sorry. Look d'you want me to come round?'

Imogen shook her head at the phone. 'No, not now. I'm going to drink a bottle of wine and smoke a packet of cigarettes and then I'm going to my bed.'

Connla was cold, darkness in his eyes. He wasn't sure if he was dead. If he was, then this darkness wasn't good. People saw light, didn't they; light and tunnels. And they felt as if they didn't want to go back to wherever it was they'd come from. This wasn't light and it wasn't warm or comforting, and he wasn't at all sure he liked it. Then all at once he felt pain, a searing, blinding pain in his legs, and he wondered for a millisecond if he was in hell. Then he felt the chill night air and his vision cleared a little and he could see the brightness of the moon above him. Not dead; he was outside somewhere, which was why he was so cold. Then he remembered the fall. He was lying on a hill in Scotland and it was night. He was freezing and he couldn't move his legs. Panic – a knot of it in his throat. He hissed breath through his teeth to quieten himself. *Crevices and ravines. Devil's Rigg. Lots of crevices and ravines.* He slipped in and out of consciousness – strange dreams, images, voices from the past.

He saw Ewan Munro's smug face after completing yet another home run in Little League. He saw his own jealousy at the attention Ewan got from the coach, the other players, everyone.

He must have woken up again, for the images cleared, and from somewhere far off he heard the shriek of an eagle. The light grew and the clouds that had gathered cleared, and the moon was pale now as a new morning threatened. For the first time he was conscious enough to take in his surroundings. He was lying in the ravine. He remembered slipping on the rock – a stupid mistake to make, not concentrating properly. Too eager to get up and get on and get something other than the lies he had created from this trip. He half lifted his head, painful but possible. Sharp pains shot through his chest and shoulders, but at least he could move his arms. He looked down at himself, his trunk, his legs. His trousers were torn and his legs bloodied; the left one was twisted out of shape and the right one wasn't much better. Then he realized he was lying on a grass-topped bluff, no more than ten feet square, with a sheer drop all round him. It was like a stalk of rock lifting from the earth below.

So what could he do? Lie there and hope? Wait for someone to come looking for him? Imogen. Imogen would come. She had been expecting him last night. She would have been worried when he didn't show up. He could see her in his mind's eye as clear as if she were looking down on him now. He closed his eyes and drew her in, holding her there in his mind, almost lifting his hands to her face which wasn't there. He dreamed, and she was a little girl and he was sitting with the Custer county sheriff and she was watching him out of onyx eyes as big and oval as saucers. She could see into his heart, and somehow she knew, or thought she knew, just as she had with Ewan.

He woke again to a new sound, grunting and heavy breath, and he closed his eyes and smiled. Mellencamp's elegant features, ears pointed, muzzle soft yet strong, yellow eyes darting. 'Hey, girl,' he whispered, 'you cubbed yet? You're late, honey. Summer's nearly over.'

He opened his eyes and stared up at the black face of a panther looking down from the hillside above. For a second he started and thought he was dreaming, then he felt the freshness of the wind on his skin and the chilled rock under his back. She was real and she was no more than thirty feet above him. He could pick out her whiskers, the rosettes beneath the darkness of her fur. Even then he could tell she was female by the size and shape of her head. She yawned and he could almost catch her breath; large canine teeth and a long pink tongue. She rose to a sitting position, licked her lips hungrily, then looked for a way to get down.

'You gonna eat me?' Connla struggled, shoving one elbow into the rock under his back and forcing himself up; his head swam and the pain in his legs reached a blood-boiling throb. The panther stood up, looked at him again and hissed; her ears were right back now, her muzzle wrinkled above her teeth. Connla felt at his neck for his camera and his hand came up with one loose and empty strap. 'Goddammit,' he muttered. He lay back, breathing harshly, exhausted and cold again from the effort. He closed his eyes, fought for breath and looked up once more. The panther was no longer there.

TWENTY-FOUR

IMOGEN MOOCHED ABOUT THE HOUSE, UNABLE TO SHIFT the feelings of betrayal and humiliation and the horrible sudden emptiness this new loss had brought with it. Her entire life had been turned upside down and now there was nothing but confusion in her head. It was the betrayal she couldn't come to terms with; the lies and deceit. Why do what he did? Why go to all that trouble unless he deliberately wanted to hurt her. None of it made any sense.

She heard a vehicle hissing gravel in the driveway and she dashed to the window, hoping. No, it was only a blue Peugeot. Her heart sank and she watched as a man climbed out, glanced at the house, briefly at the loch, then distastefully at the chickens that clucked around his feet. He wore a dark suit and his tie was undone at the neck. He looked hot and slightly flustered and he picked his way a little gingerly to the kitchen door. She waited while he knocked. A detective this time, no doubt, come to tell her they had found Connla McAdam and were detaining him on a firearms charge. Smoothing back her hair, she opened the door.

'Miss Munro?'

'Yes.' She almost invited him in, but something about the expression on his face dissuaded her.

'My name's Graham. I'm with the *Scottish Daily Post*.'

She folded her arms across her chest. 'What do you want?'

'I wanted to talk to you about this American the police are looking for. Connla McAdam. I understand you had a relationship with him.'

'Go away.' She went to close the door, but he grabbed the edge and held it.

'I just want to ask you a few questions. Did you know he had an illegal pistol?'

'Move your hand or I'll close the door on it.' It was then she saw the second man; he had been hidden from view by the sun reflecting off the car's windscreen. Now he was out and the flash of a camera blinded her. She slammed the door and leaned on it.

Graham knocked again. 'Possession of a firearm is a serious offence, Miss Munro. Have you got any comment to make about it?'

'Go away. Go away now or I'll call the police.'

'Why not give us your side of the story? The last thing you want is speculation. We'll pay. All I have to do is pick up the phone to my editor.'

'Why don't you go and drown yourself in the loch.' She yelled it at him through the closed door, then stumbled into the lounge. She slumped on the settee and burst into tears.

She sat and cried for a long time. She couldn't say exactly how long; she just let the tears fall and the sobs go, hoping the pain would recede with their passing. But it did not. It remained where it was, only worse in some ways. The betrayal was all at once matched with the loss of what she thought might have been. She got up, walked through to the studio, picked up her paints and stared blankly at the canvas. Minutes later she laid the brushes down again and took her coat from the back of the door.

She started the Land-Rover and drove across the bridge. The two reporters were waiting in one of the passing places and photographed her as she went by. Damn Connla McAdam and his lies. They followed her as far as Lochalsh, and then she stopped and told them to leave her alone or she would call the police. They photographed her again, but pulled into the hotel car park as she headed up the hill to her horse. Thankfully, nobody bothered her there and she set about clearing the stable.

She shovelled the muck into piles, then forked it into the barrow and wheeled it angrily, bumping down the track to the manure heap by the gate. Then she set about lifting all the straw and sawdust, while Keira watched from her favourite spot high up on the hill.

Imogen wheeled the last load of bedding to the manure heap and then paused for breath. The fresh bedding was stored in half-hundred-weight heat-sealed plastic bags in the horsebox. She manhandled the first one out, balancing it on the barrow, and then wiped her eyes with the back of her leather glove. Then she saw Connla in her mind's eye, pressed against a cliff, looking down. The image passed and she stared out towards Skye. She was cold; the kind of coldness she hadn't felt in almost thirty years.

She drove home, disturbed. There was no longer just the emptiness in her breast, but a finger of fear, chilled and damp and immovable. She closed the doors and switched on the television for the lunchtime news. She waded through the international bulletin, thinking she would have to wait for the local programme, and was shocked to find that Connla's disappearance was national news. She watched, hunched on the edge of her seat, her hands clasped in front of her. The bulletin was dominated by the fact that the police wanted to speak to him urgently. They showed shots of the rented Land-Rover, which had been towed in, and then aerial pictures of the area where they had lain together under the sky, bringing back the tenderness of the moment to her again. The mountain rescue teams had been out and searched the area thoroughly, backed up by the RAF helicopter from Oban. But they had found nothing; no sign of him. The speculation was that he had somehow learned of the police's desire to speak with him and had disappeared. Imogen sat and shook her head. No, he hasn't, she thought. He hasn't done that at all. But what could she do. They were still searching; they would find him. He had probably taken a fall. They would find him, then he could answer all their questions and go home to his precious mountain lions.

But she had questions of her own: why had he lied to her like that? Why not just tell her who he was? Unless, of course, he thought he had something to hide. Did he? For thirty long years she had wondered.

She felt used, abused by him. Her childhood had been betrayed, all that she had been. Everything that had been buried had been exhumed, dragged rudely into the present to be picked over and devoured. Her life was all over the newspapers. She imagined the gossip in McLaran's bar and the hotel. She imagined the parents of the children she taught – the subject matter for discussion after the children went to bed. How would they explain to their offspring why their teacher was in the newspapers? She thought of the first day of term and shuddered. McKewan would be having a field day, Patterson would be thinking how he could use all this to his advantage, and MacGregor; MacGregor would just be disappointed.

Connla heard the helicopter pass overhead; there was no change in its engine note. He knew it hadn't seen him, and for the first time he wondered if he might die up there. His body would never be recovered. Eventually, it would roll off its perch to be chewed at by foxes and whatever else was passing, consumed in time by the worms. He tried to laugh it off, going over his own epitaph: 'Here lies Connla McAdam, slightly famous photographer found in a Scottish ravine, his bones gnawed by the panther he was chasing.' But still there was Imogen, precious, precious Imogen. She had known roughly where he was going. Why didn't she come?

The second night was bitterly cold and he could feel himself slipping into a fever. Infection in his leg, perhaps. Best-case scenario: get found but lose the leg. Oh, God. His throat was dry, nothing to drink. How long could a man last without water? He was a zoologist; he ought to know stuff like that. But right then he didn't. Right then, he didn't know anything except that he couldn't move and his bones felt as though they had been fused to the rock. Sometime in the night he thought he heard the panther again, but it might have been Mellencamp in a dream.

Tendrils of grey hinted at dawn, or was that just more blurred sight, more hallucinations, if that was what he was experiencing. He wondered how many people had died on Devil's Rigg. Perhaps they had called it that because so many people got killed. *Ravines and crevices; crevices and ravines.* He tried to remember why he was up there in the first place, but couldn't. Then it came to him: eagles. He remembered what an Indian from Pine Ridge had once told him: *Where eagles fly only prayer can follow.* He should have thought of that before he started climbing.

It was fully light now and raining; he could feel it spattering the cotton of his field jacket. It wasn't waterproof, or at least he didn't think so. Lying flat out like this he would find out soon enough. He tried to decide if he was still cold, or whether the coldness had just numbed to nothing as he became part of the rock. How long had he been here? Why didn't the helicopter come back? Why didn't somebody come? And then he realized that he was wearing clothing suitable for wildlife photography, grey and green and nondescript. He even had muck on his face and the backs of his hands.

Nobody would ever see him. Survival bag. Where was his orange survival bag? In his pack. Where was his pack? He strained himself up again, almost to a sitting position this time. Incredibly, the pain in his chest seemed to have eased; either that or he had just got used to it. He couldn't see his pack. He felt for it. By rights he ought to be lying on it, but he wasn't. The straps must've broken. It wasn't on the slab of rock with him and he couldn't bring himself to look over the edge. The effort wearied him and he lay back again, closed his eyes and felt rain on the broken skin of his face. For a moment he thought this might be a good time to die.

Imogen phoned Jean. 'Hello, it's me,' she said. 'Do you know if the police have called off their search?'

'I think so, yes. They think your man got wise to them and ran off.'

'They're wrong. Why would he leave his Land-Rover? So it

had a flat tyre, so what? He could have changed the wheel. I think he's still out there, Jean.'

'The police didn't find him. They've had helicopters up and everything. Surely if he was they would've found him by now. Anyway, you shouldn't worry. Have you seen the newspapers this morning?'

Imogen shuddered. 'No. And I don't want to. Don't even tell me about it.'

'OK.' Jean hesitated. 'Look, I've got to go. I've got all the menfolk wanting their breakfast. I'll try to come over later.'

'Tonight?'

'If I can, yes. I know you're going to worry, but try not to. He'll be fine; not that he deserves to be. Just lie low till all this blows over.'

'D'you think it will?'

'Of course. Everything blows over given enough time.'

Imogen put down the phone. Jean's inference was that it wasn't her problem, but it was. Whether she liked it or not this *was* her problem and she had to do something about it. She thought again of what she had seen or felt up at the horse's field. It had been thirty years but the sensation was only too familiar. The last time she had felt it she'd found her brother dead. Again she was on that path in the Sawtooth with the darkness of the trees pressing in on her. Again she was on that cliff, crawling on her belly, with her eyes shut fast till she felt the chilled river air on her face.

Andy McKewan was at the bar when she went into McLaran's that evening. His crew were with him, and some of the other fishermen from Kyle, and they all stopped talking as she entered. Ironic this, she thought. McKewan was the one who had given her name and address to the police, perhaps to the newspapers, and it was McKewan she needed now. She was glad to see him look suddenly sheepish. He had said things he knew he shouldn't have and his neck flushed red, as if they'd now come back to haunt him.

'Andy.' He had turned his back to her and she saw his massive shoulders stiffen. He set down his pint, sighed and looked round. 'Hello, Imogen.'

'They've officially called off the search. I heard it on the news just now.' It was dark outside; if Connla was lost this was his third night of exposure.

'So?' McKewan jutted his chin at her.

'So I think he's still out there.'

He squinted at her, lip twisted slightly. 'So what? What d'you care after the way he treated you?'

'That's just it, Andy. I do care.'

'Then you're a fool, lassie. Nothing but a fool. There's good men right here in this village.'

'It's not like that.' She looked beyond him, lifting her palms and dropping them again. 'It's more complicated than that. Much more.' How could she begin to tell him, tell any of them; they were already so prejudiced. 'The police think he's taken off, but I know he hasn't.'

'How?'

'I don't know *how*. I just know. I'm going to look in the morning, Andy. And I want the local rescue team to come with me.'

McKewan gawped at her for a moment and then his face drew up. He toyed with the unlit cigarette he had just rolled and glanced at his crew. The local rescue team meant him. For all his other faults he was a good mountain man and had brought many a wounded walker in from the hills. He looked at her again, one eyebrow raised, and then he sighed heavily. 'Have you any idea where he is?'

She nodded. 'I think he's on Devil's Rigg.'

TWENTY-FIVE

IMOGEN DROVE WITH MCKEWAN IN HIS 4 X 4 TOYOTA PICK-up with the winch attached at the front. He used it to haul his brother's lobster boat up the beach. He smoked as they drove, the window rolled down, his elbow on the sill, protected from the rain by the windguard. The short-wave radio resting in his lap crackled now and again with static.

'Why's he so important?'

Imogen did not look at him or reply right away. 'Andy,' she said at length, 'he's a man lost in the hills.'

'Maybe. But they've searched and searched and found no sign. If the RAF can't locate him, what chance have we got?' He shook his head. 'You don't know that he's even out there.'

Imogen looked through the rain fragmenting the windscreen. 'I do know, Andy. And I think he's alive.' But even as she said it, the breath died in her chest and the image of him pressed against the cliff fogged in her head.

They were almost at Loch Loyne and the freshness of her time with him was with her again. The gun made no sense. The lies made no sense. She remembered him as a boy, and of course now she could see the resemblance. 'I knew him before, Andy,' she said. 'That's why he's important to me.'

'McAdam?'

'Yes. It was thirty years ago. I didn't recognize him when he turned up here. When I was a kid I lived in America for a while.'

This was hard, but she felt she owed McKewan something. 'We lived in the same town. He was my brother's friend.'

'I never knew you had a brother.'

'I don't. He died years ago.'

The radio crackled again, and a voice came over the receiver; it was Smitty, one of McKewan's crew who was ahead of them. McKewan responded, then looked across at Imogen. 'Smitty's at Peel Point,' he said.

'Tell him to wait there. That's where we parked the Land-Rovers.'

'We can't drive much further anyway.'

She nodded. 'Is there no way you can get the helicopter up?'

He shook his head. 'As far as the authorities are concerned this is a wild-goose chase. McAdam's long gone, Imogen. You ought to let it be.'

'No.' She said it quickly, sharply. 'Listen. Thank you for coming, for doing this. I really appreciate it.'

Six of them walked in, leaving Smitty behind as control. The radio signal was good for the distance they were going to cover, and if they did find anything, he could summon any outside help they required. McKewan led the way, striding out on long legs, with heavy walking boots and rubber-valanced gaiters. Imogen walked alongside him, her pack on her back, watching the line of the horizon and cutting a path towards it. She didn't need a compass or a map; she knew this part of the country as well as anyone.

After an hour of walking they were strung out in a long line, keeping together only by radio contact. Imogen walked with McKewan just behind her. They kept to the gorge, running a thin line in the lee of the Maol Chinn-dearg, Gleouraich rising over 3,000 feet to the south. Imogen retraced the steps she had taken with Connla. She saw his face in her mind, his eyes, skin and hair. She saw the shape of his mouth, his lips, and then she thought of the lies that had spilled so freely from them. But was it all lies? His identity, yes; the past, yes; but all of it? Their intimate moments – making gentle love, then lying naked in the night out here with the northern lights above them; the way he'd watched her when she was bathing, the passion deep in his eyes. She pushed the thoughts away again. Too many questions and no answers to any of them.

He *was* out there somewhere; the further they walked the more she could feel it. She was aware of his passing, *their* passing, rock and stone, tree and shrub. He hadn't come back alone, at least not this way; she would have been able to sense it. She amazed herself then, wondering at her inexplicable arrogance. But it was not arrogance, if he had come back alone she knew she would have felt it.

Another day dawned. Was it four or five, three maybe, Connla could not remember. It rained again, though, hard this time, and he was flat on his back, mouth open, able to draw some moisture onto his swelling tongue. His hair was soaked, plastered against the rock, and his clothing stuck to him. It was colder now, very much colder. If this had been anything other than the height of summer he would be dead already. He still might die. No-one had come. The chopper had made umpteen passes and hadn't spotted him. He had waved his arm and done the best he could to attract their attention, but they had not seen him. The gully he was in was partly obscured by the rest of the mountain and any helicopter pilot would have to come in really low to spot him, and then he would have a problem with down draught and his rotors being so near the side of the rock. The panther, if he had actually seen it, had not come back again.

He watched crows circling and thought they were vultures waiting for him to die. No, he told himself, there weren't any vultures in Scotland; they were just big black crows waiting for him to die. He drifted again, semi-sleep, semi-conscious, and he knew, even in his remoteness from it all, that this was hypothermia. Blood loss, probably concussion, lying on cold stone and getting soaked. Hypothermia would kill him before the lack of water.

*   *   *

267

Imogen stopped and McKewan almost bumped into her. They had reached the final camp, where she and Connla had packed up the tent, kissed for the last time and separated. All kinds of thoughts ran through her head and seemed to clog and congeal, like so much dirt in a drain. She needed clarity, hope, desire; all those things she could remember from thirty years ago, as if it were only yesterday. McKewan looked at her, then beyond her to the grim height of Devil's Rigg, partly shrouded in cloud.

'It's raining hard up there,' he said. 'If we have to climb it's not going to be easy.' Imogen was not listening to him. She stood where she was and gazed across the valley, hazy and grey now, where the sheets of rain were falling. She couldn't feel anything and she wondered if she hadn't just imagined it after all. Maybe finding Ewan had just been luck, coincidence. Maybe this was nothing to do with any of that. Maybe Connla was just the liar that everyone thought he was.

'Imogen?'

She looked at McKewan, his face earnest and bent towards hers. 'Devil's Rigg. Where would he have gone?'

'We saw a pair of eagles,' she said and pointed into the cloud. 'I only glimpsed them for a second, so I don't know where they came from. But I assumed they'd be nesting somewhere on the Rigg. He watched them for longer than I did. Maybe he saw where they went.'

'From here?' McKewan shook his head. 'I doubt it.' He looked back at the mountain. 'The Rigg goes on for ever. You could climb all day. There's a million and one gullies, and he could be lying in any one of them, if he's there at all.' He was talking more to himself than to her. The radio crackled then and he spoke to Smitty, who was checking in from the control point. Nobody had seen anything.

McKewan shifted his pack between his shoulder blades and spoke to the team over their radios. 'Rescue Unit from Rescue One. We're heading directly for the north face of the Rigg. Spread out and concentrate the search on that area. Nobody climbs without telling me and no risks are to be taken. Maintain radio contact.' As if to emphasize the point, he rolled his thumb over the volume wheel and the radio crackled with static.

They moved off once more, the seven of them spread out across the approaches to the mountain. Imogen walked with McKewan alongside her, aware of the rasp of his breathing, as if his nose was permanently blocked. She kept her eyes ahead, trying to pierce the weight of the cloud and spot something familiar. The ground was boggy now and sucking at the soles of their boots. Imogen's trouser legs were damp and mud-spattered and she wished she had worn gaiters. McKewan's pace was brisk and they made it to the lowest level of the hills quite quickly, where black shiny rocks pushed out from the bracken like bald patches on a dozen heads. McKewan glanced sideways at her every now and again, as if he was looking for a prompt of some kind. Imogen could not give him one. She could feel nothing; her mind was blank and she was beginning to believe that this was a fool's errand after all. Thirty years was thirty years and nothing was quite how you remembered it.

They walked for three hours, following a path through the foothills, looking for the easier routes up. Imogen was reluctant to just start climbing because they could be hundreds of yards out, and every lost second might be precious. At last McKewan stopped and looked at her. 'Are you following some kind of a trail, Imogen?'

She looked at him and sighed. 'I don't know, Andy. I might be.'

He scratched his head. 'You're a weird one and no mistake.' He pointed to the rocks. 'Why don't we just climb, eh? If he was looking for eagles, you can guarantee he went up.'

Imogen paused, the mountains gathering height around them, the grass soaked and greasy underfoot. Clouds curled round the upper reaches of the Rigg itself, like bandages over a wound. Since they had left the final camp area she had been wandering aimlessly, aware of nothing, sensing nothing, doubt saturating every bone in her body. Now she was staring at the slabs of granite to their right and the feelings of despair were

269

rising in her. The slabs were not vertical and you could probably just about walk up them, using your hands to balance. It
was logical to make your way up them if you were endeavouring to get a lot higher. Weighed down by McKewan's scrutiny,
she moved up the path to the bottom of the grey-black cliff, her
calf muscles suddenly straining. The rock rose above her,
broken and fissured, like seams in a coalface. McKewan, head
wagging, followed behind her. She leaned on the wall for a
moment to steady herself as the hill suddenly steepened. Then
she sensed something and the hairs lifted on the back of her
neck. She glanced over her shoulder at McKewan. 'I think it's
this way,' she said.

McKewan followed her, staring at her back as she picked her
way up the great slabs of stone like a semi-reluctant spider. The
slabs were interspersed with sections of shale and bracken, loose
soil and grass. Imogen slowed, her grip much less firm. She went
on, though, knees straining, gaining height all the time. She did
not look down, did not look back at McKewan, but kept her
eyes ahead and her body close to the rising wall before her.
He had come this way; she didn't know how she knew it, but she
did. Suddenly she was back in the forest on the edge of the
Sawtooth in Idaho, the old fears bubbling like uncorked wine in
her throat.

After that first hundred feet or so things got tougher. Imogen
paused as the wall lifted almost sheer in front of their faces. This
was the first real climbing; black rock, slimy and treacherous
with rain. McKewan came alongside her. Imogen stood for a
second, aware of nothing, doubting herself again, and then she
pointed to their right, where the rock formed a natural bulbous
pillar on the mountain. 'Can we go that way?'

McKewan was alongside her now and set down his pack. 'It's
a traverse. I've done it before. Should've left a bloody rope up.'

Imogen looked at him, as if for reassurance. 'Does it make
sense if you're climbing?'

'The traverse. Aye.' He indicated the sheer wall above their
heads. 'Once you get round the pillar the going's a lot easier.'

Dropping his pack to his feet, he bent and began to uncoil the rope from the top. 'Can you climb?'

'I don't know. I've scrambled up Tana Coire, but that's about it.' She lifted her shoulders. 'I guess we're about to find out, Andy.'

'Hang on a minute.' He checked in with the others, told them what they were planning and called them all together. 'We're going ahead with the traverse now,' he said. 'It's not too severe, but it could be tricky in this weather. Take care on the approach.' He signed off and strung out the rope.

Imogen let him lead, paying out the line as he worked his way round the pillar, heavy boots biting at the rock for grip. He moved out of sight and then, a few minutes later, she felt the rope jerk twice in her hands and his voice came over the radio. She picked up her handset from where it lay at her feet.

'OK, Imogen. It's only about fifteen feet once you pass the exposed bit. Leave your belay in place and fix another karabiner onto the rope. Leave the bits of gear I've put in the rock in case we have to come back this way.'

Imogen did as he told her and soon she was on the wall, flattening herself against it, unsure of her grip on the slippery surface. But as she sought handholds and scrabbled with her feet, pressing her body and face in close to the rock, she knew he had been there before her. Sense or smell or impression, she had no name for it, but the knowledge was firm and fast in her head. It both thrilled and terrified her in the same moment.

McKewan cracked a broad smile as she came into view. He was keeping the rope tight, so she could feel the comfort of it tugging her middle. She knew, if she slipped, he would hold her. 'Well done girl,' he said. 'You're a natural.'

She unclipped from the rope and looked up. McKewan had been right: they still had to climb, but the going was easier. Again he led, Imogen allowing him to lead now and pick out the safest route up. An hour later they were standing in a sloping boulder-strewn amphitheatre, perhaps 1,500 feet across, rising steeply to another sheer wall of granite overhead.

'My God,' she said.

McKewan looked where she looked. 'That's serious climbing, Imogen. Especially when it's this wet and greasy. I'm not sure I want to take you up there.'

Imogen gazed the length and breadth of the plateau. 'Let's worry about that when we get to it,' she said.

McKewan checked everyone's position on the radio while she stood a moment in silence. He frowned at her, not understanding, scepticism again curling his lip. He took his tobacco tin from his jacket pocket. Imogen sat on a rock, knees together, hands between them, looking up and down the mountain. Once again she had to wonder why she had brought them here. Nothing. Just the stillness of the air, the cloud overhead and the land stretching away from them. She sat for a few minutes, then a few minutes more and began to question herself all over again. Doubt.

McKewan's semi-scornful eyes were on her; he was doing his best to hide it, but every so often his mask slipped and she glimpsed it. Why shouldn't he be scornful? For God's sake, she was scornful. This was ridiculous. The whole mountain seemed to mock her and she questioned why she'd gone there in the first place. What was he to her after all this time except a cheat and a liar? And then she realized, perhaps for the first time, that she wasn't there for him at all; she was doing this for herself.

'Well?' McKewan broke in on her thoughts. 'Are we going for it or what? I can't see anything that looks like an eyrie from here.'

Imogen sat there looking at him, then lifted her hands in a gesture of helplessness.

'Maybe you're right, Andy. If the helicopter couldn't find him, what hope have we got?'

'Now you tell me.' McKewan frowned and sucked on his cigarette, picking strands of tobacco from his teeth. He called in on the radio once more. Two of the others were just beginning the traverse. He spoke again to Imogen. 'We'll let the others catch up, then we'll string a line on this plateau. We'll search it

272

section by section, and if we don't find him we'll have to think again.'

Imogen nodded and frowned, then she got up and looked at the ground: grass, heather, the broken soil where her boots sank into the earth. She looked at the scattered rocks, thick slices of stone, boulders split where they'd fallen away from the cliff face. Slowly she moved off, leaving McKewan where he was, smoking his roll-up and talking into the radio. She walked up the slope, totally at a loss now. The land seemed to yawn and stretch and mock her. Ahead was a massive ravine. She stopped, moved back again, then set off in a different direction, desperately trying to keep the sense of aimlessness from her footfall. She moved fifty yards ahead – McKewan was watching her – then she stopped again and sat down. Cold hard stone underneath her, stone all around her. She recalled her book on gemstones – the fields of electrical energy – trying to remember if it was scientific fact or just somebody's fantasy. The search party had gone off in the wrong direction back in Idaho all those years ago. She had known it. How had she known it? Had Connla known it, too? Had he sent them the wrong way? Something about his demeanour that day had told her he knew more than he'd ever said. She remembered staring at him in that clearing, staring at him across the desk in the sheriff's office, staring at him in the handful of schooldays left before her parents brought her back to Scotland.

And then she felt him and all her senses seemed to come alive, her nostrils suddenly flaring, as if she could smell the scent left by his passing. She stood up, head high, eyes bunched at the corners. She turned and stared at a fallen section of rock and moved closer to it and the same strange certainty came over her yet again. She looked back at McKewan and nodded. Rapidly, now, he joined her.

Imogen led him across the brown stain of the bracken, around the ravine towards the barrier of sheer rock. She moved more quickly now, a sudden urgency in her breast. At the wall she paused. Nothing. Then something vague and faint, like the thinnest of etchings, and then nothing again. It didn't make sense. She stared at the cliff face, then moved further to her right, then back again, and all the time McKewan stood and scratched his head, looking at her as if he were considering having her certified.

Imogen stopped and looked back. She looked at the wall once more, and whatever she had sensed was fading. And as it faded so the panic grew and the doubts returned and she wondered if she wasn't just slightly mad.

'If he went up there, we have to climb,' McKewan said. 'You belay, I'll lead. It'll be bloody slippery, so make sure you tie on fast to a rock. I need you to hold me if I come off.'

Imogen nodded, stepped back and selected two karabiners from her harness. All sense had gone now and she stumbled like a blind man in a forest. She didn't understand this sudden nothingness; only moments earlier she had been sure. She moved closer to the gully, looking for a decent rock to mount her belay.

And then she saw him, lying on a slab of stone, almost hidden from view by an overhang. His eyes were closed, his face white and he lay absolutely still. *And Ewan lay under the river, body thrashed by the waves that beat the cottonwood bough that held him.* She stared, no words, breath just lodged in her throat. Connla had fallen. He was dead. She knew that he was dead and a chill swept over her then, like nausea.

McKewan was still working at his rope behind her. Something moved in the bracken and Imogen heard a sound that dragged her gaze from Connla – half hiss, half growl. She stared at the far side of the gully. A black shape reared up from the grass not fifty feet from where she stood – a broad, flat head, ears laid back, mouth open and long, yellowed teeth. McKewan saw it, too, and took root where he stood.

Imogen stared at the panther, then down at the slab of stone. Connla's eyes were open and he was looking at her. The panther snarled again, then bounded away, racing across the amphitheatre and melting into the rock, black on black, as if she had been part of it all the time. Imogen looked at Connla and his eyes were still open. He was blinking. He half raised his head, dropped it again and closed his eyes once more.

McKewan had seen him, too, and was already on the radio.

'Smitty, this is Andy. Get on to the RAF. We've found him, but we're going to need a chopper.'

TWENTY-SIX

CONNLA WAS AIRLIFTED TO THE EMERGENCY MEDICAL centre in Fort William. Imogen sat on the hillside watching as the RAF helicopter flew in and winched a stretcher down from some height to avoid the down draught blowing him off the rock. She could see he was only semi-conscious, muttering and groaning and lying still as the grave. McKewan organized everything and she admired him for it. For all his bar-room boorishness he knew what he was doing in a fishing boat, and he knew what he was doing on a mountain. She watched as Connla was hoisted to the hovering helicopter, feeling very small, very alone and very bitter. In an instant he was whisked away. McKewan rolled a cigarette and passed it to her, snapped his zippo in the sudden stillness and lit it for her. She looked up at him and smiled.

'Shall we go down now?' he said.

Connla lay unconscious for two days, dehydrated, half starved and suffering from hypothermia. Eventually he came round, though, and again he thought he had died. He didn't mind so much, this time, because it was warmer and brighter, and then he realized he was in hospital. When he closed his eyes again he saw Imogen's face, and then he remembered: the mountain; the panther suddenly snarling, shaking him from unconsciousness, and Imogen at the top of the ravine.

The doctor came by his room and told him that his left leg had been broken in two places, his right knee was sprained and badly bruised, and he had been lucky to get away without ligament damage. They had pinned the left leg and it was encased in light plaster. He looked down at Connla through squared half-moon glasses.

'You were lucky that team of volunteers arrived when they did or we wouldn't be having this conversation.'

Connla stared at him. 'Volunteers?'

'Aye. From Gaelloch.'

Connla thought for a moment. 'Imogen must have organized it. Is she here?'

'Who?'

'Imogen Munro. She was on the mountain.'

The doctor shook his head. 'No. Nobody's been here. Except the police, that is.'

'Police?'

'Aye. They're outside now. They're waiting to speak to you.'

'Why? What about?'

The doctor moved to the door of the single room. 'I'll let them tell you that.'

Two uniformed policemen came in, their faces stern and grave. 'How're you feeling?' the older one asked him.

Connla tried to sit up, pulling on the cord above his head. 'I've been better.'

'I'm PC Soames, Dr McAdam. This is PC Gray. We want to know why you had a handgun in your hotel room in Tomintoul.'

Connla stared at him. 'Excuse me?'

'A Magnum pistol. Three five seven. Nasty weapon. While you were messing about on yon mountain we've been wanting to speak to you about it.' Soames took a chair and sat down close to the bed. 'You see, pistols have been illegal in the United Kingdom ever since sixteen children were murdered by a lunatic in a place called Dunblane. I don't suppose the name means anything to you.'

Connla stared at him. 'Of course it does. Everyone's heard of Dunblane.'

'We banned handguns after the massacre, Dr McAdam. Having one in your possession is a very serious offence.'

'I can imagine. But I don't know anything about any gun. I don't know what you're talking about.'

The policemen looked at one another and then Soames scratched his head.

'Seriously,' Connla went on. 'I don't. What's been going on?'

Soames told him what had happened, how they had had a call from the hotel in Tomintoul and, when they'd investigated, they'd found the pistol in the room he had just vacated. Connla smiled thinly at him. 'Cullen,' he said.

'Who?'

'Harry Bird Dog Cullen. You must've heard of him. Everybody else has.'

The policemen looked briefly at one another.

'You have heard of him then,' Connla went on. 'Let me ask you a question. Were my fingerprints on that gun?'

'We don't know. We haven't taken them yet.'

'Take them.' Connla held out a hand. 'Let me ask you another question. If I was packing a three fifty seven around Scotland with me, would I just go off and leave it in my hotel room?'

They looked at each other again.

'Cullen was my guide,' Connla explained. 'I'm a zoologist. I was up there trying to track down a panther. I found it: a female with at least one cub. Cullen had a pitbull which went after the cub, and the mother killed it. Natural thing to do. But Cullen tried to shoot the mother, so I stopped him. Guess he musta been more pissed than I thought.' He looked from one to the other of them. 'Any of this making sense?'

'Cullen was in the bar when we arrived,' Soames told him.

'There you go.'

'Are you saying that Cullen set you up?'

'No. But I am saying it's possible. Look.' Connla pulled himself still higher up the pillows. 'My pack got stamped on. Imogen Munro'll tell you. I had plaster casts of the panther's paw prints in the pack, together with some from her cubs. The pack was in my room in Tomintoul. Somebody came in and crushed them, stomped on my pack. I didn't discover it till the following day, but I can tell you my room was unlocked all night. I was so dog-tired I didn't hear a thing.' He shook his head again. 'Ask Imogen; she'll tell you.'

'I wouldn't bank on that.' Gray twisted his mouth down at the corners.

'Why not?'

'Because for the last week and a half she's had her name plastered over every newspaper in the country.' He leaned forward. 'Why did you call yourself John Brady when you checked into the hotel at Loch Duich?'

Connla stared at him for a moment.

'You can see why we're upset about the gun, Dr McAdam. Add a false name to the equation and we're really scratching our heads.'

Connla looked beyond him then, and his heart slowly sank. 'This has been in the papers?'

'Of course it has. The papers, television. You're big news, Dr McAdam. We've even spoken to your ex-wife in America.'

'Holly?' Connla looked back at him. 'You spoke to Holly?'

Soames nodded.

'Does she know I'm all right?'

'The rescue was on TV.'

Connla closed his eyes and thought for a long moment. 'Is it illegal to use a different name at a hotel?' he said, looking at Soames again. 'I figure people do it all the time – businessmen with their secretaries, that kinda thing. I paid for everything, didn't I. I stole nothing from anyone.'

'It's not illegal, no. Not in itself. But the gun, you see.'

Connla sighed. 'I used a different name because I didn't want Imogen to know who I was. Not right away, anyway. You see, I knew her when I was a kid in Wyoming. There was stuff to think about, to figure out; stuff from the past.' He looked from one policeman to the other. 'I can't tell you any more than that until I've spoken to her. Look, I can understand about the gun, but it isn't mine. Believe me. I think Bird Dog came into my room in the night when I was asleep. If he broke my casts, he could've planted the gun on me. He was a slaughter-man, wasn't he. I don't suppose he had trouble getting access to weapons. He has a helluva hunting rifle, that's for sure. He also had every reason to stiff me because his dog got killed, and I guess I messed up a big payday for him. Think how much his story would've been worth if he *had* shot that panther.' He broke off for a moment. 'Take my fingerprints and do what-ever else you have to. But I'll ask you both a question. Who's more likely to be packing an illegal firearm, me or Harry Cullen?'

They left him then and he lay back, head pressed deep into the pillows. Imogen knew everything. It had all fallen down around his ears, as it had been bound to do. You spin a yarn like that and what d'you expect, he told himself. At least the police would ultimately believe him; he was pretty confident of that. They wouldn't find his fingerprints on the gun, so he doubted they could link him to it. It could've been in the hotel room long before he even got there, but he was more than sure Cullen had planted it and he hoped there was some way they could link him to it. But, Imogen; she had been there on the hill. He had seen her; that bit had not been a hallucination. He pressed the bell on the cabinet and a young nurse wearing a crisp powder-blue uniform came in.

'Can I get a telephone in here?' he asked her.

He had no coins, but his wallet was in the cabinet and he scooped out a credit card and dialled. Imogen's phone rang and rang and rang. No answer. He put down the receiver and lay back again, thinking hard. He called the nurse back a second time and asked her how long he was likely to be kept in hospital.

'I don't know,' she said. 'You'll have to ask the doctor.'

Connla had to wait till the doctor came back, so he picked up the phone again and dialled Imogen a second time. There was still no answer, but he hung up and tried again. Nothing.

He lay back in the bed, staring at the ceiling, fists clenched in frustration.

The doctors kept him in hospital until the beginning of September. The police came back, reinterviewed him and informed him that his fingerprints were not on the gun and they had decided not to take the matter any further. That was one relief at least, but he had phoned and phoned Imogen and never got a reply. She didn't visit him and she didn't call. He lay there in solitude and nearly drove himself crazy.

On 2 September he struggled through the hospital doors on crutches, got a taxi to Fort William and took a bus to the Kyle of Lochalsh. He had grown a beard and it hung about his face like some throwback to his student campus days. His hair was overlong and kept falling across his eyes, but he could do nothing about it because both his hands were needed for the crutches. The bus dropped him at the castle and he wondered how he could get out to Imogen's house. In the end he hobbled into the hotel and Billy, the Irish barman, smiled at him. 'Ah,' he said. 'Dr McAdam, I presume.'

'Hello, Billy. Look, I'm sorry about the John Brady bullshit, but there was a good reason. It's just a helluva long story.'

Billy was already pouring him a pint. 'Another time, maybe.'

'Right. When you've got about a year to spare.' Connla drank the beer and waited to see who would come in, but the season was winding down and nobody did. 'Billy,' he said, 'do you own a car?'

'A battered one, aye.'

'You think you could do me a favour?'

After the bar closed, Billy drove him out to Loch Gael, but Imogen's Land-Rover wasn't there. Connla cursed silently, then persuaded Billy to drive him up to Keira's field. The horse was gone but the Land-Rover was there, and Connla told Billy just to leave him.

'How will you get back again?' Billy asked him.

'Don't worry, buddy. I'll figure it.'

Billy frowned into the rear-view mirror. 'Do you want a little advice, Dr McAdam?'

'Not really. But I figure you're gonna give it me anyway.'

'If I were you, I'd go home. Go back to the States and forget any of this ever happened.'

'You know, Billy, I'd like to.' Connla looked sideways at him. 'But it's not as easy as that. I've got unfinished business to take care of first.'

Billy leaned across him and opened the passenger door. 'Good luck,' he said. 'I think you're going to need it.'

Connla hobbled and stumbled up to the stable, which was open and warm and dry. The sun was high over the loch, bouncing back off the water so that half of Skye was obscured. He made his way to the window, rested his crutches against the flat stone wall and perched on the ledge to wait.

Imogen rode Keira across the River Leum and passed the Seer Stone, and as she did she heard Redynvre bellow at her from the hillside. She reined in the horse and shifted round in the saddle. He stood tall and grey, his antlers a headdress of fraying velvet against the skyline. He was alone, having dispensed with his bachelor band already, as if he wanted that extra bit of time to prepare himself for the rut. He was getting older and his supremacy on the mountain would not last much longer. He stretched his neck, pawed at the ground like a horse and roared at her once again. She sat and watched him; he stood for a long moment, then disappeared over the crest of the hill. She heard him bellow one more time, long and low and drawn out, echoing the emptiness in her soul.

She rode back through the gap in the hills at the top of Keira's field just as twilight was falling. The sun was low in the west, casting shadows across the twin lochs, which ended in darkness where hillside met the horizon. For a moment Imogen paused and wondered and felt a pinprick of pain in her breast, then she squeezed her knees and Keira cut through the gap in the fence. Dismounting, she let the horse go, refixed the fence, then followed her down to the stable. Keira stood patiently outside, one hoof cocked, waiting to be unsaddled.

'You're a good girl.' Imogen came alongside her, smoothing one hand through the tangles of her mane. Then she glanced into the shadows of the stable and saw Connla McAdam asleep against the wall.

For a long silent moment she stared at him, pale and bearded now, with lines around his eyes. She let go a little breath and he woke up, looked at her and his face seemed to twist in pain.

Imogen could feel the blood in her ears and she stood, one hand on the girth strap, the other resting on the bow of the saddle.

'Hello,' he said.

She just stared at him.

Connla struggled to get up, one crutch sliding in the gathered sawdust. He rooted it, applied his weight and stood up. Imogen turned her back on him, undid the girth strap and laid it across the top of the saddle. Connla stood and watched her. He said nothing. She was silent and just carried on with Keira till the saddle was off, together with the reins and bridle, and she humped it all over to the pegs fixed on the wall. Connla moved outside to let her fasten the hay net and stood in the twilight, with the mountains of Skye against his back.

'I'm sorry,' he said at last. 'Really, I'm so very, very sorry.'

She finished up, dusted her palms on her thighs and hooked her hair behind her ears. She closed the stable door, her back to him, stiff and cold.

'Imogen.'

Still she ignored him.

'Imogen, please.'

'What?' She rounded on him then. 'Imogen what? Sorry I came into your life. Sorry it's been thirty years. Sorry I lied through my teeth.'

Connla stood like a helpless child, leaning on his crutch. She stepped past him and halted; the sun was sinking into the sea, a silent ball of fire against the sky. He opened his mouth to speak, but suddenly he had no words. He sucked in breath, exhaled heavily and looked at the set of her shoulders, shunted into her neck as she stared across the loch.

'Do you want to hear something funny?' She spoke without looking at him. 'I mean really tragically stupid. I loved you, Connla. Or I thought I did. When you were John Brady, like a dumb unthinking idiot, I fell in love with you.'

Connla just stood there. He moistened his lips, but when he spoke his voice sounded cracked and broken. 'Would you please let me try to explain?'

She looked sharply at him. 'Explain? What? Why you lied, why you spun me the yarn of the century and made me look like a fool.'

'Imogen. Please.'

She drew breath through her nose and looked coldly at him. 'Is it worth hearing?'

'I'd like to think so.'

'Well, I tell you what, if you can get to my house I'll listen.' She stalked down the path, leaving him where he was.

Connla watched her for a moment, his throat dry, and then he called out, 'You've every right to be angry, Imogen. Every right in the world. But I can't make it to your house unless you take me.'

She stopped by the Land-Rover and stared through the gathering twilight. She seemed to consider for a long time, then she yanked open the passenger door.

They drove back to her house in silence, Connla's left leg thrust stiffly in front of him. The cab was cramped and his bones seemed to ache. At the house, she didn't offer to help him down and he had to work himself round in the seat. She was already inside with the kitchen door closed when he got to the ground. He thought for a moment, looked back along the rough track and almost turned and shuffled away. But she opened the door and looked him in the eye, and there was a darkness in her gaze that he hadn't seen for thirty years.

She sat in the lounge smoking a cigarette. He stood, leaning on his crutches, at the window and picked up the carved Indian. 'I saw a picture of this,' he said. 'In the store in Dunkeld. I didn't recognize the scene outside, but I recognized this.' He set it down on the window sill once more. 'You picked it up on that cliff, didn't you?'

'It was lying in a pinion bush.' She looked at the floor. 'I took it home. I kept it, Connla. And every time I looked at it, it reminded me of the day my brother died. I wasn't sure it was a good thing at first, keeping it so visible, but you know what, in a way it was a comfort. It helped me get over the tragedy.' She paused for a moment, drawing heavily on her cigarette. 'Those are the kind of memories that normally haunt you for ever, but as I grew up I really thought I'd dealt with it. Then, all of a sudden, you show up and bring it all back again.' She stared coldly at him now. 'I want to know what happened, Connla. What *really* happened that day. And I don't want any more lies. You hear me? No more lies. You tell me the truth or get out of here.' She broke off, looked at the floor, then back into his eyes. 'You knew, didn't you. Back then. You knew all the time. You knew what had happened, yet you sent the search party the wrong way.'

Connla sat down on the other couch awkwardly, wincing from the pain in his leg.

'I didn't *send* them the wrong way; they went the wrong way. I just didn't put them straight, is all.'

Connla opened his eyes as the first glimmer of dawn pressed the walls of the tent. Ewan hadn't stirred yet. Imogen lay beside him, huddled in the warmth of her sleeping bag, thumb in her mouth and blanky stuffed under her nose. He looked down at her and smiled. Ewan moved on the other side of him, opened his eyes and squinted. 'Is it morning yet?'

Connla lifted a finger to his lips and nodded towards Imogen. 'Don't wake her.'

'Don't worry, I'm not gonna. I don't want *her* tagging along.' Ewan grabbed his jeans and jacket and they crawled out of the tent.

He led the way, as always, striding down the trail, through pine trees that scraped at the sky overhead. Connla followed as always; it wasn't as if you got any choice with Ewan. He did everything first, led everything, was captain of everything. Connla had got used to it. They came to the clearing, beyond which their fathers had told them not to go. 'You wanna fish some more or hunt for Indian stuff?' Ewan said.

'We don't got no fishing poles.'

'Not with poles. We'll make ourselves some spears. Spear fish like the Indians did in the old days. You seen the movies, Connla. It ain't difficult.'

'Sharpen up a coupla lengths of pine, you mean?'

'Yeah.'

'Whatever. I don't care.'

Ewan nodded, lips twisted in a line. 'Let's head on down to the water and see what we can find. If there ain't no poles we'll just dig for arrowheads or something. There're always arrow-heads near a creek.'

Connla watched as Ewan strode off again, shoulders back, head high, chin jutting out at the world. Ewan Munro, Jackson City's finest son. He walked with a swagger and a swing to his shoulders and Connla wondered why nobody else seemed able to see the Ewan he could see. Maybe he was the one who had got it wrong. Maybe he was just jealous.

They got deeper and deeper into the forest, well beyond the point of no return, and Connla was in awe of the way the moun-tains encroached on the trail. The trees were thick-trunked and grew close together, but all of a sudden the density would be broken by a great sandy cliff, red and brown and orange in places, where the sun picked out the hollows. Ewan looked back at him. 'Imagine what this place was like when the Nez Perce Indians were hunting here.'

'I figure they'd be Shoshone, Ewan. Not Nez Perce.'

Ewan stopped and looked back. 'You do, huh? Well I figure they'd be Nez Perce.' Connla shook his head. 'Nez Perce was north of here. I seen it on a map.'

'No you didn't. Well, if you did, the map was wrong. Nez

Perce was right here.' Ewan pointed at the ground with his fore-finger.

'How the hell would you know? You ain't even American.'

'I'm as American as you are.'

'No you ain't. You weren't born here.'

'What's it matter where I was born? I can hit a baseball harder'n you, I can throw a football better and I can run faster any day of the week.' Ewan swaggered in front of him. 'Who's leading the trail, huh? Who always leads the trail?' He stepped closer. 'Who catches the most fish? Come on, Connla. How many steelhead you catch? Heck, the Twaggle Tail caught more'n you did.' He pushed him then, stiff-fingered, in the chest so that Connla had to step backwards.

'It don't matter,' he muttered. 'You weren't born here. You ain't American.' It was the only thing he could ever say, because Ewan had an answer for everything else. And it galled. It stuck right in Ewan's throat, because deep down he knew Connla was right and there was nothing he could do about it. Ewan balled a fist, his face going red as it always did when he started to get mad. 'I oughta punch you out.'

Connla took another pace backwards. He didn't want to fight: fights were another thing Ewan always won.

Ewan laughed at him then, seeing the fear in his face, and, turning on his heel, he strode on down the path. Connla tagged along behind and they could both hear the rushing sound of the Salmon River growing steadily louder. 'Like to canoe me this river one day,' Ewan said.

'You'd drown.'

'The hell I would.'

Connla shrugged and walked on.

They had been gone maybe an hour when the trail started to climb, the cliff walls rising jagged and sheer on their left, the forest falling away on their right. They went through a kind of tunnel and then the ground flattened and opened out and they could see the Sawtooth mountains, capped with snow in the distance. Before that the world dropped away and they glimpsed the rising spray from the river.

'Oh, man.' Ewan stood with his hands on his hips, then darted to the edge of the bluff. 'Hey, Connla. Come look at this.'

Connla was more hesitant, wary. He recalled his father's words about not going beyond the clearing on their own. He recalled the tone of his voice and the expression on his face. He'd tasted his belt on too many occasions and he didn't want to again. 'Hey, Ewan,' he called. 'You figure maybe we oughta head back? We shouldn't have come this far.'

'The hell we shouldn't. Who knows we're here?' Ewan smirked over his shoulder at him. 'We'll just tell 'em we never went farther than the first clearing.' He beckoned. 'Come on and look.'

Connla walked over, not getting too close, but close enough to see the racing, swirling river, choking white foam sucking at rocks and fallen trees and tearing lumps from the bank. 'Sure runs fast,' he murmured.

Ewan suddenly grabbed him from behind. 'Saved your life!'

Connla nearly jumped out of his skin and Ewan darted away, laughing. Connla stood a moment longer, gathering himself. The drop was perhaps twenty-five feet into a whirlpool that would suck him to his death in seconds.

Looking back, he saw Ewan standing with his hands on his hips. Halfway up the cliff, fastened to a ledge in a tangle of interwoven twigs and willow sticks, was a red-tailed hawk's nest.

'Eagle's nest up there. Look.' Ewan pointed.

Connla went up to him. 'It ain't an eagle, Ewan. Eagles don't nest this far down.'

'Sure they do. What the hell do you know about it?'

'It's a red tail's nest. I seen one before.'

Ewan had stripped off his jacket and was already rubbing dirt into the palms of his hands, looking up and gauging the height of the climb.

'What you doing?'

'I bet there's eggs up there.'

'Ah, leave 'em be, will you.'

'Leave 'em be yourself.' Ewan pushed him hard and he sprawled in the dirt, bruising his elbow and upper arm. When he got up he saw his shirt was torn. 'Now look what you done. My mom's gonna kill me.'

Ewan was already climbing, though, hand over hand, feet scrabbling for holds. Connla watched him, jealous all at once of his skill. He sat down where he was, close to the bottom of the wall, with Ewan sweating above him. He hoped the nest was an old nest and that it was empty. That would serve him right. He could feel the blood oozing from his elbow and he looked again at where the rough skin was chafed and split. Then something caught his eye, something in the rock, like part of the wall and yet not part of it. He crawled forward and looked closer. The dust on one part of the cliff was loose and what looked like a tiny piece of wood was poking out.

He worked at the patch of dust, ignoring Ewan above him, rubbing at the rock and loose stones. As he worked, more of the wood was exposed. It wasn't very big, no more than an inch or so, but was smooth and shaped like a carving. Connla's excitement grew and he worked faster and faster. He had to get it out before Ewan spotted him, before he jumped down and claimed whatever it was for his own.

'Ah, hell.' Ewan's voice rang out from above him. 'There ain't no eggs. Must be an old nest.' He looked down, saw Connla and called out to him. 'Hey, Connla, there's no eggs up here. Hey, what you doing?'

Connla didn't answer, he just worked more feverishly, picking and scrabbling at the dirt. He could hear Ewan descending as he worked faster and faster. Ewan dropped beside him just as Connla freed the last of the dust and pulled out a carved wooden figure. He moved away as Ewan's breath pumped over his shoulder. 'What you got there?'

'I don't know yet.'

'Let me see.' Ewan made a grab for it.

Connla was too quick, though, and he rolled back and stood up in one movement. There were three paces between them. He looked again at what he held: a beautifully carved Indian in leggings and a shirt, dancing, his head back, arms above his head and two feathers pointed at the sky. He had no idea what it meant, but it was Indian and he had found it.

'Let me see.' Ewan was in his face almost. Connla stepped back, one arm out to keep him away. 'OK. But don't touch it. It's old and it's probably fragile. And I found it, Ewan. You got that? I found it.'

'Yeah. Yeah. Let me look, will ya.'

Ewan moved alongside him and Connla stepped away again, not trusting him, knowing what he was like. He moved closer to the river, unwittingly, unknowingly, concentrating on his prize and the possible theft to come.

'Come on. Let me see.' Ewan made a grab for it, but Connla stepped back again, and then the two of them were scrabbling, tousling in the dirt. Connla held on to the figure, but Ewan was fighting him for it. 'Just let me look at it!'

'OK. OK.' Connla stood up straight, hand behind his back, the other trying to keep Ewan off. 'You can look. But I told ya, Ewan, you ain't holding it.'

He held out his hand and, as he did so, Ewan made another grab for it, but Connla was ready and he stepped away sharply. Ewan, coming forward, tripped over his feet, staggered, then toppled onto his hands and knees. He rested there for a moment, then all at once he whacked Connla on the back of his legs and they were both in the dirt again, fighting hard now, rolling over and over. Connla lost all sense of direction, still keeping one hand on the Indian. He felt something snap and he cursed. He got up. Ewan got up and went for him again. Connla pushed him off – hard this time, with all the strength he could muster. Ewan stumbled back, then took another pace to steady himself. The river was behind him now. They glared at one another, sweating and panting. Connla looked at his prize and saw that one of the feathers had broken off at the stem.

'Now you've gone and ruined it,' he yelled.

Ewan suddenly leered at him, pivoted, and then lunged for him again. The ground broke from under his feet and he fell.

Connla saw his eyes ball, heard the cry, short and high-pitched, then nothing. No splash, no scream, just the roaring of the river in his ears. He stood there for a moment, not quite believing any of it. And all he could think of was his father's last words. *Don't go farther than that clearing. You hear me, boy? The clearing.* He looked at the wooden carving he held in his hand and the Indian looked back at him. He stood there, breathing hard, then he saw Ewan's jacket lying on the ground where he had discarded it. All at once he dropped the little Indian, snatched up the fallen jacket and ran back up the trail.

He spoke as if to the empty fireplace. 'I guess I musta dropped the jacket in the clearing. I don't remember. I came back to camp and you know the rest.' His voice sounded distant, lost. 'I was ten years old, Imogen. All I could think about was my old man and what he said about that clearing.'

'So you lied to everybody.'

He made an open-handed gesture. 'I guess. I don't know why. I was scared, I suppose. I didn't know what was gonna happen.'

'But you let them go off in the wrong direction, for Christ's sake – the sheriff, the rescue team. Why on earth did you do that? Why didn't you just say that Ewan went to the river?'

He said nothing.

'Didn't you want them to find him?'

Still he said nothing. He sat with his hands by his sides and stared at the remnants of their candle, now just a twist of old wax on the hearthstone.

Imogen was quiet for a long time, just watching him. Then she got up, paced to the window and gazed across the loch. 'You pushed him, didn't you.'

Connla stared at her back. 'Of course not.'

'Why else would you lie?'

'Imogen, I didn't push him. We fought and he fell. That's what happened.'

She turned towards him then. 'Are you sure?'

'Totally. That's exactly what happened. I know. I was there.'

She laughed then, a hollow sound in her throat. 'Of course. You were there. That says it all. Get a life, Connla. You waltz in here after thirty years, lie to me about who you are and then

291

just expect me to believe your explanation when I already know you sent them the wrong way. You were scared; no other reason than that.' She snorted. 'Why *should* I believe you?'

'Because I'm not lying.' He looked her in the eye. 'I'm telling you the truth.'

'But you lied that day. You told everybody you didn't know what happened, but you did. And in the meantime my brother was drowning.'

Connla didn't say anything. There was nothing he could say. She was right. He just sat on the couch, only too aware of his helplessness. 'I'm sorry,' he said at last. Imogen snorted again and shook her head. 'Sorry! Good God, you're pathetic.'

She took another cigarette from the pack and turned to the window once more. She stood and smoked for a few silent minutes, the wind off the loch rattling the glass.

Connla sat forward and clasped his hands together. 'I don't know why I let them go the wrong way, Imogen. Honestly I don't. I guess I figured Ewan would be all right. I guess I figured he was fooling around maybe. I was just a kid. I had no idea he was dead, or hurt even.' He shook his head then. 'I was just plain scared. We'd had a fight and he went over the bluff. How was that gonna look? Nobody'd ever believe it was an accident. They'd figure I was jealous and that somehow I meant to do it. Just like you do now.' He looked up at her again. 'I don't know what went through my mind. I've been over it every day for the last thirty years. I was scared, I guess. Just plain scared.'

Imogen wasn't looking at him; she was watching the waves crest on the surface of the loch, remembering the waters of the Salmon, and the rushing sound filled her head like a memory. Ewan's white face, glassy-eyed, just beneath the surface.

Then she turned, and she and Connla looked at one another for a long time, the weight of thirty years of silence balanced between them. Connla pushed himself to his feet, biting down on his lip. 'I'm sorry. I really am sorry. I thought this thing was dead and buried, too, then I walked into a store in Scotland and there was a picture of the ghost dancer I'd found in Idaho.' He moved to the window sill. 'It was unbelievable. I felt like some-body had opened up my grave.'

She was still staring at him, the familiar darkness in her eyes, and her voice cut like a knife. 'So why did you lie to me? Why couldn't you just be honest? I mean, you looked me up. You went to the trouble of contacting my publisher. Why? What did you want to do? Just see me again? See how I'd changed? Gloat maybe?'

'No.' He held up both hands, palms outwards. 'Of course not. No, Imogen, I . . .'

'What? Still couldn't handle it, so you lied. Is that what you're telling me, Connla? You just decided to make it easier on your-self and who cares what I felt. Or maybe you just lied because you fancied your chances of getting into my knickers after all these years.'

'No. You know that's not how it was.' He snapped at her then. 'You *know* that.'

'Do I?' She stepped up close to him.

'Yes. In your heart, you do. I know you do.' Connla shook his head. 'I was gonna tell you everything. I saw that carving, and after I got over the initial shock I figured, at last, the chance to put the record straight and tell you how it was. But then I saw you, and somehow I just couldn't do it. I guess I remembered how you looked at me that day in Idaho. You were only a kid, but God you looked right through me. Somehow you knew. I don't know how but you did.'

Imogen was numb now, the memory burned into her mind like a branding mark. 'You should just've told me the truth. You should've told *them* the truth. Back then in Idaho, when it mattered. That's all there is to it. There's no excuse. I don't care how old you were or how bloody scared. A boy's life was at stake – my brother's life. And he died.'

Connla felt the weight of tears behind his eyes. He clamped his jaw together. 'I'm sorry. I'm so sorry for everything: for that day, for now. I should've told them, and I should've told you the first minute I saw you.'

'Stop saying you're sorry.' She clenched her fists. 'Sorry's got nothing to do with it. Sorry doesn't make it any better. Connla, has it ever really occurred to you that if you'd told the truth Ewan might not be dead?'

Connla looked lost. His voice was weak. 'Of course it's occurred to me. Every day of my life it's occurred to me.' He sat down again, his leg stiff in front of him. 'I can't explain it. I just shut down. I was scared. I mean, plain terrified. I panicked, Imogen. I was a kid, just a kid. Sometimes you do stupid things when you're a kid.' And then his face hardened, biting down on his teeth so the muscles stood out against his jaw. 'You can blame me all you like and you're right it *was* my fault. But there was nothing I could have done any differently. It's been thirty years and I still haven't come to terms with it. Ewan fell and I reacted like I did. I can't change it. It's happened.' He looked up at her then. 'And d'you know what, I reckon if you wound the clock back now it'd be the same all over again.'

Imogen sat on the other couch. 'Maybe you wanted him dead, Connla. Did you ever think of that? He was only friends with you so he could bully you, so he could push you around. That was obvious to me and I was only eight. Ewan was a little bastard. I knew that. What I couldn't understand was why you were friends with him in the first place.'

Connla sighed. 'I was friends with him because he was Ewan Munro. Every kid in school wanted to be Ewan Munro's buddy, and I was really too young to be in that grade at all. I only made it because of when my birthday fell. I was the youngest guy in the grade and buddies with the most popular kid in the whole damn school. Man, I walked tall over that.' He looked at the empty fireplace. 'Maybe you're right, though. Maybe I did want him gone. I have wondered.' He stared at her then. 'I don't know. I've thought about it so much my brain's been scrambled.'

Imogen held his gaze for a long time. 'Tell me the truth,' she said. 'Did you push him over?'

'I've already told you the truth. He fell. He tried to steal that carving and he fell.' He made a face then. 'Why should I push him? He was leaving the US anyway. You both were. You were coming back to Scotland. What possible reason could I have for pushing him over a cliff?'

They sat in silence after that, then Imogen lit another cigarette and paced to the empty fireplace. 'There's something I want to tell you,' she said. 'Something you need to know.' She paused and eased the smoke from her lungs. 'When you two left me that morning, I woke up and followed you. I only went a little way into the woods because I was scared to be there on my own. I'd got about fifty yards down the trail when . . .' Her throat seized up and she couldn't get the words out. She had never spoken, never practised, never articulated this to anyone before.

'What?' Connla asked gently.

She shook her head, sucked harshly on the cigarette and exhaled hard. 'I went into the woods. You'd gone. I was looking at a ground squirrel and then . . . then I saw him. I saw him in my head: Ewan up to his neck in water.'

She was quiet for a few moments, gathering her emotions. 'D'you know what that means, Connla? Have you any idea what that means? Of course you don't. How could you? *I* didn't know until I looked it up, God knows how many years later.' She broke off, a trace of spittle on her lip. 'We talked about mythology, remember? Well, there are all sorts of books about mythology; Celtic mythology. I got one out of the library and it described on the page exactly what I'd seen in my head. It's called Celtic second sight. If you see a vision of somebody up to their neck in water, it means they're going to drown. They're still alive when you see it, but they *are* going to drown.'

Connla stared at her, his tongue so thick it stuck to the roof of his mouth.

'Yes, Connla,' she said. 'When I saw what I did, Ewan was still alive.'

He was very still, the realization sweeping over him in a wave: his actions, and their consequences, were what Imogen had lived with for the past thirty years. He felt broken inside. He wanted to go. He wanted to sit there. He wanted to hold her very tightly, standing as she was now, hugging herself at the window.

But then another thought struck him. 'Imogen, how did you find me?' he said quietly. 'The helicopter must've passed a dozen times without spotting me. How did you know where I was?'

She didn't answer him immediately, then she spoke without looking round. 'The same way I found Ewan. I could feel where you'd been in the rock.'

She turned then. 'When the police told me you weren't who you claimed to be, when I first found out it was you, I hated you for lying to me. I mean, really hated you. You played me for such a fool. You betrayed me, Connla. Betrayed my trust. You took pretty much everything from me when I was very vulnerable. I wanted to forget all about you and get you out of my head, so I went up to the stable to work. I cleared out all the muck and laid fresh bedding and then suddenly I saw you in my head, just like I'd seen Ewan, only you were pressed against a cliff.' She broke off, her shoulders suddenly trembling. 'That was the moment I knew you were still out there. I knew you were alive, but I also knew you'd fall. Think about it, Connla. It happened to me again. I saw you. I knew you would fall, and if you did you would die.'

He stared at her then, eyes bunched at the corners. 'And you still came to find me?'

'I had to. What else could I do? The authorities had called the official search off. D'you know how hard that was? Wandering around out there with Andy McKewan laughing up his sleeve at me, and knowing that, even if I did find you, you'd be dead already.'

'But you still came regardless.' Connla lifted one eyebrow. 'Why?'

'Believe me, I've asked myself the same question.'

'I wasn't dead, though, was I. I did fall but *you* found me in time.' Connla moved alongside her then, desperately aware of her womanhood – her scent and the weight of her hair falling over her shoulders. 'Does that make it any easier?' he said gently. 'The past, I mean. Nothing being repeated. You must have feared that, even if you did hate me.'

Imogen made a face. 'Give me another thirty years and I might be able to tell you.'

She was sitting on a high-backed chair in the kitchen, sipping a glass of wine and staring into space. Connla leaned against the table and folded his arms. His heart was pounding. For ten minutes neither of them had said anything, and he was hoping, praying, that perhaps things would be OK. That she could somehow forgive him. He couldn't take his eyes off her: her face, hair, the imprint of her lips on the rim of the glass. Even after everything, the reality was that he had found her, and to lose her now after all of this did not bear thinking about.

But the room was suddenly cold and the wind broke against the walls of the house. Connla's mouth was dry. 'I loved you, too, Imogen.'

'What?'

'What you said to me up at the stable. I fell in love with you, too.'

'No, you didn't. You were just trying to appease your guilt.'

He shook his head.

'Yes, Connla. Yes.' She set the wineglass down. 'That's exactly what you were doing.'

'So what happened between us,' he said, gesturing to the window, 'out there in the hills, you think that was all just make-believe, do you?'

She looked at him coldly then. 'I don't know. Maybe you were just getting laid.'

'Of course I wasn't getting laid.' Connla shook his head. 'Goddammit, Imogen, you know I wasn't.'

'Connla, I don't really know anything about what I think. I'm not sure I want to think at all. It's been thirty years. Maybe I just want to forget about it again. Maybe I just want my life back.' She broke off and looked between her feet at the floor. 'I think you'd better go now.'

'Imogen—'

She held up a palm. 'No. Please, Connla. Just leave me alone.' She stood up. 'I'm going upstairs now. We've talked ourselves out. There's nothing left to say.' She pointed to the dresser. 'There's the phone. If you ring the hotel, they'll fix you up with a cab.'

TWENTY-SEVEN

IMOGEN DID NOT WATCH HIM GO. SHE SAT ON HER BED upstairs, listening to the thud of his crutches as he hobbled to the waiting taxi. She listened until the silence returned once again, the silence of her life after turmoil. And there was no sound whatsoever; no wind to press the window, the loch quiet against the shore and the house as still as her brother's grave. She remained where she was for what seemed like a long time, then she went downstairs and unlocked the door to her studio. The unfinished canvas still stood on the easel, dominated by the rock, and within it the outline of her brother. The past became the present and the future and the past again in a moment. She closed her eyes and bit down on her lip.

Outside, the wind seemed to have risen once more and the loch was alive with waves, like chips of flint in the darkness. Imogen's hair flew about her face and she hooked it behind her ears, as Connla had done before her, and peered into the gloom. Far in the distance she could see the headlights of the taxi as it wound its way towards the main road.

She lay in the bath, aware of herself and yet unaware, as if someone else was thinking her thoughts to make sure she didn't have to face them. It was gone, finished, over. She hadn't even said goodbye, just let him shuffle outside and close the door behind him. Now he would be back at the hotel, and tomorrow he would be on the bus, and then on the plane and home to

America. She sat up and stared at herself in the mirror. She could see the haunted look in her eyes.

Billy was polishing glasses and McKewan and his crew were in the bar; their conversation stilled into silence as Connla hobbled in on his crutches. He stood for a moment, regretting going in, and McKewan looked at him sourly. 'You're up and about then?'

'Yes. Thank you for what you did, coming out to find me. You saved my life.'

'Aye, you're right. We did.' McKewan turned his back on him, picked up his pint and swallowed what was left in the glass. He nodded to his crew and they trooped across the road to McLaran's.

Connla looked at Billy.

'Pint, is it?' Billy asked.

'No, thanks, Billy. I'll just go up to my room.'

He climbed the stairs with difficulty and sat down on his bed in the darkness. He hadn't switched on the light, but the room was illuminated by the glow of a street lamp. Beyond it, Lochalsh stretched in laced black to the sea. Connla could hear the waves among the boulders which littered what passed for the beach. He had heard them on the stanchions under the bridge as he crossed it one last time in the taxi. The driver seemed to know who he was and conversation during the seven-mile ride had been non-existent. From downstairs he could hear Billy stacking glasses, then there was silence as he closed the bar and disappeared out to his bungalow.

Connla knew he wouldn't sleep and, easing himself up on one crutch, he leaned on the window sill and lit a cigarette. The smoke dulled the pane of glass before his eyes, blocking his vision and forcing his thoughts back on himself. He knew he had been a fool; more than that, a coward, and look at what it had cost – not just him, but Imogen. She was right: she had probably been doing just fine with her life before he'd arrived to ruin it all for her. He thought about home, the United States and his cabin in the Black Hills. Would that he could just go

300

there and hide and lick his wounds like a stricken cougar until he was fit and strong again. But the Fall beckoned, and with it two semesters in Washington. After this he wasn't sure he could face them. Crushing out his cigarette, he stripped off his clothes and went to bed.

He left on the bus in the morning. It would take him to Perth, then he'd have to take another bus to Edinburgh and a train to London and the airport. The driver pulled over for a coffee break beyond Spean Bridge and Connla sat in the silence of the mountain road and watched as the sky pressed black clouds against the horizon. The hills dulled to the darkest green and wind ruffled the grass by the roadside. Summer was waning. Autumn was coming and the world would turn gold and brown, then white on the highest hills. The bus seemed to sit for a long time and the clouds got lower and lower. By the time the driver headed down to Dalwhinnie it was raining.

Imogen had sat in the cab of her Land-Rover and watched the bus take the bend on the road by Eilean Donan castle. Waking early, she had driven up to her horse's field like a woman possessed by a demon. Keira watched her for a little while, then took off to the highest point on the hill to chase sheep. Imogen worked until she was sweating and her hair fell in damp locks across her eyes. Only then did she realize she was crying. She had driven home and passed the bus on the bridge before the turn for Gaelloch. She'd slowed, made her turn and then swung in a loop and crawled back to the main road. She didn't see him get on, but the bus pulled away from the hotel and she followed it as far as the corner. There, she turned into Eilean Donan car park, where she sat with the engine off, watching till it disappeared into the foothills.

Nobody met Connla at Dulles Airport. There was nobody, except possibly Holly, given his semi-crippled condition, but he hadn't told her he was coming. He stood for a while, leaning on his sticks, and thought about what to do. He bought a cup of coffee and sat drinking it, looking out of the terminal window

301

at the heat softening the pavement and thinking of the complete mess he had made of everything. He was fit enough to still do the two semesters teaching, but was appalled by the thought of it. He finished the coffee, knowing he was only putting off the inevitable, and made his way outside. He took the Flyer to Falls Church and then a metro train to Foggy Bottom and the Holiday Inn he always stayed in when he was in DC. He climbed the escalator to the street and hobbled the rest of the way, not wishing to be stuck in the back of a cab. The city was still hot and sticky with the residue of summer.

He got to the hotel and stopped, laying his bag down on the sidewalk, and looked at the glass-fronted entrance. A bellboy watched him, smiling, then he came over and offered to take Connla's bags.

'Just dump them inside for me, will you? I'll be right there,' Connla said, and slipped a dollar bill into the man's hand. He took his cigarettes from his pocket and leaned on one crutch to smoke. The bellboy came outside again and watched him for a moment. Connla crushed out the cigarette and hobbled inside. The receptionist looked up and smiled. 'D'you want one bed or two in the room, Dr McAdam?'

Connla blew out his cheeks. 'There is only me,' he said.

The girl tapped at her keyboard, then looked up again. 'OK. I've put you in room three ten. That's on the third floor. I just need to take an imprint of your credit card.'

Connla fished in his wallet and, as he did so, he looked at the clock on the wall behind her. The emptiness gnawed like hunger in his gut and he hesitated. The girl had her hand out for his card. 'Dr McAdam?'

Connla made a face. 'You know what, I'm sorry. Can you cancel that and call me a cab instead?'

Very late that evening, Paha Ska, the buffalo-skin painter from Keystone, dropped him off at his cabin in the Black Hills and hefted his bags from the back of the truck. Connla had been lucky: the old Indian had been collecting his wife from the airport in Rapid City after visiting her sister in Arizona. He had to drive right by Connla's cabin to get back to his shop.

'You gonna be OK, bro?' the old man asked him.

'Yeah. Thanks, pardner.' Connla shook his hand.

'Call in for coffee next time you're passing the shop.'

'I'll do that. Thanks.' Connla struggled up the three steps and dropped his bag on the floor. The cabin was in darkness, the drapes still pulled, and it smelled of age and old leather. He didn't bother to open any of the windows, although the evening was hot. Leaving his bags where they were, he crashed out on the bed and slept through till morning.

He woke to the emptiness, that vacuum in his stomach that takes away hunger; the same hollow sensation he had felt since leaving Imogen's house. She was in the middle of his head when he woke, right between his eyes, almost like a physical pain – her face, body, scent – as if that were her space and she would occupy it for all time. He lay there in the silence, not daring to think about what might have been. Soulmates: he remembered the discussion they had had in that café in Kyle while rain ran opaque on the window. Found and lost in one terrible moment.

He didn't want to get up, but he forced himself and took a shower. His left leg was still in plaster, so he left it dangling outside the tub and washed himself down, then he scraped the beard off his face with a wet razor. When he was done, he shuffled round the huge single room, opening the drapes and windows. Then he opened both the front and back doors, creating a freshening breeze right throughout the house. He glanced at his mail, saw nothing but bills and shovelled them into one unopened pile. His eyes wandered to the walls and his newspaper clippings from Britain. The black beast of Elgin stared out of the pictures at him.

He made a pot of coffee and sat down with the photographs he had developed in Scotland. They took him back to that day by Lochalsh, before anything had gone wrong and he and Imogen had been close. He loved her. He had known it then and he knew it now. He should have been up front right away. If he had he wouldn't be sitting here like this. He wasn't one for moping or feeling sorry for himself; life had already thrown far too much at him for that. Normally he could 'cowboy up' pretty good, but this . . . this hurt with a vengeance.

Getting up from the crude wooden table that served both as desk and something to eat off, he made his way to the yard door and pressed back the screen. There was sunshine on his face now; warm mountain sunshine. Once more he was reminded of the precious time they had spent together sitting on a rock while she painted him. His breathing grew sharper as he saw her in his mind's eye, naked against the moonlight; and in the morning, when she'd bathed, and the water and sunlight had combined to raise gooseflesh on her skin.

A movement among the tree stumps at the top of the yard caught his eye and he saw Mellencamp looking at him. She had her summer coat, her muzzle flat and broad, the white fur round her mouth set off by the black of her nostrils.

'Hey, girl.' Connla shuffled off the stoop and crossed the dirt towards her. She watched him, looking at his two additional legs with a quizzical expression, and when he was about ten yards away she flattened her ears and gave a low growl of warning. Connla paused, frowned and then his face broke into a smile. He could see two spotted bundles of fur playing together beside her. Very slowly, he shuffled himself round and slid down a tree till he sat in the dirt with his back resting against the trunk, facing away from them. The cubs looked up at him, their fawn-coloured coats covered with black spots and paws that were way too big for their bodies. They glanced at their mother, moved over to nuzzle against her breast for a moment, then their curiosity got the better of them and they advanced on him. Connla watched for Mellencamp's reaction, but she seemed passive enough, ears pricked forward now, watchful but silent. He made no movement, didn't even lift his hands as first one cub, then the other, came over, sniffed at him and poked him with their paws. The male climbed onto his leg and slipped and slithered against the plaster.

Connla smiled, but still he did not make any move to touch them. He was watching Mellencamp. She had made a lair for her young in a burrow below the tree stump where she lay. Cougars had no natural predators and they were only vulnerable as cubs. Mellencamp would have sought the safest location possible for them while she went hunting, and the yard was as safe as it got. This was where she had recuperated when she was hurt and she had clearly not forgotten. Still Connla was cautious: she weighed more than 150 pounds and could kill him with one blow from her paw.

She yawned and got up, stretched flat on her stomach, her hind legs arched, tongue curling between her teeth, and then she wandered over to him and stood there, sniffing her babies. Gently, Connla stroked the head of the female, who scrabbled now at his thigh. Mellencamp watched him for a moment, then she bent and, with infinite care, lifted the cub in jaws that could snap the neck of an elk. She walked back to the tree stump and set her down in the lair. Then she walked round Connla, picked up her son and took him to join his sister. She came over to him then, yawned and rubbed herself against his shoulder like a domestic cat. He lifted his hand to her ears. 'Good to see you, girl,' he whispered.

Over the next few weeks he stayed home and let his leg heal. Then he took his truck into Rapid City and got the plaster cast removed. After that he was more mobile, and he went up into the hills and took pictures of Mellencamp teaching the cubs to eat meat. She killed a couple of young deer and hid them in the scrub, dragging them out for the youngsters to practise on. She cut through the hide with her incisors and showed them how to tear the flesh away from the bones.

The new school term started and Imogen returned with a heavy heart. There seemed to be nothing to look forward to now, save chill nights and the oncoming snow of winter. She got back into it, though, and had to rebuff Colin Patterson's advances even harder. He was very concerned about her, he told her, after what she had been through during the summer. She kept him at arm's length, however, and confided in Jean.

'You've not been yourself since he went back to America,' Jean told her as they shared playground duty one lunchtime. 'You really miss him, don't you.'

Imogen was watching two boys preparing to kick lumps out of one another. 'Yes,' she said, 'I do.' And she did. She would see his face sometimes in her mind's eye – his smile, the way his hair fell over those green eyes when his conversation grew animated. She had even finished the painting of him. She hadn't intended to; she had meant to throw it away, but couldn't quite bring herself to do it. In the middle of the night a week or two ago she had got out of bed and finished it. His eyes had stared out of the canvas at her, as if he could guess her thoughts, and in the morning, when the paint was dry, she'd found herself brushing his cheek with her fingertips.

'Can you get in touch with him?' Jean asked.

'Why would I want to do that?'

Jean smiled then. Imogen had told her the whole story over a bottle of wine one night, just before the term started. 'Because you had a crush on him when you were a kid. Because he pretty much treated you right. And because I think you've loved him all your life.'

Imogen made a face. 'He lied to me, Jean.'

'He did, aye. But I imagine he's paying the price.'

Imogen glanced sideways at her then. 'Even if I did want to contact him, I don't know where he lives.'

One Saturday morning at the beginning of October she took Keira and rode into the hills that formed the Five Sisters of Kintail. The day was cold, and it was colder still in the mountains, but the sky was clear. The cloud was high and the breeze barely caressed the grass. She rode between the first and second sister and heard the roar of a stag. A thrill took her as she recognized Redynvre, and for a moment her pain was forgotten. Keira snorted and pranced and Imogen kicked her into a gallop. They raced between the slopes and diagonally across the hillside, heather and bracken splintered by black and shining rock. At the top of the second rise she pulled the horse up short and held her on a tight rein. Below her, head dipped to meet those who pretended to his throne, she saw Redynvre in the rut.

Slipping from the saddle, Imogen sat down on a rock and reached for her sketch pad. But then, all at once, she hesitated. This was his moment, not hers to capture on canvas. Suffice enough that she was privileged to witness it.

She sat there all day and watched as he wallowed in a mud hole and urinated over his belly to make his odour strong and pungent for the females. He would stand on the hillside and roar out his lungs, longer and louder than any other stag. His antlers were full and hard; he scored the ground, frayed bushes and branches and dipped his head to fight any male that outgrew his station. By the end of the day he had a harem of ten hinds to himself and the rut was just beginning. He nuzzled them, he cleaned their flanks and kissed them and, when they were ready, he mounted them and mated.

Connla followed Mellencamp's movements till the weather turned at the end of October. She was a good mother and taught her babies well. She allowed him to trail them through the high woods to Sylvan Lake. This was a favourite sunspot of hers in summer. Many times he had seen her lying flat out on a ledge while people swam in the lake, completely unaware of her presence. But now the summer was over, the first leaves were beginning to fall and the cougar had young to feed.

Connla had not been to Washington to begin preparing for the semesters, and had suffered Holly's wrath on the telephone. He had burned his bridges as far as the university was concerned, but he just couldn't face teaching and was thinking about getting a job bartending in Rapid City to get him through the winter.

He never stopped thinking about Imogen. Every morning he told himself the pain would get easier to deal with, but it didn't get easier, and as every day passed the fear that he had missed the one and only boat grew and grew in his mind.

Then one night he woke in the darkness having dreamed of her. They were together in her house by Loch Gael, and in the dream he held her and whispered to her in the night, and they made love until the sheets were a tangle of sweat on the bed. In the morning, he had an ache in his loins and a longing in his chest like a physical pain. Mellencamp had her cubs' education well in hand, and Connla made a decision. He threw some clothes into a bag, checked the balance on his credit cards and called Paha Ska for a ride to Rapid City.

It was two forty-five on Friday afternoon and the weekend beckoned in Gaelloch. Imogen had planned to ride into the hills, but the weather forecast was bad and she could see the time ahead yawning empty. Her mind had drifted throughout the day and now she was wondering what story to tell the children. It was only as they settled down, cross-legged in anticipation, that she decided. Connie McKercher, as always, was sitting closest to her. 'Can we have the one about Olwen again, Miss Munro?' Imogen smiled at her and thought, Yes, she would've liked children of her own.

'Not today, Connie. Today I want to tell you a different story. It's a very special story and one I haven't told you before.' She looked at their faces then, each one in turn, and the rain began to fall against the window, driven in by the wind from Lochalsh.

She sat there for a quiet moment and gathered her thoughts – images in her head, frayed memories that just wouldn't flee when she banished them. With eyes closed, she began: 'Long, long ago, Connla of the Fiery Hair, the only son of Conn of the Hundred Fights, stood with his father on the mountain known as Usna. Side by side they stood, and as they looked across the sea, Connla saw a maiden, fair of face and clad all in white, coming towards them. She walked as if in flight, as if her bare feet didn't touch the ground at all.

'"Where dost thou come from, maiden?" he asked her.

'Quietly she replied, "I come from the plain of the ever-living, Connla of the Fiery Hair, a place where there is neither death nor sin. Every day is a day of peace, each hour full and free from strife."

'Connla's father, and all those gathered with them, stared in wonder. They heard the maiden's voice, soft and sweet as honey, but they saw her not.

'"Whom dost thou speak to, my son?" said Conn of the Hundred Fights.

'"He speaks to a fair young maiden," the maiden answered for him, "whom neither age nor death will beckon. I love him. I have always loved him and I come now to call him away with me to the plain of pleasure, the place called Moy Mell, where Boadag has his throne."

'She turned to Connla then, one fair hand extended and a love in her eyes the like of which he had never seen, nor would he see again. "O come with me, Connla of the Fiery Hair, ruddy as the dawn and with thy tawny skin. A new crown awaits thee, a crown to grace the beauty in thy face. Come with me this hour and never will thy beauty fade till that day of judgement."

'But Conn the king, afraid now for his son, called to Coran his druid. "Coran of the many spells," he said. "I call upon thee now. A maiden unseen has stepped these shores, and she would, by some strange power of form and speech, take my son from me."

'So Coran the druid came forth and chanted spells, conjuring the rune and rhythm of his magic, and directed his words at the very spot where the faceless voice had risen. And then no more they heard her voice, and under the spell of the great druid she faded from Connla's sight, but before she was to vanish altogether she threw to him an apple.

'From that day forth Connla would take no water; he would take no food, save from that single shiny apple. And as he ate of it so it grew again, and nothing more sustained him. All the time the yearning in him grew, the longing for his maiden, she so pale and fair of face whom only he had seen. A month passed, and on the last day of that month Connla stood again at the side of his father, this time on the plain of Arcomin, and the maiden came to him a second time.

'"Connla," she called, and her voice was soft as singing, "'tis a glorious place thou holds among the folk of the living. They love thee, yet living thou art and mortal thou remain, and as a mortal, shortlived, awaiting only the day of death. But the folk of life, Connla, those who live for ever, call to you. Come, Connla. Come to the plain of pleasure, for there they have learned to know thee, to love thee and they see thee in thy home among the dear beloved ones."

'When Conn heard her voice again, he summoned his druid a second time. But the maiden said: "O mighty Conn of the Hundred Fights, there is no love in the druid's power. Whence the law comes the druid's power will wane, these magic spells that come from the lips of the demon will be no more."

'The king had witnessed that since the maiden had come that day upon the height of Usna, Connla, his son, had spoken to none who spoke to him. Wearily, Conn of the Hundred Fights turned to him. "Speak, my son. Tell me what is in thy heart. Is it in thy mind to heed this maiden, only thou can see?"

'"My father," Connla said. "'Tis hard on my heart. I love my people above all else, but a longing takes me for this maiden that I cannot begin to understand or impart to thee."

'When the maiden heard these words she spoke with a new softness. "The oceans of the world will never match the strength of thy longing, Connla of the Fiery Hair. Come with me this day, come in my curragh, my straight gliding crystal canoe, and together we will seek Boadag's land. See now, the bright sun sinks in the west and yet we can reach that place before the darkness falls. It is a land worthy of the journey, a land joyous to all those who seek its path. If you will come with me this day, we will seek that path together and live there for all the days of life."'

Imogen broke off, suddenly irritated. A shadow had fallen across the floor through the reinforced glass of the door. Patterson had developed a habit of interrupting just as she was finishing, hovering in the corridor like some latter-day Uriah Heep. For a moment the spell of the story was broken, her thread lost completely. She stared at the shadow, frowned, then looked straight up into Connla McAdam's eyes. No crutches now, his beard gone, his hair swept back from his face. In one hand he held a small travel bag and the palm of the other was flat against the glass.

'Miss Munro?' Connie McKercher was tugging her sleeve. 'What happened after that?'

They stared at one another through the glass, Imogen oblivious to Connie's plaintive voice and the hand on her arm. A lump lifted in her throat and she tried to swallow it. She saw threads of crystal in the back of Connla's eyes, but he blinked hard and then his face creased into a smile. Imogen sat there looking into his face and let the warmth rush in her veins. After a few moments she looked back at the children once more and took Connie McKercher's hand.

'When the maiden's voice was heard no more,' she said, 'Connla of the Fiery Hair looked to his father one last time, then he walked down the beach to join her. Taking him by the hand she led him to the water's edge, and together they leaped into the curragh. Connla did not look back, and all those on the shore – the king and his court – saw it, too. They stood upon the plain, with the wind in their hair, and watched the two of them glide towards the setting sun. Connla and his fairy maiden sought their path on the sea, and they were no more seen, nor did anyone know where they went.'